Voyage to Eneh

Voyage to Eneh

Book One of *The Seas of Kilmoyn*

ROLAND J. GREEN

TOR®

A Tom Doherty Associates Book
New York

This is a work of fiction. All the characters and events portrayed in this novel are either fictitious or used fictitiously.

VOYAGE TO ENEH

This book is printed on acid-free paper.

Design by Jane Adele Regina

A Tor Book
Published by Tom Doherty Associates, LLC
175 Fifth Avenue
New York, NY 10010

www.tor.com

ISBN 0-312-87231-3

First Edition: March 2000

Printed in the United States of America

0 9 8 7 6 5 4 3 2 1

To the memory of the late Dr. Oscar Parkes, M.B.E., whose love for long-vanished warships inspired my own—and with the passage of time, the work of which this is the first volume.

cast of characters

Human

BAER, Justin
Junior commander aboard human-crew *Lingvaas*.

BORLUND, Sean Lincoln
Originally Study Group trainee; later Farer and commander-trainee aboard mixed-crew *Lingvaas*; junior commander aboard human-crew *Lingvaas*.

CHAYKIN-SCHMIDT, Roald
Junior Farer aboard human-crew *Lingvaas*; "nephew" of senior Study Group Security commander.

HOUYLAN, Bridget
Senior bearer-partner of Sean Lincoln Borlund; one child by him; Observant.

KLIMOVA, Justine
Farer; oiler aboard human-crew *Lingvaas*.

KUND, Sharil
Second Captain (Executive Officer) of human-crew *Lingvaas*.

MAARTENS, Fridrik
Gunnery Commander of human-crew *Lingvaas*.

MCCLINTOCK, Wann
Watch chief aboard human-crew *Lingvaas.*

MEDVEDEV, Sebastian
Junior official of Study Group Directorate.

PEDERSON, Ands
Farer aboard human-crew *Lingvaas.*

WEIL, Barbara
Senior human commander aboard mixed-crew *Lingvaas;* later Captain of human-crew *Lingvaas.*

YELM, Vavra
Farer Second aboard human-crew *Lingvaas;* militant Rationalist.

YOSHINO, Adrianna and Corinne
Twins; respectively Engineer Chief and Farer aboard human-crew *Lingvaas.*

Kilmoyan

ALIKILI
Jossu I Hmilra's tuunda companion.

AMATAI, Dat
Watch chief of the tops aboard mixed-crew *Lingvaas.*

BELINDOUZA
Senior cook of mixed-crew *Lingvaas.*

I DJURR, Gurgan
Senior Captain in Expeditionary Fleet.

DROJIN, Vuikmar
Rinbao-Daran merchant of Kertovan descent; Imperial spy.

EJKMUS, Ludon
Junior commander at Fort Huomikki.

FAIND, Egose
Farer aboard mixed-crew *Lingvaas*.

FOBEEN, Acht
Captain of armored cruiser *Shuumiba* in Expeditionary Fleet.

GUUNDZOUSA, Ye'mt
Teacher watch chief; senior instructor aboard mixed-crew *Lingvaas*.

I HMILRA, Elandra
Wife of Othan I Hmilra.

I HMILRA, Jossu
Senior Captain Over Captains; of old Captain-born stock; commander of Expeditionary Fleet to Eneh.

I HMILRA, Othan
Son of Jossu I Hmilra; aspiring politician and entrepreneur.

IMPANSKAA, Ijo
Captain of armorclad *Byubr* in Eneh campaign.

JUINJIJARSA
Rinbao-Daran mounted-scout commander.

KEKASPA, Moi
Saadian; chief of Jossu I Hmilra's private intelligence service; aliases include "Jornja" and "Sikoe Yuurn."

NAYTET, Kappala
Retired Farer; owner of a waterfront reliefhouse in Saadi.

REN, Shaarasti
Writer of *Songs of the House of Nilvan.*

RYNKO
Junior Farer aboard mixed-crew *Lingvaas.*

I SHTUUR, Quiusa
Farer in Women's Squadron.

SKORBEEN, Fiya
Senior Fleet Commander ashore in Rinbao-Dar during the riots.

Voyage to Eneh

chapter 1

It was not the sunbrighten Reverence bells or the lamptenders' cries that awoke Watch Chief Ehoma Tuomitti. It was the noise of hammers in the shipyard just downhill from the reliefhouse.

Tasting sleep in her mouth and feeling something more pleasant in her loins, Tuomitti lay on the pallet, eyes closed, and tried to make out the different kinds of hammers. Mauls driving steel wedges into timber. Sledgehammers driving wooden wedges under light hulls or perhaps knocking them out—the yard finished a double hand of fishing craft and ships' boats every midtide.

Carpenters' hammers, finishing deck planking or cabin woodwork. The dull thud and wheezing of the big steam-driven hammers, driving in shores for a new building way or perhaps braces under some larger ship. (Wasn't there a new gunboat within a few commons of launching?)

Then, drowning out everything else like a watch chief with a speaking horn, the fierce rattle of the riveters. Not much of that being done by hand here anymore, she judged—it was all the new rammed-air riveting hammers.

Whatever they were using, if the riveters were at work already, that meant she had overslept by long enough to be shamed, if anybody learned. If she did not launch herself back aboard *Valor* before the first watch ended, everybody *would* learn.

Her partner for the night was gone, his good manners holding to the end. He had left only a small braided wreath of heartweed, and no money. She slipped the wreath into an outside pocket of her seabag and began pulling out clean garb.

Before she pulled it on, however, she did her exercises. She had to flex her knees to touch the floor with the backs of her hands, but she hardly had to stretch at all to reach the beams overhead. The rooms on the second and third level were higher-ceilinged than those with nothing but the roof between them and the mists and flyer droppings. They also held four to twelve beds; too much like sleeping aboard ship even when one wished to sleep. When one wished to spend part of the night in a way that custom and most worthwhile partners demanded be kept private. . . .

When Tuomitti had worked up a decent sweat, she toweled herself dry, then oiled and combed her fur. A quick pass of a brush over her foreteeth took most of the sleep sourness from her mouth. The rest could wait until she'd eaten and chosen her way back to *Valor*.

Foghorns joined the shipyard din as she slung her bag, and whistles replied from offshore as she made her way down the narrow stairs. She averted her eyes as she passed the half-open door of the room that gave on the landing. Not out of shame—twenty Greats at sea left one with precious little of that—but she did not care to embarrass any of *Valor*'s people who might be amusing themselves in that writhing, grunting pile.

" 'Shore's laws are not ship's laws,' " she quoted to herself.

She realized that she had spoken aloud when a grizzled woman's head thrust up from behind the counter in the common room.

"The last man I heard saying that was explaining to the Wharf Watch why he'd set a drinkshop afire," the woman said. "Pardon me if it makes me tremble, though not in awe."

Tuomitti gave the other a mocking parody of the gesture used by Daughters of the Rock in giving a blessing. "Your pardon is gladly granted."

"At what price?"

"Price?"

"It will be sunglow, maybe even fulldark, before a watch chief *gives* anything. Has either come while I slept?"

"You *slept*? The Great Tides are overtaking you, my friend. But of course, the snaggle-toothed are never—"

"I need no teeth at all to put greenmist leaf in your morning hoeg."

Tuomitti clasped her hands over her muzzle in mock horror. "My tongue abases itself. Hot hoeg, please, without greenmist leaf but with whatever sweetener you have."

The woman bared teeth that were stained and gapped but mostly straight, poured two cups of hoeg from the pot on the stove behind the brazier, then pulled out a plate of cakes and a pot of sweetbreath spread.

"Let me put a fresh pot up to boil, and I'll be joining you," she said.

Tuomitti was halfway through her first cup and second cake when the other joined her. They clinked cups.

"To a prosperous Great."

It was one of the few goodwishes that both reliefkeepers and Farers could agree on. They were more likely to illwish one another. But Tuomitti's hostess Kappala Naytet had come ashore only after three injuries and two motherless children made it prudent, proper, and even necessary. Before that she had been at sea for more Greats than Tuomitti, enough that the smoke-darkened print of her first ship showed a high-seas paddlewheeler.

Naytet fell on the cakes as if she had eaten even less than Tuomitti. When the plate bore only crumbs, she wiped her mouth, spooned up the last of the spread, and belched with dignity.

"So, how was your night?"

"Parts of it were excellent."

"I noticed his parts. Excellent seems too strong a word for his ears."

"They made good handles at the appropriate times."

"Lord and Lady alike forbid that you should do anything inappropriate, Ehma. A watch chief's dignity would never bear it."

Tuomitti made a rude gesture, brushed crumbs from her lap, and cocked an ear toward the stair.

"I think your other guests are slept or ploughed out," she said. "Not to take you from your work, but how much—?"

"Seven and two."

Toumitti handed over eight slyn.

"Oh, and the name of your friend."

"Cradle-robber!"

"Nine slyn or the name?"

"Are you sure you never sailed with the Luokkan pirates?

"By Rock and Wave I swear it."

"You mean, by Pebble and Puddle."

"Whatever. No doubt I can learn the name myself." She ran claws through Tuomitti's ruff. "Take care of yourself, friend. I hear rumors of an expedition to the Bishak Gulf. Of all my comrades, you are the most likely to sail with it."

"How many times has that rumor floated past in the last four Greats?"

"Enough, I admit. But until the last Great, the Dhandarans had no real navy on our seas. *Valor* could have stood off half their ships on the Greater Sea by herself.

"A settlement they can feed with their own ships is different from one riding in chartered bottoms. It might even win more favor from the Empire or at least some faction in Rinbao-Dar."

"That well may be," Tuomitti agreed, reluctant to continue any conversation along this line. She had been aboard *Valor* too long and learned a warrior's closed mouth too well.

A tidal bore of guests howling for food, drink, and baggage saved both women from embarrassment by silence. Tuomitti snatched her seabag, returned her friend's farewell gesture, and bolted for the door. She was outside in the fog before she could recognize any of the din-makers or they her.

The fog thickened as she strode toward the water. Certainly more foghorns were blowing, both afloat and ashore. Piping whistles and brass trumpets from light craft added to the din. Tuomitti preferred this to silence. That would mean the fog was keeping everything at the quay, with no ride out to *Valor* until the murk thinned.

SEAN LINCOLN BORLUND REMEMBERED TO DUCK AS HE STEPPED THROUGH the door from the passenger lounge onto the afterdeck. Humans averaged ten centimeters taller than Kilmoyans, and at a meter eighty-six Borlund was taller than most humans. He had bruises and cuts on scalp and forehead from mantelpieces, beams, and door lintels that offered plenty of clearance for ninety-nine out of a hundred of either race.

The afterdeck was nearly deserted. *Aygsionan* carried few passengers this early in the season, and most of them were either still at breakfast or farther below, preparing to debark.

Borlund had been too excited to sleep, and had come on deck to catch his first glimpse of the Hask Delta and Saadi. All he saw was fog that seemed to grow thicker the closer they drew to the land. He stared futilely into the murk until frustration and hunger drove him below to snatch a plate from the buffet.

What drove him out on deck now was more than curiosity. *Aygsionan* was closing the mole at barely steerageway, with lookouts posted everywhere from the foredeck aft. More stood in the maintop, and a couple of hardy souls even out on the yardarm.

The sea around them was still full of fishing boats and small craft, raising their cacaphony of high-pitched signals among the intermittent blasts of larger ships' foghorns. Borlund was glad *Aygsionan* was taking standard precautions. He'd have been even happier if she and all the other big ones had anchored until the fog lifted.

He knew the arguments against that, not all of them economic. He also knew that they sounded more convincing if you sailed the seas of Kilmoyn in something big enough to survive a collision. Human research boats didn't qualify, and it was a Kertovan refrigerated-cargo ship that ran down *Nautilus* and drowned Peter Kilmack and three other humans.

Sean Borlund hadn't sailed with his sire-parent that day because Grace Ohama, his second bearer-partner, was having their baby. A customary, even compelling reason for staying ashore—and quite useless as a defense to survivor guilt.

Some of the guilt had weathered away in the last three years. Wariness remained. As Borlund walked *Aygsionan*'s deck, his hearing reached out into the murk, seeking a horn or whistle just a little closer aboard than the others, fearing to hear the crunch of steel plate meeting wooden thwart, driving the boat down into the gray depths—

TUOMITTI FIRST STRODE BRISKLY, THEN WALKED CAUTIOUSLY, THEN SLOWED to ambling, with her free hand held out in front of her and her ears searching the murk around her. She hardly expected to hear anything in time to be warned, the way the fog and the warren of old streets close to the waterfront distorted sound. She also hardly intended to stand like an image of the Lady of the Rocks until the fog lifted.

The fog had to be lighter offshore, or else all the captains and boatsteerers in Saadi Bay were on direly urgent business. She'd heard every signal except the three-three-three of a ship at anchor, although she might have missed some of those. Also, a ship anchoring in this murk was as likely to be run down by somebody underway as they were to ram somebody else if they kept moving at dead slow.

Please, Lord of the Waves, let them at least be able to see the channel markers.

The murk ahead of her turned solid. Tuomitti stopped abruptly, her nose a finger from the side of a large van. She thumped the wood with her fist, only afterward noticing that it showed lettering in Saadia as well as Kertovasi.

"Apologies, Farer," a plaintive voice came from the driver's seat. "There's no but all the wagons in town ahead in the Fish Street, and none of them moving. Know you a better way to Likug Wharf?"

"If I can ride with you, I think I can find one," Tuomitti said. If one was going to contemplate this murk for the rest of the morning, one might as well do it sitting down.

She stepped around to the far side of the van, to avoid frightening the dreezans. She could tell from the accent as well as the lettering that she was dealing with a Saadian, who weren't always careful about crowd-training their dreezans.

"Beg your pardon, Lady," the driver said, as Tuomitti climbed up. "I can't offer much comfort for your kindness, but—"

"The most comfort you can offer for now is a moment's silence," Tuomitti said. She pulled out her handkerchief and wiped the puddled mist off her side of the skin bench, then sat down. The driver looked at her sideways, as if wondering whether he'd lost any real chance for a friendly chat. A Kertovan watch chief might be "Lady" only by gross, almost servile courtesy, but she was under no obligation to speak to a Saadian van driver unless she was desperate for conversation.

Which I might be, if this fog keeps us here the whole common.

Tuomitti had never liked fog on land, even though it put her in less peril than at sea. Right now she would yield a quarter-Great's pay to be in the warm and fusty Watch Chief's Hall aboard *Valor*. She might even pay a few-score slyn to be standing in *Valor*'s forechains, heaving the lead as the armorclad crept toward a lee shore with a landing party already mustered by the pulling boats and the steam launch already in the water, ready to tow the others ashore when shoaling water brought *Valor* to a halt.

"Forgiveness is begged," the driver said.

Mercifully, the tone wasn't as servile as the words. Tuomitti had long outgrown the pleasures of "chasing the graveltoes," even before she began to homeharbor out of Saadi. She wondered truly how anyone her age or even a few Greats younger had the strength to spare for such nasty games.

Oh, the Saadians had been grateful enough a hundred Greats ago, when the Kertovans were all that stood between them and the anarchy spreading like redeye fever from the City-States. Their gratitude had kept them loyal and productive for most of that time, until they became the backbone of Kertovan industry, and not only in graveltoe goods but the iron and coal mining that fed the shipyards.

That gratitude, Tuomitti reflected, might not survive many more years of being called "graveltoes" behind their backs or even to their faces, or barred from the high-paying work in the shipyards and arsenals. Not when the City-States were forming the Alliance of the Hask, possibly with Aloboliran advice, certainly with excellent Imperial weapons.

"I think I now owe *you* an apology, friend driver," Tuomitti said. "At least no one is likely to ram your van in this fog and send it to the bottom of the bay."

"There's something in that, Ma'am," the driver said, in a tone that was at least neutral.

THE FOG GREW NO THICKER AS *AYGSIONAN* CREPT INTO THE HARBOR, BUT no thinner either. Her own whistle hadn't sounded three-three-three yet, but Sean Borlund had been hearing the anchoring signal from all around for a good twenty minutes. Whistles, sirens, horns, drums, pipes, bells, and more than a few sets of leathery lungs called out in three languages and half a dozen dialects that Borlund recognized and more he did not.

More passengers were coming on deck, even though they could hardly see the bow or the masthead, let alone their landfall. Borlund recognized the look on the few human faces, and supposed most of the Kilmoyans had the same thought: better to be on deck staring into the fog than below staring at a bulkhead. On deck human or Farer had a chance to swim for it if some iron prow suddenly loomed out of the murk and drove through *Aygsionan*'s side—

"Kanik!"

The obscenity shrilled in Borlund's ear, and a hurrying shape with a Kertovan headcrest slammed him back against the cabin bulkhead. The back of his head struck hard metal. Pain flared all the way to scalp and ears. With blurred vision, he saw the rapidly receding silhoutte of a deckhand with an armload of small cartons.

Borlund rubbed his head, surprised that neither his fingers nor what turned out to be a fire-hose bracket showed blood. What did that Farer have under his tail, to be in such a hurry that he couldn't keep a lookout ahead? Borlund had a brief vision of uncovering the theft of lifeboat rations or something else portable and receiving a civic award.

He wiped salty droplets from his skin and laughed quietly. It would take diplomacy, subtle negotiations, and perhaps a few not-so-subtle bribes to have a Drylander's word taken against a Farer's. Hardly worthwhile, when no one was hurt.

Badly hurt, at least—Borlund knew he would have a lump tomorrow, where skull had skull met bracket. Worth filing an Incident Report? Maybe, if only to buy off some rule-happy superior who could make his life miserable or at least unproductive. A place with the Study Group in Saadi still carried a good deal of prestige; every senior Observer and probably most of the junior ones had a friend or relative ready, possibly even qualified, to fill a vacancy.

Then he saw the color of the bulkhead, and laughed again. He had a perfect excuse for not filing an Incident Report, without having to so much as hint that the Incident File made for bad feelings and wasted expensive paper in the service of a bureaucracy that the human community in Saadi could not really afford.

The bulkhead was nearly the same medium brown as Borlund's skin, allowing for weathering, soot, salt, and dirt distributed variously over both. Add Borlund's dark brown traveling suit and dreezan-skin boots, and in lighter fog than this he'd have easily blended with the bulkhead.

The din of anchoring signals had almost died, when *Aygsionan*'s own whistle drowned out every other sound. Three blasts, three more, then a last three. Borlund braced himself into a corner as the deck shuddered from the backing propeller. Somewhere aloft a wire parted with a dismal *twunnnng*.

As the fog swallowed the signal, Borlund heard the squeal and grind of the main anchor chain running out, then from aft a milder echo as they let go the stern one. The deck was still, the water alongside motionless for the first time in three days.

Borlund walked aft toward the second-payer hall door. Being out here on deck in the fog had chilled him more than he'd realized. A cup of something hot would be worth braving smoke, ancient fish-fat, and even foul-mouthed Kertovans.

EHOMA TUOMITTI AND THE DRIVER COMBINED THEIR IGNORANCE WITHOUT achieving knowledge. At times they were as completely lost as Tuomitti had been the time she was shipwrecked on an island off the

Luokkan shore and had to flee inland to avoid the pirates. She thought afterward that the fog must have crept into their brains through their wide-open ears, as they listened for any guiding sound to fight its way through the din from the harbor.

At last they found themselves on a street sloping the right way, which said "waterfront" to both of them even if Tuomitti hadn't recognized a couple of the reliefhouses and at least one drinkshop. They waited behind a steamhauler in its turn waiting for a railsteamer to pass. While they waited the driver dismounted and oiled the hides of his dreezans in a couple of places where the harness chafed.

Then at last the railsteamer hauled its train off into the murk, one of the trainmen walking ahead of it with a lantern and two more lanterns hung from the open guard wagon at the tail end. Steamhauler, van, and all the vehicles and walkers behind them bumped and rattled across the double tracks, and onto the Stone Road along the quays.

As they turned south, Tuomitti looked back at the little quayside station. It was hardly more than a brick hut with a long passenger shelter stretching fifty paces from either end. But when they'd crossed the tracks, Tuomitti hadn't been able to see the far end of the passenger shelter. Now she could not only see it but also make out the shape of the freightyard gate beyond it, and even the wrought-iron Hand of Wealth over the heavy timber lintel.

She didn't dare say it aloud, fearing that both the Lady of the Rock and the Lord of the Wave (partners in making fog as in other things) would punish such impudence. What she saw might also be an eddy in the fog, that would pass on and leave the station invisible again.

For now, though, she would allow herself a modest hope that the fog was lifting.

chapter 2

There was silence aboard *Aygsionan* but not around her. Off in the grayness, Sean Borlund heard bells, gongs, and trumpets, as nervous souls tried to generate a reassuring echo or even reply. This thick a fog could make even Farers wonder if they were not the last thinking beings left on the face of a world at last swallowed by the Mist Demons. . . .

From close to redside came the rasping whistle of a pair of Seakin, surfacing to breathe through their double blowholes. Then they would dive again, to make their way out to sea in the narrow space between the deepest keel on the surface and the tallest wreck on the bottom.

Saadi Bay held many of both. It had been a port long before the Kertovans established their Protectorate, and human marine archeologists drooled at the thought of a license for extensive diving anywhere in the seventy-by-forty-klick stretch of water inside the hundred-meter line. None of it gave any trouble to the Seakin; their organic sonar was ahead of anything likely to be built on Kilmoyn for two more generations.

Borlund opened the hall door. The smells inside struck his nostrils like a padded club. For once he didn't mind the Kertovans who wriggled a shoulder at him, then moved out of his path.

A few of the Saadians who made up about a third of the hall's population followed the Kertovan example, politely hinting that Borlund's body odor was unbearable. Others did not. Two of them stayed so close so long that Borlund wondered if he should hug them, politely ask them to move, or try to sell them a low-rate certificate for the Luokkan labor draft.

It said something for the relations of Kertovan and Saadian that any Saadian who could afford a second-payer's passage only needed to put down his slyn, pack his bag, and walk aboard. It said something else that Saadians would refuse to follow Kertovans' lead in dealing with a Drylander—something at the heart of the human dilemma on Kilmoyn.

Too many Saadians had begun to look to the Drylanders as a force for change—a force against the Protectors who'd outstayed their undeniably sincere welcome of four generations ago. Too many humans recoiled from the thought of forcing any change in Kilmoyn's society, or even participating in anything that hadn't been classified by the Study Group as part of the world's "natural evolution."

Natural evolution, my left bean. This planet hasn't evolved naturally since Skyfall, and we're no asteroid strike.

In fact, Borlund had for years thought that relying too much on "natural evolution" went directly against the other human goal—to see Kilmoyn develop space flight.

Preferably, before the next wandering asteroid hits, or Ramparts *runs into space junk big enough to wreck her* and *her data banks.*

"Table or counter?" the steward asked. He could have been either Saadian or Kertovan; most likely he was one of those numerous mixed-bloods. Few talked about them; hardly more singled them out for persecution—the good old Kertovan middle way.

"Natural evolution" might be the way to go, on a planet where that evolution moved faster than a glacier. On a planet skewed by a millennium of survival pressures toward conservation, it seemed less wise.

"Table or counter?" the steward repeated, in a voice that made it clear he loathed indecisive clients regardless of race.

"Counter," Borlund said. He realized that he's used up too much adrenaline in the past few hours, anticipating all the problems he might face on joining the Study Group and conjuring up solutions to each one. If he sat down at a table, by the time *Aygsonian* moved again he might have his head down on the wooden mosaic tabletop.

The steward condescendingly waved him toward the counter at the rear of the salon. Only half the stools and even less of the rail space was taken, mostly by Saadians. Borlund was relieved to see no humans. Polite conversation at least was rigid etiquette when two humans met; Borlund was feeling neither polite nor conversational.

He shifted his carrybag to his right hand and steered a course for the counter.

* * *

BY THE TIME THE VAN REACHED THE BOAT LANDING, TUOMITTI HAD DECIDED that she'd seen only an eddy in fog that elsewhere lay as thick as ever. They finished the last hundred paces with the driver on foot, leading the number-one dreezan with one hand and holding his whip out in front of him to probe the way.

Tuomitti walked alongside the wagon, expecting every moment to fall or be pushed by a wheel into the water. Twice she had to swing around the outside of slippery bollards.

It was after this that she broke out the carrystrap on her seabag and slung it across her back. No Farer liked that pose, which made one look like a graveltoe landfighter under one of their spine-bending packs. At least no street squatters were going to see her and call rude remarks or toss overripe vegetables.

At the boat landing, Tuomitti judged that the first problem would not be finding a boat crew willing to sail. It would be finding a boat crew at all, without falling off the quay onto their heads or perhaps into the bottom of their boat and sinking it.

"*Kanik!*" Tuomitti growled.

"Eh, Goodfarer?" The driver had taken to using that ancient term in place of "Lady."

"I fear I've led you off in search of the Treasure of Skuun."

"No harm done. This cursed murk will be all over the city by now."

Implying that she had no need to apologize, because he wouldn't have been able to do his business anyway. Tuomitti wondered which of them was more surprised—him at her apology or she at his letting her down easily.

She slammed her fist against the van, hit an iron strap, scraped her knuckles, and both cursed at the pain and laughed at her folly. Nobody would notice if she didn't return to *Valor* until the fog lifted. Nobody would care if she spent the time in a waterfront drinkshop, as long as she returned aboard dryheaded.

Several people groped past, unseen but not unheard, their voices indicating that they'd already visited at least one drinkshop and were on their way to another. Tuomitti heard three different Kertovan accents and a Saadian who seemed to be the most wetheaded of all.

Instead of joining them, Tuomitti sat down on a bollard.

"Driver!"

"Goodfarer?"

"Here's for your time and trouble, since I've led you farther from where you were bound. If you want my advice, moor—hitch—your team some place away from the water, then go wet yourself inside."

"I might just do that," the driver said politely. Still more politely, he did not bite the half-slyn she handed him. Tuomitti wished he would show the greatest politeness of all, which would be leaving. Her charity toward Saadians or anyone else stopped short of letting them see her not knowing what to do next. It was a vice, she knew, but one hard to avoid once one put up the lantern badge of a watch chief.

Eventually she heard the squeal of iron wheels on stone as the cart turned, the whining and belching of dreezans routed out of a comfortable drowse to pull their load again, and the fog-dimmed *pok!* of the driver's whip as he worked his team up to a walk. It took longer than Tuomitti expected for the team to vanish into the mist.

She decided that to keep a light conscience, she would go seeking that boat or *something* that would take her back to *Valor*. At worst, a search of the waterfront might let her rally a few more strayed *Valors*, to make up a party when the fog did let them see farther than an oar's length beyond their noses.

Tuomitti rose from the bollard, as slowly as if the fog had rusted her joints, and began her walking.

THE COUNTER ATTENDANT LOOKED TO BE ANOTHER KERTOVAN-SAADIAN cross, with maybe a trace of ancestry from somewhere up the Finnugh Valley. He wore a work smock, with his hair in a purely Saadian style, as well as an expression that seemed to accuse Sean Borlund of being personally responsible for the fog. No doubt the attendant had some plans of his own for when the ship was safely ported, something more pleasant than waiting on pallid, hairless, smelly Drylanders.

"Hoeg or gruuyan?"

Hoeg was made from various combinations of dried seaweeds, gruuyan from a root vegetable that looked like a potato with a glandular condition. Gruuyan was a high-status drink, also high-priced (two slyn a cup, by the sign), and much easier on the human palate.

Borlund told his taste buds to go back to sleep and ordered hoeg.

"With or without?"

That probably meant greenmist; the herb almost masked the bitterness of the hoeg.

"With. Any rolls?"

"Just biscuits."

Probably half seaweed flour and half fish oil, but he was hungry enough not to care.

"One."

"One slyn three."

Borlund fumbled in his pockets for money and also for the fishskin tube of vitamin paste. It tasted worse than straight hoeg but kept humans healthy on almost any diet yet found on Kilmoyn. It might even save Kilmoyans from deficiency diseases, if the "natural evolution" leadership among the humans ever allowed the paste to be manufactured for sale to the humans' hosts!

The hoeg was hot, which was all Borlund's throat and stomach cared about now. He crunched a corner of the biscuit, and discovered that it was not only greasy but half-charred as well. Before he could decide about the next bite, he heard voices on deck, then the booted feet of deckhands running forward.

Borlund turned to ask what had happened. Someone sharper-eared saved him the trouble.

"Cursed if they're not calling the anchor detail to their stations," a Saadian muttered. "Hope the fog's lifting."

"Might well be," someone Borlund couldn't see replied. "Lookout aloft, he could see better'n we."

"Or the captain might just have a hot number waiting for her and not care 'bout much else," another anonymous voice put in.

Several Saadians looked as if they wanted Borlund's opinion, but his luck was in. The signal-din started again, building steadily. Most of it was three-two-four—"getting underway." When the whistles, horns, bells, and trumpets weren't making conversation pointless, the hiss of steam into the anchor winch finished the work.

By the time the deck started vibrating from the engines, Borlund was convinced that either the fog was lifting or *all* the captains and boatchiefs on Saadi Bay had direly urgent business elsewhere.

TUOMITTI FOUND TWO FERRIES WITH STEAM UP, NEITHER OF THEM ANY USE to her, running as they did to Yuirpesi and Kylomaak. The ferry to the Fort Huomikki landing was nowhere in sight, since it ran at all tides and was probably caught somewhere in the fog if it had ever left the fort.

She hoped any of her shipmates caught aboard the ferry were at least having a good drinkfest.

At the boat landing beyond the ferry piers, Tuomitti thought at first she would have the same sodden luck. Half the boats were drawn up on the shingle; half of those in the water were empty. Some of the grounded boat were overturned, their crews huddled for shelter underneath. One comfort-driven soul had knocked out the drain plug from his boat, run a sprayed-iron pipe through it as a chimney, and built a fire to warm his shelter. Nothing short of his boat catching fire would get him on the water today.

In her younger days Tuomitti would have been tempted to wander over to the chimney-boat and plug the chimney, then wait until the boat's owner came storming and coughing out to settle with his visitor. Fuller of years and rank and needing to at least pretend to greater dignity, Tuomitti could only mourn the passing Greats and go on.

The Tide of Wonders was not yet passed, however. Toward the end of the shingle, shadowed by the breakwater guarding the ways of the next half-dozen building slips, lay a steam launch. She was an older model, doubtless sold out of Fleet service ten Greats ago. Her boiler was more patches than original metal, but she rode clean and high, brave with fresh paint.

She even had paying passengers aboard, judging from the pulled-down curtains of the passenger cabin forward. Tuomitti scurried across the treacherous shingle, waving and calling.

"Heyo, the steam launch! Are you taking passengers?"

The woman standing at the wheel just forward of the funnel was alert if surly.

"What's it to you if I am?" she replied. She didn't cup her hands or even take her smoketwist out of her mouth.

"Let me come down and talk."

"I don't have a crankgun to keep you up there." She sounded as if this was something she regretted.

"Skoi, up the steam another quarter," the woman shouted, slapping the roof of the boilerhouse behind her for emphasis. Tuomitti decided this meant the woman would take her if she hurried. She ran across the last of the shingle, splashed through water up to her ankles, and flung herself on to the deck so hard that her seabag jammed under the railing and for a moment she was wedged and helpless.

Her belly went taut as a cloaked figure stepped out of the passenger cabin and loomed above her. Large, flabby hands gripped her, freeing her with more strength than skill. She heard her seabag rip, wriggled out of the hands, and rose.

The man facing her had the look of a prosperous merchant of no ancestry commonly found hereabouts. He reached to brush her clean; her glare discouraged the gesture.

"Glad to have you with us, Goodfarer." Somehow the title was less pleasant from this man than from the van driver.

"Glad to be aboard," Tuomitti replied. She pitched her voice loud enough for the boat chief to hear, and hoped she sounded sincere. *Never begin a voyage by insulting the captain* was not one of Ukkio's Maxims, but it might as well have been.

"Where you bound?" the boat chief growled, knocking the pleasantries on the head like a fresh-caught rilk.

"Valor," Tuomitti said.

That got her such looks that she surreptitiously examined her garments to see if anything improper was showing. *Valor* seemed to be a potent name with these folk. Or perhaps it was Captain Over Captains Jossu I Hmilra, *Valor*'s senior owner?

"Where she moored?" the chief asked.

"Too far from Iojuk," the merchant began.

"Ah—I believe, Goodfarer—"

"Yes, I asked you, Watch Chief."

"South Anchorage, Fort Huomikki. About nine casts west of the arsenal pier, when I came ashore last night."

"This fellow's first," the boat chief said. She pointed at the merchant, rather as she would have pointed at a pile of dreezan dung. He seemed deaf to her tone and blind to her gestures.

"But I can take you out to *Valor* if the fog and your money be right, afterward."

Tuomitti had no chance to ask about the money. A high, slightly quavering voice hailed them from the shore.

"Boat? Did I hear that you are going to Fort Huomikki?"

"What's it to you if I am?"

"I go to my husband there."

The accent would have told Tuomitti that the woman was Saadian, even if her headscarf and the embroidery on the blanket wrapped around the bundle in her arms hadn't already made that plain. The blanket quivered, and Tuomitti saw that the woman was holding a baby.

"After you land me at Iojuk—" the merchant began.

The boat chief frowned. It made her look almost pleasant. "Long time on the water for a baby. Eh, Watch Chief?"

Farer was appealing to Farer. Tuomitti stared at the merchant. Something about those ears—

Of course. Most likely, the woman's husband was a commander in the Saadian legion at Fort Huomikki. From the shape of his ears, it was just as likely that the merchant was a Drilion with a Kertovan earcrop. The Drilions hated the Saadians and were hated in return. They had been vocally unhappy a generation ago when the Kertovan Council of Captains allowed the Saadians to raise a landfighter legion for regular garrison service instead of just frontier patroling.

Tuomitti nearly spat over the side. She wanted to spit in the merchant's face. Drilions were not her favorite folk at the best of times. She and all true Farers loathed any form of self-mutilation except for the customary earrings and forearm scarifications. Cropping one's ears to look more Kertovan was obscene.

The woman, not having heard a *no,* was crossing the shingle. Another moment and her feet would be wet.

Tuomitti dropped her seabag, vaulted over the railing, and splashed toward the woman. The merchant shouted after her.

"She comes aboard, I find another boat."

"So be it, 'long as you leave half your fare," the boat chief said.

The merchant looked like a boiler ready to burst. Tuomitti nodded.

"She has the law with her. The time you've taken—"

"What about *her?*" No need to ask who that meant.

"So does she. You don't."

The boat chief held up both hands. Tuomitti had the notion that there'd be weapons in them if she had to do it a second time.

"You game to go to the fort?" she asked Tuomitti.

"I am. I can get a boat there to—"

"Good-oh. Crop-ear," she said, turning to the merchant. "I cut the third off your fare if I take these folk to the fort, then you to Iojuk." She turned half away from the merchant and flicked a hand at Tuomitti, behind her back. The gesture was plain: charity had its limits, and Tuomitti would be expected to make up most of the lost slyn.

Tuomitti mentally counted her remaining money. She'd be lean-pursed until next pay, unless she could arrange a loan with the store chief, although he and this boat's owner were the same breed when it came to charity. Better that than having a mother and babe stranded in this murk.

"You'll lose nothing by it," she called, then reached for the babe. The boat chief jumped down from the wheel mount to take it from

Tuomitti, leaving the Drilion even shorter of words than he was of ear tufts.

Relieved of her burden, the woman splashed boldly into the water and scrambled aboard with an agility that spoke of both youth and health. She was wringing out her skirts when Tuomitti boarded, but hissing steam and the clang and clatter of stoking made speech impossible.

As the propeller churned up mud from the bottom, then foam from the water, Tuomitti saw that at long last the fog had truly begun to lift. A land breeze stroked her cheek. Then the boat was underway, and the land breeze mixed with the passage wind, while the gurgle of water at the prow joined the chuffing of the engine.

AYGSIONAN'S ANCHOR WAS UP BEFORE SEAN BORLUND COULD FINISH HIS snack and reach the deck. As he mounted the ladder, he heard cheering. Under his boots he felt the changing rhythm of the engines as the ship got underway.

The only problem was that as he reached the deck, he heard more cheering from vessels still invisible in a fog that was clearing but far from gone. The first line or two of *Aygsionan*'s anchormates were visible even to Borlund's unaided eye from the deck; they could be avoided with ease if they were commanded with minimal skill and caution.

Five times as many ships had to be still veiled in clammy gray, as opaque as a Captain-Born matron's nightrobe and even less decorated. When *they* all got underway, this corner of Saadi Bay was going to become a demonstration of the physical law that two bodies could not occupy the same space at the same time.

The best Borlund hoped for was that *Aygsionan* would not be part of the demonstrations. Or in sight of them, for that matter. He still had nightmares about his sire-parent's death, even though he had not been a witness to it. The last thing he wanted was to have one while awake—a daymare?—when he needed to be at his best, reporting to the Study Group.

A breeze began to ruffle the water; *Aygsionan*'s straight rusty stem was now cutting through more than ripples. Borlund's greenside was becoming the windward one. Thumps and clinks came from behind him as the stewards were closing the windows of the second-payer hall.

"Keep up the fug and the fumes at all costs," Borlund quoted to himself, from the irreverent (as well as discouraged, if not outright banned) translation of Einsem's Household Maxims. He supposed that the people of a world that had by the narrowest of margins escaped becoming uninhabitably cold after Skyfall could hardly be blamed for accepting other discomforts to keep warm. It was either that or re-evolve the thick, greasy pelts of their semi-aquatic ancestors, and stoves worked faster than evolution, natural or otherwise.

As Borlund reached the redside, it also ceased to be the lee, as *Aygsonian* swung ponderously onto a course almost due north, directly into the breeze. Spray leaped higher at her prow, and a line of fishing boats passed so close alongside that Borlund could nearly have spat on the deck of the nearest.

Ahead, a tug with a string of lumber barges in tow hastily backed water, then swung to starboard. Borlund watched and sensed others watching, too, until the barges also started swinging around to follow the tug, instead of driving onward into *Aygsionan*'s path. Only when the last barge was falling astern did he realize that he'd been clenching his jaws tightly enough to grind teeth and strain cheek muscles, not to mention drawing blood from his upper lip.

No humans had been lost or even present when the passenger packet *Ilraamen* ripped her bow open on an unseen coal barge and took two hundred passengers to the bottom with her. That disaster was still in every manual of seamanship or child's book of cautionary tales printed in the fifteen Greats since the disaster.

Visibility was definitely improving. Before the last of the barges was out of sight, the South Anchorage off Fort Huomikki was in sight, almost to the breakwater that divided it from its cousin to the north.

Half a dozen warships shared the anchorage, barely a quarter of its full capacity. One lay alongside a coal hulk that must have started life as a particularly fine four-master. The graceful lines still showed under years of accumulated grime that no waves could now touch, and three masts survived as derrick stumps. Smoke curled up until it was lost in the haze, from the steam winches aboard the warship and the hulk, and from the tug waiting patiently at the hulk's bow.

With binoculars Borlund could have turned the ripples of movement on the two decks into the organized, brutal chaos of coaling ship. The Kertovans designed their more modern ships with dozens of labor-saving devices, driven by small steam engines fed off auxiliary boilers, hydraulics, or even electricity. It still took a full day to transfer the thousand tons of coal a big cruiser could swallow, then another day for the crew to clean their ship and themselves. (And even then, the beans, biscuit, and pasties tasted of coal dust for a week.)

A small armorclad was standing out as *Aygsionan* passed the buoys marking the mouth of the dredged channel to the anchorages. A long half-submerged ram, a hull like a potato sliced lengthwise, with a single turreted gun forward and a fat funnel aft—she had to be an *Illik*-class harbor-defense vessel, the ones known as "the floating turds."

From the departing ship's bridge—a platform just forward of the funnel, perched precariously over the wheelhouse on four skeletal legs—a light winked. Another replied, from the bridge of the watch vessel, an unarmored gunboat of the same vintage as the armorclad. Probably a former or future merchant ship, like half the Kertovan Warfleet. Purpose-built warships were added sparingly, since Kertovan technology allowed double-duty vessels and the Kertovan strategic situation made them adequate for many tasks.

At the limit of visibility, a third signal lamp winked in reply to the gunboat's. Borlund watched until the last ship took on a definite shape. Low-freeboard hull with a ram bow, one turret forward of the bridge, guntowers on either side just aft of the bridge and funnel, a high superstructure studded with light guns, and a second turret aft. The funnel was massive, the two masts heavy enough to spread the sails this ship would never carry.

Valor, or one of her class—the "Lords of the Fleet."

Borlund tried to make out the funnel colors, which would identify the ship, but the ship slipped tantalizingly behind a patch of fog before he could even guess. Then *Aygsionan*'s deck tilted as the rudder went hard over, in a sharper turn than Borlund thought wise, but the lighthouse at the end of the breakwater was coming up on the port bow, with Fort Huomikki squatting beyond it—

The ship's whistle screamed the four-one for an emergency back-and-turn, then went on screaming steadily as a collision warning. Borlund clapped his hands over his ears and opened his mouth to protect his hearing.

Other warnings screamed, moaned, blared, and thundered. Borlund spent a desperate moment, wanting to believe that he hadn't heard the crunch of some small craft dying under the prow of a larger one. If he just wanted badly enough not to have heard it, it wouldn't have happened. . . .

The whistle changed pitch and signaled one-one-three—"Farer overboard." Doubt became impossible; duty became certain.

Borlund ran forward, already unbuttoning his coat.

THE SCENE ON THE BAY WAS EVERYTHING TUOMITTI HAD FEARED AND SOMEwhat more. Everyone was trying to get underway at once, and a hundred craft varying in speed, turning circle, and crew skill were on the move.

Tuomitti began to regret her eagerness to return to *Valor*. It was law, duty, and custom, as well as necessary to her authority as a watch chief. It had also bound her to a ride about as pleasant as steering a raft-fort into a narrow channel with cable-guided bomb-boats converging on her from both sides!

The boat chief had not offered her the courtesy of the "bridge," which was just as well. There was hardly room for one grown Farer on the wheel platform, and on deck Tuomitti could stay between the Drilion and the Saadian woman with her babe. The Farer didn't really think the merchant would push the woman overboard, but it might help keep the peace if he knew that he would follow if he tried.

After the third near-collision, the woman turned pale and went to the railing. Tuomitti gently but firmly took the babe, while the woman thrust her head over the side and gave her breakfast to the fishes and the Seakin.

"Bearing sickness, by any chance?" Tuomitti asked.

The woman rinsed her mouth with a dipper of water from the jug racked on the cabin bulkhead, and shook her head. Then she smiled for the first time.

"It may not be long, though, after I join Paevo. He is one of stout loins. Ah, pardon."

Tuomitti grimaced. Sometimes the formalities between jouti and tuunda were more than a trifle wearying. She had to accept the apology, or be more offensive than the woman would have been by not offering it at all.

"Granted. But I have fertile kin, and because one is barren does not mean one has no use for stout-loined men."

The woman ventured a smile. "I imagine so."

The Saadian now went inside, leaving Tuomitti and the Drilion sharing the midships. This was as good as being alone, just when the Farer wanted to talk; she wondered if Skoi the stoker felt like conversation. If he existed, that is—although Tuomitti thought that if someone had really invented the process used in *The Vitalized Corpse* to make the dead walk, they would probably not use it to provide stokers for ferry launches!

They skimmed between two sidewheel steamers with barely a half-cast on either side, heeled over as they avoided a steamfisher, then slowed as three Seakin surfaced directly ahead. Tuomitti knew only a few concepts in the Seakin language, but doubted if what these were saying was in any polite text.

The boat chief used similar phrases in tongues Tuomitti knew. It was as well that the Seakin didn't hear her, likewise any Speaker for the Lord of the Waves. The rights of Seakin might be sacred, but steerageway in this kind of waterborne scrum was life or death.

The Seakin made their way off on the surface, which hinted at shoaling water below. Tuomitti peered ahead. The mist had lifted enough that she could see clearly ten casts ahead, all the way to the lighthouse guarding the Fleet anchorages, nearly all the way to Fort Huomikki.

Faintly on the breeze came the sound of the garrison's bands practicing on the parade ground. Tuomitti grinned at the pleasant memory of a shore leave spent with a senior baton bearer of the band, fur gone half-gray and one eye dimmed by cataracts but another stout-loined fellow—

The launch gained steerageway again. The wheel went over and Tuomitti gripped a railing as they swung around the stern of a heavy two-hull, lurching along with a deckload of railroad cars. Cutting it close, she thought, but there was an outbound coastal packet hard in the wake of the railroad ferry—

Two whistles and one living throat screamed almost in chorus. Tuomitti wanted to chop the edge of her hand across the Drilion's throat, to silence him.

Even more, she wanted to wish away the rusty iron prow looming over the launch, so close she could almost have touched it with an oar. The ferry hadn't hidden the northbound steamer, but it had obscured just enough to make the boat chief misjudge distance.

The distance between prow and launch shrank, then vanished. An iron wall came at Tuomitti, as fast as a shot from a hostile gun or an opponent's fist in a brawl, as slowly as the incoming tide. She saw rivets so clearly that she could count them, a horrified face peering out of a port, the launch's stern driven under—

She had just realized the deck was no longer under her feet, when she was in the water.

chapter 3

Sean Borlund's mind told him that he wasn't needed forward. His mind didn't command his legs. They answered to his guts, which told them to take him forward. If he stood here, he would always think he'd let the people in the water drown, unless he saw every one of them saved, which he wouldn't do unless he was forward. . . .

After the first dozen steps, he slowed to a walk, so as not to appear a thrill-seeker or any of the crew on their way to rescue stations. He'd barely started when the deck started vibrating, until he expected the entire high-pressure cylinder assembly to hurtle up through the deck and overside. Then the deck heeled again, as *Aygsionan* began to swing to starboard.

For a moment outrage swamped Borlund's wits and he screamed something at the bridge that held no sense but fortunately went unheard. Then he remembered a fundamental of shiphandling: the stern goes the opposite way from the bow. Swinging *Aygsionan*'s bow to redward, away from the people in the water, would bring the stern and the churning propeller right over them. Swinging her bow to greenward would take the stern away from the swimmers, at least until the ship could stop engines.

Borlund kept moving, looked up to see if the crew was swinging out the seaboat yet, banged the calf of one leg into a stanchion and the shin of the other into a bollard, and yelled again. Nobody heard him this time either. He stopped to rub his bruises and remember that a boat might not be needed.

Kilmoyans' ancestors had been a semi-amphibious biped, and they themselves still looked like a cross between an ape and a seal. When they lived near water, like the folk along the Hask or the coastal Sadians, or by and on the sea like the Kertovans, they learned to swim as fast as they learned to walk, and better than any human could hope to emulate. That was one reason for the humans' cover story of being from the heart of a Skyfall-ruined continent in the southern hemisphere: they needed to account for their almost grotesque clumsiness (by Kilmoyan standards) in the water.

It was just possible that nothing would happen today to give Borlund a new round of nightmares. Anybody from whatever small craft that had died under *Aygsionan*'s prow who'd made it safely into the water might already be swimming clear of danger, waving to show the crew on deck where to throw the floatbelts to those who hadn't put on their own. . . .

He wanted it to be that way. He wanted it badly enough to taste the wish. He didn't think his wanting would make it come true, so he kept walking. As the deck cleared before him, he began to run again.

EHOMA TUOMITTI HAD SURVIVED MOST OF THE PERILS OF THE WESTERN AND Greater Seas, as well as lesser bodies of water. In fact, she preferred natural dangers to some of the modern high-powered machinery aboard *Valor*. A Farer could fight wind, waves, or even rocks and shoals, but not high-pressure steam that could fatally sear lungs with three breaths or engines that could pulp the hand of an oiler reaching to lubricate a bearing.

Now she was fighting both water and machinery, but the water was the lesser danger. Enough of it over her would be a shield against the ship. She thrashed downward, until the light above was dimmed and she thought she could see the bottom. Then she flipped over and stroked even faster toward the surface, steering away from the shadow of the ship's hull but otherwise not wasting a moment or the few breaths left in her lungs.

She had saved herself; now came saving others.

She was maybe halfway to the surface when she felt rather than heard an explosion. The pressure wave squeezed her all over, from ears to groin. Pain raged in her head and she thought she would lose her breakfast. Half-dazed, more than half-blind, she fought to let her breath out slowly, not hold it until her lungs burst or let it out so fast that she drowned.

She was just below the surface when something lashed across her forehead and left cheek, like the whisper-cut of a pirate ghatys. For a moment everything went dark, then her head broke the surface. Her left eye was still blind, but she managed a dim view from her right.

Also, her limbs were all still attached and working, and she could breathe. She no longer even wanted to vomit.

A day of miracles indeed.

As well as she could with one eye, Tuomitti searched the water around her. The launch had apparently sunk, the ship that sank her was outside her field of vision (although perhaps the home of that chorus of whistles and screams), and floating wreckage dotted the water. It must have been one of those pieces that laid her face open—badly enough that she could see blood in the water and be glad the Seakin mostly kept the bay clear of green-gullets and their equally hungry like.

Now she could make out heads. The boat chief, swimming strongly and calling "Skoi!" The Drilion merchant, who seemed to have at least two virtues Tuomitti hadn't expected: he could swim and he hadn't panicked.

Of course, fat is lighter than water. Any Seakin could tell you that.

"Did Skoi make it out?" Tuomitti shouted. Or at least she began to shout. The pain in her face and eye reduced her to a croak. The boat chief still heard, and waved one hand in a circle, to signal that she didn't know.

Tuomitti didn't know either, but she wasn't hopeful. If the stoker hadn't made it out of the engine compartment and got well clear before the boiler exploded, he was not only dead but gutted like a hylerksh ready for salting down.

Something large broke water just behind Tuomitti. She whirled, making blood drops fly and stabbing her head with new pain. She half-expected to see a green-gullet; instead she saw the stoker's body. Literally—his head was gone and something had laid his chest open like an axe blow.

That was everybody—no, it wasn't, and the missing two were the worst of all. Forgetting her pain, Tuomitti screamed:

"Hoy! Where's our Saadian friend? Goodwife, where are you?"

The boat chief echoed her. The Drilion merchant merely seemed to draw himself up higher in the water. The stoker's body was mute. The whistles, horns, and voices continued, but they seemed to be a great distance away and getting farther every moment.

Blood loss. Scalp and face cuts will bleed freely, even when they're not deep enough to cost you an eye.

BY THE TIME BORLUND REACHED THE FOREDECK, EVERYBODY FORWARD had rushed to greenside. So many were leaning over the railing that he expected the ship to list, and floatbelts, floatrings, deck furniture, and anything else that would support a swimmer were raining over the side. Right now, anybody in the water was in as much danger of being hit on the head by their would-be rescuers as of drowning.

The Kertovans' long "bond with the sea" had driven a good many lessons deep into their culture. One was that it was better to do something adequate at once than perfect an hour late. Apparently they'd decided that a boat in the water was the perfect solution.

There was hardly room to greenside now, and not much need for extra eyes or hands, nor any need at all for spectators. Borlund wandered over to redside, where he'd at least be out of the way, and leaned on the railing.

A thin cry, almost a wail, floated up to his ears from below. He looked down. Something—a Kilmoyan woman—was bobbing alongside. Alive—she was swimming clumsily, with one arm. One arm swimming—the other holding a bundle wrapped in a Saadian headscarf.

The wailing came from the bundle. It was a baby.

Borlund was on the railing before the knowledge of what he was going to do was clear in his mind. Then he jumped back down, ran across the deck, and snatched a floatring from a deckhand just about to fling it over the side.

"Sorry, I need this worse than you do."

The deckhand was still gaping as Borlund tossed the life ring at the woman and waited to see it land just out of her reach. He opened his mouth, but his shout died silently as Borlund sprang on to the railing again and dove overboard.

TUOMITTI WAS USED TO BEING IN COLD WATER, BUT NOT WITH HER FACE gashed and leaving a pink trail as she swam toward the boat chief. She was slow and clumsy, since she could not dip her head under without her wound feeling as if it was being laid open all over again.

Water still splashed over it from the little waves, and into her mouth and nose. She began to wonder what was going to kill her first—drowning, loss of blood, or the pain. (It felt as if two clawed hands had gripped her face and were trying to rip skin and fur off it, like scaling a fish.)

At some point her one good eye let her know that a ship was looming over her. No, two ships, one larger one ahead and another smaller one off to her—right? She thought she could still tell left from right and redside from greenside.

She nearly blundered into the boat chief, which drew a nasty laugh from the Drilion merchant. She'd almost rather he'd panicked, so that they could have let him drown with a reasonably clear conscience. Somehow, though, he'd managed to find a floatbelt buoyant enough to keep even him afloat. Why had the Gray Lord done such a miracle for a Drilion, and not for the woman and her baby?

No miracle, Tuomitti realized. Even her dim vision now showed her a dozen belts, rings, deck chairs, and other oddments bobbing on the water, flung down from one of the two ships. The boat chief had a ring under one arm and was pushing out a belt to Tuomitti. Then, seeing that the other Farer was hurt, she trod water while she pushed out the ring, easier to put on.

Wonderful. Now I can stay afloat long enough to bleed to death.

But Tuomitti would be cursed if she'd give that Drilion the satisfaction of dying in front of him. She dredged up the strength to pull on the ring, and found she did feel better. She even found her voice.

"Where's the woman?"

"Gone to the bottom with her brat, like as not," the merchant said.

Tuomitti found another reason for staying alive: to permanently maim the Drilion if the woman and babe came back, or kill him outright if they were gone. The boat chief's eyes said that she might help the Fleetfarer.

The second ship now lay straight ahead. It also seemed to have shrunk or backed away. No, something was coming toward them, only a half-cable away. A boat, your standard service boat that half the ships on the bay carried, high at prow and stern, low amidships for easy work with anything in the water—

And a Drylander sitting aft, steering, while four rowers who looked like Saadians making the spray fly as they put their backs into the work. A Drylander woman.

Tuomitti needed an explanation for that. She decided not to ask even the gods for it now. Not when she might not be able to endure it. She had to wait until she was in the boat before she could lose her senses.

THE SAADIAN WOMAN WAS YOUNG, ROBUST, AND ABLE TO KEEP HERSELF afloat once she was relieved of the burden of keeping her child above water. That took a bit longer than Borlund had expected. Twice the baby slipped out of the adults' hands and the whole rescue seemed about to sink with him. (At least Borlund thought it was a boy.)

The floatbelt was too big for the baby, and too small to fit over the woman's bulky, sodden garments. Borlund realized, too late, that he'd snatched a child's floatbelt, but afterthoughts solved no problems.

They finally arranged for Borlund to put on the floatbelt, which just fit him once he'd taken off his upper garments, then exhaled. He could barely breathe, but by only needing to use his legs to stay afloat, he could use both arms to hold the baby's head above water.

The baby stared at his rescuer with those curious green eyes that seemed to run more in Saadians than in Kertovans. Then he expressed his gratitude by throwing up all over Borlund.

Borlund muttered obscenities, then stopped when he heard the Saadian woman laughing. If she could laugh at a time like this, maybe he could at least be polite.

With an admirably practical lack of concern for modesty, the woman methodically stripped off every garment except her underwear, letting it all drift away except the headscarf. She swam over to Borlund and used that to wipe his face, then laughed again.

The warmth of the laughter fought the chill of the water in Borlund's mind. He coughed and licked salt from his lips.

"Best we don't laugh. If any are dead from this, their spirits may hear."

He had to repeat himself twice, before his north-islands-accented Kertovan reached the woman. At least he supposed it was his accent. Any Saadian woman with the price of a ferry-launch ticket was likely to know Kertovan fairly well.

Before she could reply, he heard someone hailing them, from redward. It seemed to come from the water, not from *Aygsionan*'s deck. Looking around, Borlund saw that *Aygsionan* had backed off a good cast or more and dropped anchor again. The hail came from a boat approaching them, with four Saadians rowing, one Kertovan sitting in the prow and directing the rowers, and what looked remarkably like a human woman in the stern, bending over somebody out of sight in the bottom of the boat.

"Slow—stop!" the Kertovan said. The oars trailed in the water, then were thrust out level and dripping as the boat's momentum carried it the rest of the way toward Borlund.

The woman struck out, covering the last few meters to the boat as fast as a racing swimmer. Four calloused hands reached down, gripping both her and her remaining garments. The garments did not survive the strain, and the woman tumbled into the boat almost naked.

She didn't wait to borrow as much as a cloak before she was at the gunwale again, reaching down for her child—definitely a son, Borlund saw, as he held it up. The baby was nestling against his mother's nearly bare torso and a Saadian was wrapping them both in a blanket before Borlund could struggle out of the floatjacket.

The urge to keep it as a souvenir yielded to the knowledge that he really hadn't done all that much and now desperately wanted out of the water. He'd avoided appearing before the Study Group Directors sleepless from nightmares; now his danger was pneumonia or at least a bad cold. He gripped the gunwale, heaved himself out of the water, and nearly fell back as an appalling face confronted him.

It had one glaring yellow eye and the other half of the face and part of the scalp swathed in a rough and already blood-soaked bandage. Pain and rage glared out of the visible eye, and a strong arm rose, extending a large hand with a Farer's tattoo all across the back. Borlund waited for that hand to lash across his throat, opening it to the windpipe.

Instead the yellow eye blinked, then drifted shut. The Kertovan woman slumped backward, and would have fallen if the human woman hadn't caught her. Borlund heaved again, slid into the boat, and nearly laid his forehead open on an oarlock.

"Careful, I'm out of bandages," the human said briskly in Kertovan with what sounded like a Saadian accent. "And don't bounce on Ehoma. She hit her head on a piece of wreckage in the water and—"

"Who are you?"

The woman frowned. She was dark-haired and sturdily built, as far as Borlund could tell when she was swathed in Kertovan foul-weather gear modified for a human. Her eyes were large and brown, and right now also totally expressionless.

"Barbara Weil, First Watch Commander aboard the coastal service vessel *Lingvaas*."

The name was familiar, since Borlund had memorized the roster of the Study Group's humans some months before. He couldn't remember that title being associated with the name, however.

Before he could ask for a further explanation, Weil shouted to her rowers and scrambled back aft. The oars plunged in deep and the boat spun around so fast that Borlund was thrown aft. He missed hitting his head on the gunwale again only because Barbara Weil caught him first.

"You hurt?" The tone was remarkably clinical.

"Not yet."

Weil actually laughed. "Stay that way. I want to get back to that Drilion we had to leave when we saw you and the family."

"The what?"

"You didn't hit your head, did you?"

"No."

"Then it's simple. We left a Drilion merchant in the water to pick you up. You and them." Weil's tanned thumb jerked toward the bow.

Borlund strangled a groan. He didn't want to be fussed over by Barbara Weil or the surgeons, wherever they ended up. What he wanted right now was to be aboard a ship outbound for some island so distant from Kertovan rule that everybody would have forgotten today's events by the time anyone learned where Sean Lincoln Borlund was.

A human officer with a Saadian crew had left a Drilion merchant in the water, possibly drowning, to rescue a human and a Saadian. If the Drilion actually had drowned, there would be a literally howling scandal.

Even if the Drilion had been hurt only in his dignity and purse, he would try to make a scandal. Sean Lincoln Borlund had lost his last hope of slipping quietly into a place in the Study Group and doing valuable work before anybody noticed him.

Instead, he'd managed to arrive under circumstances that would make a dozen drummers and drinkshop girls throwing wreathes at him superfluous. He'd thoroughly violated the principle of keeping one's head down and mouth shut, unwritten but almost as sacred to Kilmoyn's human refugees as the more formal "natural evolution."

He wasn't the first to do so, of course, But every other one he'd heard of in the last twenty years of the Study Group's existence had also ended in serious trouble!

chapter 4

Captain Over Captains Jossu I Hmilra eased himself into his high-backed chair and reached for his smokebowl and pouch without taking his eyes off the oiled wooden wall in front of him. The chair responded with a squeak of aged joints and a faint *pok* of ancient dreezan hide splitting somewhere new.

Maybe it was too old to be moved from the Seaview Chamber, and this is its way of telling me to pension it off.

I Hmilra had surprised most of his fellow members of the House of Captains when he had the chair moved from a window that let him look far out over Saadi Bay. They had muttered about the Greats finally overtaking him.

They would have muttered louder if he'd told the truth. When he was on land, he could no longer compose his thoughts while looking at the sea. Or at least not as well as when he looked at something else—like the hornwood of the wall in front of him, gleaming and even smelling of recuin oil.

He did not care for the change. It hinted of a day when he could not stand on the bridge of a ship and plot a course to yield the best shot at a pirate encampment or match speed with a storeship. Then he would come ashore forever, and he would give no more to the seas of Kilmoyn from that day until his body was slipped over the side and his spirit set free to roam those seas forever.

However, he could at least ensure that no one followed him around, waiting for that day to come so that they could step into his boots. He was fourth among the Captains Over Captains in the whole Kertovan Fleet. If he stayed fit for sea service he was likely in time to become the first. Lord and Lady willing, he might then have time to turn some of his dreams into realities.

He opened the pouch and sniffed. Krimo, cured in ale but not oiled.

He dropped a pinch of the ruddy leaf into the bowl, then decided to add a drop of oil for easy lighting. He undid the pocket at the bottom of the pouch and pulled out the carved eihn-tooth oil bottle. The spring-loaded silver top let one drop of oil hang glimmering for a moment, then slip softly down into the krimo.

Now the lighter. A spark, and the krimo flared yellow. *A little too much oil, but no harm done.* I Hmilra puffed several times to get the pipe well lit, then leaned back again.

His spine had just touched the dreezan-hide when a discreet cough floated past him from behind the chair.

"Captain-Born?"

The voice gave I Hmilra no reason to snarl at the intruder, and a good many reasons not to. One was that being rude to Nen Makhiri would be only slightly less of an offense than setting fire to the House of Captains. The other was that Makhiri would never have interrupted a good bowl if the matter had not been urgent.

"Yes?"

"There is a message for you."

"Bring it in."

"Pardon. I meant, a messenger."

"Live and present in the flesh?"

Another slight cough, this time in reproof. "So it appears, Captain-Born. A young commander, from Fort Huomikki, with a mounted escort."

That meant a message so important that it would be the Lord's own gift if I Hmilra did not have to deal with the matter personally. The mounted escort might even mean that he was under a confinement order, unlikely as that might seem—but those more distinguished than he had fallen afoul of the Supreme Council.

Reluctantly, I Hmilra knocked out his pipe. Smoking was prohibited in the dining chambers and halls of the House, and in one chamber reserved for those Captains who could not tolerate others smoking by reason of age, failing lungs, or simple perversity of nature. He hoped that the message was important enough to justify the loss of a pleasant interlude.

Makhiri led the way with his customary dignity, as though he was an armorclad flying the High Captain's flag and everyone else was fishing vessels and tugs. Across the chamber, down the passage to the left, then a right turn into the Visitors' Hospitality Chamber.

At least the guards and (presumably) their mounts were still outside. The young commander wore day uniform, his kilt showing the red border of the Gunner Corps and his green tunic lamentably bare of medals. But then, he could hardly have been weaned the last time the Island Republic went seriously to war. He also had the look of one with more than a trifle of Drilion blood, and it was only in the last generation that they had been sending their children into Kertovan ranks.

"Captain Over Captains." The address by rank and the hands pressed palms together in front of his chest proved that the young man at least knew service customs.

"I listen." *Polite, but it should give the right hint if he can take one at all.*

"I will be brief. But could we speak somewhere more discreet?"

"The grooming chamber is over there,"

"Excellent, Captain."

I Hmilra's whiskers twitched. He had meant the suggestion as a joke. *Was* the message something dire?

The only place to sit down in the grooming chamber turned out to be a bench facing the necessary pots. The commander looked at them sourly, then went to the door, hung the UNFIT FOR USE sign on the handle outside, closed the door, and locked it.

If you can't justify this carnival of secrecy, my young friend, I will have one of your ears decorating my cabin aboard Valor *and send the other to Alikili.*

"There has been an incident in the Bay."

"Not another case of public indecency aboard *Valor,* I trust? If someone has his bones rattling over that, they will rattle even louder when I'm done with them."

"No, Captain. It is a matter of possible negligence in lifesaving, involving a Saadian woman, a watch chief from *Valor,* and a Drilion passenger, among others."

"A Saadian woman?"

"Yes, and with a baby in arms."

I Hmilra noted that if one closed one's eyes, one could not tell that the commander had Drilion blood. His voice held as much outrage at unnecessary danger to a Saadian mother and child as if he were Saadian himself.

"Names?"

"The watch chief is Ehoma Tuomitti. The woman's name is—curse the writing—ah, I think it was Sikoe Yuurn, or something like that. They were in a ferry launch to the fort when—"

I Hmilra had turned into a statue at the two names. The commander did not notice. He sailed briefly through the remainder of the story, and only then saw that his listener was on his feet.

"What touches *Valor*'s name touches mine. Wait in the Vistors'. I will be garbed and with you as quickly as I can."

The commander's, "Yes, Captain" was addressed to I Hmilra's rapidly retreating back.

THE NEXT FEW MINUTES AFTER HE ROLLED INTO THE BOAT MADE SEAN BORlund regret that his pistol was in his baggage aboard *Aygsionan* instead of at his waist. It was ten years old and had not been the best brand even then, but it was a metallic-cartridge model whose six bullets should have survived a soaking. (Of course, being old and cheap made it heavier than newer models, and he might have had to discard it to stay afloat and fit to save others.)

The rowers thrust the boat vigorously through the rapidly vanishing fog to where the Drilion merchant bobbed like the cork from the lord of all ale jugs. They needed no orders from Barbara Weil. Just as well, too, as she was busy swathing the wounded Warfarer in so many bandages that the other might have been laid out ready for sliding overside into the sea.

When Weil started wrapping the Warfarer's left arm, totally unhurt as far as Borlund could see, he was bold enough to raise an eyebrow. That drew a glare from Barbara Weil, which in turn drew a laugh from the Saadian woman.

She was sitting in the bow, still wearing only the blanket, rocking her baby and patting him on the back. He was coughing and wheezing, not sounding particularly healthy, but definitely alive and breathing. Kertovan medicine was largely fit to handle the other conditions.

"Hush, brother," she told Borlund. That would have been somewhat bold on the part of a Saadian woman under most circumstances. In a boat full of Saadians and with a Drylander who'd just saved her life and her baby's, she doubtless thought custom fit only to feed a green-gullet's intestinal parasites.

"Good move," Weil said.

This brought the woman around to glare at Weil. "Do not treat him as a crippled child, either. You wish to keep peace between the merchant and Warfarer Tuomitti—"

"Thank you for the name," Weil said.

The woman glared again at the interruption. "To keep the peace, by making her seem so hurt that even a Drilion merchant in a rage would not quarrel with her."

Weil looked eloquently at her rowers.

"So they are not mute slaves?" the woman said. "I did not think so. But they must have learned to be deaf to you and dumb to others, or they would not be rowing for you."

The rowers proved that by not missing a stroke or batting an eye. Borlund felt less calm. This was when he first wished for his pistol, if only to fire a shot in the air to interrupt the argument.

Interruption came nonetheless, as they pulled alongside the Drilion merchant and another live Kertovan, floating to either side of an uncommonly ugly corpse. The Kertovan woman, in boatcrew garb, swam lithely over to the boat, then peered at the bandaged Warfarer Tuomitti.

"Does she live?"

The other three all looked at one another, each daring the others to speak. The boatcrew—boat chief, from the earrings and lanyard—took the right cue and nodded.

"Pray to all." She turned toward the merchant. "Can you swim? Or just float like a—driftwood—until the tide carries you somewhere?"

The merchant replied with several tedious obscenities and a good deal of thrashing and splashing. Apparently he could swim well enough that there was no need for anyone to tow him to the boat. It took him long enough that Borlund began to be afraid the boat would have to move to avoid another collision, but the merchant finally floundered alongside.

It took Weil, Borlund, and the boat chief to haul the merchant over the side, with little help and not much more cooperation from the man. Either he'd exhausted himself swearing and splashing, or he was in an even worse temper than before. Twice Borlund wasn't sure they were going to be able to land this particular fish. After the second time, he began to wonder if they could find some excuse not to do so.

At last the merchant landed with a soggy thud in the bilges, narrowly missing Tuomitti and not missing her at all when he vomited what seemed to be half the harbor. Borlund resisted a strong urge to kick him in the stomach only because that might make him vomit again.

Instead he grabbed a bailing bucket, dipped it over the side, and began cleaning the Warfarer as best he could. He'd succeeded in getting the worst off when he realized that Barbara Weil was trying to talk to him.

"You hit your head or something, Citizen—?"

"Borlund. Sean Lincoln Borlund."

"Well, Citizen Borlund, does your ship have a doctor aboard?"

"Ah—I never saw one. But then I didn't ask."

Weil looked ready to spit over the side or possibly on him. "Very observant. If she doesn't, she can't do more than first-care, and that's not worth hauling our friends up and down ladders. They can't endure it."

The boat chief started on what sounded like an indignant rebuttal, until the Saadian woman (unseen by the merchant or Weil, seen by Saadian woman (unseen by the merchant or Weil, seen by Borlund) kicked the boat chief in the small of the back. The boat chief's mouth stayed open but no sound emerged.

"Right. No doctor aboard *Lingvaas* either. So we're bound for the fort. They've a doctor, even stretcher-bearers."

Now it was the merchant's turn to start expostulating, about his reluctance to be handled by landfighter healers. Weil cut him off briskly.

"Don't talk so much, and *don't* try to get up. You might have internal injuries, or have swallowed contaminated water."

The second was possible but unlikely. Any Kilmoyan folk who depended as much as the Kertovans on working with the Seakin acquired a nose for pollution control even before their industrialization. The Seakin were probably tougher than some of the Earth sea creatures wiped out by pollution, but they still had a low tolerance for raw sewage or toxic chemical wastes. Saadi Bay was probably cleaner than a good many comparable bodies on environmentally conscious, Gaaian, harmonious-technology Esperanza.

The Drilion merchant lay back down again with a melodramatic groan. Maybe he was good enough at reading human faces, voices, and body language to realize that if he didn't lie down as if he were injured, he would be lying down because he was injured.

Borlund was cold to the bone, drenched to the skin, and feeling soggy inside as well. He was tolerating his present and prospective situation only because he'd put himself into it in a good cause.

He still wished Barbara Weil would moderate her tongue. If you wished this kind of business to end tidily, you did not publicly slash to ribbons the pride of Drilion merchants.

But Weil, the boat chief, and the Saadian woman seemed to be working almost as a trained team. The best that a mere male could do in a situation like this was keep quiet or at least out of the way.

Weil raised a hand and the stroke barked an order. The Saadian rowers spun the boat around until Borlund could see Fort Huomikki over his shoulder, dead ahead.

JOSSU I HMILRA LEFT THE HOUSE OF CAPTAINS AS QUICKLY AS HE COULD without calling attention to himself, which was not as quickly as he could have wished. The young commander had brought his message and a decent escort, but neither a spare riding dreezan, a decent carrier, nor hire-fare to find one on the streets.

The man was young, perhaps too newly registered to have faded the dye in his first dress kilt; he could not appreciate I Hmilra's, "When I was your age, I did that sort of thing too." The Captain discreetly counted coins into the hand of one of the escorts and sent him out to ambush a hire-carrier.

That took long enough for I Hmilra to study the weather board with more intensity than the readings themselves deserved. A balanced tide, wind from the north-northeast and freshening, barometer falling but so slowly that it said little about today's weather—not much to concern Farers by sea or common folk by land. But if he made a ritual of studying the weather, it might discourage the curiosity of fellow Captains long enough for him to take evasive action.

Not the politest term, when applied to his peers, but right now their curiosity would be about as welcome as a shore-commanded mine exploding under *Valor*'s engine room. It would inevitably drag him into political talk, and also delay him.

If he went down to the fort quickly enough, he might settle matters before the leaf-scrap press, the wall posters, and the street-corner howlers flung it about like a bump-ball. If not that lucky, then at least some of the tales would tell of efforts made to settle the matter justly, by a commander trusted more than many.

The hire-carrier rattled up before I Hmilra needed more than a few polite excuses. Cross-sashed, he strode out into a wind that was definitely freshening and climbed into the carrier.

"Fort Huomikki," he told the driver.

"Low road or high road?"

"What say you of the wind?"

The "high road" was shorter and all downhill, but ran along the top of a steep slope. It could be perilous on a windy day.

"I say you be a Captain, not I."

I Hmilra mentally conceded the first two touches to the driver. "High road will be safe enough, if you don't dawdle."

"I won't, but if we end ahind of one who does—"

"I do know about streets, believe me."

The driver pulled at his whiskers. A hundred Greats ago, he might have been fined or even (if unfree) flogged for insolence. The laws had been changed; the memories had outlasted them.

No surprise, really, when the cast of mind that made those laws has done the same.

"Jeh—yaaa!" the driver called, and the carrier rolled forward. One of the escort's mounts swayed nervously from side to side. The commander looked at the rider with an "If you dare to fall off . . ."expression.

Then they all stepped off downhill.

SEAN BORLUND SPENT MOST OF THE BOAT JOURNEY TO FORT HUOMIKKI TRYing not to shiver, and the rest trying to read the signals now darting in all directions.

Lingvaas was signaling to *Aygsionan*. Both were signaling to the big *Valor*-class armorclad, and the warship was signaling to both of them and to Fort Huomikki as well. The fort seemed to be using both lantern and flag signals to talk to everybody at once, including the shore. Borlund thought he'd heard them firing signal guns as well, but that turned out to be only firing practice at the Kwinmouth Battery.

Borlund began to feel as if his arrival in Saadi could hardly be more conspicuous if he'd arrived wearing a glitterskin robe and a golden crown, in a ceremonial barge rowed by twelve silver-collared slaves. There were those in the human community who felt that perhaps humans ought to seek "higher visibility," but Borlund trusted neither their motives nor their political influence.

Certainly they wouldn't be too numerous in the Study Group, let alone its Directorate. There wasn't much they could do to punish him if they lacked either a case against him or the courage to raise a scandal by sending him home. However, they could see that he spent his first and only three-year term in Saadi working on petty details with little contact with any breed of Kilmoyan.

That would be a sad waste, nor did he think that was overestimating his own talents in believing so. More likely, the Directorate was overestimating the resources the Kertovan portion of Kilmoyn's human community could devote to political games among themselves.

The political games hadn't escalated to the point of nearly open warfare, as had relations between the descendants of those humans who'd made the Great Migration sixty years ago and those who'd remained behind under the authority of the Confederation of Dhandara. Of course, the easterners weren't entirely their own masters; the Dhandaran landholders knew a valuable and exploitable resource when they saw one. But to Borlund's thinking, that made a united front that efficiently used everybody's talents all the more important for the westerners.

The shriek of a steam whistle interrupted Borlund's internal monologue on political philosophy. A steam launch in Fleet colors was turning in front of them, a brawny Farer standing in the stern with a coiled line. Then the Farer spun around; the line uncoiled like a whiptree shoot, soaring over twenty meters of water toward the boat.

Without thinking, Borlund got his feet under him, crouched to guard his head, and plucked the weighted end of the line out of the air. The boat chief moved to take it, but Borlund was already knotting the end around the towing bit in the bow. The sailor in the launch waved, the whistle shrieked again, and foam curled alongside as the tow gathered way.

As he sat down, Borlund noticed that Barbara Weil was smiling. She might even have been smiling at him.

chapter 5

Jossu I Hmilra's progress to Fort Huomikki was slow enough to unsettle his temper, in spite of taking the quicker high road. There were long stretches of narrow street, the bricks or stones slick with the early morning's mist and the late morning's dreezan dung and spilled barrels. One crossing was completely blocked by an overturned charcoal burner's wagon; I Hmilra prayed briefly that the furnace wouldn't set anything afire before the Watch arrived. And always there was the din of the city—squealing axles, bellowing and whining dreezans and mustekkas, people cursing, complaining, or sometimes even being happy at the top of their lungs in half a dozen different languages.

I Hmilra could not shut himself away from the din with his own thoughts, nor could he say a single word to his escort without shouting. The only man he could reach was the hire-driver, who had long since proved that he was not being paid enough to be a conversational partner.

It was a weary journey, until they reached the high road which twisted down the bluffs above Kwinmouth. At the foot it joined the sea road, but on the way down it gave a fine view of Saadi Bay to the south and the city to the east.

Fort Huomikki and *Valor* were doing a fair bit of signaling, however, and two other ships also had lamps winking. One was a smallish red-hulled deep-sea mixed-carrier, with nothing to distinguish her but a taller funnel than usual. Probably *Aygsionan*. The other was a propeller-driven coaster, with three masts and a funnel aft that suggested she'd been built as a deep-sea huntership.

"Captain-Born?"

The commander had ridden close enough that he could lean from his saddle and reach I Hmilra's ear without shouting.

"What now?"

"I saw signals from the Drylander's Council House."

"What of that? If a Drylander is involved in the accident—"

"They were signaling that ship. The smaller one, with the black hull."

I Hmilra reflected wearily that recruiting Host commanders from Drilion merchants' sons might serve justice. It did not make them less ignorant of ships and the sea.

"Unless my memory is failing me—" in a tone that promised a slow death to anyone who suggested that it was "—that ship is *Lingvaas*, the coast patroller with the half-Drylander crew. Doubtless the Study Group wishes her to become involved, if she was not already."

"You may well be right, Captain-Born. The more so in that I see on the road below us several Drylanders seemingly bound the same way as ourselves." The commander's youthful face was as bland as his voice, but I Hmilra could not doubt that the man was enjoying bursting a rocket over his superior's head.

Even from well above, the Drylanders were hard to mistake. Two of them rode dreezans and sat them better than Drylanders usually did; they had either practice or perhaps specially made saddles. I Hmilra would not begrudge them the latter; Drylanders' legs were far longer than those of any Faring race.

Two other Drylanders rode in a single-pole speeder, one driving and the other clutching the rails for dear life. A swift conveyance moving even more swiftly—perhaps too much so for the wet sea road? Perhaps the commander was right in seeing meaning in those signals.

It was easy to say (as I Hmilra had done many times), "Don't take every Drylander fart as a portent of the next Skyfall." It would also be moderately easy to reach Fort Huomikki ahead of the Drylanders, or at least not far behind.

"Ten more slyn if we reach the Fort before those Drylanders," I Hmilra called.

"Aye. And if we go off the road?" the driver replied, unblinking.

I Hmilra laughed and passed a ten-slyn piece to the commander. "If we do, see that his family gets this as well as his fare."

"Just see that you don't ride off after your lord," the driver added. "Loyalty's loyalty, but a workingman's family needs a roof and a bed more."

Then the driver's whip cracked, and they were off again.

* * *

A BAND WAS PLAYING AS THE LAUNCH AND ITS TOW APPROACHED THE FORT Huomikki boat landing. Practicing, rather—Sean Borlund didn't have much of an ear for music, but he could tell seasoned bandsmen of either race from novices. A bunch of novices today, it seemed—the brass section in particular sounded like some large barnyard animal having a difficult delivery, and no two drums were quite on the same beat.

The Saadian woman shifted her now-sleeping baby to the other shoulder and grinned. "Look at the clear sky, not the clouds. Noise is supposed to drive away evil spirits."

Borlund managed to return the smile. He couldn't tell from her tone whether she believed the old tale or not. The open boat was no place to ask when any answer was bound to offend someone.

At times Borlund almost sympathized with the official human ban on religion, in spite of what he'd seen the ban do to his two bearer-partners who were secretly Observant. Their broad tolerance of other ways of looking at the cosmos wasn't always the norm for Kilmoyans—and it apparently had definitely *not* been the norm in pre-Esperanza human society.

Borlund ducked as the cast-off bowline whipped over his head, then nearly took the weighted shaft of an oar in the ribs as the rowers returned to work. The next moment they were alongside the landing stairs. Borlund was the second out, following the bow man, and it was to him that the Saadian woman handed her baby.

Fortunately it didn't wake up. Borlund had spent enough time with human infants, his own and others', to know which end to burp and which end to diaper, but the morning's events seemed to have driven that knowledge to the back of his mind.

Delayed reaction was also weakening his legs, and he had to sit down on a bollard to avoid putting the baby down. He was immediately chased from his perch by several aggressive pierhands handling lines from the launch and the boat. Then what seemed like half the garrison of the fort swarmed toward him.

Borlund saw commanders and troopers from both the Saadian and Kertovan infantry, plus a self-sufficient band of hospital attendants of both races, a couple of doctors, and an artillery battery leader who looked as if he would take charge of the mob scene if he could only make himself heard over the uproar. Since even the loudest wrong notes from the band recruits were lost in the shouting, this was a vain hope.

Somehow, though, the dead boilerman was bagged, Ehoma Tuomitti and the Drilion merchant ended up on stretchers, and a woman who looked like a commander's wife all but kidnapped the Saadian woman's baby. This forced the Saadian woman to dash off after her, but before she did, she called over one bare shoulder to Borlund.

"This will be remembered, and others will learn of it."

Borlund was not so ungracious as to say the first thing that came into his mind, which was, "That's what I'm afraid of." Instead, he cupped his hands and shouted, "I was just the first one to see you. I wasn't the only one who would have helped."

The effort at modesty was lost in the din, and also because as Borlund spoke somebody threw the woman a second blanket and a cloak and she was too busy wrapping herself up to listen. She vanished, leaving Borlund hoping that he'd heard a promise, not a threat.

Barbara Weil stepped up behind him and said, "Come along."

"The next time somebody tells me to come along without telling me why or where, I may push them into the bay and jump on top of them until they sink."

Weil flushed under her tan for a moment, and her mouth tightened. Then she shrugged.

"If you don't need a doctor—"

"No. Maybe a healer and some hot hoeg. Make that a *lot* of hot hoeg, and I don't care what formula."

"Sweetened?"

"As I said, if it doesn't drink me first, I'll drink it. Then I think I want to lie down—"

"Better not count on that. The Study Group is sending down representatives, to interrogate—ah, interview you."

"Me?"

"Us, actually. So if you want to talk things over with me beforehand—"

"That sounds like plotting against the Group." As her face hardened again, he added hastily, "Or at least that's what the Directorate will call it. You may have nothing to lose from such a charge, but what about—?"

"You? How important are you?"

Borlund wouldn't have understood, let alone answered, that question if he'd had his wits clear. "Ah—how important *is* any new assignee to the Group?"

"Important enough—oh, floods, there's no way to talk about this now, but if I don't, you might foul us both without knowing that you'd done it."

"Is it enough if I watch my tongue, and meet you someplace afterward to hear the explanation?"

Weil smiled. Her face was round and weathered, and her best feature was enormous brown eyes, but that smile seemed to light up the whole landing.

"Glory and wonder! He doesn't think he knows everything!" The smile took the edge off the words, and Borlund wanted to squeeze her hand or commit some even more flagrant breach of intergender customs.

What saved them both was a quartet of hospital attendants—no, the red kilts said artillery, in spite of the stretcher—coming up.

"Sean Borlund?" one of them said.

"Guilty," was the first word that came to his lips.

"Into the litter, please," the leader said.

"Why?"

"Into the litter." Borlund noted the omission of "Please," also the gray eyes fixed on him like the muzzles of twin crankguns. The woman wore the badges of a battery subchief, which meant she was probably sterile, but she could have acquired that tone and presence just as well by years of drilling recruits.

He looked at Barbara Weil. She obviously knew quite a bit more that she wouldn't or couldn't tell him, and was even more obviously trying not to laugh.

Borlund sighed and climbed on to the stretcher. Obviously his day's quota of being ordered around by totally strange females wasn't yet filled.

THE WAY THE CARRIER PLUNGED DOWNHILL MADE JOSSU I HMILRA WONDER if the driver *had* a family. He looked old enough that his children's children might already be seeking mates. Or could he be a veteran racer from the days before the railsteamers, when a crack carrier driver was written up in more than the leaf-scrap journals and his share of the wagers made on his runs could leave him a wealthy man?

I Hmilra had been a fair whip in his younger days and could recognize the embers of old fire still glowing in the driver. They shot down the road at a pace that always allowed them to swerve around or aside from other traffic and kept the wheels firmly on the pavement. But the margin between the carrier and disaster was always as thin as a drinkshop brawler's patience. Only his position and experience with a few such runs himself kept I Hmilra able to seem calm.

The commander had no such experience, and was too busy controlling his dreezan to have any strength left over for hiding his fear. His troopers clearly found this entertaining; I Hmilra found it all the more reason to keep his own face an impenetrable mask, which he vowed to maintain even as the water closed over his head. . . .

They reached water level only a trifle behind the Drylanders, but on this last stretch before the turnoff to the fort, traffic was still heavier. I Hmilra stared glumly at the water curling over the beach, almost to the foot of the stone causeway. Between tide, wind, and probably a storm far offshore, the water was too high to allow passage along the beach.

I Hmilra had seen pictures of the early days of Fort Huomikki, twenty Greats before the Drylanders came to the Island Republic. It had been an island surrounded by water deep enough for the early harbor steamers. Now, often as not, a well-shod walker could pass at low water dryfooted from the mainland to the gate of the fort.

I Hmilra bent forward to call to the driver, then sat back, he hoped, before anyone noticed him. More slyn would not draw more speed from a team and driver already doing their best, any more than overpressuring boilers could take a ship through the Driomehen Passage in a half-watch.

By now everyone for within three or four casts had seen the race, and I Hmilra wondered how many slyn were going to change hands over bets. He could not see if the Drylanders were still signaling; a bluff cut off his view of their Council House and most of the city, and two big merchanters did the same for *Lingvaas*.

Those on the road had done more than see the race. They were trying to clear the way for the racers, as eagerly as wingfish seeking shoal water to evade a band of Seakin. Walkers and those aboard dreezans left the road entirely; mustekka riders and anything with vehicles slowed to a crawl, to let their fellow-travelers by.

One carter who left pulling aside until almost too late cost I Hmilra some distance. The driver made up for it in the next few moments, cutting across a stretch of hard-packed gravel. The larger stones in the gravel made I Hmilra think of his teeth and the carrier's springs, but slowed nothing. The commander and his outriders kept up as if invisible ropes bound them to the carrier, and when the whole party regained the road they'd picked up a good cast on their opponents.

By now I Hmilra could see the Drylanders' faces clearly enough for a clear conscience about this mad dash. They might well have legitimate business at the fort. Certainly it would be as well if they had to carry it out under the eyes of I Hmilra or some other person equal in both rank and knowledge of the Drylanders.

Three casts to the turnoff to the fort—and suddenly one of the Drylander riders was pulling his mount savagely around. I Hmilra saw the dreezan scrabbling for a footing, then complete the turn and come pounding back toward him. The forward riders pulled rein and turned inward, trying to block the Drylander's path without blocking the carrier. The commander's curses filled the air, so loud that I Hmilra couldn't have heard his own even if his mouth hadn't been suddenly dried into silence.

The driver's whip cracked like a rifle shot, and the Drylander's mount reared. I Hmilra had an unpleasantly good view of a discolored nail on a foretoe, and a brown patch across its belly from rear rib to male organ.

Then the dreezan lost its balance, skidding and toppling to the right. I Hmilra saw the Drylander in midair, wished him a landing with only painful injuries, then needed all his strength and every hand and foothold the carrier offered in order not to follow the Drylander.

The dreezans swung hard to the left; smoke rose as the driver locked the brakes on the left wheels. That kept the carrier from riding up and over the falling dreezan, perhaps even from overturning. As the team and carrier hit the edge of the road, the driver unlocked the brakes, cracked the whip, and sent the dreezans lunging ahead.

The Drylanders in the speeder had stopped to watch their comrade's fate. Now they were trying to get underway again. They were too late. The driver turned again, this time swinging the stoutly built carrier against the lighter speeder like a whiplash against a dreezan's flank.

The speeder came apart. Its two occupants were suddenly only two more pieces of debris flying through the air. One of them landed rolled up into a ball, and when he stopped moving, uncurled himself without apparent injury. I Hmilra thought it was the driver. The other flew like a rocket clean over the boulders, which would have cracked his bones to powder, and landed with a mighty splash in a weed-slimed tide pool. He also rose, sputtering and cursing in a way that no mortally hurt creature could have managed.

I Hmilra established that his legs would support him and that his teeth would not chatter. Then he rose, gripping the back of the driver's seat.

"You don't get ten slyn for that, my friend," he hissed.

"That's gratitude as the Captain-Borns—"

"You get a hundred, whatever comes of this day." I Hmilra started to hop out, turned the hop into a more dignified slide, and found himself on the road facing the young commander.

His eyesockets and lips were the color of Seakin milk and his hands shook on the reins. If he'd had any foreknowledge whatever of this, he could pursue an acting career after he was dismissed from the Republic's service.

And that suspicion itself is my fear speaking. I Hmilra commanded his voice.

"Where is the last Dryland rider?"

"He dashed off toward the fort before we—ah—encountered the speeder."

"Send two riders ahead to make sure that he is constrained. Have the rest tend to our friends here, except for one to escort me to the fort."

"You—"

"I could ride, in a dim and distant day before your dam proved her fertility. Perhaps I still can. Certainly there is something at the fort that has the Drylanders mightily perturbed. I still need to know what it is, the more so in that they seemed ready to commit murder to keep me from learning."

"Ah—perhaps they didn't recognize—"

"Perhaps Seakin will also grow wings tomorrow. But if if you are wagering, put your slyn elsewhere."

I Hmilra looked around him as the riders dismounted. Some held the mounts, while others drew healing packets from their waist pouches and converged on the fallen Drylanders.

As I Hmilra found a likely dreezan, a shot told him that the fallen beast was now out of its pain.

SEAN BORLUND WAS IN A FULL DOCTOR'S EXAMINING CUBICLE WHEN the riot started. Or at least it was his first thought, that the incident had touched off violence among the various races of the fort's garrison.

Then he heard heavy guns firing. His thoughts turned to even worse possibilities, such as an attack by the Imperial Hask Squadron, at long last come out from behind its minefields—

"Damned recruits," the doctor muttered. "Even at drill, they can't get four guns off within a six-breath of one another."

"Oh, and when were you a gunner?" someone muttered, just loud enough to be heard.

"I helped defend Fort Kirja when the pirates attacked overland," the doctor snapped. "That was three days of battle. The only powder you've ever smelled is what you put in your hair."

The same or another someone made a rude noise but no other reply. The doctor stepped back from Borlund.

"All right, my young friend. To the best of my knowledge and belief, you're none the worse for your bath. Go take that hoeg for its heat, and some herb water and wafers to balance your fluids."

The idea of eating anything solid made Borlund's stomach shudder. To cover that, he looked at the clock on the wall. His nerves were *not* what they ought to be, if he thought the noise of firing practice and recruits going out to drill meant serious trouble.

Fort Huomikki was a key installation; a third of its garrison was picked Host regulars, half artillery and half infantry. It was also a major training camp for the Saadian Coastal Defense, whose recruits supplied a good part of the rest of the garrison.

Then an unmistakably human voice rose above the din:

"In the name of the Drylander Study Group, I demand entrance."

An unintelligible Kilmoyan reply.

"Very well. Then I *request* entrance, to speak to Sean Lincoln Borlund."

Another unintelligible reply, sounding vaguely affirmative. The door opened and a tall human male with a square-cut beard strode in.

"Candidate Borlund?"

"Yes. Are you from the Directorate?"

"Sebastian Medvedev, Directorate Junior, at your service."

"I thought I was supposed to be at yours."

"That attitude will hardly help when you appear before the Seniors." Medvedev brushed dust and dried salt off his tunic, although he kept his hands away from his holster.

Borlund stood, reaching to the right to brace himself. His hand encountered a hot cup. He lifted it to his lips. It was the sweetened hoeg he'd requested.

"Thank you," he said, to the air in general.

"You're welcome," came Barbara Weil's voice from somewhere behind and to the left. Medvedev's eyes swiveled that way too. He seemed about to sprout fangs.

"Is this your—?" he began.

"I'm a witness. Under Kertovan law, I can claim the right to be here, or at the Directorate's judgment, or both. So can a few others. You can't snatch Borlund off like a stolen load of firewood, hoping you can burn up the evidence before the Watch arrives."

"I have no such intention."

"What about before your speeder accident?"

"That was no—"

"Ah, here we are," the doctor said, sidling in and past Medvedev with a pewter jug. From the condensation on its exterior, it had to be straight out of the cooling pit. "What were you about to say was no accident?"

Medvedev looked briefly torn between answering, walking out, and telling the doctor to leave. He took a deep breath and seemed to remember the dictates of both prudence and manners.

"The Study Group was sending a party to take Candidate Borlund to the Group House," he said. "It was sufficient to both carry and guard him and his baggage. No, I don't know who we were supposed to guard him against—I was the junior member of the party."

Medvedev was not too junior to be free with accusations against a Kertovan or Kertovans unknown for assaulting the party on the high road just outside the fort. He was not so free with the names of the Kertovans. Barbara Weil finally lost what remained of her patience over that.

"The one you suggest may have assaulted you is Captain Over Captains Jossu I Hmilra. Very senior, very well-connected, and under the Fleet Reserve Law my superior and patron."

"I know all that, you garcik!" Medvedev snapped, using the most obscene form of the word for a sterile female. It implied that she was sterile due to vice or excess.

Weil's return look should have peeled paint off the walls. Borlund felt like throwing his cup at either of them, but decided not to waste the hoeg. Instead he stepped between them.

"Am I supposed to be quartered at the Group House or not?"

"Yes, as soon as we can take you there."

"When will that be?"

"Ah—as soon as I can gain access to a telephone."

The doctor, who'd managed to listen to the whole exchange in silence until now, laughed. "You can send word faster by walking, or hiring a recruit as messenger. We've only been on the wire-speaker net for two Greats, and the sea air puts it out half the time. Besides, it will take longer to get permission than to send the messenger. May I offer one of my orderlies, if they're all free?"

Refusing hospitality was a cardinal sin in Kertovan etiquette. Offending the doctor with that sin might make him willing to tell other Kertovans about the conversation he'd just overheard. Borlund saw those thoughts play across the other human faces, and heard them in his own mind.

"I am grateful," Medvedev said finally.

"Then let us go," the doctor said. He put a hand on Medvedev's elbow and ushered him out.

Borlund and Weil looked at each other. "You sure you want to go to Group House right now?" she asked.

"I said, that until I know more, I'd rather go by the rules."

"What rules? This is the Directorate's whim," Weil snapped. Borlund looked at the door.

"They already know," she said, with a shrug. Her shoulders, Borlund noticed, were broad, but not out of proportion to the rest of her large-boned frame. "You can do as you please, but if they can't get you up to the House tonight, you can sleep aboard *Lingvaas*."

His face must have told several different stories. "Oh, we have a spare cabin and plenty to eat, for a night or two," Weil said. "Just get to the Stores Quay and ask for Eldunkaa or Suun. One of them is sure to be on duty."

"Eldunkaa or Suun. What if I want to spend the night at the fort?"

"They may not have a bed, they won't have good food, and they may interrogate you privately."

Borlund recognized the euphemism. He wouldn't have to fear that in the Group House or aboard Weil's ship, no matter what the magistrates decided to make of this case. Aboard *Lingvaas*, he might even have a better chance of learning what was going on here.

chapter 6

"Wan'wa crossing! All out for Wan'wa Crossing!"

"I heard you the first time," Jossu I Hmilra muttered under his breath. The steward either didn't hear or thought a Captain Over Captains was beneath his notice. He tramped aft down the passage between the seats and vanished, still bawling, through the rear door into the next wagon.

I Hmilra was long since on his feet and heading for the front door, his attendant behind him. The man was really not needed for such a short journey, ending at the estate, but I Hmilra had not brought him for the work he was expected to do.

He had come out of town because the newsgatherers were on the prowl like Seakin on the flanks of a school of miuni. I Hmilra had never in ten Greats caught the man yielding to any temptation that a good servant was expected to resist, but why expose him to more? Slyn flowed like drinks, and drinks flowed like a broken feedwater pipe as newsgatherers sought to amuse themselves and perhaps even their readers by gathering fact, stories, rumors, and outright lies about today's unseemliness at Fort Huomikki.

There was such a thing as exposing a virtuous man to too great temptation. As the Watch made no objections (or at least no more than formal ones), the attendant boarded the fourth-twenty train with I Hmilra.

The captain would gladly have taken his driver and Commander Ejkmus as well, to also free them from temptation and harassment. However, the Watch had other ideas, which they expressed with a firmness not even a senior Captain Over Captains could ignore. One could not politely speculate whether they had been paid by newsgatherers; most likely they merely lacked imagination rather than ethics.

These thoughts took I Hmilra and his attendant out of the wagon and on to the platform beside the rails, gritty with damp cinders. As the attendant set down the baggage, the railsteamer whistled for departure. It was a humpcab eight-wheeler, and I Hmilra could see the pilot in the cab, waving to the invisible stoker at the rear. Then the couplings rattled and banged, as the steamer pulled the slack out of the train and the wagons began to move. Almost before one could draw a breath they'd vanished into the twilight.

"This way, Captain-Born," the attendant said.

I Hmilra saw that the estate had sent a whole squadron after him, not only the high-wheeler but two freight wagons as well. Both wagons were well loaded, and what spare crates, sacks, and barrels didn't take, servants did. Mostly well-built farmhands, I Hmilra noticed, and he would wager that some of them were armed with more than sticks and clubs. Was it bandits they feared, the merely hungry, or today's events?

They'd need no arsenal at the station tonight, for all that it was nearly dark. The new self-lighting gas lamps carved yellow circles out of the smoky darkness, and most of the passengers who'd left the train had already left the station as well. The only exception was a party of schoolgirls, waiting under the eye of their mistress like newly aboard Warfarer recruits waiting under the eye of a watch chief.

Praise Lord and Lady, that Tuomitti would live. She might be one-eyed and would certainly be worse of temper, but the Fleet could live with her temper and she would see more with one eye than most did with two.

A pity that it will be hard to procure justice against those who hurt her. Perhaps favor to the Drylanders who saved her will be easier?

Several servants now climbed down to load the baggage and help I Hmilra up into the high-wheeler. He brushed them off and scrambled up beside the driver.

"After that train ride, I need fresh air more than invisibility," he said.

"Aye, those rail-riding things lock you up and then joggle you all about until you've less teeth than a new babe," the driver said. He was the last of the estate's original staff still on duty, and he'd come to the I Hmilira household even before then, a fisher lad with youth-tufts still covering half his face. All those Greats of service had earned him a free tongue, as little as I Hmilra felt like chatting.

"I once felt the same," the captain said. He grinned. "Particularly after hearing one of Othan's lectures on the future of railsteamers!"

"The lad did go on a bit, he did."

"Oh, he's put his money where his tongue wagged, and done well enough by it. Besides, there's more than money coming out of the rails. They're one way we can hope to build up the metalworking, for when we need more ships."

"Then you think it's coming to war, Captain-Born?"

The whistle of an approaching train saved I Hmilra from an embarrassing silence. By the time the twenty wagons of baled tasselroot, lumber, and canned oil had rolled by, he'd chosen words to the purpose.

"There's more than wars needing new ships," he said. "The Confederation will be many Greats buying ships before they can build them in their western provinces, and better they buy from us than from the Empire."

"Better still they stay ashore altogether," the driver said, and cracked his whip twice as a signal to the other drivers, once as a signal to his team. The dreezans leaned into the harness, and leather, wood, and bone joined metal in a ragged chorus as the high-wheeler began to roll.

"WAY, THERE!" THEN CAME "TOSS OARS!"

The boat slid alongside *Lingvaas*'s gangway and bumped the pontoon. Comments and orders mixed, floating down from the deck and rising from the boat. Sean Borlund heard without listening as he worked his way from boat to pontoon, trying to lose neither bag nor balance.

He wasn't sure what he expected aboard the ship, but he saluted the steerpost as he stepped on deck, and asked the greasy darkness:

"Permission to come aboard?"

"Welcome aboard, Farer Borlund," a voice came from aft. Borlund wouldn't have been surprised at a Saadian accent; instead he heard someone who had clearly grown up speaking the purest High Kertovan, even if sea service might have roughened the voice.

"Sorry to impose on you—"

"We have duties to Farer Veal," the high-accented Kertovan said. Borlund frowned, then remembered the usual Kertovan difficulty with the letter "W."

"As have I," he said. What his duties to Barbara Weil might be, he could only guess, but he would perform them even if the Directorate did whine and squeal. He owed her that much, for offering him a bunk aboard her ship until the "wise and honest" of the Study Group charter prevailed, found him space at Group House, and put the investigation of his day's work on a civilized basis, preferably a long way from the newsgatherers.

He was also beginning to look forward to another stay aboard ship, even a cramped one at anchor. The possibility of more of Barbara Weil's company also appealed more than it appalled. It would take the edge off his curiosity about her, at least.

Not that he expected much to come of the curiosity; at her age she doubtless had two or three children by as many different sire-parents, as well as the responsibilities of her position. Second-in-command of a Fleet vessel (even a shorehugger) was high Kertovan rank for a human, and the negotiations for it might well have taken longer than the gestation of a baby. (Would have, if any Fleet priests put their hands into it!)

"Follow me," came another voice, this time with the expected Saadian accent but the flavor of education as well. Borlund followed.

He followed the Saadian accent across what seemed like hundreds of meters of smooth, slick deck, coated with dew over a light-toned varnish that made it just possible to see where one was going. Oil lamps burned in the standard positions at bow, stern, and along either beam. Also as usual, they helped more with the navigation of other ships than with the navigation of *Lingvaas*'s own decks.

The journey couldn't have been that long—*Lingvaas* was just over sixty meters from bow cap to banner pole—but it was long enough for the sudden blaze of light from below to dazzle Borlund. Carefully using both hands and feet, he descended the ladder, then realized that he'd forgotten his bag on the deck. He started back up the ladder, and a familiar voice spoke behind him.

"Don't worry. I'll have one of the hands drop it in your cabin. Come on around to mine for some hot hoeg?"

Borlund would have accepted hot Seakin milk; he was chilled and aching on top of his fatigue. He nodded, and Weil gripped him by both shoulders and turned him around, then squeezed hard.

"Welcome aboard," she said, then frowned. "Was that doctor right, about you being fit?"

Borlund shrugged. "I feel as if he was," he said. "Even if he was wrong, you have at least a healer aboard, don't you?" She nodded. "And no newsgatherers, either."

"You think that's the problem?"

"I'm almost sure. I think the Directorate would have let me bunk down almost anywhere I pleased, if they hadn't been afraid of newsgatherers crawling down through the skylights and up through the pipes. Also, that junior who galloped in—"

"Sebastian Medvedev."

"Anyway, he was too busy with the watch, the garrison, that high-ranking Fleet lord—I forget his name—"

"Jossu I Hmilra."

"—and not having a public fit, to send a messenger to Group House. You offered first." He kissed both hands toward her, in the adapted gesture of formal gratitude.

"I thank you likewise," Weil said, repeating the gesture. Her hands, like the rest of her, were rather heavy—one might say workmanlike—but not without the dignity and grace of a highly functional instrument. They displayed the calluses and scars of many years of seafaring.

She led him to her cabin. It was designed for two, with an upper bunk now loaded with crated and bagged supplier and a rack for a second sealocker over the one holding Weil's. Another rack held a washbasin and a water jug, and Borlund's face stared back at him from a mirror over what he suspected was a pull-down desk.

Weil sat down cross-legged on the bunk—there was no room for two to sit in the cabin otherwise. "Since you swore that you didn't know everything, I can tell you more than I would otherwise. As long as you know that I have a pronounced viewpoint, which isn't the Directorate's.

"Being my guest will make some of them suspect you by the time you go ashore. Spouting my line will make most of them sure I've recruited you. I have an informal agreement with them not to do that. So keep your tongue between your teeth."

If you knew how many secrets I've been keeping since I was fourteen Standard, you wouldn't be fussing at me like Melissa the morning after our baby had the belly cramps!

"I'll keep my tongue anywhere you want it—"*not quite the way I wanted to say it* "—if I can thaw it out with that hoeg first."

"I can live with that bargain."

* * *

THE HIGH-WHEELER ROLLED UP TO THE GATE WITH THE MIST TURNING TO rain that would hurt the crydo, and that the tasselleaf, already peeping over the lower fences, didn't need. The freight wagons turned off to the rear as the high-wheeler pulled to a stop. I Hmilra slid down from the seat, gripped a rump strap as his feet skidded on wet stone, then regained balance before he lost dignity.

"Many thanks, Pian."

"Pleasure's ours, Captain."

On the long walk through the entry hall, the reception hall, and the art gallery, I Hmilra caught the whiff of cooking, succulent if unidentifiable scents. So he was not surprised to find the study in order, with a fire in the hearth, his chair drawn up to it, gruuyan, biscuits, and the day's post on the brass tray on the sidetable, and Alikili nowhere in sight.

That meant she was back by (please, Lady, not *in*) the cookhall, and watching or at least listening to every move the cook made. He would be in a broth of injured vanity tomorrow, probably needing to be solaced with a raise or a banquet large enough to make him feel needed.

I Hmilra mentally composed the guest list for such a banquet as he sorted the post. A double sheaf of invitations to affairs given for no better or worse reasons than the one he'd considered. The day's journals—which he refused to face on an empty stomach. No bills—Alikili would be tending to those, muttering that accountkeepers were no longer discreet in their dealings with the Captain-Born, and what was the world coming to anyway?

Alikili was in her thirty-eighth Great but at times she seemed older than Pian.

Last, a few letters. One from Othan, fat as only letters from the rest of the family could make it. Several whose penning made I Hmilra sure they were from old shipmates—jointlock ruined the handwriting of too many Farers, even if it survived Greats of scribbling logs in half a gale on a pitching deck with the ink either turning to water or freezing solid.

And a final letter, from the Vathuvo Partnership—which meant Moi Kekaspa.

By pure reflex, as automatically as he had once checked the set of the sails or the propeller revolutions repeater, I Kmilra lit the spirit lamp. By the time it was aglow, he had the letter open. Three beats of holding it over the lamp, and the real letter started to form. Three more, and it had swum up clearly into view.

> Elder Friend:
>
> One who was at the center of recent events may be seriously ill. I have arranged for departure to the country until the danger is past, and perhaps for a foreign journey if health requires it.
>
> Reliable attendants are with the patient. I am confident that they will do their duty so well that we need have no further concern for his welfare,
>
> Respectfully,
> Jornja

Even using invisible ink, Kekaspa insisted on keeping her messages cryptic—sometimes, as now, almost too much so.

"One who was at the center" was almost certainly the driver; of the others who might qualify Ehoma Tuomitti was not fit to be moved and in no danger of legal trouble, and the other two were Drylanders. Kekaspa was not so fond of Drylanders that even for one in danger of serious legal attention she would use so many favors to take him safely out of town.

There was more room to wonder about the nature of the driver's "illness." Was he merely likely to be punished with unjust severity out of a desire to make an example and pacify the Drylanders? Or did Kekaspa know that the driver was active in some cave of Saadian rebels—and if she had learned that, how, and had she traded secrets that were not hers to give away?

Also—and I Hmilra looked at the letter's wrapper—the letter had come in the form of a regular posting, complete with the pay-seal, but it could not have come out from the city in time to be found in the post bin at the gate this day. Somebody had brought it and slipped it in with the rest of the post. Who?

Better not ask, I Hmilra realized. He had already been made sufficiently conspicuous by his own curiosity and the driver's—*let us call it, bold initiative*. Making his own household even more aware than they already were, that he was at the center of irregular events, would be foolish.

One question he could ask, however, because it would be asked of one who already knew enough and more. Had Kehaspa given the driver's "attendants" (presumably among her trusted streetprowlers) instructions to kill the man if he was in danger of capture and interrogation?

A question that could be asked, but need not be. Kehaspa would know that her streetprowlers would not risk their freedom for the driver beyond a certain point—nor would she risk hers, or her husband's rank. She would leave that matter to their discretion—but had probably ordered them to take the driver so far upcountry that bandits were more dangerous than the Watch.

Moi Kekaspa's hands had proved steady many times before. Better leave matters to her.

I Hmilra had just finished burning the letter, when the gong summoned him to dinner.

SEAN BORLUND'S CHAT WITH BARBARA WEIL—OR RATHER, HER LECTURE TO him—lasted through three rounds of hot hoeg, a trip to the head, and Weil's changing from deck clothes into a sleeping robe.

She changed in front of him, without waiting for his visit to the head, and even brushed her teeth and hair before she pulled on the robe. That was clearly showing complete trust in Borlund's adherence to the Kilmoyan refugees' sexual code, or at least the part that said mere nudity did not mean a sexual invitation.

Borlund had to admit, however, that Barbara looked better nude than she did clothed. You could see all the well-toned and shapely muscle that held the chunkiness together. After a while, in fact, he found it useful to stare at the wall occasionally, counting the knots in the primwood paneling or trying to decide if a particular plank had been brushed with oil, waxed, or pressure-boiled in tarat sap.

After a while, Borlund no longer had to pay this silent tribute to Barbara Weil's unclothed charms. He was young and vigorous, but he'd also had enough to do with women to be sire-parent three times. It had also been a long day.

In fact, the danger of Weil's lecture turning it into a long night finally exhausted Borlund's patience. He yawned so wide that he nearly dislocated his jaws, and leaned back until his head rested against the locker.

"Let me see if I understand you correctly," he said. "The Study Group Directorate has over the last eight years acquired a veto over most of the Group's activities. Any Member or Candidate who doesn't go along with them is left hewing wood and drawing water—"

"Are you Observant?"

"I've known a few who were. That was one's favorite phrase."

"Don't slip like that when you face the Directorate."

"If I get a good night's sleep, I'll be awake when I do."

Weil looked embarrassed, annoyed, and amused all at the same time. Amusement won out. She winked.

"No, that's not an offer," Borlund added, managing not to be hasty. "I said a good night's *sleep*, not a good *night*."

"A useful distinction, I admit."

"One question. I can see this cult of doing nothing growing out of the cult of 'natural social evolution.' But I never heard any of this back on the Island."

"The old guard of the Study Group Directorate has too many friends on the Island Council, and you must know what they're like."

Borlund nodded. "They'll accuse you of wanting to turn rogue if you offer to teach a night-school course in engineering at a level the Kertovans reached fifty Greats ago. I suppose they give the Directorate a free hand. But what about the ones the Directors send down? Don't they talk? Or do they fall overboard?"

Weil's face showed that he'd gone beyond a joke. "I've never been willing to believe all the 'accidents.' Don't you believe them either. And watch your back."

That opened more questions than it answered, but dealing with a quarter of them *would* keep them up all night. Borlund also admitted that his curiosity now went beyond his own survival, into how Barbara Weil had ended up in as high a rank as any human held at sea among the Kertovans.

The humans ran part of the coastal traffic around their own island of Yproga, as well as fishing and research vessels. But the custom of a Kertovan monopoly of high-seas bottoms was almost as firm as law. There had been 'accidents' to humans who tried inter-island trade too.

Borlund lurched to his feet and kissed one hand to Barbara Weil. He needed the other to hold himself upright. "Which cabin is mine?"

"Greenward as you go out, two doors down on the redside. Look for *Gruauni* on the handle."

"Aye aye, ma'am."

Weil grinned. Borlund would have extended the parody with a mock salute, if he hadn't been holding on to the doorjamb with his right hand.

DINNER WAS FRUIT SOUP AND FISH WITH A LIGHT HERB SAUCE THAT I HMILRA recognized as one of Alikili's own inventions. The cookhall staff looked much too cheerful for her to have prepared it herself, however.

With that uneasiness removed, I Hmilra enjoyed the meal thoroughly—and the aftermath even more. Ever since he'd confessed that a full stomach made him inept in the bedchamber, such a light, elegant meal had been Alikili's sign of how she intended them to spend the sunfade time. (Were the cookhall folk grinning or passing bawdy jests about restorative food for the old one?)

They slept after a while, and it was nearly sunbrighten when I Hmilra awoke. Alikili was already astir, although she wore nothing but her short kilt. The line of her back was so exquisite that I Hmilra wished he could write a poem about it, or that she would cover it before it awoke him even further.

As if his mind had touched hers, she came over to the bed and touched his ears, both of them at once with her hand spread. "Are you flattering an old woman?"

"Old woman, by Gulit's whiskers! There is a difference between old and ripe. If you do not know it yet I shall have to spend more time teaching you,"

"Have we the time for such lessons?" But she was smiling and unhooking her kilt as she said it, and proved herself as both pupil and teacher once she had rejoined I Hmilra in bed.

They chatted, cuddled together under the furs as the chamber servants brought hoeg, soup, and biscuits. Alone again, they threw off the furs and ate in bed, not clothing themselves. I Hmilra could be past desire without being past admiration.

"Thank you for keeping the peace with the cook," he said. "Unhappy cooks have led mutinies in times past."

"Uitso seems not the sort to mutiny," Alikili replied. "But I imagine that we will be doing more entertaining than before, if you are going to seek the High Captaincy."

"Am I?"

"You have said nothing to make me believe otherwise. Or rather, you have left unsaid everything that could do so."

"That could be from having my thoughts elsewhere."

"Not with you. I have spent too much time with you off the couch."

"And not enough time on it?"

"I did not say that or even mean it. I meant that one learns different things about one's beloved in each place."

"Indeed." Such frankness deserved to be repaid in kind. "Whether I am High Captain or not makes little difference to the course of the next few Greats. We need to strengthen our friendship with Eneh, if only to have allies behind the forts on the Hask."

"The City-States will not be enough?"

"Remember the map. Two-thirds of them are downriver from the forts. None of them have the strength to do more than defend their walls and storehouses, provided that they are not attacked by modern artillery. Few will offer a single hair to us, unless they are satisfied with our treatment of the Saadians."

"Have they the right to sit in judgment?"

"The Saadians do, but tell that to the first three folk you meet on the road—and be riding a fast mount when you do."

"Why do I feel that it's really neither war nor Saadians that is making you uneasy?"

Because it is something else. I Hmilra sighed. "As High Captain, I have to justify our—us."

"Our irregular connection, you mean?"

" 'Irregular' is a word to use for Enehan mounted troops or Farers fed too long on salt rations. Lord, Lady, and all their lawful kin together could not use it about us."

"Lord, Lady, and others can afford to be so easy-minded. Our connection does not stand in the way of their inheritance."

"My children have said nothing to suggest discontent."

"Silence does not always mean consent," Aliniki said. "And your son's wife's kin have not been silent at all."

"Regrettably true. They make such an uproar about their sister and her children coming here that one would think you were fertile."

Aliniki could laugh at that. Not many tuundas could. It was one of a number of reasons why, speaking as a private citizen of the Republic, I Hmilra would invite his son's kin-by-marriage to go leap into the Boiling Gulf if they made a public uproar about Alikili.

However, as a candidate for high Fleet command in the coming campaign—perhaps even war—or the High Captaincy, he was not a private citizen. He would be one of the twenty or so citizens who among them held more power over the Island Republic than the Emperor wielded over Alobolir. He would be scrutinized like a new coastline through an explorer's telescope, and not everyone would care for what they saw.

Taking your dismissed tuunda back to your house and your bed after your jouti died was—"anomalous" was one word I Hmilra had heard used. He had even used it himself, liking the sound if not the sense.

Other language, with greater penetrating power and less savor, had also been used. Particularly by the kin of his son Othan's jouti, driven by greed and perhaps by political enemies of Othan's father. At least so far the wrangling had not been made public outside the kin-borders.

This could easily change. Would change, because even if Othan and Elandra held their tongues, they could not turn aside the political ambitions of her brothers, who both saw themselves as future Councillors of the Republic. They would use any weapon that came to hand.

This prospect was something best contemplated after sleep, but it was too late in a busy day for more sleep, and indeed for much contemplation.

"Arrange another light meal tonight."

"By your command, Captain-Born." She rested a hand on his chest.

"Woman, consider that my wits also grow sluggish after too much—"

"Indeed, it has been said that the wits are more vital to happy joining than—"

I Hmilra gave something between a laugh and a cough, wrenched himself out of bed, tripped over the dislodged furs, and sprawled full-length on the floor.

chapter 7

Sean Borlund spent three days aboard *Lingvaas* before the Directorate sent a representative with orders for him to come ashore, expressed in terms that it was impossible to ignore.

They'd previously sent at least one polite request that he heard about, possibly others. He'd also heard a rumor that the ship's healer had provided a certificate, either immaculately documented or else interminably long and boring, to the effect that Drylander Borlund needed an indeterminate but long period of seclusion and sea air.

Ordering him ashore in the face of that might put the Directorate on the wrong foot legally; the authority of healers compared to that of full doctors was still being debated. He'd learned from Barbara Weil, however, that that the Directors were prone to ignoring Kertovan legal niceties—at least when there was no danger of its reaching the newsgatherers or offending some local potentate.

Which implies that Jossu I Hmilra is not a local potentate, in the opinion of the Directorate of the Study Group.

If they thought that, they were clearly even more capable of gross errors than Borlund had believed. Unfortunately, they weren't likely to pay the price for that mistake—at least not until other, lesser or even innocent humans had paid the first few installments.

He would have liked to sit down with Barbara Weil over anything drinkable, water included, to discuss the Directorate's anomalous behavior. Unfortunately, by the time the pressure increased, Weil would have needed to be twins to have time for anything but her ship.

Lingvaas was preparing for sea, and Weil had not only responsibility for her own work but for seeing that the rest of *Lingvaas*'s humans did theirs. Being senior over three other commanders (two deck and one engineering), nine watch chiefs, and thirty-one common

Farers of every shipboard speciality except stoker, Weil had enough headaches of her own without listening to Borlund's.

But she kissed him good-bye when he climbed down into the shoreboat. The gathering sunfade didn't hide it that she was a sweaty, filthy mess after a day spent sending down the old mizzen topmast and sending up the new one, but Borlund did not care.

"When are you sailing?" he asked.

"Before you're done with the Directors or they with you, I suspect."

Borlund's determination grew firmer, to do or say nothing that would bring immediate action from the Directorate. With *Lingvaas* at sea, his only other line of retreat led all the way home—which was disgrace and rout, not honorable retreat.

Unless I want to throw myself on the mercy of I Hmilra the Inscrutable?

The Captain Over Captains had plainly interested himself in Barbara Weil's career and *Lingvaas*'s mixed crew. For Borlund to presume on his slight acquaintance with Weil to ask for similar favors from I Hmilra seemed injudicious, to put it mildly.

"Who knows? They may decide I can be disposed of without so much as delaying lunch."

Weil cocked her head. "You're picking up the right degree of cynicism. Just don't flaunt it in the wrong place, which is everywhere off *Lingvaas*."

"I wish I was sailing with you."

"Don't even *think* that too loudly." She paused to cup her hands and shout for the painters to bring the proofing buckets *now*, not next midtide. Then she lowered her voice and put her mouth to his ear. Her breath tickled pleasantly.

"But if you can make them think being aboard *Lingvaas* would be a disgrace to your family and a punishment for you. . . ."

"I didn't come down here to learn acting."

"Learn what you need, Sean. And be a good judge of what that is. You do that, and you'll do all right even if *Lingvaas* goes down with all hands on this trip."

He wanted to hug her to drive away that grim thought, but the deck was too public and the boat crew were beginning to cough and whistle rudely from alongside. Instead, Borlund punched Weil lightly on each shoulder, tossed his seabag down into the boat, and swung himself outboard onto the ladder.

* * *

CONSIDERING THE TONE OF THEIR LAST MESSAGE, BORLUND HAD EXPECTED the Directorate to send Security people into the boat, rush him ashore, confine him, and quickly bring him before the Evaluation Committee for what would be in all but name a trail.

He was less sure about the verdict or the sentence even if he was found "guilty." Staying out of the Kertovan-Saadian tension was one unwritten rule in human-Kertovan relations. Obeying local laws and customs was another—and those laws and customs were tolerably strict about aiding those in distress.

As he climbed into the boat, Borlund had decided one thing. If the Committee's decision showed that they did not regard the woman and her baby as "in distress," they were going to have to find a penalty for his laughing in their faces—at least.

Or perhaps slapping them like that would do more harm than the pleasure justified. If the obsession of the Directorate was not rocking the boat, arguing politely that such a finding would do so might permeate even the thickest Directorial skull and reach the vestigial brain within.

And, of course, Barbara Weil could be wrong about the whole Directorate, thanks to some personal grievance she hadn't mentioned. That degree of paranoia gave Borlund no pleasure, but under the circumstances he couldn't abandon it either.

The journey ashore was much less disagreeable than Borlund had anticipated.

His first surprise was the boat. It was a regular hire-craft, with two rowers and a steersman, all Kertovan. It took him in to the closest landing stage, where a human waited on the boat pier.

The human might have been from Group Security. Certainly he was even taller than Borlund, and looked as if he lifted baby Seakin or wrestled sand-apes as his morning exercise. He was also singularly taciturn, whether by order or inclination.

If he was armed, however, the weapons were well hidden. His clothes were a prosperous Farer's shore-going kilt and tunic, modified for human anatomy, with only the brass-studded shoulder loop that was the Study Group's one concession to Kertovan uniform regulations for registered Watch members.

"Can you ride?" the man asked. "I have mustekkas waiting."

Borlund's first thought was that he had never seen a mustekka large enough to carry this man's weight; it should be an interesting sight. His next thought was wondering if his answer was part of his examination.

His third thought was that paranoia had gone far enough when it made him afraid to do anything. He nodded.

"What about my baggage?"

"I have a hire-cart coming."

"It's not here yet?"

The escort swept his hand along the quay. "What does it look like?"

A look at the quay told Borlund little. It was a tangle of porters, carts, carriers, and a couple of streetsteamers hauling heavy loads, coal or iron plate. Correction: it told Borlund that any cart not hired on the waterfront would be a while in arriving. Too long to wait; much too long to leave anything remotely valuable completely untended.

"I don't want to have to fill out a theft report the moment we reach Group House."

"You don't trust the—the Farers."

Borlund wondered what word had nearly come out instead of "Farers," and shook his head. "I don't trust *anybody* exposed to too much temptation."

The escort's face told Borlund that he would like to order the newcomer into the saddle and off to Group House, and green-gullets devour the baggage! What he would like and what he had the authority to do, however, might be two different things. Borlund decided to gamble.

"If I'm on the roster for a meeting today, I certainly won't keep the Examiners waiting over a seabag or two and a trunk. But if all I have to do today is sign in to my quarters—"

"Very well. We can wait."

One test passed.

BORLUND HAD TO DO MORE THAN SIGN IN TO HIS QUARTERS THAT DAY, BUT not much, and hardly more during the next two days. This left him leisure, and the choice of using it by worrying about his fate, catching up on the news, or exploring Study Group House.

On the first day he divided his time between the last two, the first being certainly futile and possibly dangerous. His room was a sparsely furnished one in the Guest Section of the Quarters Wing, not a cell in the Security Section two floors below. However, it was right next to the Security guardpost for its floor, and it might not be entirely his imagination that the Security people gave him particularly close scrutiny when he entered or left.

Trained to recognize signs of stress or impending "deviant behavior," the Security muikken could not be given the slightest opportunity to believe that they'd found it. Borlund had enough practice in deceiving less trained people who knew him much better that he was cautiously optimistic about able to veil Security's eyes.

He didn't know what to feel about the news. What he had expected to be an "eight-Tide wonder" had barely reached the evening editions on the fifth. Either he'd overestimated what the involvement of Drylanders and Jossu I Hmilra would do to an otherwise minor incident in Kertovan-Saadian relations, or somebody was trying to discourage public attention to the affair.

Probably the latter, with several somebodies putting their oars in, half of them for legitimate motives. Too much news coverage had been know to corrupt or confuse Security investigations, or even lead to riots, which did the same job even more thoroughly.

Borlund decided to go on reading the papers. Otherwise something vital to his own case might arise unexpectedly, to leap out and bite him at the examination.

He would not read them in his room, however, since he had the freedom of the public areas of Group House. He used that freedom to walk out whenever the weather allowed, with a jacket, canteen, and reading matter in an oilskin pouch. Sometimes he sat and read, sometimes he walked and watched the city and bay, sometimes he ran with no thought but to fill his lungs with smoky, salty air and push his muscles until they sent twinges of healthy pain up and down his body.

He certainly had plenty of room. Borlund had grown up with the joke that Group House should really be called "Group Castle." Actually being there instead of listening to the stories and looking at the photographs on school walls and in museum exhibits made this less of a joke.

The Saadians had not been notable seafarers before they came under Kertovan tutelage. Across the bay and up the Hask was as far as their water traffic took them. But even this much meant ports, ports meant wealth lying ready to hand for pirates, and keeping off pirates meant armed ships and coastal fortifications.

The Old Princes of Saadi hadn't had to do much with Group House to turn into their main fort for this stretch of coast. It had been founded as a godhouse by one of the monastic orders of the Warring States that had preceded the Empire of Alobolir, and the priests and readers had definitely been of the "church militant." The shrines were encased in enough stone to resist artillery, their quarters were like barracks, and a wall surrounded the whole complex.

Then they built a second outer wall, around the storehouses and servants' quarters. After gunpowder came into regular use, they raised a third wall wide enough to mount artillery, with a ditch and a cleared space all around the foot of the rock that was the original site of the godhouse.

The power of the Princes rose; eventually they laid siege to the godhouse and starved out its defenders. It was said that the ghosts of the thousands who died in the stone warren still drifted about on certain inauspicious days. When the Drylanders chose the old Princely fortress as their home in the City, it had been widely predicted that the ghosts would quickly drive them out, or perhaps into madness and evil.

So far this hadn't happened. Lack of imagination and a taste for intrigue—even if Barbara Weil was right—were neither insane nor criminal. At least not yet.

The world was turning toward sunfade on the third day, and Borlund was watching the gaslights come on in the city, when he sensed someone watching him. He half-turned, to avoid both vulnerability and confrontation, recognized even in the twilight with his peripheral vision his escort of three days ago, and saw that the man now wore a Security tunic with full insignia. Not to mention a pair of ostentatiously expensive and laboriously polished boots.

"Good day to you, Farer," Borlund said. It was an opening to which no one could possibly object, unless they were determined to find something to object to.

"It is a good enough day," the man replied. "Tomorrow may not be so good, at least for you."

"Do I see the Directorate or merely an Evaluation Committee?"

"The second, Farer," the man said. "I doubt that your actions loom so large that the whole Directorate will devote itself to them."

Borlund wasn't sure if this was meant to be encouraging or not. At least they were following standard procedure, and the Security man was definitely being polite, which was more good than bad.

Unless I'm being soothed in order to be caught off-guard tomorrow.

That was the paranoia rising too high again. "Is there anything I have to do tonight?"

"Most of the people you're likely to see are early risers. I suggest a bath, dinner, laying out your clean clothes, and retiring to bed early."

Borlund nodded. He could not read much into a Security man's giving him commonsense advice. It did seem to argue against any plans to throw him to the sand apes, to be pulled apart until his gnawed bones were good only for the cubs' playthings.

"Thank you." Borlund remembered just in time not to offer the man money or promise favors. Both would be considered bribes. Apart from the strict ethics of Security, the man was old enough to be his sire-parent.

"Good luck to you, Farer Borlund," the Security man said. He slipped away with that peculiar stance and stride of theirs, that let them see immediately if you were as much looking after them, let alone following them.

Borlund sighed. At least he could choose or not whether to be paranoid. Some were not so fortunate.

BORLUND WAS AWAKE AND DRESSED BEFORE HIS ESCORT CAME FOR HIM, AT an hour which proved the wisdom of the Security man's suggestion. The escort was civil staff, not Security, a gray-haired man and a young woman, auburn-haired and noticeably pregnant, which was reassuring. Neither was armed, and even if they had been armed they didn't look like the sort of people sent to escort suspected violent criminals.

Borlund was wearing his best tunic and trousers, a plain heavy vest under the tunic, and belt, boot, and other leathers not of the best quality but greased and polished until they looked better than they were. Time was the one thing he'd had plenty of, and nobody raised an eyelash at his requests for more cleaning gear than he'd packed.

Borlund himself raised both eyebrows as his escorts led him down one endless corridor, then turned in to another, and finally a third that led to a spiral staircase. By the time they'd gone down at least seven flights of the staircase, lit only by smoky oil lamps, Borlund was beginning to take comfort in his sidearm.

No one had told him not to bring it. He was, after all, fully weapons-qualified and had applied for a position that required him to go armed. Not to mention that with only the six rounds in the cylinder he could hardly be plotting insurrection or mass slaughter of the Evaluators.

They passed the tenth level in their downward passage. Borlund began to wonder if the Directors had assigned his examination to the Cold One, and they were going all the way down to the Dark Lord's lair in the Cavern of Stillness. Certainly the timeworn carvings he saw in corridors leading off the stair landings made it plain that the folk of the godhouse had once been friendlier to the Dark One than anyone cared to be now.

Of course, the humans of Kilmoyn had also used their share of caves and deep tunnels in their time on the planet. On the island, they'd even built an underground complex deeper than this one. It held the computers, classrooms for covert-knowledge training, machine shops and arsenals for the reserved weapons, and a hydro-electric plant driven off an underground river. All of it high value, if not outright irreplaceable, and all of it material that would produce not just cultural contamination but cultural chaos if spread generally across Kilmoyn.

Group House wasn't supposed to have anything like this, although there were rumors of an improvised computer and reserved weapons disguises as standard ones. The Study Group had to be more careful than most humans about keeping up the Drylander image, so that all the dire repercussions from the advent of "sky gods" would not bring Kilmoyn's natural cultural development to a sticky end.

Borlund wondered about the rumors. He wondered if "supposed to" wasn't the critical phase. Then he stopped wondering, as the fif-teeth door opened on what at first glimpse seemed another endless corridor.

It ended after only six paces, in a trio of doors set into the far wall of a low, hemispherical chamber. The walls were bare stone, although ancient brickwork showed in the doorsills. This place had to be as old as the godhouse, if not older; it might even be pre-Skyfall. That could explain how it had come to be; pre-Skyfall societies had abundant labor, slave and free, that few of their successors had been able to emulate after the meteorite strikes, tsunamis, earthquakes, and "secondary kill" (what Bridget had called "the Four Horsemen of the Apocalypse") had done their work.

"Candidate for Study Group Service Sean Lincoln Borlund," the woman said. Her pleasant voice also brought back thoughts of Borlund's parent-partner Bridget Houylan.

"Does the Candidate wish entrance, to be examined as to his fitness to serve the Study Group?" Maybe the voice was more doleful because it had to filter through a grille in the door. Borlund still didn't care for it.

"Yes." A brief but acceptable reply. So far the formalities were being observed on both sides. Borlund mentally crossed his fingers that this would continue.

"We who represent the Directors of the Study Group at this evaluation grant Candidate Borlund entrance."

The middle door opened with a faint protest of ancient hinges, and Borlund stepped forward into what seemed complete darkness.

THE DARKNESS LASTED ONLY A FEW STEPS, AS HE PASSED THROUGH A STONE wall so thick that the doorway was nearly a tunnel. Then he stepped out into a low-ceilinged room about five meters on a side, with a table for the Examiners to the left and a chair for the candidate on the other.

So far, quite orthodox, including the electric lights in three marine-bronze fixtures—although the electricity was a bit of a surprise. Borlund hadn't thought there was a place for a generator in this warren of ancient stone, or resources to run wires from the main plant, by now a good forty meters overhead.

Also, one almost *expected* candles or at most gaslight after this kind of trek through darkness. Candles burned down to stubs, casting a flickering, uncertain yellow glow over figures in dark robes, their faces invisible in the shadows of hoods, while masked figures flanked the hooded ones, masked figures with bare chests and huge swords in their muscular hands. . . .

Borlund had to smile and wanted to laugh regardless of the impression that might make on the Evaluators. This setting looked right for a persecuting religion's torture chamber, but was probably only intended to discourage eavesdroppers—particularly eavesdroppers with holes in their pockets, who might listen to the clink of coins from leaf-scrap newsgatherers. Once upon a time it had been assumed that no human would deal with those, but the assumption had been plainly a fairy tale well before Sean Borlund was born.

The Examiners were seated at a long wooden table, with inkwells and papers in front of them, and a recording book in front of the junior member. Two from Security, their chests covered even if they did carry swords as well as holstered pistols. The swords were light dress weapons that would snap like fishbones if they ever met one of the heavy-bladed cutlasses in *Lingvaas*'s arsenal. All very orthodox.

So was the first part of the Evaluation. Borlund identified himself, verified that the documents submitted in his name were authentic, summarized his life and skills, and stated his intention to serve a full three years with the Study Group.

The second part was more orthodoxy in action. It was a series of questions, some of them more personal than Borlund cared for, others intended to test his ability to think on his feet or hold his tongue in the face of provocation. He'd already answered many of the questions for his qualifying tests or discussed them with veterans of service with the Study Group.

This last wasn't strictly legal, but only people who intended to go back for further terms fretted about the law. Borlund began to wish that he'd thought more about the implications of this before he came to Saadi. He might not have found Barbara Weil's suggestions so startling.

"Why is the Study Group in Saadi instead of Kehua?" the middle Councillor asked. It sounded like a low-pitched woman's voice, although it was hard to tell from the face.

"Because the Kertovans—the Island Republic—did not wish us in their capital city?"

"Why have we never raised the issue since the original refusal?"

That question was less than orthodox, but the answer was obvious.

"The Kertovans have the full range of their institutions here. It's also easier to observe the Saadians and the Empire. The only way to get a mission established in the islands would be to overthrow the present government, and that would be worse than cultural contamination."

"Oh? Is there something worse than cultural contamination?" the man at the right asked.

"Yes. Stupidity."

Borlund thought he heard someone laugh. He kept his face blank.

"Would you be in favor of overthrowing the current government?"

That was definitely an unorthodox, not to say imprudent, question. This far from any possible Kilmoyan eavesdroppers, it might at least be safe.

"I can see no possible circumstances under which that wouldn't be the worst thing we could do. Well, maybe one circumstance. If they began a campaign of systematic persecution of the Drylanders, either on their own initiative or with Fugitive help. Even then, if the opposition to the campaign wasn't capable of setting up a stable government, we might do better to flee.

"The Kertovans have done well for us. Helping throw them into anarchy would be a bad return, and kill many innocent people."

Borlund half-expected questions about the logistics of another Flight, with eight thousand humans and everything that gave them a claim to civilization needing to be moved in the face of the Republic's superior naval strength. Instead he saw the three representatives look at each other; he thought he saw one nodding.

"Very well. What about the Saadians?"

"What about them?" was what Borlund did *not* say. He also rejected handing the Evaluators the answer they clearly wanted to hear. The simplest answer was always the safest. From the age of ten, he'd learned that authority figures didn't care to learn how easily you'd seen through their attempts to fool you.

Borlund took refuge in formality.

"Exactly how are the Saadians connected to this line of questioning?"

More exchanges of looks. This time the exchanges included the two Security guards. Borlund wondered if they were getting bored with the chase down a theoretical blind alley, or something more. Did Security have a different perspective on human-Kertovan relations, being at the sharp end of it more often than most other humans?

Something to bounce off Barbara Weil, if he ever had a chance to talk to her again.

"Would the position of the Saadians affect your loyalty to the present terms of our relations with the Island Republic?"

Borlund had to run that one through his mind twice before he understood it, and a third time before he could reply.

"I think the Kertovans and the Saadians are going to have to settle the future of their relationship themselves. We can't offer them much advice that they'd be willing to take, even if we were willing to risk our cover story."

"Then you think the relationship may be adjusted peacefully?"

"If it needs adjusting, and I'm not an expert on that, maybe. Even if it comes to a fight, we ought to stay as neutral as we can and be able to deal with both sides after peace breaks out. That will help more than anything else."

This time the nods were unmistakable. Borlund didn't allow himself to relax; he had the distinct feeling it wasn't over yet.

Now the man on the left spoke. "Could you describe in your own words the incident that took place in Saadi Bay, the day of your arrival aboard *Aygsionan?*"

Borlund's first feeling was resentment at this obtuseness, then he realized they had a point. Every other report they'd had so far had either come from a Kilmoyan or had a Kilmoyan somewhere in the circuit. It made sense to get the unvarnished word of the human principal, with no string of relays through people who might have their own agendas.

"Very well. *Aygsionan* entered the bay at approximately 0800, about an hour behind schedule. She proceeded toward the anchorage. . . ."

He ran through the whole story, up to his falling asleep aboard *Lingvaas,* using human terms of measurement even when he had to think twice to do so. He wasn't sure what this accomplished, other than reminding the Evaluators that he hadn't "grown fur on the brain," but even that much would be useful.

"You never thought about the political implications of the incident?" the woman asked, when Borlund had finished.

Borlund's temper nearly snapped.

"No." If he'd said anything more, they would have heard his anger.

"Sorry. Not at the time, not that day, not since?"

Borlund took a deep breath. "Not at the time, no. Since then, everybody has been screaming 'politics' at me or at least in my hearing. Including you. If I wasn't aware of it by now, I'd be deaf and mentally incompetent.

"But I wasn't trying to commit a political act or criticize anyone's conduct when I jumped overboard. I was simply the handiest person for doing what needed doing. If anybody wants to complain about that, let them complain to my face, and I don't care what culture or race they belong to!"

He had to take several deep breaths after that, but nobody noticed. The three Evaluators had their heads together and were whispering. The Security were exchanging looks that to Borlund showed infinite boredom. He sympathized.

The woman cleared her throat. "Candidate Borlund. Clearly you have caused a good deal of trouble without any intention of doing so. In fact, your motives were humanitarian and highly honorable.

"The trouble is just as real. Would you be prepared to take as your first assignment one that would keep you out of this city for the rest of the year at least? By that time, you will not be trailed by news-gatherers every step you take."

Borlund nodded. The speech didn't tell him what further response they expected.

"You don't feel that your parent-partners and offspring will be disgraced?"

This time Borlund wanted to laugh. Two of the women had thought it was almost supernatural that he had passed the tests at all!

"I seriously doubt it."

"Do you have a preference for assignment, within these limits?"

Time to start the game in earnest.

"Something as far inland as possible. I can do without seeing any more saltwater for a while."

This time it was headshakes. "Not possible, I'm afraid," the woman said. "The border areas are unstable, and the telegraph and railroads are in everywhere else. "No, we'll have to send you to sea. You've dealt with the humans aboard *Lingvaas*. Do you think assignment aboard her would work out—?"

Borlund's efforts to strangle a laugh nearly strangled him. The woman actually looked concerned.

"Did you have any problems you would care to discuss?" one of the men asked. "We know that ship's something of an experiment, and with a garcik running the human side of it . . ."

Have to tell Barbara about this one. Sebastian Medvedev had been in a rage when he used that obscenity. Hearing it from one of the Evaluators who had no such excuse was disquieting.

"I didn't have any problems. I've been to sea often enough, on coasting voyages. I don't suppose I will. But wandering around the seas of Kilmoyn wasn't exactly what I expected when I boarded *Aygsionan*."

"Duty to the future of all races frequently calls on us to face the unexpected," the other man said. He sounded as stiff as a reader of the Cold One giving the lesson in a Temple of the Lady. The manner was correct; belief was almost painfully absent.

"All right. When do you want me to leave?"

I hope it's before I break out laughing.

"*Lingvaas* has sailed," the woman said. "We will have to learn her schedule and find you a berth aboard some vessel touching at a future stop. I hope you don't mind traveling lower-pay, if necessary?"

The interrogative tone was purely a formality. Fortunately, Borlund would gladly have gone chasing *Lingvaas* aboard a Drilion-crewed fishing boat rather than stay around here and keep up pretenses until the ship returned from her rounds.

"All I'll need to pack is a few personal items, if *Lingvaas* is expected to outfit me."

He intended to pack more than a few. Barbara Weil was like any good commander, not likely to be impressed if a new Farer came aboard with only the clothes on his back.

"We'll telegraph her—"

Borlund coughed. "I don't know if the newsgatherers monitor the telegraph. But why take the chances?"

They went on for a while, letting Borlund essentially plan his own assignment. He was having so much fun that he almost forget to play the reluctant traveler. However, his act held through to the end, and the Evaluators' apologies sounded almost sincere as they wished him well in this challenging and unpleasant assignment.

Even the privacy of his room wasn't enough for Borlund. He stuffed his head under the pillow and two blankets before he let out half a Watch's pent-up laughter.

When he caught his breath, he realized that he'd naturally thought in Kertovan units of time. Maybe he did have "fur on the brain," but if so he was going to one of the few places where that was safe or even desirable!

chapter 8

"Fisher buoy one mark, green!" the foremast lookout called. Sean Borlund shaded his eyes against the glare from the blue-green water and saw it too—a red can that marked one end of a floatnet longer than an Island packet-steamer.

He didn't need to do anything about it, though—nor about any other maritime hazard. This freedom might last as much as another watch, if the boat to *Lingvaas* was late or slow.

After that, it would be, "Look lively there, Farer Borlund!" He expected to start in the ranks, although he had qualifications for several different departments aboard a ship the size of *Lingvaas*.

Or so he hoped. The idea of being refused because of Barbara Weil's feud with the Study Group presented itself for about the tenth time in the last six commons. The same willpower he'd used nine times before drove it back into the shadows where nightmares lurked.

He would be in what he had heard called "a position of exceptional awkwardness," if he was refused. Unless he could work his passage back to Saadi, and even then it would not be aboard *Igrinsaan*. The freighter that had brought him (as well as a thousand tons of cloth, canned food, fine-cut lumber, and machinery) from Saadi to Joku had a Drilion purser, the real power aboard.

Also a thorough bigot. In Borlund's position aboard *Aygsionan*, the purser would have let mother and child drown, possibly even smiling as they sank, certainly muttering, "Well, if the shtrug couldn't swim, why didn't she wait for a ferry?" He'd heard of Borlund's feat, hadn't been happy to see him turn to in the storm three commons ago without going overboard, and would be loudly unhappy about letting such a Saadi-lover contaminate his ship's decks any longer.

Igrinsaan was turning redward, but not hard enough to heel. The screw was slowing, however, and the topcrew were scrambling aloft, managing to look both quick and clumsy at the same time, as Kilmoyans so often did to the human eye. The foresail and fore topsail shrank, and soon *Igrinsaan* was ghosting in toward her anchorage with barely steerage way from her propeller.

Borlund was below decks when the anchor went down and the steam shot up the whistle, venting boilers and signaling the shore at the same time. It didn't take him long to finish packing, since he'd brought only a Farer's seabag and a hundred slyn in small bills and coin.

The balance of the letter of credit was on deposit at the Study Group Financial Cooperative. After some mental debate, he'd finally decided that implying he didn't trust them by depositing it elsewhere would be rudeness without good purpose, at least for now. (Which was a phrase he found himself using quite a bit lately.)

There was *Lingvaas*, close inshore, her after topmast missing and only shreds of sail on two yards on the mainmast. The storm had also scoured paint off her funnel, making it look fungus-splotched, and a repair party was over the side in two workboats.

Lingvaas had been to the wars, or at least through the same storm as *Igrinsaan*. With that much work to do aboard, they'd certainly not be quick to refuse able-bodied Farers, and if they had crew in the sick berth (not that Borlund wished any such bad luck)—

"Huh, Farer Borlund."

It was the first boat steerer, and he was looking from Borlund to the shoreboat.

"Aye, Steerer?"

"We called all ashore to the boat a while back."

"I thought I'd wait—"

"*Lingvaas* most likely hasn't a boat to spare for the likes of you, and here you can buy a boat for what the fare'll take."

"Oh."

"It's the most thanks I can make you, for your turning to in the storm. That was done like a Farer. More'd—well, the Ledger Commander's a bad one to cross."

"I won't argue that."

"Then you won't mind taking yourself off to the boat, either?"

Borlund knew an order when he heard it.

Igrinsaan's crew also knew their work, and the boat was alongside *Lingvaas* in no more than an eighth-watch. Borlund fished his seabag up from the bilges, shook the green slime off it, and hooked the carry-strap over his shoulder to leave both hands free.

"Ahoy, the deck," he shouted. "Farer Sean Borlund, reporting for duty."

Now, assuming the storm didn't snap the telegraph lines. . . .

"Permission granted to come aboard." The voice was human, but with a Saadian accent one could have recognized at the height of the gale.

Borlund jumped for the ladder; the freighter's boat was backing water before he reached the third rung. He scrambled up the rest of the way, glimpsed himself in the bronze bollard across from the entryway, and decided he would serve.

Skin boots, properly loose trousers (the Kertovan kilt was not designed to look well on humans), storm jacket over striped shirt since this was a formal occasion, belt with sheathe knife and purse, seabag serviceable but not shiny-new. Hair short (the alternative to long enough to braid) and face clean-shaven (again, the alternative to a full beard).

"Permission to come aboard?" he asked, not sure which of the two Kilmoyans and three humans in sight was in charge—"had the deck," was the term he remembered.

"Permission granted," one of the humans said, in High Kertovan. "I'll inform Ladysoul—ah, Second Captain—Weil, that you've reported."

That seemed to settle any question of his being accepted, but where did that nickname come from? It was a high compliment, implying that someone's soul had been passed down from the time of the Lord and Lady creating water and land. A rare privilege, granted only to those who did well with each reincarnation.

Not to mention the other title. It was a title, not a rank—Barbara was no doubt still some level of watch commander. But as a title, it meant that she was now officially third-in-command of *Lingvaas*, next to Captain Viligas himself and a Kertovan Second Captain whose name Borlund could not for the moment remember.

No calling her "garcik" here! Borlund felt even more kindly toward *Lingvaas* than before.

But here came "Ladysoul" Weil herself—and Borlund had just time to salute the sternpost before he saluted her. (Again, the safest course. Fleet discipline wasn't strictly enforced aboard survey ships the size of *Lingvaas,* but he'd wait for someone to tell him that officially.)

"Welcome aboard, Farer Borlund." Weil returned the salute, then held out a hand. Borlund took it, as gently as if it had been made of glass.

He thought Weil was trying not to laugh, and he knew he saw her wink. Then she squeezed his hand and stepped back.

"Report to the steward for a bunk assignment. The Captain will want to see you before lights' out, but he's ashore now. Be ready to report to his cabin as soon as he's reported aboard."

"Yes—ah, aye aye, ma'am."

Another burst of laughter never got past Barbara Weil's disciplined lips. But her shoulders quivered slightly as she turned away toward where the workboats were tied up.

Borlund looked after her, wishing he dared ask her or *somebody* one question. Was the Captain in the habit of meeting all new hands? Or was this meeting because the man wanted to see what strange fish had been washed aboard his ship?

If it was the second, Borlund's (and the Study Group's) plans for him to be inconspicuous aboard *Lingvaas* were going to have a rough voyage.

HERE IN THE HIGHLANDS, A COMMON'S RIDE NORTH OF THE RAILHEAD, spring had not yet given way to summer. Another day's ride north, into the Pyaltis Mountains with their permanent snowcaps, and one could believe it was still winter.

Jossu I Hmilra had no intention of taking himself or sending anyone else of his household that far north. The Pyaltis Shield was the home of the Saadians' poor relations, living only a step or two above tribal and clan organization and that in the last hundred Greats. They'd gone from barbarism before Skyfall to barbarism after it, and any tinges of civilization they'd developed were buried many spans below the smoke-blackened stone walls of their villages.

They were defending their way of life, however, and their warriors made travel in the mountains hazardous for strangers. The last time they'd raided across the mountains was only twenty Greats ago, and the problem of resettling those who'd been burned out still sprouted in one Hall or the other every year. Meanwhile, the Highlands were a refuge for the landless, the lawless, the homeless, and the rootless, few of whom murdered cold-souled but most of whom would get away with anything (or anyone) they could.

Hence the armed guards on this picnic, four of the household's best, rifle-armed, vigilant, and carefully placed. Also two more, even more carefully placed, to be invisible to anyone who crept close enough to note the places of the first four.

But Alikili was holding out a plate loaded with smoked meat and salt fish, topped by sweetcrusts, and a full cup in the other hand. I Hmilra decided that he'd let the landscape take his attention long enough, and took the offerings.

This left him with nothing to hold the knife and fork, but Alikili's ingenuity came to their rescue. She popped both handle-first into I Hmilra's mouth, and watched while he tried to thrust them into the food.

With immoderate self-control, she didn't burst out laughing until I Hmilra had managed to impale the food without impaling himself. She was still giggling when he set everything down on the Hyolian-weave blanket.

"We are really too old for this," I Hmilra said. As an effort to subdue the lady, it was an abject failure. She laughed again, until she finally had to lie back on the blanket and pull her shawl over her face.

I Hmilra felt his own self-command slipping away. It would have departed entirely, except that he had a mouthful of pickled yoritsk and he was afraid of choking on the odd bone.

He finally swallowed. Then he swallowed again, as Alikili undid the top three thongs of her tunic. He wondered if the guards were looking their way.

"Lady, I'm an old man."

"Age is in the mind. I found none this morning."

I Hmilra remembered the morning, with the room sunwashed by the south windows, and how long it had been after they awoke before they left the bed. Perhaps she had the right of it.

He also remembered going back to sleep, then waking to the shouts and cheers of the guards as they watched Alikili scrambling up the cliff to the north of the house. She moved with the assurance of a seasoned Farer on a mast in a gale and the lithe grace of the herder-girl she had been, climbing about the rocks of Torhaania to bring in her father's strayed flocks.

The guards had been vigilant as well as enthusiastic; I Hmilra had felt no fear of hostile locals. But he shuddered at an image of Alikili lying broken at the foot of the cliff—and he shuddered again as it returned.

Her embrace drove the image from his mind. Then she rested her head in his lap and they finished their meal that way, he popping tidbits into her mouth and she holding up cup after cup for him to sip. They were neither of them quite sober by the time they'd reloaded the hamper.

"I was thinking of making the Highland estates over to you," I Hmilra said, after the breeze had blown some of the drink from his mind. "The marriage-kin hardly know that they exist, and I prophesy that Othan will be in no great haste to tell them."

"How much are they worth?"

"Mercenary wench!"

"That's an epithet, not an answer."

"They bring in about sixteen thousand slyn in an average Great. Sometimes less, sometimes more. They also have their own estate account at Irongate, by way of a reserve."

"I am honored. But how secure are they? Some of those bad years, I suspect, are from mountaineer raids or bandits."

"The raids and banditry are diminishing. In twenty Greats there will be none."

She looked up at him, with that curiously aggressive tenderness that he had always found so irresistible. "That was what they were saying in the year I first came to your bed. What has been the problem?"

"Too few landfighters, I assume."

"Indeed. And where are they to come from?"

I Hmilra started to reply. She ran her fingers along his lips. He smiled and pretended to bite.

"No, hear me out. Where are they to come from, but from Saadi? And will they come from there, with relations between the Saadians and the Republic as they are now?"

"A good many Saadians will come forward, for a chance to learn warriors' skills."

Alikili replied with a silent but speaking look that mirrored I Hmilra's own thoughts. *The Saadians will come forward, to learn what they may someday use against us.*

"You doubt the value of the estates?"

"Their value seems to depend on how we and the Saadians go on with each other, over the next generation. Even if there is peace, in twenty Greats I will be too old to take much pleasure in wealth."

"Now it is my turn to remind you about age being in the mind."

"They say age is in the mind. They also say death is in a lonely bed."

He bent down and brushed her forehead with thumbs and lips. He wished he could do more. That was her plainest statement yet, that she did not really care to outlive him. The thought was flattering, but also a death sentence for someone so much younger. He swore himself to say or do nothing that anyone could imagine as encouraging her in that notion.

Instead he considered this new aspect of his old dilemma. He had begun to realize that he would decide between the High Captaincy and leading the expedition to Eneh mostly on the basis of profit.

High Captains wielded more power. But the leader of a larger expedition than any sent against the pirates of Luokkan would be no petty leader, and custom and distance from the Islands tolerated certain financial privileges for such. If he could not gather in a few hundred thousand slyn that could be conveyed where he wished without ruffs rising or teeth bared, he should come ashore now.

This left open the question of whether there would be a war. I Hmilra did not intend to provoke one merely to provide for Alikili. It also left open the matter of Kertovan-Saadian relations. In either position, he could work actively to alter them—Lord and Lady willing, for the better.

Which should he choose?

SEAN BORLUND HAD MET *LINGVAAS*'S CAPTAIN VILIGAS BRIEFLY DURING HIS previous stay aboard the ship. The man had not been too forthcoming to an unknown guest, one whom he doubtless saw as the eye of a storm of leaf-scrap headlines and suspected of sharing Barbara Weil's bed.

Something had clearly happened to change his mind by the time Borlund entered the Captain's cabin that night. Viligas wore a formal tunic and embroidered vest, kilt, and sash in the colors of some Captain-Born house Borlund didn't recognize.

He'd heard rumors, however, that Viligas was the son of the tuunda to a very high-ranking Captain-Born. His mother had been dismissed before being tested for pregnancy—and in due course returned carrying evidence that her dismissal for sterility had been both unjust and unlawful and would be highly embarrassing if it came to public notice.

Thus Viligas's right to wear the family colors on the sash and probably some of the other signs of wealth around the cabin. The bulkheads were paneled, the decks carpeted, the table covered with an embroidered cloth, and the artwork on one wall included not only original paintings and engravings but some exquisite framed mosaics in both wood and fishbone.

Barbara Weil had led the way in. Now both humans saluted, open-palmed. Viligas returned the salute and motioned them to the other two chairs at the round table.

"Welcome aboard, Farer Borlund. Weil's sponsoring you says much. Your file says more."

Not half as much as I'm sure you'd like to know.

Viligas asked half a dozen questions, all intelligent, none idle, and most capable of being answered without revealing any secrets. However, the one exception needed all Borlund's tact and ingenuity.

"You are not being seriously punished for your actions, it seems," Viligas said. "Is your Directorate viewing the matter less seriously than we had expected?"

Borlund wondered, among many other questions, who "we" were. However, what he was expected to produce was answers, not questions. *Preferably without discussing a meeting the Directorate would prefer to keep secret from any Kilmoyan.*

Borlund cleared his throat, not only to delay his answer. His throat had been tickling since he came aboard and was beginning to hurt. He hoped his drenching in the storm hadn't finally caught up with him. Spending his first few commons aboard *Lingvaas* in the sick berth was for many reasons a dismal prospect.

"I don't have any access to recent information," Borlund said cautiously. "Not even the leaf-scrap ravings. The storm ruined them all before I had a chance to read them."

"I also imagine that aboard any ship with old Zaalpotz as purser, the cabin lighting was cavelike," Viligas said.

"That also," Borlund replied. He looked at the overhead and lined up his thoughts, forming a sequence that he hoped would be both informative and discreet.

"The more serious part of the day's incident was the confrontation with Captain Over Captains Jossu I Hmilra. I know nothing about that except what I read, and I'm not sure that is knowledge."

Viligas smiled. His teeth were not only intact but dazzling white. "Neither am I. The newsgatherers are like pilots without charts. A wise captain gives them only moderate trust."

"As for my part, both law and custom seem to support me," Borlund continued. "The Directors do not have the reputation of fools or brutes. Nothing I heard or saw at Group House has led me to believe otherwise."

Borlund saw Weil frown at this. He hoped Viligas didn't notice. If she wanted secrets, she could go whistle for it until they were alone and out of hearing of any Kilmoyans. Weil could make his term aboard this ship difficult; the Directorate could cause him trouble for the rest of his life. An independent mind was not the same thing as enthusiastically seeking martyrdom.

"So you do not expect the Directorate to interfere with our ways of running this ship because you are aboard?"

Was that all that bothered Viligas? Probably, *Lingvaas* was already the best-known mixed-crew ship, and Directorate interference with her would immediately put her in the searchlight beams of some high-placed politicians. Any Captain could be pardoned for preferring to run aground.

"If I was betting, I'd bet against it. Not much, but I don't have much to spare for betting on anything."

"Then stay out of bone-rolls with the stokers," Viligas said. "They will win your crest ornaments and daughter's dowry."

Viligas slipped Borlund's papers back into their folder and handed them to him. "You have done more aboard ship than you perhaps realize. The Directorate may wish to see you a common Farer, and you seem to have come aboard ready to serve as one. This does you honor.

"However, *Lingvaas* does not waste good Farers. You will be assigned to the steward's division, because that is the most under-crewed. However, while performing duties there, you will take instruction in deck seamanship, navigation, and engineering. As soon as we can do so without any protesting, you will be declared a Command-Candidate and allowed to sit for your Deck certificate. Is this fair enough?"

Borlund had not expected half of this, let alone being asked if it was enough. He decided that false modesty wouldn't go over well, and besides, right now he felt very little modesty of any kind.

It didn't hurt that Barbara Weil was grinning at him, with a complete disregard for what this might tell Captain Viligas.

"I hope I'm worthy of your trust, Captain."

Borlund didn't remember if he was offered a drink or not, or if he took it if offered. He did pocket a certificate for an impressive list of clothing and gear, all to be deducted from his next pay bag (or next three or four, from the likely cost).

Then he was climbing the ladder to the main deck, to be greeted by a large, stout Kertovan woman.

"You Borlund?" she asked. He couldn't place her accent, except that it made him wonder if she had a speech defect.

"Yes."

"That's aye-aye, Farer," the woman said.

"You must be the steward."

"Always that bright, are you? Let's see how bright you can make the pots. We've a few needing cleaning."

"Aye aye, ma'am."

At least that couldn't hurt. What did hurt was the laughter from farther forward, both human and Kilmoyan. Clearly the mixed crew was successful in one way—they all found that breaking in a new hand offered first-class entertainment.

interlude

The most common name for the planet came out in Anglic as "Kilmoyn."

A thousand years before humans needed to name their world, Kilmoyn's most advanced societies had reached something like our late Renaissance. Its inhabitants (resembling a cross between an otter and a chimpanzee) had printing and some notion of the scientific method. Thanks to a hazy atmosphere and a location close to an interstellar dust cloud, they had little notion of astronomy.

Then the sky literally fell on them. The head of a comet struck, obliterating civilization in the southern hemisphere. The north survived and so did some knowledge, but too many Kilmoyans did not. The survivors lacked wealth and labor to do much with that knowledge for centuries.

It didn't help that the water vapor thrown into the atmosphere brought on an ice age. Also, as a result perhaps of volcanic gasses or some element in the comet, about half the women were now sterile. The Kilmoyans had this much luck: about twice as many women as men had always survived to reproductive age. But the effects on marriage and family were many and various, and ultimately added a whole mass of nonfertile females to the labor force, with further consequences all across society.

Centuries passed. The Kilmoyans groped their way back to their previous level of civilization, then passed it. Three major power centers developed around the Western and Greater Seas: the Empire of Alobolir to the west, the Kertovans on the islands in the middle, and the Confederation of Dhandara on the continent to the east. A multitude of lesser powers, City-States, tribes, and other entities flourished or faltered.

But the upward urge continued. In the tenth century after the comet, a late Victorian Englishman dropped in a Kertovan city might have found much of the technology familiar. He also might have noticed a lack of noisome slums (preventive medicine was developed early, to hold down infant mortality), women laying out along the yards of ships, privately owned ironclads, domesticated killer whales (or their first cousins, anyway) used as coastal tugs, and much else to make him wonder if he had fallen asleep while reading one of H. G. Wells's tales.

If he had looked and listened long enough, he might have discovered that the Kertovans also had a streak of optimism. But it was not the complacent optimism of a Britannia that ruled the waves, it was the hard-won confidence of those who have taken the worst the seas of Kilmoyn could throw at them and wrested prosperity from the waters.

THE STARSHIP *RAMPART* WAS HALFWAY THROUGH A FIVE-YEAR, THOUSAND-light-year voyage when she struck the dust cloud on the fringes of the Kilmoyn system. She survived; her ability to travel faster than light did not.

Most of the hundred crew and two thousand hibernators aboard survived. So did nearly all the eight thousand suspended embryos. With a reasonably large and carefully screened gene pool, if the Ramparters could get safely down on Kilmoyn they ought to survive.

By the skin of their teeth, they did. They'd hoped to leave the ship crewed (at least by hibernators) and in shape to be repaired for the rest of the journey in a couple of generations. Instead they had to cannibalize much of her to increase the shuttles' capacity by enough to land every living thing and all the vital data and equipment. This included a heavy load of medical supplies, since the first priority was getting the embryos turned into viable babies.

The Ramparters landed in the northwest corner of the eastern continent and spent a generation surviving and trying to keep a low profile. (It was felt by the leaders that playing gods from outer space would create dangerous chaos rather than advance local civilization.) They survived diseases and mineral deficiencies, if not in fine style, then well enough to give hope for the future. In that future, they would have living space, then a viable society, then (probably in conjunction with one of the local civilizations) a space program. *Ramparts* would need replacement parts and the great-grandchildren of her original crew would need training, but if both were available she might take to space again.

High hopes for the long term were dashed, however, when the humans ran into the expansion of the Confederation of Dhandara toward the west. Some humans tried to arm the aboriginals, which provoked full-scale war by the Confederation. More humans than the gene pool could afford were killed. Others fled, either north into the wilderness or south of Lake Jazar. The largest single group fled to sanctuary with the Kertovan settlement along Muosi Bay. All used the available modern weapons, and retained some of them, but nearly exhausted their ammunition supply.

After some consideration, the Kertovans took the humans off and gave them the island of Yproga, offshore from the Kertovan colonies on the western continent. They were more or less dumped because the Kertovans at that time wanted no war with the Dhandarans.

The humans survived, however, clawing back from the edge of disaster to regain a reasonably advanced technology, including medical research and a limited production of modern weapons and the stockpiling of their ammunition. In order to avoid inbreeding, they also worked out what amounted to a system of group marriages, with genealogical records rigorously kept pending the restoration of DNA typing. The social arrangements and taboos supporting this system were complex, including a near-ban on recreational sex.

In time, the Kertovans allowed a human settlement in their colonial capital of Saadi. Nobody on either side had illusions about generosity: this was an experimental laboratory that let each side study (and spy on) the other. But the benefits went both ways. Three generations after *Ramparts* entered orbit around Kilmoyn, it has become a high honor for a human to be chosen for the Study Group in Saadi.

chapter 9

"Borlund!" the cook shouted.

"Aye aye, ma'am?"

"Don't call me 'ma'am.' I work for a living. You're supposed to, but these kiviriks—you call them peeled?"

They had looked all right to Sean Borlund when he brought the basket down to the galley. Maybe Belindouza the cook was just chasing the new hand. Or maybe he wasn't a very good kivirik-peeler.

Borlund was learning that he knew much less about the work of ships and Farers than he had thought. He hoped he would not have to use on filling in the gaps all the time that Barbara Weil expected him to devote to the tutoring program.

He looked at the basket of bilious green tubers again. "Peelings too thick?"

Belindouza looked away. Borlund still saw her ears twitching, although her voice was as gruff as ever when she turned back. "Got that much right. You think kiviriks grow on the masts? Ever seen them growing there?"

"No."

"Right. You don't drink that much. What does that mean?"

Borlund decided that the cook wasn't referring to his drinking habits. "We have to buy kiviriks."

"Right again. On shore, which we don't get to every day. With slyn, which we don't have enough of. I could feed this whole crew like Captain-Borns if I had enough slyn, which I don't and won't. So I have to throw myself on the mercy of fumblehands like you, who carve off half a kivirik trying to peel it!"

The cook brandished the ladle, until Borlund wanted to back away. He couldn't, or Belindouza would bully him even more than she did already.

He took a deep breath. "Give me a whetstone. I thought the peeler was sharp enough. Maybe I was wrong."

"No maybe about it. Sharpen it until you can split a hair with it, and keep it that way."

Borlund wanted to groan and knew he didn't dare. Peeling vegetables was either the last job at night or the first in the morning. Making it longer could only cut into his sleep or his study time.

It would have to be sleep, he decided. He couldn't let Barbara down—and he had the feeling that behind her were quite a few other people, some of them present only in spirit, whom he'd also be letting down if he didn't make himself into a proper Farer.

The whetstone clunked down on the deck at his feet. He picked it up without taking his eyes off Belindouza, and she favored him with a brief, teeth-baring sort of smile.

LINGVAAS WAS RIDING UNDER FORE AND MAIN TOPSAILS AND A REEFED aftermast lower. Not a way to get anywhere fast, but she was two commons ahead of schedule and Captain Viligas wanted to give the crew shore leave. So they were dumping ashes from cold boilers, painting the funnel, and so forth, while the winds pushed *Lingvaas* across the Osorikin Gulf as they had pushed her forerunners in the years when *Rampart* was still a file in a computer on Esperanza and no human now living on Kilmoyn was even a gleam in their parents' eyes.

The quartering sea still sprouted whitecaps and made the deck sway gently under Borlund's feet. He was no more likely to be seasick today than any other; sea legs came naturally to him. It was less natural to navigate a swaying deck when he had four large flasks of hot hoeg in a carrying harness, and a pail of biscuit-and-fish mash.

"Food!" he shouted, cupping his hands to carry to the four Farers dangling from the funnel. Two wielded chipping hammers, the others brushes dripping oily primer. Seasoned for a day or two by heat once the engines started again, the primer would halt rust and make a better base for the normal orangish-red topcoat.

"Right down," one of the Kertovan Farers called. A human named Bernsdorf didn't bother to shout.

He also didn't bother to see that his harness was properly locked before he began his slide to the deck. Suddenly he was in midair, falling free.

Borlund acted entirely by instinct, and luck was with him as well.

He was under Bernsdorf when the Farer came down. They both crashed to the deck, but Borlund had softened a bone-breaking impact to a bruising one for both men.

"Gaah," Bernsdorf said, slapping at steaming patches on his clothes where hot hoeg had splashed from the flasks. "Next time don't be so messy."

"Next time he can throw you neatly over the side," the Kertovan called. She slid down to the deck and helped Borlund to his feet. "Thanks, shipmate. I call this hairless windbag a friend, though the Lord only knows why. This isn't the first time I've had to be his tongue when he couldn't shape it to polite words."

"You're both welcome," Borlund said. He picked up the flasks and examined them for damage.

"Borlund!" thundered from below. "If you've broken any of the deckware—"

What will you do, Belindouza? Make me stay up all night repairing it? Or take the price out of my pay, if there's any of it left unclaimed?

Borlund handed out the two intact flasks and the bucket, only dented instead of cracked. Then he lifted the broken pieces into the harness and stood up.

Or, rather, he tried. His leg joints seemed rusted, and he could have sworn *Lingvaas* was lying far over to both redside and greenside at once, which was impossible.

"You all right?" the Kertovan said.

"I think so."

"You might have hit your head," she added, taking his arm. After a moment, Bernsdorf came up on Borlund's other side.

"Sick berth?"

"Back to the galley."

That finally drew sympathy from Bernsdorf. "Send you back to Belindouza's mercy? When Seakin mate with jouti!"

"I'm on duty."

"After the healer sees you."

Borlund wanted to shake off both sets of hands and tell them that he was just tired. He didn't want anyone standing between him and Belindouza, and not just because the cook was a law unto herself and even Captain Viligas couldn't protect most of the crew from her wrath.

He could take it. He had to—and everyone had to see that he could. Particularly the ones who didn't know it already.

* * *

FARER STEWARD'S MATE BORLUND, ARE YOU LISTENING?:

Borlund was ready to put the point of his knife under his chin if he could think of a way to do it without being noticed. Instead he jerked his head up and back. The pain in his neck and shoulders sharpened, then eased a little.

"Yes."

"What was the last passage we discussed?"

"Passage?" For a moment Borlund couldn't remember if Watch Chief Teacher Guundzousa was referring to a geographical feature or a part of a book.

"Yes, which passage?"

Memory crept back. So did the power of speech. Thick-tongued and dry-mouthed as he was, Borlund managed to describe Woilko's Nine Principles of Design, as applied to ships.

"Eight: Strength must be in proportion to purpose."

"What does that say about *Lingvaas*?"

"It means she has to be a good deal stronger than a regular merchant vessel. We work close inshore, where we face more danger of running aground. We also have to keep the sea off lee shores in worse weather, which is why we have two propellers *and* a full sailing rig.

"We're not as a good a cargo carrier as a purpose-built merchant ship of course. The heavier frames and plating takes up more space. We're almost a warship, in some ways."

"Been listening to the gabbletongues?"

"Eh?"

"The ones who talk about the expedition down south."

"Just rumors, I thought."

"Then why did you listen?"

"When your bunkmates are talking loud enough to be heard on deck—"

"Stow that. You've committed a mastheading offense. Take yourself aloft to the aftertop and stay there until sunfade."

"Aye aye, Teacher."

"You can do that right, anyway."

BORLUND WANTED TO WEEP ON HIS WAY UP THE MAST, BUT DIDN'T DARE IN sight of the deck. Once in the aftertop, he still didn't want to cry but the smoke from the funnel stung his eyes until he did.

Lingvaas was on her way out of the Osorokin Gulf, after three days cruising along the shore, unloading shipments at small posts that regular merchant vessels either drew too much water or couldn't afford to visit. Everyone had been working harder than usual, so Borlund was not the only one who'd gone short of sleep.

Except that he'd been short of sleep before the coastal excursion began, and not because he'd gone ashore to visit the drinkshops and pleasure halls. The cook wanted the gallery turned out and scoured before the fresh stores came, the teacher wanted seventeen navigational problems solved, both of them wanted the work done yesterday, and neither of them seemed to have ever heard of sleep deprivation, let alone Barbara Weil.

He didn't mind it that Weil might have been on another ship for all that she seemed to be doing for him. If she'd decided that he had to prove himself to her as well as everybody else, he could live with that. He'd rather live without her afterward, but that prospect certainly wouldn't affect Weil's judgment. She couldn't afford to be suspected of favoritism, and he had nothing to offer that could outweigh that risk.

He did mind being so tired that he might be scalded in the gallery, swept overboard, or fall from aloft before he took his deck qualifications. He'd already learned how little sleep he needed; now he was learning how to catch that minimum in naps even when his bunkmates were arguing or singing.

It was a race between fatigue and learning, and if he hadn't been able to sneak bowls of commander's chowder and fat-loaded biscuits from the gallery, he'd have bet on the fatigue. But extra calories really could substitute for sleep—up to a certain point, at least.

Hand over hand, Borlund climbed the aftermast shrouds. He did it properly, pulling himself up the vertical wires and only using the crosswires to brace himself. He was horribly tempted to go through the newlies' hole, in the top platform itself, instead of outside on the shrouds, but did it proper Farer-style.

There was a bad moment when *Lingvaas* heeled sharply to redside and one of Borlund's feet slipped out of the shrouds. But instinct aided fear, and two hands and a foot held their place. The next moment he was in the top.

It was varnished wood with a netting of heavy canvas over freshly painted wire hanging from the railings. Borlund clung to the railing and looked forward. One of the lookouts in the midtop waved; Borlund waved back. Wind blew the funnel smoke out over the redside quarter, but the plume was too wide for Borlund to escape. He leaned over the windward side of the top and stared at the ocean.

The only land visible was the Spesyo Archipelago, a mountain massif submerged except for a few peaks. The *Instructions to Seafarers* warned that their underwater formation was largely unknown, and Farers could expect close approaches to be dangerous as the sea level continued to fall. The Seakin seldom visited the area, so their knowledge of the bottom was impressionistic and unreliable.

As if thinking about them had called them, a family of Seakin rose to blow. One turned on its side, then rolled completely over, giving Borlund a clearer view of the big mammalian than one usually managed even from aloft.

It was ten meters long, with a high-crowned skull and a humped back that sprouted a dorsal fin larger than a longboat's sail. The pectoral fins were bifurcated; no two scientists had the same opinion about whether they were degenerate or evolving limbs. Borlund didn't much care; if the Seakin ever did evolve enough to play the flute, it would be long after his time.

The big one, apparently the family head, flung himself—no, herself, the family head was always a female—into the air. She practically turned a somersault, landing on her side. Then another, more agile Seakin burst out of the water almost vertically, rising completely into the air. That one did turn a somersault.

Borlund watched the Seakin cavorting long enough to hear the drums beat twice. He also saw the deck fill with Farers tossing lines over the side. Seakin sometimes drove schools of fish toward Kertovan ships. Other times, the remnants of their own meals brought scavengers who also made good eating after a final swim through cooks' pots.

Borlund remembered a particularly good fish stew, loaded with hotleaf that he'd minced and pickled himself, and bread that he'd baked that even Belindouza said was fit to eat. He was learning to cook; maybe he could find work in a waterfront cookshop if he had to leave the sea.

He didn't want to, though. He would miss the wide waters, and the Seakin blowing, and laying aloft when the wind was enough to be exciting rather than frightening, and listening to squeezepipes and five-strings on deck on a fine night.

He would miss—oh, he'd miss a hundred things that he hadn't

really learned about from coasting voyages, things that were part of the Faring life such as you could only live aboard a deep-sea ship like *Lingvaas*.

Many more than a hundred. Borlund sat down, braced himself in a corner of the top, and began the list. He might have reached fifty—he could never remember—before he fell asleep.

LINGVAAS WOKE BORLUND BY TAKING ON A CORKSCREW ROLL THAT SMELLED of bad weather even to a sleeping Farer. He awoke, in rain blown by a gusty quartering wind that at least kept the top clear of smoke.

The next thing he noticed was that it was dark; he might have been at the bottom of an inkwell save for the masthead lights above and the riding lights below. It was only after counting the lights that Borlund realized he was not alone.

"Farer Steward's Mate Borlund, accepting relief," he said. He had to cough twice and try three times before he could get the words out intelligibly.

"I relieve you, Farer," the visitor said. Then a hand came out of the darkness, holding a hoeg flask. It was hot to the touch, but it wasn't the heat that made Borlund nearly drop it.

The voice was Barbara Weil's. Which seemed a little hard to believe, but there was one way of finding out—

"Thank you, ma'am," Borlund said.

The reply was laughter so soft that he could barely hear it above the wind, but unmistakable.

"Remember what I said about relaxing when we're alone?"

"It's been so long since that happened that my memory failed me." Borlund heard an edge in his own voice.

Weil's reply was bland. "Mental aging already?"

"You know why my memory *should* be going, as well as anybody." Borlund didn't know how long he'd slept, but it was long enough for him to feel combative. "Even if you didn't order it—"

"You think that?"

Borlund swallowed. Just because he felt strong enough for a fight didn't mean that he had cause for one.

"You know why I had to leave you to your own devices," Weil said. "Not just for the sake of discipline, but so you wouldn't appear to be one of my faction in the eyes of the Directorate. Your shipmates I could trust you to handle. The Directors are above your fighting weight."

"And *you* didn't want any more trouble with them either. If they were angry enough, they might appeal to the Fleet to send you ashore."

"Exactly. Or at least off *Lingvaas*. I'm not indispensable, but I am one of the people determined to make the mixed-crew experiment work. I think you're another."

"Then I'm one of your faction, whatever the Directors don't think."

"You might be. But I think you're more. You're a Farer."

"I am?" Borlund almost croaked. Then he shrugged and said quietly, "I suppose so." He wasn't going to talk about watching the Seakin, even to Weil.

"You are," she said. "Even Belindouza thinks so. She thinks you'll be a better one if you learn the way she did. Guundzousa doesn't agree. That's why he sent you to the aftertop. Not for listening to gossip, but to get you away from old Belindouza long enough for you to catch up on your sleep. If you were Farer enough to sleep in an aftertop at sea, that is."

"What if I couldn't sleep, or fell out of the top?"

"Then I suppose you wouldn't be a Farer."

"Cold comfort, Commander Weil." He didn't want to insult her with "ma'am," but he couldn't let that remark pass completely. He'd studied the concept of "survival of the fittest" in biology and in the history of science. It was the first time that he'd been the subject of an experiment in it, and he was not going to pretend that it was at all pleasant.

"Say that again when we return to Saadi. If you can say it with a straight face, I'll let you go ashore without prejudice."

"Aye aye, ma'am," Borlund said, but he said it so that Weil only muttered a mild obscenity. Then she added, "Are you going to drink that hoeg before it freezes, or let me drink it before I do?"

chapter 10

The Divusoros Club offered as much privacy as any place in the Island Republic or its territories, and more than all but a few. Five inner rooms could accommodate fair-sized gatherings (up to twenty or so) for the discreet discussion of indiscreet topics.

The builders of the club had even guarded against indiscreet servants. Three of the five rooms were designed so that food and drink could come in without those who delivered it hearing more than a mumble or two of what was being said within.

Also, it was generally suspected that the leaf-scrap journal chiefs had spent all their money trying to unearth scandal from the incident at Fort Huomikki. For a while at least the newsgatherers would have to pay bribes out of their own pocket—and a bribe to the club's well-paid servants was more than most newsgatherers could afford. Nor was it likely to yield anything that wasn't available in the streets for a tenth the price. (Even the most incorruptible servant saw no harm in profiting by pulling the fishskin over a newgatherer's head.)

At the moment, nobody could have heard anything except breathing and the occasional *skritch* of a firelighter, because there was nothing else to hear. Everybody was staring in succession at a piece of paper making the rounds of the big table, without doing more than raising an eyebrow or quirking an ear.

The paper with the complete attention of fourteen Captains and Captains Over Captains was a proposed list for the fleet sailing to the Bishak Gulf. On that gulf was the Kingdom of Eneh's only seacoast. Someday rails might pierce the mountains south of the Hask and provide a shorter route, but for now, if one was carrying any sort of burden, one voyaged to Eneh.

"A question, and not just out of curiosity," one Captain said. "Are you sure we need so many heavy ships? That means more coal, more provisions, more storeships to escort."

"I thought the plan was to purchase anything we might need along those lines in Rinbao-Dar," another Captain put in.

The first speaker shook his head and pulled at one ear, which was no more than a stump thanks to a Luokkan pirate's blade. "I have problems with that. Or, rather, I have problems with relying on the goodwill of two cities where Imperial agents have been running openly down the street like stray fowl these past two Greats.

"Even if we can buy, the price is likely to be higher. Then it will be either ask the Halls for more slyn, or dip into our own bags, and I have even more problems with either course."

"All the more reason for a generous allowance of storeships," Jossu I Hmilra said. "If we have enough heavy ships, their escort will be no problem. We simply sail them in the same convoys as the transports, and we *must* provide a heavy escort for those. One hostile cruiser among the transports could be a massacre."

"How many 'hostile cruisers' do we need to guard against?" yet another Captain said. He was old for his rank, unlikely to receive further rank or honors, so had nothing to lose by being an earstinger. Certainly most of what he'd said was along such lines.

I Hmilra was relieved to see another Captain save him the trouble of refuting such pestiferous optimism. "The Dhandarans had at least eight regular warships or big packets that could be converted to raiders, the last time I looked at a reference book."

"Mostly built by us," someone muttered.

"Never mind the Great Debate," the first speaker replied. "Do we know where all of them are? No. Could one of them slip in among unescorted ships? Yes, unless we threw a patrol line all the way across the Western Sea. That would take either the whole Fleet, or else squadrons of converted light vessels that could neither fight nor flee. Either would also mean even more coal and stores, shipped unguarded, carried in unescorted traders.

"I don't think the proposal includes too many heavy ships. The only point I question is whether there are enough armorclads, not too many. Remember, we don't know what kind of shore batteries we may be engaging. Field guns can damage lightclads, and heavier guns can sink them outright. Armorclads can do double duty, escort at sea and bombardment vessels inshore once the convoy is unloaded and moored in a protected anchorage."

"Thank you for your Elementary Strategy lecture," another someone muttered.

I Hmilra smiled. Gurgan I Djurr had taught at the Higher Fleet School, and did tend to lecture. He also tended to make sense, more often than not.

"I would agree with Captain I Djurr," he said, "if we had armorclads to spare. But the last time I looked at a Fleet roster, we were scraping the bottom of the drydock for ships that float only thanks to their last coat of paint. I am the first to regret that armorclads don't grow on bushes, but the first to admit its truth.

"I don't, however, propose to mourn our inability to do the impossible. I suggest two things. One, we take a page from the book that the Dhandarans may have also read. Convert packets into escort vessels and arm the storeships and transports.

"Two—I seem to recall a shipyard report a few years ago that mentioned a huge store of plates, frames, and engine components for the *Illiks*."

Some of the other Captains looked as if I Hmilra had performed an elimination on the table in front of his associates. He tried not to smile at the reaction.

"I admit the floating turds have an evil reputation. But that's the harbor-defense model.

"Suppose we used those existing stores and a few more to build a more seaworthy version? Higher freeboard, more deck space, more ventilation—"

"More hatches for the crew to escape when the Lord-forsaken things do capsize," was the latest mutter. "Or are we breeding a new race of Farers, with teeth to gnaw through iron plates and lungs to let them swim up from Seakin depths."

"—and all of it, in sum, more ships fit to stand up against heavy guns. We might have to lighten the armament and even the gunhouses, but that's not likely to draw the wrath of either the Lord or the crews."

"I suppose we could do—what's that term the new school-trained engineers are using— a 'design study' for both," I Djurr said. "I've even seen a list of ships for conversion, although I think it was ten Greats old and not amended since it was written."

"Would you care to take command of finding the list and amending it from the surveys of new ships?" I Hmilra asked.

I Djurr tugged at his lower lip. "Only if I can have an associate. It is more work than I and my household could manage alone. If Captain Kwinzuzuurus is available—"

Kwinzuzuurus, the elderly "earstinger," looked bemused, as though he could not decide whether he had been rewarded or trapped. Finally he nodded, although his ears were twitching. That might be from uneasiness, or perhaps only from age.

I Hmilra decided that Gurgan I Djurr was going to be surprised with a most generous gift next Greatday, or perhaps even sooner. He had deftly given his aging associate work that he could not only do but would make him a responsible worker instead of an irresponsible pest. Scholarship, I Hmilra decided, could teach as much about intrigue as command.

I Djurr was not the only one going to be surprised, either. I Hmilra had examined in detail the concept of "design study." So had Peros Dlaaro, a Captain Over Captains now gone ashore but still maintaining a controlling share in *Byubr,* one of the older *Illiks* still in service and commanded by his son.

A "design study" of how to use the floating turds on the Fleet like fertilizer on a garden, to make it grow, was well underway. It would be showing results well before Clearsky ended, and the dockyards would be at work, one could hope, before Barebranch was far advanced.

EHOMA TUOMITTI SWUNG HERSELF OUTBOARD AND ONTO THE LADDER FROM *Byubr's* bridge to the main deck. She went down slowly, since she was still getting her workstrength back and wore a patch over one eye.

The doctors had a notion that the eye might recover in time; it had been damaged but not destroyed. Meanwhile, it was ugly enough to scare children into fits and overly sensitive to sunlight and salt wind. Hence the patch—which Tuomitti had to admit gave her an exotic look, rather like a Luokkan pirate.

Also one that appealed to some men, at least if their words could be believed. Ehoma was too old to believe men's words and still tired too easily to let them prove their opinion by deeds. She'd made an exception for one old friend, but he would have called her fine-looking when she was laid out and dressed for slipping overside!

She was still a good few Greats from that condition, thank all those responsible. She was not so sure about *Byubr.* Her job was to overwatch the engine and deckhands helping the four engineer-designers with their study of the old harbor-defender, or at least to keep them from falling into the bilges or off the roundbacked foredeck. This gave her plenty of time to listen to the rude remarks all ranks were making about *Byubr* in particular and the *Illiks* in general. Compared with some of the terms she'd heard, the old "floating turds" was almost praise.

She vaguely understood that the plan was to make the *Illiks* more seaworthy, for some unspecified (or at least unspoken) purpose in the near future. The silence was not so much a concern for secrecy as universal knowledge that someone had the notion of taking the *Illiks* to the Bishak Gulf. No doubt they would do well enough there if they could survive the voyage; they had been designed for shallow or confined waters and the Gulf offered plenty of these.

But between planning and doing lay a great deal of rust, many loose rivets, bent frames, cracked plates, propeller shafts as twisted as a Drilion's ethics, and doubtless more horrors not yet discovered. And this was apart from the vices built into the *Illiks* from the time the moldings were laid out on the loft floors twenty Greats ago.

Tuomitti walked aft, thinking rude thoughts about hands who left so many loose lines and wires on deck. But most of them were newlies or gray, either with much to learn or with all forgotten.

Fresh-combed or gray and balding Farers were coming aboard Fleet ships every day. Nor were they turning too only for the Fleet. Merchants were launching new and crew-hungry ships almost every day.

Near the chopped-off stern, Tuomitti leaned against the aftergunhouse and watched two engineers and two deck Farers measuring beam and other dimensions with long folding rules and string. They were silent except for calling out lengths and widths to a third Farer, a gray woman with a slate and stylus who was writing them down as carefully as if they were her sister's children's names or the namingdays of old shipmates.

With nothing being said that she didn't already know, Tuomitti turned her ears to the din of the dockyard. Huddled low in the bottom of a drydock that could take a large armorclad, *Byubr* was out of sight of practically everything except the cranes and work parties on the edges of the dock. One work party also squatted on the floor of the dock, some scraping slime and picking up debris while others unrolled a gumcloth hose dangling down from an airdriver above.

Tuomitti could only hope that the hammer wouldn't drive a hole through *Byubr's* hull plates when it started working on the rust.

Other hammers, cleaning, chipping, and riveting, were hard at work all around. Cranes puffed steam as they swung loads of plates, timber, or machinery with the ease of a sounderman casting the depth line from the bow of a ship. Workmen shouted, cursed, cheered, or even sang in the usual host of languages and dialects. Draft animals bellowed and shrieked, whips cracked, and the wheels of carts almost drowned out the puffing of steam tractors.

A whistle screamed, and others took up the scream, like the singer and chorus in a song-play. Every other sound died before them, and when the whistles finally died so had most of the other sounds.

The gray sky said nothing to confirm that it was the lunch halt. Ehoma Tuomitti's stomach spoke louder. She rather wished she'd brought her lunchbox down from the bridge, but perhaps her dignity demanded retracing her steps.

JOSSU I HMILRA HAD RIDDEN TO THE DIVUSOROS CLUB AND WAS NOW riding back to the hire-stable next door to the rail station. Two Watch commanders flanked him at a discreet distance. Both were armed, as well as close enough to move in and settle trouble without shooting. They were also close enough that the Captain Over Captains was painfully aware of how much better they rode than he.

Jossu I Hmilra had never been a good enough rider to enjoy it, and he thanked all who might be responsible that he had been born a Kertovan and not in the Empire or on the plains of Dhandara. In both lands, riding with pretentious skill (or at least the pretense of skill) was an essential mark of one born high enough to deserve social acceptance.

In the Island Republic to this day more tencasts were covered on foot and many more by ship, than on the back of any animal. There were still growing inland towns that could be reached from the coasts only by rail.

However, today Jossu I Hmilra was riding, where hundreds of eyes would fall upon him while he did. There was no riddle to this: he had to prove to all that he was fit to command the fleet being born for next Great's campaign.

He had presided over the meeting at the club, but there he had been among friends or at least those who respected his judgment and experience. In law, the expedition commander had not been chosen. Intrigue was in the wind, the water, and the rock itself; those seeking reasons to eliminate aspirants for the position would certainly use physical unfitness as one. Anyone of I Hmilra's age would certainly be suspect (testimonies to his health and vitality from Alikili would hardly weigh much in the official balance). It was up to him to prove otherwise.

Thus he rode, although gratified that today he could take a level route along wide, clean, and dry streets. Traffic was as thick as usual, more than he had ridden in for Greats, but he usually had room to maneuver. His dreezan was also a respectable middle-aged female, used to the city's hurly-burly and unlikely to do anything embarrassing, let alone dangerous.

They rattled across the Dzern River bridge, just as a tug with a string of rock-oil barges steamed out of the lock upstream. I Hmilra reined in and watched as a several commons' worth of oil for the lamps of Saadi slid past beneath him.

He added another letter to the long list he intended to write before he again met with the Cabal of Fourteen (as they called themselves, only half in jest). Rock-oil deposits in Saadi—were they sufficient to support the use of oil engines such as the Aloboliri had invented? Kertovan steam engines depended on highly skilled metalworking that would make such engines easy to produce in large numbers, if the fuel for them was available.

If the rock-oil deposits in Saadi were not sufficient, might there be others safely within the reach of the Republic? (Ask a rock-studier, I Hmilra reminded himself, but don't expect a swift answer or one easy to understand.) Was Luokka safe territory, or would moving inland bring the folk there up in arms, leading to a war that might not be just and certainly would not be prudent? Not when the expedition to support Eneh might lead to war with the Empire.

They were almost at the station. I Hmilra turned the dreezan toward the stable, where one of the hands had already sighted him and was coming out to meet him. I Hmilra reined in, dismounted, pulled his workcase out of the saddlebags, and tossed the reins to the hand.

"Put it on my account," he said, as he turned toward the station with more haste than dignity. He badly wanted privacy to pull up his kilt and see if there was any skin left on his posterior.

Off to one side, one of the Watch commanders dared a grimace. It was plainly his opinion of Captain-Borns who could run up debts in a way that would mean a Watcher's dismissal.

Justice be cursed. Right now, I feel as if I might have to stand up all the way home!

* * *

THE COMMON ROOM OF THE GREEN NET WAS ALMOST FULL BY THE TIME Ehoma Tuomitti entered. Most of the crowd was the usual Farers and dockworkers, getting outside hoeg or something stronger as fast as their gullets could deal with the servers' offerings. The servers were already looking harried.

Tuomitti waved to two or three old friends, as she pushed through to the counter with more determination than tact. On the way she noticed a few unusual guests, such as a quartet of Saadian Farers, all watch chiefs, in one corner table, and of all unlikely things a Daughter of the Rock with five children in two, in another corner.

Kappala Naytet slid the usual free first cup of hoeg down to Tuomitti, loaded a server's tray with five cups and two jugs of something else, and grinned at her friend.

"You look hungry. Even the sacred room has people in it, but there are seats left."

The "sacred room" was a small chamber off the common room, fit to accommodate eight friendly folk or four on more polite terms. It was also Naytet's private dining room, when she didn't have to eat off the serving counter or off the top of the stove (when the cook had his back turned).

"Blame it on yourself," Tuomitti retorted. "You didn't pack me enough lunch."

"Oh, I gave you all I thought you could carry in your weakened condition," was the reply. "Would I lay heavy burdens on an old woman who is also an old friend?"

Tuomitti regarded her host with the eye of one contemplating where the knife would hurt most as it went in, even before she twisted it. Then a voice came from behind.

"Old woman, my pubic hair!"

Tuomitti turned. "Zhohorosh!"

"So it seemed, the last time I looked in the mirror."

"No doubt only a drink or two ago," Tuomitti replied. "You always were vain of your looks."

"Too vain, to hear you called an old woman," Zhohorosh said. "Handsome men like me cannot be found in the company of old women."

"And what is said of women, old or young, who are seen with the swollen-headed like yourself?"

"Many things, but few of them fit for the hearing of a Daughter of the Rock and children," he said, nodding toward the corner.

"If she's foresworn chastity at least five times—" Tuomitti said.

"They're not hers," Naytet put in. "They're from an orphanage, and were out shopping when someone snatched the Daughter's purse. I won't say anything against any particular folk, but it was down by the market, and you know what kind you find down there."

Zhohorosh met the owner's eyes with a cool, level gaze. "The sweepings of every folk in the world, from Drilions to Drylanders. None of them pious, either. So the Daughter and the young ones needed help getting home. Naytet let them stay here until she could send a messenger to the hire-stables."

Naytet looked away. "I could hardly let children stand in the street with it coming on to rain."

A sudden hiss and patter in the streets told them that the rain had now come on. Tuomitti hoped the engineers aboard *Byubr* would at least have the sense to take shelter below. When she had come off duty, they had been perched like cliff-screamers atop the forward gunhouse, and looking ready to stay there arguing about the right size for the new gun until they rusted in place and would have to be pried loose.

Zhohorosh took Tuomitti's arm, and led her toward the sacred chamber. A hastily summoned server followed with a loaded tray, collided with a rain-soaked hire-driver dashing in to shout for the Daughter, and nearly dropped the tray. Zhohorosh fixed the server with an even colder look and gently took the tray.

"If you've a hand free, Ehomatsi," he said, nodding toward the server.

Zhohorosh was one of the few men allowed to use the diminutive of her name in public without getting at least a sharp rap across the nasal forebone. She grinned and fished in her pocket for a handful of coins, which she handed over without bothering to count them. She was on full pay even on light duty, doubtless arranged by old I Hmilra, and Naytet was not charging her anything like full fees for her board and lodging.

The sacred room had been occupied until moments before. Now only a server remained, hastily clearing the tables. The two Farers watched him leave with an armload of dishes that he could barely see over, and even more barely avoid a collision with the Daughter and her charges as the driver led them out.

"Am I getting old in truth, or are they hiring younger and more soft-green servers in every drinkshop in the Republic?" Zhohorosh asked.

"The second, I should say," Tuomitti replied. She gripped his upper arm and squeezed. The corded muscle under the hair was as firm to the touch as ever. Zhohorosh was a Gunnery watch chief these days, and probably above helping move ammunition, but he could certainly do it if he had to.

They sat and ate porridge well seasoned and laced with lumps of saltfish, an omelette of cliff-screamer eggs with diced snouter, and fruit soup. They washed it down with enough hoeg to float a lifeboat; Tuomitti was still on an abstinent diet and Zhohorosh was on one for life after an engine-room accident left him with half a normal stomach.

"So, how goes the work down at the yard?" Zhohorosh asked, when both had their mouths free for talking. "Are they sending you back to sea once it's done?"

"That I don't know, and if the doctors do, they aren't telling me," Tuomitti replied. "As to the work at the docks, there's not much to say about following landbound engineers around and trying to make sure they don't fall down a hatch or offend a Farer's custom. Some of the school-trained folk they're sending out these days know the bow from the stern and not much more. I never thought I would take up nursing as a second calling at my age!"

Zhohorosh put a hand over hers. She felt the familiar calluses and could see without looking the powder and grease that would never wash out of the hair or from under the nails.

"You're saying that if there was a good deal to tell, you still might not talk about it?" he said, putting it as a question.

She warmed to his tact as much as to the hoeg. "We're being asked not to talk to people not doing this particular work, at least before it comes out in the *Bulletin*. You know how fast tales swim."

"Aye, and more than enough. There's a tale already swimming, about a move against the Empire's Hask Flotilla."

"Well, they certainly force us to keep enough of the Fleet at home that it would do no harm for the Flotilla to be farther upstream. With the fortresses blocking the river as they do, what the Empire worries about is beyond me."

"Losing the power to play knuckleball with the City-States, as always," Zhohorosh answered. "And there's no reason in that, either, although maybe it's my grandmother's blood speaking when I say that."

Tuomitti smiled. Zhohorosh was a quarter-Saadian and could have hidden the fact, but never had, even in the early days of their friendship. It was possible that this had cost him his chance at command rank, but he never speculated about that nor allowed his friends to do so.

"Your grandmother's blood also endowed you with a keen ear and a nimble tongue to repeat what that ear takes in," Tuomitti said. Her smile was even wider. "I should know."

"What vile rumor is this, that I babble secrets in bed? I am as close-mouthed as a scoopshell."

"Then you must have fallen far from your old standard, my friend."

"Are you asking for proof?" He looked sober. "If it will be hard for you, or cause tales to swim—?"

"I am well enough," Tuomitti said. "And no one has told me what to do ashore and still been heard politely, these last ten Greats. The engineers will be no exception to that rule."

"Then—shall we have some more hoeg sent up to your room? Or more?"

"Just the hoeg, my friend. I admit that an over full stomach no longer leaves me at my best."

THE RAIN CAME DOWN SO LONG AND SO HARD THAT BY THE TIME JOSSU I Hmilra left the train, the platform was three lines deep in water and everyone was huddled under the canopy. He himself was wet from feet to knees with just the short walk from the train. His kilt might have to be wrung out before it was hung up over the fire, lest it drown the blaze.

The journey from the station was no pleasure either. They had to take the longest of the three roads to the house, because water was knee-deep over the shortest and a bridge was closed on the second. Both master and driver reached home almost as wet as if they'd swum all the way, and I Hmilra refused to even drip on the post until he'd bathed, then let Alikili comb him in front of the bedroom hearth fire.

The post included several of the quarter-Great's share payments that he had requested now be forwarded as negotiable certificates to his home, instead of deposited directly into his pages. He intended to make them over to Alikili, giving her an account that was beyond serious legal question hers. With fifty thousand slyn or so in her own name plus the upland estates, she would not starve if she kept her wits about her.

It also included a coded letter from one of the upland deep swimmers. I Hmilra did not recognize the writing, but from the text he recognized that the man had served as the guard for the fugitive driver from the Fort Huomikki incident.

The tale was not pleasant. The driver had disappeared one night, and a body found well downriver three commons later could be his. Identification would be hard, though; the body had been battered against the rocks, or so it appeared. The Watch-healer had examined the body and declared drowning to be the cause of death, but could not rule out injuries inflicted before death.

None of this could be called good news. The driver's family would have to be provided for, discreetly but generously. I Hmilra had been an accessory to flight from justice (if one could call the driver's likely fate by that name); now he was an accessory to the driver's death. If the death was murder, he had not struck the blow, but he had marked the driver for whoever had.

I Hmilra had hardly any appetite that night, and they dined in his chambers. By the end of the meal he was wondering aloud if he should think again about his intention to secure command of the expedition to the Bishak Gulf and Eneh.

"I would be thinking less and less of it, if it were not for the prize-rights. You deserve more than I could leave you without them."

Alikili laughed, a laugh that turned into a coughing fit. He had to hold her close until she could breathe again, and when she spoke, it was into his shoulder.

"I won't say that I love you more because of the lies you tell, but this one is special. You would go even if they finally did outlaw prize-right. You would pay to go, and to raise the payment I think you would beggar your household, your kin, and even me."

"Not you. Never you, Alika."

"So you say. You may even believe it. What I believe is that you plan to return a hero, prize-right or not, so that you can lead the Republic in the next war against the Empire."

"It would really be the first war. We haven't fought the lands on the Hask since before the Oompleenas started calling themselves Emperors."

"Names, names. The name you want is 'hero'—"

"As long as I deserve it."

"I think you will. I also think that many people will be surprised at what you do about our relations with the Drylanders and the Saadians, when you have the power to do so."

I Hmilra was silent for a long while, his arms around Alikili. Finally he discovered what seemed like the right words.

"I am selfish. I like to see everyone around me happy, even my tuunda and the Saadians."

"The Drylanders seem to go their own way, as to happiness or misery."

"They can continue to do so, for all of me. But they are a mystery. I would like the answer to that mystery before I die."

"You think they are dangerous?"

"They have not been, so far. But the rumors of those who remained behind in the Confederation make one wonder. The Drylanders could be the greatest blessing our folk have ever known. Or they could be a greater menace than a second Skyfall."

After that they held each other in silence, too tired and lost in sober thoughts to do more.

chapter 11

The yard dipped toward a sea that was unfortunately not quite invisible. In spite of the darkness, the blowing spray, and the acrid smoke from *Lingvaas*'s funnel, Sean Borlund could see clearly how far he would fall if he lost his grip.

The ship had been on the second leg of her homeward voyage, off Lesser Turha, with a good south wind that let her set sail to save on coal. The voyage had not been as quick as usual, but it had been quite economical. If expenses remained below margin all the way home, Captain Viligas would not need to draw his Fleet subsidy for the first half of this Great.

At least that was the least inaccurate name for it. Borlund was doing well enough in shipkeeping, deck seamanship, and mechanics, and he thought he was doing well in navigation. He still wouldn't pretend to understand how a ship like *Lingvaas* could be both publicly and privately owned, as well as being a ship, a corporation, and a legal community of residence, all at the same time. He hoped that somewhere in the Island Republic was a Kertovan who would someday have time to explain these arrangements to a Drylander.

Then the wind rose halfway to a gale. They no longer needed to set canvas to save coal. Now they needed to take in sail to save canvas, and use coal to keep them off the reefs north of Lesser Turha.

It was as well they were north of the island. South of it, the reefs rose, fell, and thrust out fangs at random intervals, few of them fully charted. The islands set among the reefs like glass ornaments on a cheap brass chain were inhospitable even when uninhabited. When inhabited they usually held the sort of people who did not extend a warm welcome to shipwreck victims.

None of this was relevant to what had brought Borlund out on the swaying, dancing yard in the rising storm. That was a simple mechanical failure in a reefing winch, and the advantage that Drylander physiology gave Borlund in fixing it.

The short-legged Kilmoyans were not built for laying out along yards to set or take in sail. In their earlier ships the sails had been handled from the deck. In their later ships they used winches mounted in the tops. These slid the sails in and out laterally, rather than hoisting and lowering them vertically, as Borlund had read sailing ships used to do on Earth.

In the last generation of sailing vessels before steam began driving them from the oceans, the Kertovans at least used their compact auxiliary steam engines to drive the winches. Large ships mounted the engines in the tops, smaller ones on deck at the foot of the mast, with the reefing and furling chains running inside the hollow iron or steel masts and yards.

With two propellers, *Lingvaas* had not been much dependent on sail for safety, more so when she needed to turn a profit from fishing alone. Turned to Fleet service, she had not been allowed the kind of refit that would have given her steam winches. With a mixed-race crew, she was well toward the bottom of most lists of ships on which to spend bulging sacks of slyn. The Drylanders weren't sea-minded and few Kertovans besides Jossu I Hmilra and his faction thought her more than an interesting experiment that somebody else could underwrite.

So she still had hand winches in her tops for Farers to crank the sails in or out, and now one of the winches had jammed. Half the mid-uppersail could not be reefed, and was likely to do expensive damage to itself, the rigging, or both. Even wire rigging could be flogged out of its turnbuckles by a large sail running wild in a storm.

Thus the need for somebody to lay out along the yard (the term Borlund remembered from the well-thumbed copy of *The Maritime Compendium* that Barbara Weil had loaned him) and unjam the winch. Nobody had looked at Borlund directly, but only because they were all looking at his long legs.

Those legs were now clamped around the spray-slick yard, only meters from the end of the yard, while he studied the jammed winch traveler. For the third time he wished that it had been the winch itself, repairable (if at all) in the comfort of the top, instead of requiring acrobatics on the yard and tools clutched in teeth or slung from the yard.

"How goes it?" came the hail from the top. The voice was old Dat Amatai's. He wasn't exactly unfriendly, but he'd been a Farer since well since before Borlund was born. He was not above making it clear how nominal was Borlund's "command" of this working party.

"I'll need some of the pieces on the other belt."

"What other belt? You took both, even if you did not sling everything proper."

"There was a third belt. Rynko had it on."

"Aye?"

A confused noise that might have been Rynko protesting innocence. A less-confused shout followed.

"Lifeboat ahoy, three lights off the red bow!"

Amatai replied with asperity, "The belt, Rynko lad. Bring it over, and don't drop it or I'll send you after it to apologize to the Ladysoul for gouging her decks. *Then* you can run about and tell the world about lifeboats that they've doubtless already sighted from the other tops."

Borlund was creeping in along the yard as Amatai leaned over the top's railing to hand him the third tool belt. Suddenly *Lingvaas* took a perverse roll to redward. Amatai was off-balance, with one hand for the belt, one hand for the ship, and none to spare for himself. His full weight came against the railing.

Borlund was already reaching when he heard the railing crack. By the time Dat Amatai fell through the gap, Borlund had both hands free and extended. One snatched the tool belt out of a gray-furred hand that was within a heartbeat of letting it fall. The other gripped the back of the old Farer's jacket, until the Farer could get his own arms and legs around the yard.

"While you're visiting—" Borlund began.

Amatai laughed. It was not a very convincing laugh, but that might have been the wind. Was it still rising? Even if it wasn't, it was already making the sail crack like a drover's whip.

Borlund lifted the hand-candle and by its guttering yellow light examined the traveler. Nothing bent, nothing broken—as far as he could see. No, wait. A small gap in the track—the track displaced just enough to block the free passage of a rider (he guessed at the last, because he couldn't see it, but it made sense). . . .

"Hand me a file," Borlund said. "Please," he added, since this was as much request as order. "No, just a moment. I have two—can you hold the candle?"

Amatai looked reluctant to move so much as a whisker, but after allowing himself a half-glare, half-grin, he took the candle. Borlund quickly filed the lip of the visible crack smooth, grateful that by chance he'd picked the hardest of the files.

"Now, push the traveler outboard."

"Out—?"

"Yes, curse you!" Amatai didn't look hurt, so Borlund didn't apologize. If the traveler slid outboard too fast, it stood a good chance of taking toes off Borlund's foot or Borlund off the yard.

The traveler squealed loud enough to be heard over the wind, as Amatai pushed hard with first one hand, then with both, holding on with feet, stomach, and prayers to the Lord of the Waves. Whoever had the duty of oiling the gear on this yard had been slacking off.

Borlund swore into the wind. He was a naturally tidy man, with two bearer-partners who were almost fanatical about cleanliness. He found the standards of a well-run ship congenial, and lapses from them offended him even when he didn't have to imitate a road-show high-flyer act to repair the damage.

Another few moments with the file smoothed the lip of the other crack and stripped away rust. One of the slings had an oil can in it; Borlund groped for it until Amatai held the candle closer.

"Careful, I think this is rock oil," Borlund said, as a raw greasy smell made his nostrils prickle. "Burns easier than fish oil."

"Don't teach *me* how to shuck dzrik," Amatai growled, but he held the candle downwind as Borlund pulled out the oil can. He nearly emptied it on the track, but when he was done the traveler moved as if on glass.

"Ready on the winch," he called.

No response.

"Ha, get your mind off the grateful wenches in the lifeboat and bend onto that winch, you stone-ear," Amatai shouted to Rynko.

This time the reply was the clanking of the winch handle going into its socket. It should have already been there, but for once carelessness was good luck.

"Don't start cranking or you'll slice us both off the yard!" Borlund yelled. "Drylanders have powerful ghosts, too." The clanking stopped.

Borlund's mouth was dry and he saw Dat Amatai's hands shaking by the time they scrambled back into the top. But work to do calmed shaking hands, and the sail was hauled in and lashed by the time Borlund remembered to ask about the lifeboat.

"Oh, they said they'd already sighted it," Rynko said petulantly. "They haven't said anything else. Now can I go down?"

"Oh, yes, you can go down, to the galley," Amatai said. He slapped Rynko on the shoulder. "Mr. Borlund's going to want somebody to help him, when it comes to tending the survivors."

Rynko's stunned look made both Amatai and Borlund laugh, just as well for Borlund. His voice would have shaken if he'd had to reply in words.

BORLUND DIDN'T NEED RYNKO'S HELP AND BELINDOUZA BARELY NEEDED Borlund's. The lifeboat held no handful of survivors of an epic of Farers against the sea, but the passengers of a small freighter battling a fire in the cargo.

"Now if that cargo didn't contain twelve drums of disstul oil, we'd all be better off," the boat chief in charge of the lifeboat explained. "But that stuff's of an uneasy temper. Captain Suibaar, she reckoned she'd be better off with just folk who could take care of themselves if we had a leak and a flare-up. So we went off in the boat, and it's as well you came along with the sea kicking up, but I doubt we'll be presuming on your hospitality more than overnight."

In fact, it wasn't even that long. The steward's gang had barely time to provide dry clothes (with clean binders for the two children in the boat), hot towels, clean combs, and cups of hoeg or mklk, with sausage and pickled-vegetable soup for those who wanted it. Then the word came down from the deck that the freighter *Uillam* was in sight and wanted her people back, as soon as they'd finished drying, grooming, and eating.

Dat Amatai helped Borlund get the people up on deck and into *Lingvaas*'s steam launch, then vanished. Borlund was sure he was going to cajole Belindouza to give him and his mates first share of the leftover food and hoeg. For himself, a cup of hoeg almost too hot to drink had been enough.

He was still running on raw energy and the sense of having done well for his ship and himself tonight. In fact, if somebody had asked him to jump over the side and tow the launch to *Uillam*, he would have been in the water before he realized that he was being asked to do the impossible.

Somewhere about the time the launch returned from *Uillam*, the energy began to fade. By the time Borlund had finished as one of the working party getting the launch winched aboard and snugged down in its chocks, he was yawning.

By the time Barbara Weil was leaning against the foremast, watching Borlund and Dat Amatai inspect the glands of the launch's propeller shaft, Borlund felt as if his eyes needed propping open. All his fingers were thickening into thumbs, his stomach growled as if he hadn't eaten for a week, and every so often his legs seemed clad in trousers woven of anchor chain.

At last the launch was done; he mumbled something to Weil that it wouldn't sink right away the next time it went into the water.

"More than I can say about you," she said, or so he thought. She pointed at Dat Amatai.

"Take him below."

"Aye, Lady."

Borlund navigated the ladders and passages to his cabin, but his legs gave way as he stepped through the door. Fortunately his bunkmates were too soundly asleep to wake up, even at the clang and clatter of everything that fell along with Borlund.

He recalled dimly Amatai and somebody else (human, female, maybe even Barbara Weil?) heaving him into the bunk. He thought one of them tried to get his clothes off, and had the still dimmer notion that the woman was taking a personal interest in this process. But that had to be a fantasy spawned by exhaustion.

IF BORLUND HAD NEEDED ANYTHING BUT SLEEP AND FOOD, HE COULDN'T TELL when he awoke. He was ravenously hungry, and Belindouza seemed ready to cater to his appetite as she never had before. There was even a hot gignel pie, which turned out to be the result of a little trading between Belindouza and *Uillam*'s cook, who had been in the boat and been much relieved to find his galley and stores nearly intact when he reboarded his ship. He'd sent wholemeal, canned and dried fruits, honey, and a large jar of preserved gignels back in the returning launch.

Gignels were a long way from Borlund's favorite food, in any form. Preserved, they were always too salty. But Belindouza looked as if it would break her heart and other organs if Borlund refused at least the first three slices she offered him. He also remembered that a heartbroken Belindouza was quite capable of breaking his head once the fit of generosity wore off.

So he stowed away a breakfast even bigger than his ferocious appetite demanded. Then he washed, shaved, and went on deck to take his place on watch.

Lingvaas was bound north again, with the highest of the islands north of Lesser Turha just peering over the western horizon. To the east, open sea stretched nearly a thousand kilometers to the nearest island of the Republic, the gray horizon unbroken except for a distant and unidentifiable masthead and a still more distant smoke trail.

Borlund went through the coming-on-watch routine. He recorded the depths read by the sounderman ("No bottom with this line," which was hardly a surprise since they were off-shelf and the charts showed a kilometer of water below *Lingvaas*'s keel). He noted in the deck log the set of the sails (both mainsails and the after-triangle with a single reef), the strength and direction of the wind (still brisk from the south), the revolutions of the engines and the coal consumption as the Engineer Commander's messenger reported, and anything else he thought worth noticing.

With the steersman's permission he oiled the bearings of the wheel, inspected the fire-dampers, floatbelts, floatjackets, and flares, counted the scrubstone party on deck grinding away at the night's accumulation of salt, and examined the funnel for blistered paint or rust spots. He examined the boats and launch for stowaways or illicit lovers (the first unlikely this far out at sea, the second less uncommon), and did everything else that he could think might need doing.

By the time he ran past the end of both his memorized checklist and his imagination, the drum told him that the watch was a quarter over. His eyes also told him that the commander of the watch hadn't come on deck yet. Nor had a messenger, to tell him that the man was on the sick list.

Something had to be done, even if *Lingvaas* was sound and in relatively safe waters. At least he was senior to the messenger of the watch. He tapped the boy on the shoulder and was telling him to go below and find Egose Faind, when he saw Teacher Guundzousa coming on deck.

The watch chief was unusually well turned out this morning, and had a skin-wrapped parcel under his arm. Borlund thought irreverently that he was coming to Borlund in search of advice on how to conduct a shipboard romance with a Drylander female.

The prudent seldom talked about it, but it was hardly a secret that human and Kilmoyan sexual anatomies were compatible. The handful who knew the most, those who had put the matter to a practical test, said the least.

Instead, he stepped up to Borlund and gave him the open-palmed salute reserved for those of command rank. Borlund stared. He stared so long that Guundzousa laughed.

"I suppose it would be best to end the suspense," the Farer said. He handed Borlund the package. "You may find it useful enough to open here, and you will not offend me if you do so."

Not opening gifts in front of their givers was such a rigid point of Kertovan etiquette that Borlund looked dubious. Then he saw the helmsman so carefully not smiling, and the messenger doing a little dance as if the deck made his feet itch, and decided that he might as well offend all of them to get back for whatever game they were playing.

The package was two books, *The Practical Farer and Commander* and a blank personal log. The first was the standard reference for registered commanders, and Barbara Weil had let him dip into her well-thumbed and gravy-stained copy a few times. This copy that he held was so new that the sea breeze couldn't blow away the scent of the binding.

The log was also brand-new, and seemed to have something inside it. Borlund opened it, then gaped and dropped both the logs and its contents.

"That is no way for a new commander to treat his certificate," Guundzousa said reprovingly. Or at least he tried to achieve that tone. His voice didn't entirely cooperate.

Borlund snatched up the elaborately engraved certificate and held it up. The words danced before his eyes until they blurred, and it wasn't entirely from the breeze.

He didn't need to read it all, however. He could make out the crossed ship, sword, and Seakin of the High Farer's Council of Delegates. He could make out the words "Certificate of Command Education." He could even make out his own name, although those were the hardest words to recognize. They were the ones he had least expected to see here, at least this soon.

He neither wept nor embraced anyone. Instead he clasped hands all around, glad that tradition called for silence in this moment. Then Guundzousa went below, leaving Borlund alone with only the stray thought that Barbara Weil should have been here for this moment.

* * *

WEIL CAME ON DECK JUST BEFORE THE END OF BORLUND'S WATCH. SHE WORE a working kit and led a working party, whom she promptly turned over to the watch chief and sent forward. As she sat down on the bench behind the helmsman, Borlund noted that Weil was carrying another package.

"Another book?" he asked.

"Yes, but you surely aren't satisfied yet? A commander's professional library—"

"—would never fit in the size of cabin I'm likely to have for quite a few Greats," Borlund finished for her.

"So? If you were living entirely on shipboard it would be one thing, but you have a home."

"Yes," Borlund said, and before he could stop himself he added, "It's here."

Weil gave him a long, hard look. "Don't give up on your family until they've given up on you, and don't assume that they've given up on you until they tell you themselves." Borlund heard in those words the voice of experience that had left scars fit to hurt in fine weather as well as foul.

"I'm not giving anything up," Borlund said quietly. He wasn't sure this was the truth, but for the first time in their acquaintance that now deserved the name of friendship, Barbara Weil seemed to need reassurance from him. "I've just added something to what I had already."

He looked at the waves rolling away to the east, then up at the masts swaying and the brown smoke streaming against the gray sky. "I—if I had never come to sea the way I have, I would always have felt something was missing from my life. Now, if I go ashore, I'll *know* what I am missing, and I won't be happy until I go to sea again."

"Damn," Barbara Weil said softly. Borlund didn't think she'd intended for him to overhear her, nor for him to notice that her eyes were wet.

Suddenly she gripped him by both shoulders, then hugged him hard.

"Welcome to the sea, Sean."

"The Lord of the Waves told you to greet me, of course?" he said.

Weil wiped her eyes and smiled. "He did not. But I've served him long enough, Drylander that I am. I should have a few privileges."

The smile turned into a grin. "Aren't you going to open your present?"

It was a copy of *The Maritime Compendium*, as elegantly bound as the other two books and inscribed to him. (At least as far as he could tell. Barbara Weil had many virtues; legible handwriting wasn't one of them.)

"Don't flaunt this one ashore," Weil cautioned him. "It's not precisely banned like the Devotional List, but having a copy is nailing your flag to the masthead."

"What flag? It might be one I don't mind flying."

"No, I don't suppose you would. It's the flag of those who want the Drylanders to take their place on the seas of Kilmoyn. Not all of our friends are Drylanders, and many of our enemies are. But the enemies outnumber the friends, for now."

More words danced on her lips like the whitecaps overside, but the wind blew both away. Borlund wanted to hug her back, to show he understood, was grateful, would talk with her some other time when there was no one to hear.

Instead he saluted, the double palm of highest respect. He did it so awkwardly that Weil returned it with a smile.

Then Captain Viligas came on deck, and both commanders saluted him. It was time for the serious work of *Lingvaas*'s day to begin.

chapter 12

"I was thinking of the green robe," Alikili said, holding it up in front of her and turning toward her mate.

Jossu I Hmilra contemplated the woman, then shook his head slowly. She had the figure of a much younger woman, but her hair had lost some of the gloss it needed to go well with the green robe.

"The earth-tint goes better with your hair by gaslight," he said.

"I will also disappear, if what I have heard of the Solvarsen's decorations is true."

"You seem to have been uneasy about attending this opening ever since I bought the tickets," I Hmilra said. They had little time and he had less inclination for verbal duels, as pleasurable as it often was with a woman of Alikili's seasoned wit. "So why not seek to be inconspicuous?"

"Because then too many would say I was afraid of being there, or of embarrassing you."

I Hmilra decided that subtlety would waste time they did not have. "Aren't you?"

"Would you prefer delicate manners or the crude truth?"

"If you suddenly develop delicacy of manners when we are alone, I will summon a mind-healer."

"Very well. I would rather we were not going at all. You know what *Songs of the House of Nilvan* is about?"

"Yes. A song-story that purports to tell the truth about how the Saadians felt at coming under the rule of the Republic. From the Saadian viewpoint, although this is hardly surprising. Both the composer and the writer are not only Saadian, but flaunt the fact."

"It is pleasant to know you are not walking blindly into this snarebed."

"I will be most unpleasant if you do not speak plainly."

"Very well," Alikili said. She took such a deep breath that I Hmilra had a moment's vague apprehension that she intended to bring on a self-induced faint.

"Every political Saadian in the Republic will be there. Every leaf-scrap newsgatherer will be there, watching the Saadians, the singers, and anyone else interesting they see in the audience. Your presence there will draw more attention than the affair at Fort Huomikki."

"They will probably revive that, too," I Hmilra said, musing aloud. "And all of this, less than ten commons before the vote on the command of the expedition to Eneh."

"I had not thought you were consulting the calender lately."

"You lack a talent for sarcasm, good lady. It is true and worthy to be remembered, that many folk of the Republic suspect me of sympathies for the Saadians. Add that to the fear of the Drylanders somehow allying themselves with the Saadians, and one can understand why harsh and thoughtless words are sometimes said."

"More of them may be said if you are at the Solvarsen Theater this afternoon than ever before."

"So be it. Or do you really think that, knowing I was cautious, even a coward, the Council for War would appoint me to the command?"

"Not seeming too friendly to the Saadians is wisdom, in some people's eyes."

"In my eyes, such people are fools, and I hope they are not prevailing in the Councils. Perhaps hearing *Song* and talking to the newsgatherers afterward will be the best way to smoke these particular vermin out of the bilges."

"You would divide the Councils?"

I Hmilra realized that there was no reversing his course. Or at least none that would allow him to face Alikili with a clean conscience, which he realized was as good as the same thinbg.

"I would force into the open those people who fail to realize that the expedition to Eneh may be the opening of a war larger than the one against the Luokkan pirates. A war in which our main base will be here in Saadi, instead of in the Islands. A war in which the labor of the Saadians will be as essential as that of our own folk.

"If there is anyone who thinks to sow trouble here, I would like to be able to toss them into the Bay and see them properly drowned before we sail. So will anyone who receives the command. I would not willingly weigh anchor on a single coal-carrier if we had Saadi in turmoil behind us, thanks to the folly of our own hardheads."

Alikili looked ready to laugh and weep at the same time. I Hmilra realized that he had been addressing her as if she were a Council meeting, or perhaps an invincibly obtuse newsgatherer. Also, he had probably been talking loud enough to be heard all through the house.

"We will take some of the most robust of the servants with us," he said. "We will be staying in town until the Council votes, and that means a good deal of baggage as well as guards at whatever hostel we find. Not enough to be called a private army, I think, but enough to keep the random hardhead of *any* folk from making more trouble than his modest talents deserve to let him."

"If the servants do not mind guarding me as well, in the face of more danger for them than usual—"

I Hmilra put a hand under Alikili's chin and lifted her head until her eyes met his. It was amazing how he had not thought yellow eyes attractive when he was young, and now thought they were a quite extraordinarily beautiful hue.

"If you think that, then you have not been listening to the servants' gossip nearly as much as you wish me to think. They would defend you as they would me. Perhaps some of them will do it because they dislike Othan's kin by marriage rather than because they honor you, but—"

She laughed and dropped the gown, then came into his arms. Her hands roamed until he was able to stop them. Then he had more work, fighting the temptation to let his own hands roam.

"I suppose if we are driving rather than going by rail, we must make haste," she said at last. Her quick breathing and bright eyes told him that her regret in this matched his own.

However, once they had survived *Song*, the reception afterward, and whatever the newsgatherers might conjure up, they planned to escape to their hostel suite. There they would be their own master and mistress until sunbrighten.

SEAN BORLUND STOOD ON *LINGVAAS*'S BRIDGE AS SHE STEAMED INTO SAADI Bay. This was no particular honor, as all the other watch-standing commanders from the Captain on down were also there. The only exception was a Kertovan watch commander-second who was up on the foredeck, with the the anchoring crew and the lookouts perched on either bow and on the bowsprit itself.

Captain Viligas had taken no pilot entering the Bay, as he had been sailing in and out of it for thirty Greats and knew every possible danger spot new and old, that could endanger a ship of *Lingvaas*'s shallow draft and high maneuverability. He also knew that even on a clear day like this, there was no such thing as too many lookouts watching for small craft.

Borlund wished that *Aygsionan*'s captain had been as cautious. But then, if she had been, then he might now be dutifully serving out his three Greats as a low-level Study Group administrator, concerned mostly with the daily flow of paperwork, most of it containing nothing that hadn't been known about the Kertovans a generation ago.

If he'd pleased his superiors (something that now seemed unlikely) he might have been allowed a second term, if he'd signed on for a more active post, such as the Watch. That would have looked better in his career book, and certainly been more fun than sorting papers.

Or at least it would have been, until the time came for him to act against some near-innocent who had somehow disturbed the barrier of ignorance and obfuscation that the witlings of both races were trying to erect against one another.

Instead, he himself had been the near-innocent, and believing that they were exiling him, the Directors had sent him out to a new life, one that might not be profitable within the Drylander community—although the humans seemed to be getting less dry with each generation; Barbara Weil could not have dreamed of her present career twenty-five Greats ago. But it suited Sean Lincoln Borlund more than anything else he could now imagine having done.

It would probably be just as well, he realized, to occasionally act as if he were being punished. His enthusiasm at taking to the sea could be no secret to his shipmates of either race, but most of the humans seemed to be as cool toward the official Study Group position as Barbara Weil. What the Kertovans thought—other than generally approving anyone who went to sea—needed some guesswork, but Borlund was sure of one thing.

The Kertovans were not going to babble the details of his new career to the Directorate, or possibly even speak of it where anybody loyal to the Directors might hear.

Lingvaas was now coming up on the guardship, which had to be taking on stores and crewmen back from shore leave, judging from the number of small boats alongside. Borlund heard an order to the steersman to turn a trifle more greenward, in case one of the boats suddenly had urgent business elsewhere.

Then a signal lamp flashed from a wing of the guardship's piled-up bridgework. Borlund looked at that bridgework with an eye he had not known he would ever have, the last time he saw the guardship. There was one vessel that would never be voyaging to Eneh or anywhere else beyond Saadi Bay. Then reading *Lingvaas's* code numbers triggered another set of new reflexes.

"Signal from the guardship!" he called.

His voice was lost as two lookouts, the signaler, and three other commanders all saw the same thing and shouted almost the same words. They all looked at one another, then Captain Viligas laughed and raised his telescope.

When he turned back inboard, the smile was gone, and his face had the look of one who has bitten into an oversalted fish. "We are to anchor off the Englanti Mole," he said. "It seems our regular anchorage is full—with what, they did not say."

"That's right by the Solvarsen Theater, isn't it?" someone said.

"Yes, and at low tide we'll barely have a safe span of water under our keel."

"Oh well," another somebody said. "Perhaps we can watch the theater crowd, or even hear some of the music if the wind is right."

"I hope it blows dead toward the theater," Captain Viligas said with dignity. Borlund swallowed a laugh, remembering that the captain was completely tone-deaf.

THE BIG HIRE-CARRIAGE PULLED TO A STOP IN FRONT OF THE SOLVARSEN Theater. I Hmilra's servants dismounted from the dreezans and the outside seats first. Their imposing size and brusque manner cleared a space around the door large enough to let I Hmilra and Alikili climb out.

The space did not last long, thanks to the flow of the crowd and the advent of several importunate newsgatherers. The servants looked ready, at a signal from their Captain Over Captains, to lock arms and push a way to the theater door, with one or two remaining behind to improve the manners of the newsgatherers.

I Hmilra raised both hands for silence. After what seemed long enough for a medium armorclad to raise steam, he gained as much as he could reasonably expect. He raised his voice to carry over the remaining crowd murmurs and addressed the newsgatherers.

"If you're here to ask me about matters of state, this is a social occasion and I'd rather not discuss them even if I could. If you're here to ask me about *Songs of the House of Nilvan,* I have to wonder how much my opinion of a song-story that I haven't heard could be worth."

That inhibited most of the newsgatherers, but inevitably there was one who could not be silenced by anything short of brute force, which I Hmilra refused to contemplate. Instead, he grinned.

"I have heard about the scene that is supposed to tell the truth about the Saadians falling on their knees to welcome their deliverers. I don't know what he heard from his grandparents, but I can tell you what I heard from my grandfather, who was there.

"*Everybody* was on their knees. Many of the Saadians were picking over the wreckage on the foreshore, because one of our storeships had gone to pieces in the storm just before the landing. They were making sure not to overlook anything that they could use or eat.

"The rest were on their knees or even on their bellies for the same reason as their Kertovan deliverers. The mercenaries had mostly retreated, but a few hardheads stayed behind to snipe at the beach. Anybody who struck heroic poses risked an arrow in his liver or a bullet through her brain.

"Beyond that, I have nothing to say worth anybody's attention. I would like to get to my seat in time to let the performance start as scheduled. When it is done I will answer questions for as long as they make sense, or maybe even a little longer. Until then, I am going to be very rude to anyone who bothers me, my lady, or anyone else for whom I am responsible."

He used his command voice for the last few sentences, which forced the hardy newsgatherer back. The crowd made a path, but made up for that by talking even louder. I Hmilra's ears were ringing as if he'd just left an engine room running at full speed, by the time they reached the forehall.

"At least we can listen to something more pleasant once the performance starts," he said, as he led Alikili up the stairs to the Presentation Boxes.

"I hope so," she said, making a gesture of aversion.

"How not?"

"I've heard that the music—at least some of it—is supposed to be an experiment. A special Saadian mode, or so they call it."

"I see. And we are to be experimented upon, rather as a healer-candidate dissects a live vruil?"

"I fear so."

"If that is the worst thing that happens today, I expect we shall all survive."

THE ANCHOR CHAIN RAN OUT SLOWLY, CLANKING STEADILY LIKE THE BEAT OF a blacksmith with all the time in the world. *Lingvaas* had nearly come to a stop before the anchor went down. Captain Viligas was reluctant to risk any dragging this close to the Mole.

For good measure, the stern anchor went down as soon as the bow one had gripped the mud. By the time both anchor chains had drawn taut, *Lingvaas* was anchored securely enough to hold against a gale.

With no more duties either on deck or below (except updating his journal, and that was now more pleasure than duty), Sean Borlund stared at the land. He could have sworn that the vast yellowish stone bulk of the Solvarsen Theater at the foot of the Mole was staring back at him. Then he realized it was only the stained glass in the windows of the two towers that adorned the waterside corners. Over the swell of the green-tiled roof, he saw four more towers sprouting from the facade.

The Englanti Mole was in a quarter of the city that had always been Saadian, almost entirely so in the old days of legally controlled residence and still with a sizable Saadian majority. However, it now resembled any other mixed-status portion of the city, as Saadians not descended from the old merchant families found their way to pride and prosperity. Quite a few of them, too, or the Solvarsen Theater (named after one of the last of the independent Prince-Priests of Saadi) would never have been half the size it was.

Around *Lingvaas* floated more traces of Saadian prosperity. Yachts and smaller, daysailing pleasure craft, fishing boats (mostly converted to yachts; the fish docks were on the other side of the Mole), and ferry craft from two-oared skiffs up to paddlewheel steamers all bobbed at anchor. A steam launch very much like the one *Aygsionan* had rammed was tying up at the Mole, her decks crowded with people.

Barbara Weil stepped up beside Borlund and stared at Borlund, who remembered just in time that she didn't like to see people leaning on the railing. The people aboard the launch were now streaming ashore, scrabbling up the stairs and almost running toward the theater.

"They must be afraid of being late," she said. "Although from what I've heard about the new song-story, I don't know if they're missing much."

By force of habit, Borlund looked around. Weil grimaced. "None of that paranoia now, my friend. Remember, your rank is legally the gift of the Republic. The Council has nothing to say about you keeping or losing it."

"Barbara—" Borlund said, hesitating over using her first name in public.

"Yes, Sean?"

"That doesn't mean I want to look foolish over political issues. I'll leave that to people like the anti-Saadians."

Weil smiled, then pointed at the paired chimneys just to the right of one of the theater's waterfront towers. "Look at that smoke. Somebody's going to catch it for burning trash now."

Borlund looked at the curling smoke. It was blacker and thicker than he usually associated with a disposal furnace, although he didn't know what might be burning in there.

Then smoke curled out of the turret, a window first darkened, then began to glow, and Borlund saw wisps of smoke seeping out from under the eaves.

"That's not the disposal, he said quietly. "The Solvarsen's on fire!"

JOSSU I HMILRA DID NOT FEEL QUITE AS IF HE WERE BEING DISSECTED ALIVE during the overture to *Songs of the House of Nilvan*. He did, however, feel that his ears were being aggressively bludgeoned.

He had been too close to too many large guns for too many Greats to have retained all of his hearing. He hoped to keep what was left for his remaining Greats, and doubted that too much listening to music like that of *Songs* would help.

He also resolved to give no watcher of any folk or political allegiance any cause to note his behavior. He would maintain the bearing of a Captain-Born if stinkworms began crawling up under his kilt and polluting his organs of generation!

The writer Shaarasti Ren's contribution to the production made the ordeal a good deal more bearable. He was not as experimentally minded as his musical collaborator, except in the technique of using a speaking narrator to bridge the events between scenes. I Hmilra recalled that this was also used in a good many of the longer-surviving pre-Skyfall dramatic works, so he was prepared to let it pass as long as Ren did not claim to have invented it.

Indeed, as the first act flowed on, I Hmilra decided that he preferred the narrator to what he'd often seen in its place—characters expounding to each other at great length matters they would logically already know as well as they knew their mates. This was commonly intended to avoid confusing the audience about what was happening. I Hmilra admitted that the device might avoid confusion; he was less sure about boredom.

It helped that the narrator was considerably more in command of his part than most of the other players were of theirs. The pure singing was excellent, the song-speak acceptable, but the rest of the plain dialogue was delivered rather as a hire-cart might deliver a barrel of saltfish to a cheap drinkshop. "Ponderous" was a description that came quickly to I Hmilra's mind, and from Alikili's face other still less polite ones had occurred to her.

The newsgatherers were still in the lobby during the intermission between the first and second acts, but I Hmilra and his lady had no reason to run their gauntlet, or that of the horde of latecomers who had missed being seated for the first act and were now claiming vacant spaces for the second. Two of the servants remained on guard at the rear of the box, while the others went down to the refreshment hall and brought up the trays and bottles delivered that morning and kept in the coldbox until now.

I Hmilra personally enjoyed pickled erskin better hot than cold, but he was too hungry to be particularly fussy. He also realized that the fare at the reception after the performance might be lavish, but would hardly be as delicious as his cook's work.

The intermission and the meal both passed so quickly that the lights were going down before I Hmilra had finished grooming his face and whiskers. Alikili ran a brush through his crest, then hers, just as the curtain rose. They settled back to watch the long-awaited scene of the Great Landing.

I Hmilra was so intent on comparing the song-speak passages with his readings in history and his grandsire's tales that he did not notice at first the glow from above the stage. He smelled the smoke first, then heard people calling out and saw them pointing.

He looked upward for the first time, just as the flames followed the smoke out of the vents above the stage. It was then that he heard the first scream, and saw the first swirl of panic in the seats closer to the stage.

For the moment, there was more smoke from the Solvarsen Theater than there was steam in *Lingvaas*'s boilers. Fortunately, the fires hadn't been fully banked, let alone drawn. At a nod from Weil, stokers who'd come on deck for a breath of air dashed below again.

Meanwhile, the trumpet and drums sounded, "Ready fire and rescue party," so loudly that they must have heard it at Fort Huomikki. Everyone rushing on deck to collect axes and hoses and lower away the boats ran into the stokers rushing below, and for a few moments the scene aboard *Lingvaas* looked more like a panic than a crew preparing for action.

Eventually everybody reached their destination, about the time Captain Viligas decided to weigh anchor and put *Lingvaas* alongside the rear of the theater. The anchor detail put down their rescue gear and ran forward and aft, leaving the boat crews with steam to the boat booms but not enough hands to get the boats overside or crew them when this was done.

"Do they need us alongside?" Borlund heard Barbara Weil ask the Captain.

"It depends on who 'they' are," Viligas said. "I don't like the way that fire came up so fast. There'll be people needing to leave through the rear. Besides, we've more hoses than a whole company of the Fire Watch."

Borlund watched two Farers, one human and one Kertovan, trip over a length of hose they were trying to stretch clear of the boat chocks. He hoped there would still be uncut hoses by the time *Lingvaas* was in range of the fire.

He also watched Barbara Weil's face. The Captain's reply must have raised the same suspicions in her as it had in Borlund. He only hoped nobody idle or indiscreet had heard it.

The fire looked more ominous with each passing moment. The flames now crept back across the roof and across the rear toward the other tower. Smoke was already trickling from the second tower, and so far nobody had opened the doors to the two fire escapes on the rear wall.

Borlund began to see why Viligas thought of laying his ship alongside the burning theater. The fire escapes ended on a narrow and ill-maintained wharf, only a few paces wide. Stairs led up from it to the Mole at one end; at the other was only water too deep to wade.

Viligas wasn't the only one to have noticed that. By the time *Lingvaas*'s bow anchor was aweigh and she had steam on both engines, launches and even rowboats were converging on the wharf.

"Unshackle the stern anchor and buoy it!" Weil shouted, as Viligas nodded approval. Borlund was nearly trampled flat as deck crew charged aft with hammers and wrenches.

Then they discovered that there was no anchor buoy within a dozen casts, and the emergency one on deck had a leak. Some eager Kertovan flung herself over the side and swam to a moored small boat, then towed it back alongside. It made a reasonable buoy until the full weight of the unshackled anchor chain came on it, when it promptly sank.

At least it didn't take anyone with it, and they had the registration number to help them find and compensate the owner if the boat was ruined. It was probably Saadian-owned, and if the fire was really sabotage intended to influence Saadian-Kertovan relations for the worse, the fewer Saadians who had grievances against the Kertovan Fleet, the better.

Also the sooner *Lingvaas* was alongside, the better for the people in the theater. As *Lingvaas* got underway, both rear doors opened, and both people and smoke poured out. Borlund ran forward to join his fire and rescue party, and reached the foredeck just as one of the fire escapes pulled loose from the building.

Not all of it—the section leading up to the roof still hung on its brackets. But the lower section was gone, ripped loose and fallen to the wharf, in a tangle of splintered wood, piled bricks, and twisted iron. The wharf itself was quivering, looking as if it might collapse next.

The balcony by the door had room for a few people, but even from *Lingvaas* Borlund could see many more crowding up behind them. Nor was the path to the roof a way to safety. Flames flickered and soared all along the upper rear of the theater, and the roof was beginning to smoulder. Borlund wondered how long before it fell in.

As *Lingvaas* came about to lay herself alongside the wharf, Borlund realized what offered the best hope for the trapped people.

"Do we have a rope ladder aboard?" he shouted, not caring who heard as long as someone answered and the answer was "Yes."

"Oh, aye," somebody said behind him, "Want it, Commander?"

Would I be shouting for it just to entertain people about to burn to death? was not Borlund's answer. The look on his face had the crew moving before he could find milder words.

Then he studied the crew on *Lingvaas*'s deck. There were three hose parties now, which was none too many. Could they afford to divide their strength? Even then, they would not be doing much more than the Fire Watch in front of the Solvarsen.

But there was fire here, and no Fire Watch. As simple as a mathematical equation and as deadly as the formula for a poison.

Borlund turned and ran to the foredeck ladder. He went down it three rungs at a time, to meet Weil hurrying forward to finish having the boats swung out.

She kept her face blank, but nodded slowly, as he explained his plan.

"You're less of a glory-hunter than any man I've known," she said finally. "As long as Viligas knows that, too . . ."

Suddenly the musing tone left her voice, and it was as brisk as ever. "How many hoses will you need?"

chapter 13

I Hmilra could tell confusion, doubt, and fear from the panic that turned a crowd of people into a mindless, clawing monster. So far he'd seen more of the first three than of the last. But the last would come, it spread like a disease once it did, and if it infected the whole audience of the Solvarsen, many would die who might otherwise have lived.

I Hmilra did not intend to let anyone, mortal or otherwise, play such a ghastly joke on the Island Republic or its friends.

Fortunately the Solvarsen was only six Greats old and created according to the latest standards of both design and construction. For it to start so quickly and spread so fast, the fire must have started (or *been* started) close to a supply of flammables.

It was also going to reach a new and even larger supply very quickly. Tons of sets and scenery, mostly painted wood or canvas, were hung high above the stage, close to the fire. If those caught alight, heat and smoke would wreak havoc even among those well clear of the flames.

While all these thoughts paraded through I Hmilra's mind, his feet and voice seemed to act of themselves, like ship's repair parties cut off from the bridge by flooding or fire. He marched steadily down the broad stairs from the box, Alikili on his arm, two servants ahead and two behind. From the way they were patting their pockets and looking about them, he knew his four stalwarts were armed, in spite of his orders. He prayed briefly that he would remember to be grateful even if they had to use their illegal weapons.

The mere example of I Hmilra's party kept more than a few people from breaking into a run. It also helped that all the exits were clearly marked. Now that the alarm was up, the theater attendants were lifting the security bars on the outward-opening doors, unlocking the gates on the stairs, and holding everything wide open. As more attendants came on the scene, they waded into the crowd, pulling the laggards along, holding back the overly eager, supporting the elderly, lame, ailing, and very young, and generally acting like engineers ensuring a regular flow of feedwater from the filter tanks to the boilers.

None of it was going to be enough if the rest of the theater's crew didn't get the fire curtain down. It had started down, then jammed a good two stories above the stage. That sight alone was enough to clear the stage of both cast and crew, and the orchestra looked ready to follow them.

There was no help for it. Either rallied theater crewpeople or Jossu I Hmilra with his own hands and his household's was going to have to get that curtain down. It was heavy gaisol-impregnated canvas with an inner layer of metallized mesh, heavy enough to stop rifle bullets—or keep almost any size of fire out of the main area of the theater long enough for the audience to reach safety.

Jostled and bumped as they were, I Hmilra's party was able to stand its ground, an island in a steady (thank Lord and Lady!) outward current of people. The Captain Over Captains gave orders rather than making a speech, but it was not only his servants who obeyed. A good score of able-bodied men and women were behind him as he led the way toward the stage.

I Hmilra contemplated the sight with brief but real pleasure. Either these people were ready to follow anyone who looked as if they knew what they were doing, or he was more recognizable than he had thought, even in the murky theater.

There were advantages to having your face in the leaf-scraps and even on the wall posters, he decided. There was also the disadvantage that a few hardheads (even on the Councils, perhaps) were going to believe he had done this to make himself known.

Less pleasant was the knowledge that Alikili was going to be right there with him, in fame or oblivion, life or death by fire. But there were other women in the newly enlarged band, and some of them were dressed as if they were both jouti and of bearing age. With these women risking their lives, Alikili would laugh in his face if he even thought too loudly of ordering her out of danger.

The front rows of the theater were almost empty as I Hmilra led his band toward the stage. The smoke was curling thickly along the ceiling, and the overhead gaslights were going out one by one, as fumes choked them or their lines burned through. I Hmilra wondered how many small gas-fed flames would be creeping through the storerooms between the ceiling of the theater and the roof.

The orchestra was down to half its strength, and half of those left were looking uneasily about them rather than at their music. The mentor was still on his stand, holding his staff as if it was a magical talisman.

Alikili sprang lightly up onto the stand beside the mentor.

"Get your people back a few rows, and then have them start playing."

"Who are you?" the mentor said, gaping.

He gaped wider when I Hmilra stepped forward and identified himself. "Captain-Born!"

"Yes. As my lady and second commander said, *Play*!"

"What?"

"You mean, what should you play?" *Artists do not have to turn witling in a crisis to prove their honesty.*

"Yes."

"Anything that will keep people moving," I Hmilra snapped. " 'Chant to the Prince of Peace!,' for all I care!"

The mentor gaped, not sure whether he'd heard the command of a sane man or the jest of a mad one. The chant was as close to the national song of the Saadians as any piece of music. Even rumors that it had been included in the third act had brought out suggestions that *Songs* be banned. When I Hmilra was already a Captain in his own right, as well as by birth, a street entertainer singing it (badly) had led to a riot in which twelve people died and a hundred were hurt.

Then the mentor shook himself and turned to his musicians. What passed in the looks mentor and players exchanged in that moment, I Hmilra did not know. Nor did he ask.

But when the orchestra's fifteen or so hardheaded players had taken their new seats, I Hmilra heard over the rumble of the fire and the tramping of feet the opening bars of "Chant to the Prince of Peace."

SEAN BORLUND NOW FELT MORE LIKE AN INSECT ON A WALL THAN A FARER ON the end of a yard. He could see the whole scene of the action spread out below him, as most of the smoke was rising clear of it.

In fact, he could see and feel almost too much. He felt a chill at seeing that the two rear doors were not, as he had thought, connected by a balcony that would have allowed the people from both to use the single remaining fire escape to the ground. Some of the framing for such a balcony was in place, enough to fool the eye from a distance, but not enough to really help anyone without wings.

A simple omission—careless or perhaps lack of money; but a potentially lethal one, not only to theatergoers trapped meters from a furnace, but to Sean Borlund if his feet slipped, and to *Lingvaas* and everybody aboard her if the rescue effort kept her alongside the Solvarsen Theater too long.

How long would be too long? Borlund would have given a few Greats off his life to know. The fire had to be eating away at the roof, and when it fell in, the walls might very well follow. If they fell inward, that was the end for everyone inside.

If they fell outward, it would not save the theatergoers, while *Lingvaas* sank under a red-hot rain of bricks and steel beams.

Borlund wondered briefly if Viligas and Weil really knew what they were doing, in assuming so blithely that *he* did.

Then it was back to work, as two Farers scrambled up to the top, carrying the rope ladder. Borlund took it, slung it across his back, and stepped back out on the yard.

At least he had the undivided attention of those Kertovans on the balcony who were still alive and conscious. He took a moment to look down, and was relieved to see that a party had scrambled ashore from *Lingvaas*, and was spreading a sail between the wharf and the ship to act as a net for anyone leaping from the balcony.

The Kertovans who had come down from the other balcony were helping, and there was no shortage of hands for the work to be done below. Borlund refused to think about their chances if the theater's rear wall collapsed, and instead estimated the distance to the balcony. Then he uncoiled the rope from around his waist, and tied one end to the bundled ladder. The other end was already tied into a loop, and he began swinging that end toward the balcony,

Somewhere around a half-Great later (actually on the fifth swing) somebody on the balcony realized what Borlund was trying to do. They grabbed the loop and starting hauling in so vigorously that they nearly jerked Borlund off the yard before he could unsling the ladder.

The moment he saw enough hands on the rope, he let go of the ladder. It swung down like a fuzzy pendulum, danced back and forth three or four times, then began to rise as the balcony party hauled in.

It rose nearly halfway to the balcony before the line broke and the ladder fell. It might have fallen straight into the water, but instead struck the sail, which quivered but didn't collapse.

Borlund wanted to scream curses. Instead he snapped out just one, and hoped that the sail wasn't so tight that *Lingvaas* couldn't cast off in a hurry. He was less worried now about the falling wall than about staying and watch the people he'd tried to help burned alive. Without someone to take the ladder up to the balcony, there was little chance of anyone there now coming down.

Then a cluster of smoke-darkened Kertovans popped out onto the other balcony and trotted down the fire escape. Borlund looked at them, alternately veiled and exposed by the swirling smoke. Then he stared. He'd thought that everyone who was going out the back way had already done so.

What was harder to believe was that one of them was wearing the formal tunic and kilt of a Captain Over Captains. Another was a woman who had been dressed with equal splendor before the fire ruined her gown.

IN THE REAR OF THE STAGE, THE ROAR OF THE FLAMES ABOVE ALMOST drowned out "Chant." It would have drowned out "Krimzaan's Triumph" if the musicians had been playing that particular march, the most ponderous in the standard books and one that I Hmilra cordially detested.

The fire had clearly gone up rather than out, and this was keeping the theater itself just barely habitable, at least for those with strong lungs and hearts. Matters would take a sudden turn for the worse when the roof supports burned through or the fire ate holes in the outer roof and could feed its hunger on fresh air.

I Hmilra had no idea where to find the cables for the fire curtain, but the guards spread out quickly in search of it. Alikili watched them go, and I Hmilra put an arm across her shoulders, knowing that she would want a living touch and that her pride would keep her from asking for it.

"Let's stand as far to one side as we can," he said.

"If the scenery falls, the heat will kill us even if we remain uncrushed," she said. "I would prefer not to end huddling in a dark corner."

So did I Hmilra, but he wondered if he would have dared say it. But then he was male as well as Captain-Born; he was supposed to be fearless without proving it by fine phrases. Alikili was a woman of mixed blood and uncertain rank; perhaps she felt he needed reminding.

He had just vowed to discuss that with her after they escaped, when the fire curtain suddenly dropped with a crash that made I Hmilra jump. Alikili laughed impudently.

"You look as if you would rather not end at all."

"So I would, but you will pay an obscene forfeit if you ever—"

I Hmilra broke off as two of the guards returned, both now openly wearing pistols and knives. One of them carried a fire axe, the other had a watch chief's disciplinary grip on one of the theater stage crew.

"Once we found him and told him we needed his help, it wasn't hard," the man said. "Now, Captain, wouldn't we be better off out of here?"

The fire curtain blocked the way back into the theater, but the stage attendant guided them swiftly to a spiral stairway on the right. Either the man was regaining his wits or didn't dare lose any more of what he had, surrounded by four large armed men.

I Hmilra's lungs and eyes had long been reminding him that he was really too old for this sort of work. As the party pounded up the stairs, his legs joined the chorus of disapproval. He refused to slow down, however. He did not feel that it was his time to die, and even if it was he intended to die as a Farer should, at least drowning in the harbor instead of being burned like an untended shank of yeris.

EHOMA TUOMITTI WAS INSPECTING PAINTWORK IN *BYUBR*'S NEW MILITARY top, so was the first abroad to see the smoke from the Solvarsen Theater fire. She signaled the deck, but by the time anyone paid attention, she could also see the duty fireboat getting up steam.

Long before the fireboat had even cast off, however, she had seen *Lingvaas* going alongside the rear of the theater. What her old shipmates expected to do there, she had no idea. For the moment, her mind had room only for the thought that she should be there to help them do it.

She was not going to get there aboard *Byubr*. The old ship was afloat now, with one boiler in service for utility steam. Dockyard workers still infested the other three boilers and practically every other part of the ship. Even if she'd been ready to steam, *Byubr* would likely as not run aground before she reached the theater, and wipe out a dozen Saadian boats into the bargain! For coastal-defense ships, the *Illiks* drew a lot of water, and bulges, shifting weights, and a lighter secondary battery hadn't helped *Byubr* that much.

But a waterfront fire was always an all-hands emergency, which meant *Byubr* had to send a fire party if not a boat. If there was steam for the crane to hoist out the launch—

Tuomitti was calling the real Farers on deck as she scrambled down the ladder from the top. She cursed as a rung wobbled and scraped her shins, then jumped down the rest of the way.

The dockyard watch chief was coming on deck, trying to call the Farers back to work and having about as much success as he would have had trying to halt the outgoing tide. With no commanders aboard (and Tuomitti was carefully not going to look for them pier-side), the two watch chiefs were the senior Farers aboard. Not that Tuomitti considered someone who'd not served aboard ship for twelve Greats a real Farer, but he was on the Fleet roster and had as much claim under Farer-law to make trouble for her as if he were a Captain.

"This is not our work," the man exclaimed. "Keep your people at—"

"*My* people? Are yours so lazy they can't keep this ship afloat while we help at the fire? What good is the dockyard for, then?" She refrained from the mortal insult of wondering aloud if the dockyard hands were brave enough for firefighting.

Short of a brawl, however, the other had no way of stopping the Farers from manning the winch controls and swinging out the launch. The launch was one of the new models, with a steam engine so light that it was permanently installed, and a stoker was firing the boiler even before the launch touched the water.

As the Farers started scrambling over the side and dropping into the launch (even lightly loaded, *Byubr* had no more than three heights of freeboard), it occurred to Tuomitti to ask if anyone would be in the theater.

Then her hands froze on the railings, as she remembered the notices for today's performance of *Songs of the House of Nilvan*. She also remembered the lists of notables expected to attend—Jossu I Hmilra among them.

She could not see anything but disaster coming of a fire in the Solvarsen today. Not with perhaps two thousand people in it.

"Ho, Chief! Coming w' us or no?"

The shout that broke into her bleak thoughts came from alongside. The stokers must have done miracles—no, the launch was even newer than she'd thought, with a compressed-fuel boiler—because smoke was already pouring out of the stack.

She vaulted over the railing and dropped into the launch as the lowering hooks swung free. The impact jarred her from head to foot and sent pain shooting from her bad eye all across her face and down her throat to her chest. She didn't care at all, now that she was underway to do something about the fire—

THE SPIRAL STAIRS LED I HMILRA'S PARTY CLOSER TO THE HEAT, AND THE AIR seemed to grow less vitalized as well as hotter. Before their lungs gave up entirely, they reached an open door and staggered through it onto a balcony.

I Hmilra blinked soot and smoke from his eyes, spat black phlegm from his mouth, and finished restoring his senses by taking deep breaths of air that he would usually never have called fresh. At this moment it had the effect of a large draft of the Lady's nectar.

With his ability to evaluate a tactical situation as restored as it would be today, he quickly understood what was needed. The two hoses that *Lingvaas* had playing on the balcony where the people were trapped bought time, but no more, and perhaps not enough of that. But there was a third hose—and also, that line dangling from the balcony might be scaled by a Farer.

A young, limber, agile Farer, I Hmilra reminded himself. He was no longer any of these. He was one who ordered someone else to climb, as soon as they reached the ground.

"Yovair," he called. "Retrieve that rope ladder and climb the line to the balcony. Raitzo, go down and tell the *Lingvaas* people to send the third hose ashore and lead it up their fire escape. If we can take the fire in the rear—"

He broke off, as Alikili dashed past and down the stairs, taking them two at a time. She was also stripping off her gown as she did. I Hmilra did not fear for her modesty, which was protected by ample undergarments, but if she tripped over a swathe of the heavy cloth she would reach the bottom of the stairs on her head.

She reached the rope ladder and had it slung on her back before anyone except I Hmilra realized what she was planning. She had started climbing the dangling line before anyone was close enough to stop her. After that there was nothing anyone could do that would not endanger both her life and her mission.

So no one did anything, least of all I Hmilra. He did not even shout. Alikili would definitely not appreciate the distraction, and he himself would look like a fool or at least one lacking in self-command, in front of more witnesses than he had faced for his Captain's Oath.

Somebody—several somebodies—on the balcony had yet-unbaked wits. They reached over to pluck Alikili up the last half-span to the balcony, and one held her up while others tied the ladder in place. I Hmilra saw his companion grip the railing for a moment with one hand and shove her helper away with the other. He had to bite his lip now to keep from calling out. The thought that he had somehow *driven* her to this roared in his mind like breakers on a rocky shore.

Then he had to step lively, out of the path of a hose party from *Lingvaas* charging up the stairs without regard for the rank or indeed presence of anyone in their path. I Hmilra had the feeling that they would have trampled the Lord of the Waves flat if he'd been in their way, and knew that the time had come to make a dignified descent.

He did, after all, have also the right to embrace Alikili when she came down. He also had the right to say a few words to her, but that right he would only claim when they were alone.

SEAN BORLUND RESISTED THE TEMPTATION TO CLIMB DOWN ONE OF THE stays to the deck. His hands were shaking too hard, and *Lingvaas*'s people had enough work to do without scraping him off the deck.

So he went down sedately to the deck, reaching it as as the hose party vanished inside the theater. Clouds of steam and smoke poured out of both doors, completely hiding the last few survivors on the balcony.

When Borlund could see the balcony again, it was empty, and the ladder nearly so. The two hoses playing on the door kept at their work—until suddenly the hose party came out of the theater even faster than they'd gone in.

Borlund couldn't hear what they shouted, over the roar of the fire. Everyone on the wharf seemed to have no trouble hearing and understanding. The hose parties started backing away, faces to the fire and water playing, with the look of folk who would gladly be somewhere else.

The last hose party simply wedged their hose in place and sprinted down the fire escape, reaching the ground just as the fire escape ripped free at the upper end. Hose and ironwork crashed to the ground.

Then the other hoses went from a stream to a trickle, then dry, then fell as their parties abandoned them. The retreat to *Lingvaas* increased its pace, some of the Farers stationing themselves with axes to cut the sail loose, others helping the hurt or the weak on to the ship's deck, *nobody* lingering.

Borlund used his height and reach to help lift people over the railing, Kilmoyan theater-goers first, most coughing, some showing singed hair or even skin burned hairless. Then came *Lingvaas*'s Farers of both races, some trying to look over their shoulders while climbing, then falling at Borlund's feet as a result.

The last Farer aboard actually ran up one of the mooring lines just as an axeman amidships cut it loose. Borlund caught the woman as she leaped down, then over her shoulder saw cracks running across the rear wall of the Solvarsen Theater.

The cracks widened, then vanished in the smoke pouring out of them. Tongues of flame seared through the smoke, and debris began falling, with thuds and crashes now almost lost in the fire's roar.

Then the entire rear wall of the theater gave way in a moment, falling with thunder that drowned out the fire in the moments before the roof joined the wall. After the roof came the left wall, and after that Borlund could not see what was happening as dust joined the smoke to make a cloud that not only enveloped the ruins of the theater but nearly swallowed *Lingvaas*.

It was mostly dust and smoke that reached the ship. The flames tongued out briefly before the falling walls crushed them, and quite a few pieces of wreckage also made the leap. *Lingvaas* came away with scorched paint and rigging and hot lumps of wreckage smoldering all over her deck.

One bit smoldered on Sean Borlund's back as he crouched to shield three Kertovans, until someone dashed a bucket of water across it, him, and them. He grabbed the rest of the bucket to rinse his mouth, then handed it back to the Farer.

"What about the people from the other balcony?" he asked. He couldn't say "Jossu I Hmilra," and not only because he might have been mistaken about the man's identity. He was discovering that one could survive intending to be a hero but failing and then watching someone else succeed spectacularly. But the experience was still embarrassing enough to affect his voice.

The Farer pointed forward. A line of Kertovans was straggling out on to the Mole, now appearing, now disappearing as *Lingvaas*'s funnel and rigging blocked Borlund's view. He didn't recognize any of them, although two were standing so close that they might have been embracing.

Closer, a steam launch crowded with Farers in working garb was cutting in toward the pier. Borlund recognized Ehoma Tuomitti and gave a half-hearted wave. Then the launch shot out of sight, across *Lingvaas*'s bows. It reappeared greenside, backing water to come alongside the water steps on the Mole, as *Lingvaas* turned her bow toward the open harbor and her stern toward the smoking rubble that had been the Solvarsen Theater.

chapter 14

Sean Borlund was writing in his journal by the light of a candle when Barbara Weil knocked on his cabin door. He could recognize her step and knock by now. His first thought was to tell her to go away.

But she was the last person on Kilmoyn whom he wanted to know that he was feeling sorry enough for himself to forget his manners. Sixty were dead from the fire, two hundred more in bed with burns and smoke-seared lungs, and his own grievance over not having been able to finish his own rescue work was trivial.

Now all he needed was to make himself believe it, which would have been easier alone, but at least Barbara wasn't going to make things worse—

"I can come back later if you want to be alone," she said, just loud enough to carry through the heavy wooden door.

Borlund couldn't even contemplate rewarding that courtesy with a "Go away" that would also come from his guts instead of his wits. He rose and opened the door.

Weil sat down on the bunk and looked at the overhead while he blotted the journal page and closed the book.

"You take that journal seriously," she said. "I wonder if I could look at a bit of it someday."

"Not today's bit, please."

"I already know you're feeling sorry for yourself, so I wouldn't learn anything I didn't already know."

"If that's your notion of sympathy—"

"Sorry. That was putting it badly. You're feeling *guilty*. Would that be closer?"

"Somewhat."

"The rope breaking wasn't your fault, and if you hadn't arranged for the ladder, it might not have been there for Lady Alikili to pick up."

Borlund swallowed. "Alikili? Jossu I Hmilra's companion?"

"I didn't know he had more than—"

"Barbara. *She* had to risk her life because of my bright idea?"

"Sean, I don't know whether to kiss you or slap you. Or maybe kick you in the part of your body you're using for thinking, even if nature didn't intend it for that."

The light tone didn't hide crackling anger. Borlund said nothing. He had the feeling that even clearing his throat without Weil's permission would be a bad move.

"Alikili chose to finish work that you'd begun," Weil said, with equal care to keep her voice level and not meet Borlund's eyes. "If I Hmilra respects her choice, anything he says will be said to her and end there. Why are you afraid he might have a grievance against us?"

Borlund started. The surprise of having your mind read came hard at the end of a long, wearying, and frustrating day.

Weil surprised him even more with a brief hug and a kiss that was more than a brush of lips against lips. "I know," she added. "You've gone right on driving yourself too hard. That's no way to lead."

Borlund didn't know what she read on his face to make her go on. "And you won't always be the junior of four human commanders aboard a ship with fewer crew of both races than the population of most small towns. You'll have responsibilities that mean saving your strength for when you're needed. You didn't kill anybody today, but if you aren't careful, someday you might. Possibly yourself."

Borlund forced a smile. "I suppose if you can read minds, you can tell if the Study Group is planning on bringing me ashore."

"The worst I can see is that they'll request it. You'll probably have the right to refuse, and certainly friends to support you, from both races."

"Which means making enemies among the Directorate."

"Do you care?"

"For myself, maybe I don't." Borlund considered that, decided that there was no "maybe" about it. "But I've got three bearer-partners and their children to think about."

"Are you the only one they've partnered?"

"No, fortunately."

"Then the Directorate will have to deal with all the other sire-partners as well. If they think they can afford that, maybe we'd better find *Rampart* and make a quick escape from Kilmoyn."

Borlund pointed at the door, to remind her that she'd been talking on forbidden matters not only aboard a Kertovan ship but loudly enough for eavesdroppers to hear. Probably they hadn't heard anything they could use to make trouble for the "Drylanders," but why borrow trouble when they were already getting so much thrust upon them?

Weil sat back on the bunk and crossed her legs, then rested her chin on her knees. "I think that journal of yours will help," she said. "If it has in it half of what I think it does. You wouldn't mind my reading one volume, from your training time?"

"If you can deal with my handwriting without going blind—"

"I'll come around and ask you to decipher anything I can't read," Weil said. She hopped off the bunk with the familiar briskness she showed when she'd decided on a course of action. "Pick a volume, and I'll be out of your cabin and your hair."

Borlund handed her the third volume which covered the middle portion of *Lingvaas's* voyage and impressions of several of her ports of call, as well as notes on mooring, coaling from lighters, and other ship's business. She tucked it under one arm, and for a moment he thought she was going to kiss him again.

But she only gave him a half-wave, half-salute, then went out. He felt him feeling almost as confused as before, but a great deal less gloomy.

EHOMA TUOMITTI HAD STOOD ARMED GANGPLANK WATCHES BEFORE, BUT IT had been in Luokka or similar uncivilized lands. She had never before stood an armed gangplank watch pierside from a ship tied up safely in Saadi's Fleet Dockyard. The pistol in its holster under her left arm and the weighted fighting stick at her belt both felt like unnatural growths, that she expected any moment to burst and spew suppurating matter—

"Oha, the gangplank watch?"

"Who goes there?"

"Friend."

"Advance and be recognized." Tuomitti raised her left arm a trifle, so that she could cross-draw the pistol smoothly.

The speaker advanced from the darkness of the alley into the circle of pallid yellow light cast by the gangplank lanterns. He was a stoutly built male with a Farer's skin bag over one shoulder and a small dreezan-hide carrycase in the other hand.

"Hello, old friend but not old lady."

It was Zhohorosh. A welcome sight, even if she had no idea what he was doing here at this hour, forsaken by all gods fond of a decent dark's sleep.

"Are you coming aboard?"

"I don't see how I can obey my orders otherwise."

Tuomitti's eyebrows rose. "You're assigned to *Byubr*?"

"By the highest command of the Fleet Farer File. Would you like to see my orders?"

Tuomitti nodded. Not that she thought Zhohorosh unqualified, or feared the problems that sometimes arose when bedmates became shipmates. But he had been a watch chief aboard a *Valor*-class armorclad. What had he done to make the Farer File assign him to *Byubr*?

Or what had *Byubr* become, to draw a Farer of such experience?

The orders had all the proper stamps and seals in all the right places. It even had Zhohorosh's family name—Lyd—which he never used aboard ship, for reasons which no one had ever been brave enough to ask him. The clerk's handwriting was no more legible than usual, and the paper smelled as if it had been steeped in flower-fowl droppings, but otherwise Tuomitti found neither irregularities nor answers to the mystery of Zhohorosh's presence here.

She sent her messenger for one of the steward's watch, to lead her friend to the chief's quarters, and meanwhile decided to get some good out of him while she could. She'd returned straight to *Byubr* with the launch, once they'd landed Jossu I Hmilra and the rest of his party at Fort Huomikki (more to hide them from the newsgatherers than for any other reason, she suspected). Half-expecting to see Saadi in flames and mobs storming the dockyard before dawn, she'd instead seen only the distant glow of torches and heard the (fortunately) still more distant din of streets full of drunken people trying to sing.

All of which left her sadly ignorant of what was going on in the wake of the Solvarsen Theater fire, and unable to even guess intelligently as to what the light of tomorrow might bring. This was not a situation that commended itself to her—or, she suspected, to anyone responsible for the safety of ships and Farers.

"How go matters in the city?" she asked, in a more casual tone than she had expected to muster.

Zhohorosh made a not-good, not-bad gesture with head and hands. "In the upper town there's a good few folk wandering about the streets with bottles and torches. But they're emptying the bottles and waving the torches, and hadn't started throwing either when I passed by. It's all mostly quiet in the lower town."

Tuomitti began to allow herself a sense of relief, even hope. The folk of Saadi were not at each other's throats yet, and no one was invading the heavily Saadian lower town for looting and fire-raising, let alone massacre.

A peace that had lasted thus far might last until most folk were too tired to break it. Those left on their feet might be honest or even wise enough to *want* to keep it.

"There's some folks who say the Saadians deserve it for what they were putting on," Zhohorosh added. "But they don't say it too loud, not when I'm in hearing anyhow."

"Oh?"

"Stands to reason anybody raises a fire in a place like that, they don't care who dies. Oldsters, joutis, babes. *I* don't care to have that sort thinking they can escape, even if they burn Imperials!"

Tuomitti nodded. Zhohorosh's firm stand for justice had for many years outweighed his Saadian blood. A watch chief could hardly be any other way, in fact, although it had been Tuomitti's misfortune to know some who failed to remember this minor detail.

" 'Sides," he continued, "I hear there was so much junk upstairs waiting to burn that somebody could have raised the fire by knocking out his pipe in the wrong place. And if he did that, I hope the babe-molester fried slowly."

The steward arrived at that point, to Tuomitti's initial frustration. She'd wanted to ask Zhohorosh about the reaction to what I Hmilra and Alikili had done in the fire. It had certainly saved a good many lives and would keep public attention shining on I Hmilra like a searchlight on a floating mine for a good long while.

But that was hardly something to be talked of where others might hear. Also, Tuomitti remembered the conversation between the two lovers as the launch carried them to their landing. Conducted entirely with gestures and looks, it was still eloquent to one who saw most of it.

Tuomitti would have given all of her coming-ashore slyn, to be able to listen to what I Hmilira and Alikili had said to each before they turned out the lights.

BARBARA WEIL RUBBED HER EYES, BLINKED, AND REALIZED THAT THE LIGHT really was dimming. The oil in the lamp must be just about down to the bottom.

One more day's entry, she said to herself, and turned the page.

> At sea through midlight, then entering Tzigas harbor at six beats of the midlight watch. An easy two-common trip from Eltsisas, so the captain decided to coal ship immediately.
>
> Coaled from lighters. Nothing much out of the ordinary, except that Tzigas is a harbor with a strong lighter folk Guild. They would not let our people into the lighters even to speed passing the coal.
>
> Note: There ought to be a list of ports classified by Guild strength. There are some where it's worth your life to say a word against the Guilds. There are others where it's worth your life to try to organize a Guild. This makes a big difference to Captains, who certainly need to know, although it might not be wise to make the list public. The strong-Guild ports might be unhappy, to put it mildly.

Weil smiled. Word of mouth had done well enough in place of such a list for longer than she had been alive, and only a fairly new commander would think this was an original suggestion. Weil recalled the phrase "reinventing the wheel."

Except that there were always new Farers who didn't have to reinvent the wheel, exactly, but needed to learn some of its uses. Here and elsewhere, Sean was doing a fine job of setting down things that a more experienced Farer might assume a new hand could breathe in with the spray or pluck from the standing rigging like fruit.

Borlund was far enough along in his learning the art of Faring to be able to teach it. Yet he was not so far that he'd forgotten how little a new hand was likely to know.

In short, he was (accidentally and in installments) writing a Kertovan Drylanders' appendix to *The Maritime Compendium*. And if

Sean Borlund would be the last Drylander—the last *human* (no penalties for thinking forbidden words)—to need to learn the way of the sea, then she, Barbara Weil, was the mother of seven healthy children.

Here in her cabin she could afford to let her eyes mist at that thought. Well, perhaps she could never be a bearer-parent. But she and Sean might take his journal, and through it become midwives to a whole generation of human Farers.

It would help if she knew what might come of this day's work, as far as the Study Group was concerned. She could make shrewd guesses here in her cabin until sunbrighten, but a short talk with a certain man in the Watch was worth all the guesses in the Fleet. . . .

She picked up her carrycase and rang for a messenger.

"Commander Weil's compliments to the Watch, and would they signal me a boat for going ashore?"

The Kertovan messenger looked bemused but not disobedient. Then she grinned.

"A good one ready, eh?"

"You might say that."

Although notions of breaking her long Greats of celibacy had been occurring to her lately, they remained notions. Even if she decided to turn them into realities, her friend on the Watch would remain exactly that. He was a man of sense and even some compassion, not a rebel as she'd been for Greats—or as Sean Borlund might become, with a little careful handling. . . .

THE LAST MESSENGER WAS GONE WITH THE LAST WIRE-POST, AS WAS THE last of the late supper from the tray on Jossu I Hmilra's desk. So, very nearly, was the last of his strength.

It had not been part of his plan to work so late after a day spent in a way that would have taxed a much younger Farer's strength. However, what he had seen and heard, and the wire-post waiting for him when he returned home, had convinced him that opportunity beckoned in the dark but would be gone like a seaflyer by sunbrighten.

Hence the work. Hence, in due course, the inevitable bills for the messengers and all the rest. I Hmilra decided that he would pay them himself, as the messenger services were seldom generous to their workers. Even if he could reconcile it with his conscience to send the bill to the Fleet Pay Office (and tonight's work would benefit the Fleet), reimbursement would be slow.

He closed his eyes, stretched, and found his right hand touching a familiar, slightly curved, comfortably textured surface.

"Is silent approaching another of your talents?"

"Not one I worked on as a girl, the way I did climbing. But bare feet and thick rugs make up for lack of practice."

"So I see." She was barefoot, and wearing a nightcap and an old chamber robe as she stood by the desk. I Hmilra stood up, began an embrace of welcome, and had to fight not to turn it into one of passion.

The thought of losing her was the thought of a darkness entering his life, which all the light in the world would find it hard to break. He rested his cheek against hers, first right, then left, tousled her hair, nuzzled her ears, then stepped back.

Her smile and a slight glistening in her eyes said that she'd received the message. Then she looked at the desk and frowned.

"What did you say once, about having a private wire-post line or even a wire-speaker connection put in?"

"We can do the wire-post any time. This far out from the city, the wire-speaker service costs more than it's worth."

He put both hands on her shoulders and held her there, neither drawing her close nor pushing her away. "But that's not what I wanted to ask you."

"Why did I do it?"

"You've put it crudely, but—yes."

"I won't do it again, if that's what you're afraid of."

Generations of Captain-Born blood rose up in I Hmilra and tempted him to a rude answer. "I'm not *afraid* of that. Although I hope you realize you were lucky. How much climbing practice have you had since our picnic?"

"Not enough to succeed without luck, truly. Which is why I am promising that the next time, you can send someone else to do it. And I wasn't afraid of gossip, about you having to order others to go where you could not. You are a Captain Over Captains. It is your right to do that."

She sounded half angry and half amused. I Hmilra decided to keep his mouth shut, lest opening it reveal that his beloved had suddenly become wholly a mystery.

Or was she? I Hmilra remembered taking *Yuurgin* into Sihals Bay with nothing but sweep wires and lookouts to guard her from the pirate-laid Imperial mines. He suspected he was risking as much now, letting the question that had formed in his mind now rise to his lips.

"You wanted to do something that would be yours alone, and that everyone would know was yours," I Hmilra said. He began slowly, but as Alikili's smile widened the last words rushed out.

This time it was she embracing him. "Yes. I trust you. I even trust your kin. So—so this was not anything against you. It is just that a woman placed as I am—or any woman who has neither fertility nor profession—"

"Would you rather we of the Republic followed the Imperials or the Luokkan tribes, with their fertile women kept in strongholds and their infertile ones nearly slaves?"

"I do admit that being Principal Wife to an Imperial magistrate might have certain advantages—"

"Alikili!"

"Ask a question in jest, receive the same kind of answer." She was not completely jesting; her voice said that if her face did not.

"Forgive?"

"Forgiven," she said, with another brief embrace. "But remember that a woman is seldom allowed into a profession until after she has proved herself infertile. That gives the men a good few Greats' head start. We run the race with one weighted boot, against opponents in a pair of light shoes."

Kertovan life had always seemed fairer than that, to I Hmilra. But he had never doubted that those who were not Captain-Born males saw the world otherwise, and had several times been impatient with those who flattered him by pretending otherwise. He would *not* allow himself to be angry with Alikili over her offering the truth without being asked!

"Well, I do not think that you will have the chance to do this every third day," I Hmilra said. "I cannot afford to go to the theater that often, for one thing. For another, I sincerely hope that we do not have another such fire in my lifetime."

"What of the tales of the fire being set?"

"I have heard none such."

"Neither have I, but I have learned to hear your thoughts. Or perhaps read them from your face, would be putting it better."

"If you are going to be so fussy over proper phrasing, perhaps I should put you to work drafting the next batch of wire-posts."

"I would rather be put to work massaging you into a decent sleep."

"That's asking too much—"

"Jossu, beloved, I *am* younger than you. Also, you have doubtless been too busy to notice that I slept for half a watch after we came home."

"Very well." I Hmilra pulled down and locked the cover of his desk, then turned to Alikili. "Lead onward, lady, and I shall follow."

AT SUNBRIGHTEN, FORT HUOMIKKI SIGNALED THAT THE STATE OF EMERGENCY was lifted. However, Captain Viligas still insisted that a commander lead any shore party.

Since Barbara Weil was ashore "on private business" and there was nobody else Sean Borlund really felt like talking to, he volunteered to be the commander. His short list was provisions, paint, fresh canvas, and seeing about the coaling schedule, but Viligas gave him authority to accept whatever else the shore establishment offered and *Lingvaas* might need.

"They'll be more in a generous mood now than they will be in a few commons," the Captain added. "A hero-ship is favored only as long as memory runs, and you know how long that is."

Borlund found himself with even less to do ashore than he'd had aboard, with the repairs underway. The watch chief of his party was the oldest Kertovan of his rank aboard, and the least willing to let commanders look over his shoulder while he worked.

Everyone knew that this came from certain private arrangements he had with the shore establishment that added comfortably to his savings. But he never scanted in anything that would affect the safety of the ship or the health and comfort of his shipmates, so he was seldom afflicted with more supervision than he could readily evade.

Borlund found moorings at a waterfront drinkshop whose owner had enough confidence in the civil peace of Saadi to have not only opened but fired up the stove, broached a fresh case of hoeg, and set out tables on the lawn running down to the beach behind the shop. It was at one of those tables, halfway through his third cup of hoeg, that Barbara Weil found Borlund.

One look at her made him summon the attendant with a whole fresh pot of hoeg and a plate of biscuits. She looked as if she had not eaten for three commons and had either cried or been working all night.

By the time she'd emptied her first cup and demolished three biscuits, she was coherent if not cheerful.

"Those idiots of Directors have done it again!"

Borlund braced himself for bad news. "It" could cover what his Observant partners called "a multitude of sins," but from Weil's tone, this time the sins were larger or more numerous.

"Actually it's something they haven't done, or so the story goes," she added, reaching for another biscuit and refilling her cup. "It's no secret that we have a good deal of scientific detection technique available," she went on, lowering her voice, "but security and fear of cultural contamination have always kept us from releasing it.

Innocent people have been executed or exiled because of this."

So far she hadn't told him anything either portentious or even surprising. Then insight struck—or at least tickled his mind.

"They won't help investigate the Solvarsen fire?"

"No. That would reveal too much of our knowledge, and raise suspicion. Of course, there's already enough suspicion going around to start riots and lay half of Saadi in ashes, but we'll just lock the gates, issue the secret weapons, and ride out the storm."

She looked sharply at him. "Or is your conscience tough enough to ignore that possibility?"

Borlund glared. "My conscience sent me out on that yard. Any further stupid questions, or can I return to my party?"

Weil put her face in her hands, but her shoulders didn't shake. Borlund reached across the table and gently laid a hand on them anyway, brushing her cheek as he did. She reached up and clasped her hand over his.

"Thank you, Sean." Then she straightened and was her commander's self again, but with a new note of excitement in her voice.

"There's another rumor, foggier than the first. The Directorate has a request from the Fleet to supply a Drylander-crewed ship for the expedition for Eneh."

"*Lingvaas* already has—" Borlund began, then stopped. This time insight struck like a sledgehammer knocking loose an anchor chain's pin.

"Our own ship," he said. "A ship of our own."

He realized that he was babbling and didn't care. To the Kertovans, ships were both the basis of community and very nearly sacred sites. Letting Drylanders form their own crew for their own ship was conceding not merely legal equality, but equality on a higher plane. Equality in the sight of the Lord and the Lady and all the other gods of the folk of the Island Republic, who did not of course officially exist as far as the Drylanders were concerned and even less so in the eyes of the Drylanders' rulers.

The Study Group can go piss up a forest, Borlund thought. *I am going to the nearest House of the Lord when I leave here, and make the biggest offering I can afford.*

I only hope the line won't be too long.

Then he realized that Barbara was going on, not quite babbling but not quite making sense either. Something about a journal—*his* journal—

"What are you planning on doing with my journal?"

"Not all of it. Just parts. You see—"

"You drink." He refilled her cup, and pushed it and the biscuits at her. Eating brought silence, and silence bought Weil time to organize her thoughts.

"—you as my Third or Fourth," she concluded. "But you'll have a better chance at Third if you've done something that proves you're a true Farer by Kertovan standards. Which turning your journal into a manual of seamanship would do."

A whole fleet of questions sailed through Borlund's mind. What made her sure that she would be Captain of a Drylander-crewed ship? And what made her sure that the Kertovans, after allowing this break with tradition, would then turn around and dictate the crewing of the ship?

Most of all, how had she learned all this?

He stopped her in the middle of another cup of hoeg with that last question. The look she returned wasn't quite a glare, but definitely not a smile.

"Barbara, there are a good many worse things that could happen to me than going to sea under your command," he said. "In fact, most of them would be worse. But is this really a prospect? I don't want to neglect my duty to *Lingvaas* while chasing—"

"Suppose *Lingvaas* is the ship?" Weil asked. That silenced him. She went on.

"It's early to be sure of anything, but I do have a source close to the Directorate that lets me know what's at least being discussed. I shouldn't even be telling you this much, but if otherwise you're going to think I'm making it all up—"

This time insight was more like a gentle tap with a carpenter's maul. "Is your source in Security?" He swiftly described the man who'd been his shadow during his time in the Castle awaiting his examination.

Silence lasted for a good long while, broken only by conversation from nearby tables that had filled up while Weil was talking. Then Weil looked around her, seemed to notice the crowd for the first time, and nodded.

"He is getting indiscreet," she added, in a whisper.

"If the Directors are going to behave like this, he will have a good deal of company," Borlund said. He also forestalled further conversation by signaling for the attendant and the bill.

That didn't stop Weil from giving him a vigorous and lingering hug as they stood up, one long enough to raise bawdy chuckles from nearby tables. There were a good many arguments against hugging or being hugged by your prospective Captain, but right now none of them seemed relevant. Weil felt good in his arms, and the look on her face made it plain she thought the same about him.

interlude

FROM *THE FLEET COURIER,* FIFTEENTH FROSTTIDE:

When interviewed by our Special Gatherer, Captain Smeeyon Viligas allowed himself to be quoted about the new squadron of coastal-service vessels under his command.

> The notion that having separate Drylander and Kertovan-crewed ships represents the failure of *Lingvaas*'s experiment in mixed crewing is an insult. It's also nonsense.
>
> The seasoned Drylander Farers under Captain Weil are folk I would sail with at any time, on any voyage. But there are too few of them to take *Lingvaas* into battle unaided.
>
> They will need to draw heavily on their kinfolk on Yproga Island. Some of these know the coastal waters, all are brave and strong, but most are not trained, let alone seasoned, Farers.
>
> The task of training them properly is best left to their own folk. I am sure that they will do it well, and that *Lingvaas* will be honored in the Fleet when she joins it.

Our Gatherer further asked if Captain Viligas had any comments on the rumored influence of Expeditionary Fleet Commander Captain Over Captains Jossu I Hmilra on the creation of the first-ever Drylander-crewed Fleet vessel.

Captain Viligas replied (impatiently, we are told):

> It would be grossly improper for me to speculate about my commander's motives for any lawful order. Almost as improper as it is for you to ask me.

He then continued, in a more agreeable manner:

> It would also dry my throat and weary your ears to no purpose, and waste the paper of your publishers and the time of your readers into the bargain. Jossu I Hmilra's views on almost everything in the Lord's and Lady's domain are a matter of public knowledge. He has never failed to speak his mind, and I fail to see the reason for that question, unless you were too lazy to read your own files before you came out here to bother me.

Sixteenth Frosttide:

That was not the end of the article, but it was where Alikili had to stop reading. She was laughing too hard, and Jossu I Hmilra was too comfortable on the rug in front of the fire to roll over and finish reading the *Courier* for himself.

It was the first uninterrupted day he had spent with Alikili since his appointment to the command of the Expeditionary Fleet. It could well be the last for a midtide, or even until the Fleet sailed. He agreed with Captain Viligas—some things were not worth the time and energy they demanded.

"Was that article scraped and painted before the *Courier* ran it?" Alikili asked. "Or has Viligas suddenly become a rhetorician?"

"He's had three Greats to practice diplomacy with his mixed crew, not to mention its equally eager friends and enemies. He's avoided both mutiny and madness, which speaks well for his success.

"So those might very well be his own words. Remember that his mother became First Scribe to the House of the Lady in Vuisto before she died. That 'bluff old Farer' act of his is just that, more often than not."

Alikili leaned back and pillowed her head on his shoulder. "Are we getting up to dine or having a tray sent in?"

"Have you sorted the correspondence?"

"Yes."

"Nothing opened?"

"Nothing with a GUARDED grading on it."

"You're sure?"

"Being told that kind wire-posts from your family mean nothing to the Fleet is not something one forgets, particularly when you add a few words of the sort you do not commonly use."

Jossu I Hmilra felt blood rushing under his skin and his fur trying to stand up, at the memory of that quarrel. For a heartbeat he had almost been ready to sit down and draft his resignation from both his command and the Fleet, if the price would be Alikili. She had both forgiven him quickly and remembered thoroughly—her usual habit.

"Speaking of Scribes and Houses of the Lady," she went on, "our local one has visited me."

"More for the orphans and fosterlings? Not that she will not have it if they need it, but—"

"Not money, Joso. There are a number of the older girls, nearly women, who would like to join the expedition."

"The regulations are quite specific about what we can do with women before they are proved infertile."

"She wasn't thinking about having them go to sea for life before they've been tested. She's skeptical about the Riisval Test, anyway. She was thinking that we might form an auxiliary corps of women, even the young or fertile, who could serve for the duration of the war."

"That's not likely to be long enough to make it worth training them."

Alikili sat up abruptly. Jossu I Hmilra had an upside-down view of her face looming over him. A face fighting *not* to twist and spew anger.

"Do you believe that, or are you saying it to make me feel better? You are a fool either way."

"That's no encouragement to an honest answer."

"I have other methods."

"If you apply them, we will be here far after the dinner time with nothing settled." I Hmilra sat up, pleased that he could still do it with something of a young Farer's speed and ease. He crossed his legs and faced Alikili.

"Do you support this Scribe's—idea?"

"Of course."

"It will set a precedent—"

"As indeed it should."

"—of a kind that will not please everyone. Displeasure can make for division, when we need unity."

"There is danger either way," she replied.

"Do you wish to command this—ladies' auxiliary?"

"Jossu, two of your partner-Captains in *Valor* are women. There are at least thirty other women of Captain's rank in the Fleet. I would rather serve under one of them, whose knowledge I could trust, than ruin the auxiliary from the beginning by seeking power I do not know how to wield.

"Also, there would be gossip about you. And finally, if that question was a test, I may condemn you to celibacy even after you return from Eneh."

Jossu I Hmilra mock-grimaced in not entirely feigned horror and placed both hands protectively over a relevant portion of his anatomy. "It was a serious question, and if you had said *yes* I would have tried to arrange for the highest rank you could properly fill."

Alikili now looked torn between tears and rage. After a moment she blinked, sighed, and rested a hand lightly on his forehead.

"My dear one, thank you. This war will be longer for those at home, if they have nothing to do but fear for those gone to Eneh."

TENTH LONGDARK:

For a moment, Ehoma Tuomitti thought that it was the swirling snow that distorted *Lingvaas*'s silhouette. Then the gusty wind curled the crests on the waves sliding past *Byubr*. At the same moment they blew aside the veil of snow.

Tuomitti thought many vulgar words and uttered a few.

"First time you've seen *Lingvaas* since they started her refit?" came Zhohorosh's voice from behind her.

Tuomitti nodded, unable to speak or look away from *Lingvaas*. Her masts were stripped bare, her funnel had vanished completely, something that looked like scaffolding was creeping aft from her forecastle, and sparks sputtered into the gray water from riveters at work in at least five places. Compared to what *Lingvaas* was enduring, what even the school-taught engineers had caused to be done to *Byubr* and the other four converted *Illiks* was a mere earbobbing, with perhaps a ring-piercing in the nose thrown in on the side.

At least the conversions had worked better than Tuomitti would have dared wager, even a single block. There'd been a few lively arguments when the engineers stubbornly insisted on rebuilding one *Illik* that really shouldn't have been put afloat again. The old cookpot had finally settled that matter by capsizing and going down one night, so slowly that the two shipwatchers aboard had been able to scramble over the side.

Otherwise, the best proof of the success of the conversions was that *Byubr* was outward bound to take her station on the Haskmouth Patrol, watching the Imperial Riverines from a distance that was intended to prevent incidents and sometimes did. She was the first of her class to be assigned a regular mission beyond the channel buoys in ten Greats, and she would not be the last.

By spring, the five *Illiks* would be a potent force for inshore work anyplace the depth allowed them to go. Where was *Lingvaas* going to be be assigned?

She must have asked that aloud; Zhohorosh shrugged. "My guess is inshore work too. I've heard that she and Viligas's flagship *Suumalin* will have two medium guns for'ard, one on each bow, and a big pivot aft. Then they'll have that flying deck running forward and aft, with crankguns and maybe searchlights. Extra boats, too, for landing parties or maybe hauling troops."

"What about the masts?"

"They may stay, they may go. I doubt me they'll stay if the ships'd need ballast otherwise. Probably leave two masts cut down for lookout platforms and maybe a gun apiece."

Tuomitti tried to imagine *Lingvaas* after such a conversion. Anyway she formed the picture in her mind, the results were hideous.

"I think this will be a short war," she said. "We'll steam up to the Great Delta with all our new ships. The Imperials and the mercenaries and the local levies will come down to fight us off. Then they'll take one look at *Byubr* of *Lingvaas* or one of those torpedo-carriers with the 'invisible-smoke' generator, and they'll all fall down in a fit laughing. We'll walk ashore dry-shod."

"May it be so," Zhohorosh said. He looked as if he wanted to put an arm around her but commanded himself in time. Tuomitti grinned thanks and perhaps a promise. Two watch chiefs were setting a bad enough example lolling around on deck, even when they had no duties. Their embracing would absolutely befuddle the new hands—and while the Fleet wasn't dealing with as many newlies as the Drylanders, there were enough to keep watch chiefs from wanton idleness or idle wantonness.

Lingvaas vanished into another swirl of snow, and *Byubr*'s whistle signaled her turn at the next buoy. It was a deep-toned, almost majestic whistle, easily worthy of a ship three times *Byubr*'s size and five times her fighting power. Tuomitti hoped there was steam for the auxiliary engines left after blowing it; she wouldn't trust some of the newlies not to kill themselves doing Farer's work by hand.

"What's this about a women's force, or maybe farce?" Zhohorosh asked.

"Oh, the Women's Squadron? Nothing much to it that I've heard. Just a few hundred volunteers to keep the bases running while everybody else sails off to Eneh."

"That's not what I've heard."

"What have you heard, besides your organs of generation?"

"I don't think with them, and—"

"At your age, Lord be merciful if you do."

"—I never did as I was about to say before a certain sharp-tongued female assumed the worst about me."

She ventured to pat his shoulder, as he sounded genuinely hurt. "Pardon. I meant the number they'd likely have trained and ready by spring. There may be a deal more learning their way around a dockyard all through the war."

"Why didn't you volunteer? I'd wager that they'd make you a commander for the asking."

"You'd win that. I offered a wager, that I'd spend the next Great training rich merchants' daughters, and they said I'd win that one, too. I'd only just failed my Riisval when we went into Luokka, and I'll be too old and stiff for Faring if I miss out on this war."

"You'll be old and stiff three Greats before the next Skyfall." Then Zhohorosh hastily made a gesture of aversion.

Tuomitti hardly noticed. They were clear of the last breakwater now, with an outbound passenger liner whistling her way down their greenside. Then she felt it—the deck lifting gently as the sea waves rolled in under *Byubr*. Old and sluggish she might be, but she was a ship now coming alive to the call of the sea.

Tuomitti blinked her eyes, not entirely because of the snowflakes stinging them. She was too old to feel this way, really.

Or maybe she wasn't, and should say as much. The newlies who were fit for Faring at all would feel the magic of the sea on their own soon enough. But it might encourage them, to know that they might not lose that feeling with the passing Greats.

Byubr punched into a bigger wave than usual; spray fountained up on either side of the bow. Some of it fell on the trampled snow on the forecastle, and Tuomitti mentally counted the moments before a working party ran forward to check the capstan. Snow and spray joining to build up ice on the deck was bad; ice inside machinery could bring its own lesser trouble.

The people came out fast enough, but there were too many newlies among them, and the one chief in the party didn't seem to have them in hand. Some of them were working without buckling on their safety lines, and Tuomitti saw one slip and fall as another big wave sluiced more water onto the deck.

"Come on, Zho," she said, slapping him on the shoulder. "Ourkan's got more than he can handle down there."

The spray flew higher as they scrambled down the ladder as fast as their feet could find purchase on the snow-slick rungs.

FOURTEENTH BRIGHTENING:

"Staaannnndddd *easy*!" Watch Chief McClintock shouted.

The forty screened and sworn-in human Farers standing in front of McClintock and Sean Borlund had been enlisted long enough to know most of the basic commands. They put their hands behind their backs, relaxed their shoulders, twisted aches out of their necks, and set their feet wide apart.

Borlund contemplated the forty faces contemplating him. Men and women alike, most of them had lost the air of wondering what was going to happen next and suspecting that they wouldn't like it. The few who hadn't were mostly on a list for reassignment to the Directorate Fleet Base Unit.

Nobody who'd volunteered for *Lingvaas* was going to be sent all the way home. That would be a scandal and a disgrace; the political waves it would make could easily swamp a ship the size of *Valor*, not to mention any hope of Drylander participation in the Kertovan Fleet.

However, *Lingvaas*'s crew of seven commanders, thirty chiefs, and one hundred and ten Farers of one sort or another could not afford any dead weight. Not even in the stokehold, where humans would be working for the first time—that was an unwritten part of the agreement that had brought *Lingvaas*'s all-human crew into existence. (*Especially* not in the stokehold, where fire and steam waited in ambush to exact a deadly price for carelessness, and heat, fumes, and dehydration surrounded a stoker at every moment.)

It was safety, it was seamanship, it was common sense, and it was a political necessity. *Lingvaas*'s mixed crew had helped the Drylanders pass one test, in the eyes of most reasonable Kertovans (who seemed to have a slight majority for the moment). Her all-Drylander crew was an even more important test, one that might make the difference between humans staying on the fringes of Kertovan society for another century and their full integration into it within Sean Borlund's lifetime.

At least that was the theory, as Barbara Weil had quoted it with her tongue only slightly thrust into her cheek and her face almost straight. It had occurred to Borlund, as it doubtless had to Weil, that the theory did not take into account the activities of the Tribalist and Confederate humans across the ocean, normal Kertovan curiosity (and the abnormal curiosity of people like Jossu I Hmilra), and Murphy's Law.

Once more, the Directorate and its allies saw a way to retain control of human destiny on Kilmoyn. Once again, Borlund thought they were hallucinating. Once again, however, their delusions were giving him work that he thoroughly enjoyed, and probably helping the human future on this planet of exile more than anything the Study Group had ever done intentionally!

Borlund turned his thoughts outward and his eyes on the men. He nodded to McClintock.

"Kiiiiit—inspec-*shun*!" the Chief bellowed.

Borlund wished for the fiftieth time that watch chiefs, junior or senior, human or Kertovan, could learn a variety of tones and volumes. At drill or aboard, anyway, they always spoke as if they were addressing the deaf or the witless in a howling gale or perhaps an engine room at full speed.

By the time Borlund's ears had stopped ringing, everyone had unslung their kitbags and unsnapped them. There was a standard layout for such inspections that let the inspecting officer see at a glance whether the Farer had the basic kit and in proper condition. Layout-on-the-bunk inspections were strictly indoor affairs, as the kit allowance for *Lingvaas* came from the Fleet, and so far the promised supplement from a Study Group appropriation had not materialized. So Farers could be exposed to this day that couldn't decide if it was late winter or early spring, but their kit had to be treated more tenderly.

Borlund let McClintock take the lead as they walked along the line, studying each bag from two or three different angles as they passed, occasionally stopping to rummage for some particular item. Even now, Borlund sometimes felt eyes focused with cold distaste on the back of his neck.

But that sensation was part of being a commander. So was learning to live with it. Command was not courtship; consistency and justice counted for more than warm feelings on either side.

It seemed half a Tide before the last Farers buttoned up their bags and snapped to attention at McClintock's bellow.

"Very well," Borlund said. "Most of you passed admirably. A few of you did not. I expect that most of you know who you are, and your consciences are saying harsher things than even Chief McClintock could. However, just to make sure that you understand the importance of proper kit, he will—privately, of course—say those things.

"I will just say this, which I'm sure you've heard before but remains important no matter how often it's said—Not having a full kit before you sail can put you in three different situations, each one worse than the last.

"The first is having to borrow from your shipmates, which is disloyal to them and makes you enemies where you should have friends.

"The second is being unfit or unequipped for duty. That can spoil your record at best, at worst endanger your shipmates or ship. Your shipmates will not be grateful.

"The third and worst fate is being turned into a thief. That can put you in the confinement quarters afloat or ashore. Or it can put you over the side some dark night, far from land, if your shipmates detect you before your commanders do."

Borlund looked at the trickle of sunlight from the gaps in the clouds. "All right. We'll have PT when the chiefs join us."

McClintock again raised echoes from the barracks walls and the men stood easy. The wind was beginning to get up when the eleven men and women who were candidates for the rank of chief came jogging up behind the forty.

Most of them had some sea time in research or coastal trading vessels, or some special skill like boiler repairing, that made it prudent to let them try leading from the start. So they did not have to stand kit inspections, but they did do Physical Training with the two sections of recruits, while their classroom day was even longer and harder than Sean Borlund's had been aboard *Lingvaas*.

The PT started with isometric stretching, then went on through the whole list of conditioning exercises and finished with a five-klick run (twenty circuits of the barracks square). Borlund had thought he'd left that particular ordeal behind with school, before *Lingvaas* had taught him new lessons.

One was that it could be a pleasure to feel your wind, your limberness, your endurance and strength all increasing under a demanding physical regimen. He'd gone right on enjoying it after he'd been assigned to training, and that more than setting an example was why he always did PT with his sections.

Borlund led off the run around the slick but mercifully not icy brick of the yard, which had on other days sprained ankles and wrists, scraped knees and elbows, and generally made the recruits' life more miserable than even the brass-hearted McClintock would probably have wished. Borlund could have easily lapped half the section in the first quarter of the run, but paced himself to be ready to help the laggards and keep an eye on the rest.

It was past the halfway mark when he saw the two men standing outside the fence side of the yard. No, a man and a boy—and the man was his acquaintance from the Watch (he would not even *think* "Barbara Weil's informant").

The boy looked to be about fourteen Standard, hands and feet too big for a lanky frame but with a square stance and wide blue eyes that seemed to take in a lot without making a big fuss about it. There was a family resemblance to the Watchman, too—nephew, maybe, or even son?

Borlund waved at the two the second time he went past. The third time he waved again—and this time the boy returned the greeting. His companion did not move; he did not even seem to be breathing. Borlund wondered if he'd frozen stiff in the rising wind, and looked at the clock on the barracks tower.

Then he tapped one of the leading runners, a rangy young woman with an Asian flavor to her features and complexion, on the shoulder. "You've proved you can do it. Pick a friend from the leaders and go fire up the baths. We'll all need to thaw out by the time we finish this run."

"Aye-aye, sir."

TWENTY-THIRD SALTSTOCK:

The hatch slid shut above Barbara Weil, cutting off the last of the watery morning light. From the buzz of voices ahead, everyone was already in her cabin, waiting for the briefing. Suddenly the portfolio of orders under her arm seemed to weigh fifty kilos, and with dagger-sharp points digging into her ribs as well.

Nobody shouted attention when Weil entered the cabin, because that was her standing order. Nobody even had to rise, because there was no room to sit. Seven commanders and the eight senior chiefs—two each from Deck, Engineering, Gunnery, and Stewardry—hardly left room to breathe in the cabin.

Opening a scuttle did something for the atmosphere, but it took judicious elbowing and a few rude words to clear a space for laying out the portfolio and spreading the map. It had HIGHLY GUARDED stamped all over it, in large red letters that seemed to impress everyone.

"All right. We now have our official orders. We'll be part of the Second Division of the Inshore Squadron of the Expeditionary Fleet. Our mission is stated in some detail in the orders. I have two copies, one for me and one for everyone else to read and memorize. Neither leaves my sight."

This brought a ragged chorus of "Aye-ayes." Weil pinned down all four corners of the map with spare lampbases and drew her dagger to use as a pointer.

"Just for background, our mission is to eliminate piracy in the Bishak Gulf and establish secure communications with the Regality of Eneh." She pointed to a blotchy blue area just north of the long bowed range of the Kayosi Mountains.

"Now, I assume you all know how to reach the Gulf in the first place," Weil said. "Who can tell me?"

The Third/Gunnery Commander spoke up. His name was Fridrik Maartens and he was older than most of the others, as welling as having a rather blatantly good opinion of himself. But you couldn't draw in people who knew weapons and could be spared from the secret arsenals every time you dropped a line over the side. Maartens might be hard to live with, but he would probably be even harder to live without.

Maartens gave the standard sailing directions for the Saadi–Bishak Gulf voyage, then added, "But if I was sailing on this kind of work, I would swing far to the south. Not to landfall on Luokka, because somebody unfriendly might be watching from there, but just short of that. Then I would turn north and enter the Gulf close inshore to the eastern end of Fuori Island, which is near enough uninhabited. Anyone waiting for me on the western shore of the Gulf would have less time to put to sea and attack.

"I'd also steam with the heavy ships and torpedo craft on either flank, and the transports in the middle, in a square. There'd be searchlights crewed at all times, also the crankguns, and everyone on deck with floatbelts on. A surprise attack—"

Weil nodded. They didn't have time for Maartens to show off his tactical notions, even if they seemed sound enough.

"Are we going to be attacked?" one of the Engineering Chiefs asked.

Weil recognized Adrianna Yoshino, one of a pair of twin sisters noted for their magic touch with machinery. She and her sister, Corinne, were partnered to twin brothers, irregular enough even if they hadn't also been suspected of being Observant or at least Believing. But the sisters had produced four children in five years, so there was no real cause not to let them join the Fleet.

"The assumption is that we will be, at some point," Weil said. "I can't give you the final strength lists, because I don't have them myself. But the talk is about a four-regiment landing force, each regiment with its own scout and gun detachments, supplies for several fights or sieges, and plenty of construction equipment for opening up the route to Eneh."

She turned back to the map. "The route is mostly water anyway. We'll have to do some dredging before heavy ships can ascend to Lake Bhir. The locks on the Shubirani are supposed to need repair, and of course we'll need to build rails over one of the lower passes in the Kayosi. I think they've all been surveyed, but which one will probably stay a secret for a while."

"And nobody around the Gulf is supposed to object to this?" Yoshino asked.

"I answer that if you'll tell me what you object to first."

Yoshino frowned. Weil tapped the map with the hilt of her dagger. Reasonable doubts were one thing, and she would allow them to be discussed openly. Insubordination based on militantly orthodox pacifism was another matter. Weil had long since decided that this issue would sooner or later divide the Drylanders, and known from that moment which side she would be on.

"I'm merely thinking of the Luokkan situation," Yoshino said slowly. "Nobody missed the pirates when the Fleet suppressed them. But everyone in Luokka expected the Kertovans to leave after that. They didn't."

"How hard have the tribes and towns fought to get rid of the Islanders?" Maartens put in.

"Not at all, from what we hear," answered Sean Borlund. "But are you sure we're hearing everything? When was the last time enough Drylanders went to Luokka to see anything that the Principal Governor didn't want seen?"

Borlund, Weil decided, was taking to the role of rebel with a bit too much enthusiasm. She did *not* want him to talk himself out of the Fleet and commander's rank even before they sailed for Eneh.

"Enough," she said. "I think we all have part of the picture, and nobody has all of it, including our Kertovan friends. They're obviously assuming that there will be some fighting, or at least some people ready to fight if we don't enough strength to make that look like a bad idea.

"But the day when the Island Republic has to go up against the Empire or the Dhandarans or both is going to come in our lifetimes. The Regality of Eneh is one of the few likely allies they—we—have against the Empire.

"We owe the Kertovans too much not to pay at least some portion of our debt to them, even when their cause may not be absolutely just. How far will our plans be set back if the Kertovans feel that we've been parasites? Far enough to help the stay-behinds who chose to kiss the Dhandarans' asses, I suspect."

She knew that she had their attention now, even if it was from a melodramatic, even pompous bit of word-flourishing. She smiled.

"Besides, safe navigation from the foothills of the all the way down to the mouth of the Gulf will make everyone around there prosperous. They may not be grateful, but they could end up too busy making money to worry about whose fleet patrols the Gulf.

"And if the Kertovans cheat the local merchants, and we have a few hundred trained Farers to spare, what's to keep us from setting up our own shipping line?"

She didn't know which of several emotions was making everyone smile. As long as the smiles were real, she didn't particularly care.

chapter 15

It was what the old Farers called a "mizzling sort of day," and Sean Borlund liked it no more than he liked the rest of the breed. Rather less, in fact, because today was sailing day for the Expeditionary Fleet, and sixty-odd ships would be heading downchannel at once, then trying to take formation in the Outer Bay so as to be in reasonable order before they reached the open sea.

Sixty ships, from the flagship *Valor* in her fresh coat of dark green paint down to a pair of converted fish-catchers barely half the size of *Lingvaas*. Sixty ships, of varying speeds and turning circles, all belching smoke to thicken the mist, rain, and low clouds, some of them towing torpedo-carriers or barges destined to be converted into piers if the expedition couldn't use any of the existing ports on the Bishak shore. . . .

A seagoing crossroads snarl waiting to happen, in short. The one virtue that Borlund could see was that the fleet speed would be so low, to accommodate the older ships, that collisions would be easier to avoid, also less damaging when they happened.

Meanwhile, *Lingvaas* had her own problems from the damp and dreary weather. The keenest-eyed lookouts in her new fighting tops could barely see *Valor*, let alone hope to read flag signals. Every ship in the fleet had two reliable new Utoiki signaling lamps and Farers trained in their use. Borlund still kept fingers mentally crossed for at least vital signals being seen and read in time.

The fingers of his body were otherwise occupied. The last shipload of stores for the fleet had only arrived from the islands last night. *Lingvaas* had sent ten Farers to join the emergency work party, then turned out all hands before sunbrighten to unload the lighter that a tug had brought alongside with *Lingvaas*'s share of the wealth.

Now the lighter was empty, and the slick decks almost so. Farers still had to maneuver around the guns, the boats, and the close-woven net of stanchions and wires holding up the flying deck. But the coils of wire, the cases of canned fish, the igniters in their double-layered red boxes—these were mostly stowed below now, no longer laying traps for Farers' shins and toes.

A horn blared, and Borlund heard the hiss of steam and the squeal of the boom winch. Another slingload—crates and sacks, anonymous at this distance, filling a net to bulging. Borlund watched the hoisting cable tighten, groaning as the weight of the net came on it. Somebody had loaded that net nearly to the limit, in their haste to get the loading done.

The net rose, now suspended two men's height above the deck, swinging slowly toward the midships hatch—hatches, now, one on each side of the flying deck. A working party with hooks held in gloved hands stood ready to ease it down the last meters.

One of those workers was the Security officer's nephew—or at least everyone aboard called him that—Roald Chaykin-Schmidt. Borlund had guessed right about his age, but he'd celebrated his fifteenth Naming-Day ten commons after his uncle brought him to the training depot. Now he was a Farer Junior, the youngest hand aboard *Lingvaas* and the particular pet of the Farer-Instructor Chiefs.

Borlund doubted that the boy's austere uncle wanted him made a pet by anyone, any more than he wanted those aboard *Lingvaas* to know the true reason for the boy's enlistment. Since Roald Chaykin-Schmidt was only the youngest, not the least useful Farer aboard, people had tended to stop gossiping—a couple of them after being thoroughly thrashed by a youth who was stronger than he looked and better coordinated than usual at his age.

The accident came in the time a man needed to draw a quick breath. One rope in the net snapped, then a second. Then the whole bottom ripped out of the net, and the crates and bags plummeted to the deck with the crash and impact of a giant's hammer.

The first rope had given just enough warning for most of the work party to run clear. Only two laggards were still in the danger area when the net gave way completely. One disappeared in a cloud of dust and a scream that ended with awful suddenness.

The other might have gone the same way, if Chaykin-Schmidt hadn't run in rather than out and snatched the woman free of the worst of the fall. The only thing that hit them was a bag of some sort of dried seaweed, that burst and coated them from head to foot with all the blue-green powder that didn't litter the deck.

"Murphy's Curse!" someone shouted. Then there was a general rush forward, to haul the other crates and bags aside and find the man underneath.

Everyone worked fast, if not always together; Borlund found himself having to tell a pair of hands that they were trying to pull the same crate in opposite directions. He was close by when the last crate came off the man—close enough to hear someone gasp a name, which was more than Borlund could have done for a man who now had neither an intact chest nor a recognizable face.

Borlund was trying to find the idiot who'd invoked Murphy, although he remembered only that Murphy was an ancient Old Myths bad-luck spirit. Probably not a very major one, or his name wouldn't have been invoked so publicly.

Unable to put a face to a voice he hadn't recognized either, Borlund knelt and took off his jacket to cover the dead man's head and shoulders. Fortunately it was the older of his two working jackets, and a few bloodstains or even more wouldn't do it any harm. But he realized he would have used his best dress tunic or kilt if there'd been nothing else at hand to hide the bloody horror that had been a Farer.

As Borlund straightened up, he heard the sound of a scuffle behind.

"Mindless Believer!" someone snarled.

"You cold-hearted—" a female voice began to reply.

Borlund whirled, saw Corinne Yoshino fending off the clenched fists of another woman, and stepped between them. He did this just as Yoshino counterattacked, and the edge of her flattened hand caught him across the side of his neck.

"Skyfall take your ancestors!" he snarled. "What's this about, if anything?"

The two women looked at each other, then at him.

"Well?"

The looks went farther, to the circle of shipmates who'd left off picking up crates and bags or their remains and stowing them below, to watch.

"This isn't a street and we're not entertainers," Borlund snapped, which at least got the hands as far as pretending to go back to work.

Borlund remained conscious of attentive ears and an occasional head turned his way, but managed to ignore them enough to listen to the women.

"The first thing you can do is get a litter from the Healer and take your shipmate's body below. Both of you," he added. "If you cooperate that long, then go back to work, I may not say anything more about this."

"You want—?" both of them began at once.

"I want no brawls aboard this ship, whatever the excuse. If you have some real difference, settle it ashore. If you're just imagining things, give your imaginations a rest. Nobody's paying you to use them, anyway."

"No, but she's been spouting superstition—" the other woman began.

Borlund tried to dredge up her name; she had been in one of his training sections. "Vavra Yelm?"

"Farer Second, at your command, sir," the second woman said. Reluctantly, Yoshino also came to attention.

"Farer Yelm. You are charging Farer Yoshino with public preaching of superstition? Formally, as in I should take it—and you both—before Captain Weil?" Borlund's tone implied that if he did, they might wish he'd let them beat each other to a pulp instead, but he would do his duty regardless.

"I do so charge Farer Yoshino," Yelm replied. "She has been saying that our expedition to Eneh is contrary to the teachings of an Old Religion. She has said that this accident is a sign of that. She even invoked the Lady as well as—ah—"

Yelm groped for words, as militant Rationalists frequently did when trying to find a circumlocution for the name of some sacred figure.

Borlund sighed. *Bougu, Buddha, something like that,* his memory told him, in Bridget's voice. That helped somewhat. Borlund doubted that the Buddha, even if he existed, could do much more, in the face of invincible ignorance and carefully cultivated stupidity.

He thought that last so loudly that for a moment both women seemed doubtful about pursuing the issue. Then Yoshino made an obscene gesture at Yelm, Yelm stiffened and glared, and Borlund had to step between them again.

He looked around, for a messenger. Most of the hands were really back to work now, and the only spare one was young Chaykin-Schmidt. He was actually doing something, but it seemed to consist mostly of brushing the seaweed dust off the shipmate he'd rescued. She was somewhat older than he, but not much, and she didn't seem to be minding his hands on her, or perhaps it was just human touch after her narrow escape.

"Farers," Borlund said. "Chaykin-Schmidt, go to the Arms Watcher and have him place Farers Yoshino and Yelm under arrest, then inform the Captain that we need a Judgment. Farer—"

"Reza." At least her voice was steady, although her hands weren't and there were tear tracks in the dust on her dark cheeks.

"Farer Reza, report to the Surgeon, and have him send up a couple of litter-bearers."

"Aye-aye, sir."

The two culprits looked at Borlund. He replied with a glare. "It's too late for either of you to get out of this easily. And I'm certainly not going to let you carry the body of a shipmate when you've dishonored his memory by a silly quarrel before he's grown cold!"

He knew that sounded pompous and might even be so. He also knew that he'd have to be careful about that when he was angry. Commanders who didn't ended up making themselves both ridiculous and ineffective.

Right now, however, he was too angry to care how he sounded, as long as what he *said* penetrated the thick skulls of Yoshino and Yelm.

BARBARA WEIL HAD SUSPECTED THERE WERE BAD TIMES AHEAD AS THE LIST OF last-moment preparations for sailing grew longer each time she looked at it. Suspicion turned into certainty when ten of her best people were pressed into a working party intended to correct somebody else's laziness or incompetence.

She went beyond certainty when she heard of the accident and its sequel. By the time Deck Chief Second Peller had been pronounced dead (a mere formality in his case) and the Arms Watcher had reported Yoshino and Yelm confined on charges placed by Fourth Commander/Deck Second Sean Borlund, she had gone beyond certainty into a conviction that indeed Murphy was loose in the expedition or at least aboard *Lingvaas*.

This did not improve her mood as she faced the culprits, and her mood did not improve the atmosphere in her cabin. Fortunately, the atmosphere in the literal sense was agreeable—two scuttles were open, a light breeze was at least shifting the mist about if not blowing it away, and there weren't enough people present to make a stifling crowd.

There were in fact only the two culprits, Sean Borlund (in a hastily donned dress jacket and working trousers), the Arms Watcher, and herself. She debated whether to stand or sit, and finally compromised at standing beside her desk.

"You have agreed to accept Captain's Judgment, is that correct?"

"Yes," one of them mumbled. Weil couldn't tell which.

"Both of you?"

This time the "Aye-aye, Captain," unmistakably came from both.

"Good. We don't have time for a Council of Judgment before we sail. You would have to be put ashore, and remain under Restriction or Extra Duty in the barracks until we returned. That might be the best part of a Great.

"Or you could both resign. However, you would undoubtedly be fined heavily, and you would have to pay your passage home from what was left of your money. You might end up living on the Study Group's charity. Personally, I would rather dance in a waterfront drinkshop, so I think you've made a wise decision."

She folded her arms. "Now, I would like to hear each story from your own mouths. I will not interrupt, and neither will Commander Borlund, as long as you do not interrupt each other. If you do, any and all means necessary will be used to restrain the interrupter."

It loomed large in several sets of regulations and many books on leadership that a commander should never put him or herself into a physical confrontation with an offending Farer. Maybe this made sense for Kertovans or for drunken or drugged offenders.

Yoshino and Yelm, however, had made idiots of themselves while sane and sober. They had no excuse, and Barbara Weil realized that she would not much regret an opportunity to knock either of them even sillier than they already were.

Her eyes briefly met Sean Borlund's; she thought she read the same sentiments in them. Then she nodded to Yelm.

"Farer Yelm, you may begin."

BORLUND HAD NEVER BEFORE ADMIRED BARBARA WEIL SO MUCH AS HE DID now, standing and watching her try to administer justice when she would as gladly have committed mayhem. He wondered if this urge came from more than fury at the utter pointlessness and wretched timing of the quarrel.

Was Barbara really Observant—possibly even an Observant Jew? Or was she more like him—not a Believer, not at all Observant, but knowing enough Believers and Observants to realize that the Rationalists had simply invented a new set of myths to intimidate those who held to the old ones?

He wondered. He also wondered how many more of that kind there might be, among the human exiles on Kilmoyn, and if they, the Believers and the Observants, might not add up to an unofficial, illegal, but very real majority of the exiles.

It hardly mattered for now, of course. The settlement in the Island Republic at least was no sort of democracy, and not much the worse for it. Dissidents who carried their disputes beyond what survival allowed were a menace to everyone and all joined to put them down. Those who merely chose to live apart could do so, at some risk to their lives and more to the lives and futures of their children, but without anyone trying to arrest them for it.

It was a delicate balance, which had so far survived for two generations and part of a third. However, the time seemed to be coming when it would take more than silence about the delicacy of the balance to keep it from being upset. There, at least, Borlund knew that he and Barbara Weil were on the same side.

Borlund forced his mind back to listening to the two offenders' tales. If by some quirk they changed their mind about submitting to Captain's Judgment, it wouldn't help if they could claim that the principal witness had stood there with his mouth open wide enough to catch seafliers and his mind halfway up the Hask.

Both offenders had obviously had time to mentally rehearse their stories and tighten up their presentations. They might have been presenting reports at a school seminar rather than arguing something that could end their careers and blot the records of their families.

Borlund mentally awarded them each five points for cool heads. He would have awarded them more, if they hadn't lost those heads in the first place. On the whole, he hoped they would remain aboard *Lingvaas,* if they could keep their tempers. Dealing with Adrienne Yoshino if they sent her twin sister ashore would not be pleasant for anyone aboard *Lingvaas*.

Weil listened in silence and with so little expression on her normally mobile round face that Yelm finally faltered twice and Yoshino once. A curt "Continue," from the Arms Watcher got them both started again.

By the time the testimony was done, Borlund was conscious of silence from on deck, and less noise than usual in the passageways and cabins below. Even the normal metallic din from the engineering spaces was subdued. It was as if not only the offenders but the whole ship was waiting.

Weil took a brief turn on deck after the testimony, which if anything deepened the silence. She didn't invite Borlund and he wouldn't have accepted if she had. The Arms Watcher had a mind more Security than Farer, and had once suggested that disciplinary cases like this could be handled by throwing the offender overboard and taking bets on how long they could stay afloat.

This was the first disciplinary case aboard *Lingvaas* that the politically minded would notice. Justice not only had to be done, it had to appear to be done.

Weil came below able to manage a thin smile. "Good news," she said. "It's clearing up, although the breeze may have a chop kicked up outside the Bay by the time we sail. Anybody who hasn't got their sea legs *or* memorized the location of the slop buckets may be in for a bad time."

She looked at Yelm and Yoshino. "You still wish to accept my Judge?"

Both nodded.

"More good news for me." Weil put her arms behind her back again. "Farer Yoshino. Your beliefs, observances, and faith are none of my concern, nor anybody else's, as long as you do your duty and help maintain discipline aboard this ship. To do anything else is failing your shipmates, a far more serious offense than reading religious books or attending a religious service.

"You have committed this offense. Trying to make an ordinary if tragic accident an omen is nonsense. Accidents in loading cargo, like people saying stupid things, are not omens. They are part of life, no more, no less. You could have undermined discipline if you'd gone on as you began.

"I do not accuse you, without evidence, of wishing to undermine discipline. That accusation might have been raised if you'd chosen a formal trial. However, I do remind you that carelessness can do as much damage as conspiracy, sometimes more. Good intentions seldom count against bad results, and this was not one of those times.

"Farer Yelm. Your saying that Farer Yoshino was talking nonsense in this particular case would have been acceptable. Attacking her beliefs in general was not.

"All the people who had anything to do with the decision to crew *Lingvaas* for Fleet duty rejected the idea of a Belief or Observance Test for assignment aboard. Do you think you are wiser than they?"

Yelm shook her head. Borlund hoped she was telling the truth. Although he had experience with militant Rationalists who would have said yes, she didn't seem like one of them.

He also suspected that the Belief/Observance Test had been turned down by a narrower margin that it would give anybody comfort to know. It had been rejected, he was sure, because no one wanted to sabotage this high honor to the Drylanders from the Kertovan Fleet over a matter that was ultimately Drylander internal politics.

It might have done more than that, too. It might have brought about the long-deferred confrontation between Rationalists and their opponents. Both sides had shied away from that so far because they knew that Lord, Lady, and human Higher Authorities working in concert could not keep the Drylanders' secret in the face of religious brawls.

"Very well," Weil continued. "You are being realistic. Your attack on what Yoshino believes was therefore as big an attack on discipline as what she said. From where I see it, there isn't a single strand of rope's difference between your offenses. Both of you let your mouths get ahead of your brains, and as a result we had a silly brawl over a shipmate's dead body.

"I won't have it or anything like it again. If I do, the offenders go ashore, because I will not have them on my ship. I will also wash my hands of what may happen to them ashore.

"Since this is your first serious offense and both of you have pulled your weight until now, I will be lenient. You formally apologize to each other, here and now, swearing by what you believe in most strongly to keep the peace.

"You will also work one watch's extra duty every common for the next thirty. During that period you will also be fined half your pay."

"Do you accept this Judgment, on your Farer's oaths?"

Neither was slow to agree. Yelm had delivered her apology and Yoshino was beginning hers, when a messenger hurried in.

"The compliments of the officer of the deck, ma'am, and the flagship is flying 'Prepare to get underway.' "

"Thank him and say I'll be on deck directly," Weil replied. "Farer Yoshino, continue."

Yoshino practically gabbled the rest of her apology, and both she and Yelm seemed to fly out of the cabin when Weil dismissed them.

Borlund followed Weil on deck. He felt a weight lifting from his shoulders, although it was hard to tell how much of that was justice done and how much of that the sight of the fleet getting up steam.

Smoke was already curling from *Valor*'s funnels, and with his binoculars Borlund could make out not only the rainbow of signal flags but the crankguns and lookouts in her fighting tops. Seeming through the binoculars close enough to touch, an oceangoing tug was already underway, pulling three snugged-down barges in a line behind her.

Borlund jumped as *Lingvaas*'s whistle blew, the four short blasts for "Getting underway." Then more steam moaned and whistled as the capstan began its work on the anchor chain. Two hands cast off the last line from the lighter, and a smaller tug whistled as it began to haul the lighter clear.

The breeze was freshening, and Borlund wanted to open not only his eyes but his nose, mouth, and ears, to let it blow the sour taste of death and stupidity out of his head.

chapter 16

FLAG LOG OF KERTOVAN REPUBLIC EXPEDITIONARY FLEET, FOURTH HARVEST:

> Five beats of the sunbrighten watch, detached first-class torpedo-carriers. Two making rounds of fleet to collect mail. At five beats fourteen Boat I/45 came alongside *Valor* to receive flag despatches and mail.
>
> At five beats twenty-one, Boat I/56 reported unable to proceed and requiring tow. Detached open-sea tug *Vayat* to tow I/56 either back to Saadi or until able to proceed.
>
> *Vayat* obliged to cast off tow of heavy lighter (landing-stage type). Flag ordered armorclad *Azuuva* to tow lighter until further notice.
>
> Six beats: lighter under tow by *Azuuva*. All other vessels proceeding normally.

Jossu I Hmilra let his binoculars dangle from their straps and turned inboard on the flag bridge. The torpedo craft and their lame cousin were now hull-down to the west. Only their smoke was now visible from the bridge, although any eyes studying the sea from Mount Kaksi on Guvitha Island below the horizon to the west-southwest would probably be able to make out more.

I Hmilra hoped the eyes would be friendly, but could do no more than hope. To set groundfighters ashore at every point where hostile eyes might watch the expedition's progress or hostile small craft lie in wait would take more than the Island Republic possessed. Only the

Empire could raise such a host, and they only by stripping lesser garrisons and forts.

Before I Hmilra's eyes lay part of the alternative. The ships he was leading south were only two-thirds of the expedition, the larger ships or at least those with speed and endurance to take the long way around to the south. Thus they had begun by steering due west, and would only be turning south tonight, with darkness blotting them from all eyes, friendly or hostile.

Meanwhile, the torpedo-carriers would return and join the twenty-some Expeditionary ships and the squadron of coal- and store-carriers sailing down the Turha Strait. Only the torpedo-carriers and some of the converted fishing vessels would rest the main burden of patroling the seaward flank of the southbound convoy, along the coast of Turha.

The great island had harbored every sort and condition of Farer, many short of both scruples and skills, since before Skyfall. Pacifying it might be a necessary sequel to opening the route to Eneh, as it squatted hard on the flank of the inshore route.

Protecting thirty irreplaceable merchant ships had received some thought and much argument. I Hmilra had been adamant about leaving neither convoy without a heavy escort, and reluctant to divide his four armorclads. *Valor* might be worth a whole squadron by herself, but neither she nor any other vessel could be in two places at once.

So fourteen more heavy ships would be sailing with the inshore convoy, eight armorclads and six protected cruising vessels. Only the Hask Squadron and its supporting torpedo craft would keep watch on the Empire and the City-States for a few days. Saadi's own defenses should stand off anything that came out of the Hask and slipped past the watchers inshore.

This "Fleet exercise" would raise the cost of the expedition's coal, stores, and spare parts to a still more formidable figure. By the time the Fleet had compensated the last Drilion Steward Chief whose mistress's shore quarters had been robbed in his unexpected absence, questions would not be asked in the Assembly. They would be shouted at the top of powerful lungs, possessed by Assembly folk also too powerful to ignore.

Unfortunately for both them and for Jossu I Hmilra, the "Fleet exercise" suggestion for solving the escort dilemma came from the High Captain. When the High Captain wanted to join some maritime enterprise, with any or all of the Fleet, it was not well done for a mere fourth-ranking Captain Over Captains to argue too loudly.

If he did, he could wave farewell to his chances of sitting in the High Captain's chair of state someday. He might even find his command of the expedition to Eneh dragging its anchor.

Waving farewell brought Alikili to I Hmilra's mind—and she was never that far from it. Had either of them been other than they were, I Hmilra was tolerably sure that at least the leaf-scrap rags would have cast him as an old man afflicted with senile lust. When he had been as young as some freshly hired newsgatherers and as wanting in experience of the world, he might have agreed with them.

But he and Alikili had finally achieved in the eyes of the world some of the dignity that they had so long held in each other's. That made for a restful darkness's sleep even in the narrow, solitary, and celibate bed of the flag cabin.

Steam hissed and metal squealed, followed by sharp-voiced commands that I Hmilra could practically recite in his sleep even now, twenty Greats after he last gave direct orders to his own gun crew. He did not need to walk to the bridge wing to know that the crew of one of *Valor*'s amidships citadel guns was at their exercises.

In fact, there was really nothing he needed to stay on deck to learn. I Hmilra took the salutes of his flag secretary and the two signallers, then went below. If he could manage a short nap, it would be easier to be awake tonight, when he needed to be on the bridge for the course change.

FROM THE DECK LOG OF KERTOVAN REPUBLIC VESSEL *LINGVAAS*, SEVENTH HARVEST:

> One beat ten of sunfade watch: Watch came alongside stores transport *Guilin* to transfer cased stove oil. Operation completed successfully by one twenty-five. Light breeze from S during operation, medium swell from SSE.

Sean Borlund read down the rest of the Deck Log for his watch, signed it, then saluted his relief.

"I relieve you, sir," Justin Baer said.

Borlund was in no mood for casual chatting. But both regulations and ordinary good manners toward a shipmate and fellow commander demanded more than simply dumping the watch on your relief and diving below. "Everything as one could wish it," he said.

"Any spills from the oil?"

"A couple of small ones. I had a working party sand the deck. We can scrub tomorrow."

"If the weather doesn't do it for us," Baer said. "I don't like that swell. Five times out of six, I've heard, it comes from a Disputable storm coming at us."

Borlund nodded, more out of politeness than agreement. Baer had five times as much schooling in the art of Faring as he did practical experience at sea. But much the same could be said about Sean Borlund—had been, a few times, coupled with remarks about the possible reasons for his promotion. (Borlund had reminded himself that punching out everyone who insulted Barbara Weil would undoubtedly break both his hands and his prospects, as well as reinforcing the rumors.)

Still, one of the big storms come up from the subtropical seas off the Disputed Lands south of the Confederation would not be good news. The ships taking the offshore route were all big and supposedly seaworthy, but some of them were half-crewed by newlies and the stiff-jointed, and most ships were carrying heavier loads than usual. Not to mention the crowded transports, which could turn into a Punishment World in half a watch if the groundfighters started getting seasick in really large numbers.

"Do you think we should rig for bad weather?"

Baer looked at the sky and shook his head. "The light's almost gone, so all we'd do is wake up the nightsleepers just when they've put their hammocks up and their heads down."

That was the answer Borlund had been hoping to hear. He had learned even before the thought of coming to Saadi entered his mind, that a leader who makes unreasonable demands on the led just to look good does not lead well. He or she may lead for too long, but never well.

As Borlund descended the ladder, he thought he heard a shout of "Captain on deck." But he would be seeing Barbara—seeing *Captain Weil,* he told himself firmly—at the Commander's Conference tomorrow morning. Tonight she was probably even less in the mood for idle chat than he was.

At least Yoshino and Yelm had both been on the working party that took the stove oil aboard and sanded the spills, and managed to avoid either speaking to each other or neglecting their duties. As progress, this was like the swimming of a sloughfish, but sloughfish covered great distances if they lived long enough. Yoshino and Yelm might at least keep the peace until they were no longer shipmates.

FLAG LOG OF KERTOVAN REPUBLIC EXPEDITIONARY FLEET, TENTH HARVEST:

> At six beats of sunfade watch, launch from courier vessel *Virgaadz* alongside with passengers and mail.
>
> Sea moderate, fresh breeze from west, sky overcast. Cape Zibir bearing green five zero, distance fourteen posts.

Virgaadz had steamed into sight around the cape halfway through the previous watch. She closed rapidly until she was in signaling distance, then flashed the message that she carried dispatches, mail, and passengers for the fleet.

The courier ship did not slow as she approached. Yet I Hmilra was wondering if the mystery of the Drylanders had been solved on another Skyfall became imminent, before *Virgaadz* drew up abreast of *Valor* and signaled that she was sending a boat. He knew that he owed the Fleet at least the semblance of calm, and thought he was giving it that much.

Within, however, taut anticipation of orders and letters from home warred with the relief that the storm was past. Not the work it had made necessary—from where he stood he could see carpenter repairing one of *Valor*'s workboats, and more hammering floated up from below where they were repairing his own day cabin. Fully loaded with coal and stores, *Valor* sometimes took green water over most of her main deck, only the citadel guns could fire and they not accurately, and anything near a leaking hatch or scuttle risked flooding.

Fortunately I Hmilra's cabin had escaped with nothing much more than sodden rugs and smashed furniture, and the rest of the fleet had also suffered more lightly than anyone had been prepared to wager. Two lighters had to be cut loose, one was still missing, but a crew placed aboard the other at the last moment had cranked a flypump until the weather moderated, then burned signal flares to bring help.

Paint showed scars, deck planking rattled loose, water sluiced back and forth in bilges and passageways, and the inventorying of damaged deck cargo promising to be a long and tedious process. Also, most ships reeked of spilled food, vomit, and overflowing heads; cleaning parties had a busy few commons ahead.

But every ship was fighting-fit, every Farer and groundfighter soon would be, and even butting this west wind to the rendezvous would not fatally delay matters. I Hmilra made a mental note to visit *Valor*'s House of the Lord as soon as his duties allowed.

That would not be for a while. The launch from *Virgaadz* would be alongside before a Farer could recite the Three Prayers. I Hmilra lifted his binoculars and studied the courier ship.

Virgaadz had begun life as a fast packet on the Saadi-Kehua run, carrying three hundred passengers ready to endure vibration and small cabins in return for speed. Now she carried despatches, urgent reinforcements, and valuable stores for the Expeditionary Fleet.

She also carried a quartet of five-line guns and two heavy crank pieces. She was faster than any armorclad and most cruising vessels, although unarmored except for light plating around the guns and extra coal in the bunkers abreast her boiler room. So it had seemed a good idea to equip her to make a prize of any hostile vessel she could catch. If she or any other vessel of the expedition encountered such.

I Hmilra had begun to wonder if all the other Faring nations had left the seas to make room for the expedition to Eneh? Or if the Confederation's Ocean squadrons had merely withdrawn to Imperial ports, to load guns and groundfighters and bide their time until the Island Republic had committed its forces? I Hmilra could not be unaware of the very long flanks and supply line he would be maintaining even if the expedition went well.

Now the launch was alongside, and a bright young commander-in-training dashed up to the bridge with the oiled, weighted packages for the Captain Over Captains. I Hmilra held on to the shreds of his courtesy long enough to thank the lad, then abandoned deck and dignity alike for the privacy of his sea cabin.

The despatches held his attention long enough to ease his hunger for the letter addressed in Alikili's handwriting. The expedition would meet the main Fleet at Skirmana Bay, which offered protected waters for coaling if not enough good holding ground for such a multitude of ships. Two balloon sections had been added to the convoy, one to be landed on the shore of the bay, the other to go on the Eneh. Efforts to secure the assistance of Enehan forces in opening the last stages of the route were going forward, discreetly to be sure, as Eneh was riddled with Imperial spies.

Discretion indeed! This was not the first time I Hmilra had considered the wisom of asking the Regality of Eneh to send a few of its sturdy groundfighters over the Kayosi passes and help secure the shores of Lake Bhir. He'd even gone so far as to suggest it.

The answer had always been that he was not responsible for such strategic issues, and would be told what he needed to know when he needed to know it. (The language was usually politer than that, but the meaning always as edged.)

I Hmilra made another mental note, to geld the person responsible if he did not receive full information when the fleets made their rendezvous, then tore open Alikili's letter.

> Beloved friend Jossu,
>
> I write more briefly than I intended, for darkness has come after a very long work session and I must finish this letter before I retire.
>
> However, I can say that my work goes well, and my health likewise. I have several new friends besides the ones I named to you, and I have promised them hospitality in some neutral place that will not embarrass them, when you return.
>
> Most notable to report is that I am to be made a commander in the Women's Squadron, one of eight being promoted from among the new volunteers. We number now some five hundred who have passed their training, and the commanders sent from the Fleet are too few to both continue the training of recruits and command actually on duty.
>
> There will apparently be a new table of ranks within the Women's Squadron, with at least four grades of commander. I will be neither the highest nor the lowest.
>
> I am satisfied that no one I know has procured this commandership for me to please you. The reports rendered upon me are sufficient to bring the blood to my face, although I believe I have at least been doing satisfactory work.
>
> This scheme of new ranks gives me some pause, and rumor runs that some wish it to discourage fertile women from entering the Squadron. (Women holding one of the

> four special ranks will not have authority over anyone holding a regular rank.) However, I will not suffer personally from it, as far as I can see now, and would not take sides on the issue if it were to embarrass me.
>
> The reports from the northern lands . . .

I Hmilra smiled. He would have given his share in *Valor* to hold Alikili in his arms until sunbrighten. Ever conscientious, it had not occurred to her that the stewards of the family lands were rendering reports directly to him, with copies to her out of courtesy.

The matter of ranks was something he would discuss with the High Captain when they met in Skirmana Bay. For now it did not matter if the commanders' ranks in the Women's Squadron were called Leika, Leja, and Lehna, after the legendary first three Ladyspeakers. Five hundred women was less than the crew of one of the larger armorclads, and would not need more than a score of commanders.

But fertile women should not suffer dishonor during even brief terms of service, if they and their kin were willing to come forward to the aid of the Republic. For the future, it would be best if the commanders of the Women's Squadron held regular Fleet ranks—or even that the Women's Squadron cease to be a separate body, and fertile women serve alongside their tuunda sisters and men.

And wouldn't that make the Drylander spies perched in their castle above Saadi Bay rend their hair and soil their garments!

FROM THE DECK LOG OF KERTOVAN REPUBLIC SHIP *LINGVAAS*, TENTH HARVEST:

> Seven beats fifteen of sunglow watch, anchored fore and aft off Ulus Creek in the Inner Roads of Skirmana Bay. Depth twenty-six heights nine spans.
>
> Seven beats twenty-five: hoisted out launch with watering and wood party.
>
> Changed watches. At ten into the thirdlight watch, coal-carrier *Beszoiko* came alongside. Took lines aboard; ordered all hands to prepare ship for coaling.

Twenty of thirdlight watch: armorclad *Byubr* moored to greenside of *Beszoiko*. Sent away coaling-assistance party to *Beszoiko*, Deck Commander Second S. L. Borlund in charge.

One beat fifteen: served hot soup to all hands.

Two beats ten: commenced coaling ship.

Sean Borlund tightened the damp handkerchief over his mouth. It didn't help much. Already he felt the grit of coal dust between his teeth.

Through the haze of dust he saw other ships presenting the same spectacle as *Lingvaas* and *Byubr* did, nestled up to either side of *Beszoiko*. It looked as if the whole Inner Roads was full of ships ablaze, as the coal dust rose in gray-brown clouds to scar the blue sky or drift out across the green water until it fell to make a scum on the pond-smooth surface.

In and out of the dust darted figures clad in very little or sometimes even less, both male and female alike. "Coaling modesty" had been a proverb in the Fleet since about a Great after it was discovered just what a filthy operation coaling ship was.

It wasn't as filthy and exhausting now as it had been twenty years ago, and Borlund had no shame in thanking Higher Powers for that (with the usual near-ritualistic mental reservation about their existence). About that time, metallurgy, factory capacity, and coal supplies all came together to make an all-steam Fleet practical. About that time several wise Farers also realized that there weren't enough folk in the Republic to crew such a Fleet if coaling ship needed a horde of strong backs every few days.

Hence the endless-chain bucket boom, a variant of a device already used in the boiler rooms of some of the larger ships to save Farers' sweat. Each coal-carrier that received a Fleet subsidy had two or four of the booms, each driven by its own steam winch. The boom was swung out over the warship alongside, and as fast as Farers in the hold loaded the buckets they carried the coal up and across, to dump it down the coaling chutes of the warship.

A large improvement over the old days, when every piece of coal had to be handled manually, in bags no larger than a single Farer could lift. *Then* coaling a large ship meant three commons' backbreaking work for everyone but the Captain and cooks, and another day scrubbing the ship, the Farers, the livestock, the carpets, and everything else into which coal dust had infiltrated.

Now it was simply a matter of feeding the buckets aboard the coal-carrier and hauling away the dumped coal aboard *Lingvaas*. Borlund has still taken a quarter of *Lingvaas*'s crew aboard *Beszoiko* to help her crew feed the hungry buckets and the boilers that fed the boom winches, and most of the other three-quarters had turned to below, hauling away coal to distribute it properly so that it would drive *Lingvaas*'s engines, instead of shifting to capsize her in the next bout of rough weather.

That cut the work down to a single common at most, for any size of ship. *Lingvaas* would be loading two hundred tons off a single boom; *Valor* would need to load five times as much, but she would doubtless have the undivided attention of two coal-carriers and four booms.

Borlund went to the water barrel and drank deeply. Unlimited fresh water was an unwritten law for coaling day, especially this far south. While no one was looking, he sneaked a few handfuls of water onto his handkerchief, rinsing it enough so that he could wipe his face without merely redistributing damp coal dust. Then he tied his mask back in place and strode aft. Another unwritten rule was that if commanders weren't taking their place in the work parties, they should not sit down until the rest gong sounded. (All other Fleet ships used drums or trumpets for time signals; coal-carriers used gongs.)

Halfway after, Borlund entered a particularly thick cloud of coal dust. Halfway through that, he bumped into somebody—two somebodies, and Kilmoyans from what he judged of their stature and skin in the murk.

They staggered out into comparatively clear air holding onto one another. Borlund stepped back and recognized Ehoma Tuomitti and a male Watch Chief. Both wore loinguards and sandals, headbands with their ship and rank badges attached, and nothing else.

"Farer—no, Commander Borlund," Tuomitti said, grinning. Her teeth were the only visible white on her. "How flows your world?"

"Well enough," Borlund said. "May I have the honor of an introduction?"

"Zhohorosh," the man said, saluting. "I am reminded that I owe you much for Ehma."

The look he threw his shipmate told Borlund all he needed about Zhohorosh's relationship with Tuomitti. His first thought was: *Aren't they too old*? His second was to realize that Tuomitti was no farther along her life-course than Bridget was along hers; if she had been fertile, Tuomitti would still have been of child-bearing age. It was unlikely that she needed a winch and cable to find a bed partner.

"I will do the same for you if fate calls me," Borlund said, "but let us hope that it does not. If I want to join a bathing party, the Inner Roads of Skirmana Bay is not my favorite place for it."

The others laughed. Borlund squinted against sun and coal dust and tried to get a good look at *Byubr*. It was hard to tell under the coal dust and salt-smeared paint, but the old "floating turd" looked a trifle more efficient than she had before her refit. Her main gun still looked impotent against anything faster than a log raft, but her upperworks bristled with two-line and crankgun mountings that would certainly stand off torpedo-carriers.

Certainly a refit and modernization had improved *Byubr*'s looks more than *Lingvaas*'s. Without her masts and sails, the smaller ship looked oddly out of proportion.

"What's so amusing?" Tuomitti asked.

Borlund realized that he must have let his thoughts show on his face. "Just that I've been a Farer for less than two Greats, and already I'm thinking of how much better it was in the old days."

Zhohorosh frowned. Borlund pointed at *Lingvaas*'s naked and warlike masts. "You know. When *Lingvaas* had sails, and a Farer could prove what she was made of by laying aloft and taking a turn on the furling crank—"

The Kertovans laughed, which turned into a coughing fit for Zhohorosh, which made Tuomitti slap him on the back. A whistle interrupted them, and all eyes turned seaward.

Valor was coasting by, with barely steerageway and only a faint curl of water over her ram to match the wisp of smoke from her funnels. Her crew was already on deck rigging out boats and coal chutes. Several white-kilted figures clustered at one end of her lower bridge, several more on the upper one.

"See how right she's aimed, for the space between those two coalers?" Zhohorosh said, pointing. "What'll you wager I Hmilra's bringing her in himself."

"He always was a canny shiphandler, I'll admit," Tuomitti said. "But that was in his younger days."

"Aye, grandmother," Zhohorosh said, putting a tremulous rasp of age in his voice. "Is the wager on?"

"I'll hold the stakes if you wish," Borlund said. "Or even inquire."

"Na, na," Zhohorosh said. "You'll just be talked down as a nose-poking Drylander. Let me and Ehma do our own dirty work. And speaking of work—"

Nobody had actually downed tools, but it seemed as if the party on the winch was mostly at the water barrel, and the sound of shovels and wheelbarrows from below was not as loud as it had been. Borlund nodded.

"Everyone who hasn't taken their rest, take it now," he called. "Then back to work for everyone!"

FLAG LOG OF KERTOVAN REPUBLIC EXPEDITIONARY FLEET, FIFTEENTH HARVEST:

> Three beats fourteen of sunbrighten watch, launch lowered to take Captain Over Captains Jossu I Hmilra to highship for conference with High Captain.
>
> Five beats six of sunglow watch: highship made signal that Captain Over Captains was returning. Fleet also raising steam.
>
> Five beats twenty of sunglow: *Valor*'s launch in sight from the bridge.

The launch was butting into a light chop thrown up by the rising west wind, and spray had already come over the bow several times. Jossu I Hmilra pulled the hood of his waterproof up and hooked one arm through a grab-iron, but otherwise left matters to the boat chief. She was an old, short-tempered, and thoroughly reliable Farer who would have the steering gear, engine, and if need be pumps and life-saving gear in the best possible shape.

Off to redside a small clan of Seakin was raising breath-sprays, preparing to dive deep for feeding. The High Captain had said nothing about the attitude of the Seakin toward this expedition and the war it might lead to, which left I Hmilra hoping that this meant nothing had changed.

When they last expressed themselves on the subject, the Seakin had said (or rather, the Lordspeakers had said they said) that they passed no judgment on the cause of Kertova, friendly or unfriendly.

They would hope that all sides in the fighting would observe the long-established customs for keeping the seas clean and fit for all folk using them. They would also continue their work in the waters of the Republic but would not accept work in the fighting area.

This was less favorable to the Island Republic than the judgment of the Seakin on its last major campaign, against the Luokkan pirates. But, then, the Luokkan pirates' treatment of the Seakin had been stupidly cruel, even deliberately barbaric. They could have hoped for no friendship from the Seakin and had indeed found none when the Kertovan flags sprouted on the northward horizon.

Not much had changed, indeed, in most other aspects of the campaign. According to the High Captain, the diplomatic overtures to the Regality of Eneh were now a matter of public comment, which meant that they had to be known in the Empire.

"The Empire cannot act against Eneh without either stripping the Fortress or calling on the City-States to honor their treaty quotas of mercenaries," the High Captain added. "They won't have much help from their subjects to the south of the Kayosi."

"Why not? We've always acknowledged the Empire's claim to the land west of the Bezelyon. That's everything we could give them, short of the line of the Bishak itself."

The High Captain had lowered both eyes and voice. "We might alter our opinions, if we can't bring Eneh in on our side any other way."

I Hmilra swallowed an oath. The High Captain nodded. "Foolish, unless we are desperate, and that desperate we will not be unless we—you, especially—are foolish beforetimes.

"Left to their own devices, however, the Imperial folk south of the Kayosis will fight to defend their own lands. From us, if we tresspass on them, which we should not. Also from the Empire, if they send a mighty host over the passes and begin eating the land bare to supply it. The rails over Redrock Pass are at least two Greats short of complete. Without them, an Imperial army will have to live off the land or be supplied by sea."

Unspoken was the implication that preventing resupply of an Imperial army by sea might be one task falling to the Expeditionary Fleet. Not even wisely thought about was the implication that the Republic was indeed prepared for war with the Empire if necessary—and the commander on the spot, who had no power to judge the necessity, would have the responsibility for fighting the first campaign of the war.

At least the Republic had the power to reinforce him if he needed it. I Hmilra watched the sky turning gray-brown over the main Fleet as its ships raised steam, and long plumes of coal smoke trailed away on the wind. The launch had come far enough so that individual ships were beginning to overlap, even blur. The Fleet now looked rather as if the Fortress on the Hask had dispersed into its individual bastions and gone afloat for a breath of sea air.

Now signal guns began firing, adding their flat, distant thudding to the thump of the launch's engines and the slap of water at the prow. A breath of sea that held more than air showered over I Hmilra, and the chief hand-signaled a small course change to the boatsteerer.

Guns reminded I Hmilra of another matter still more uncertain than he cared for.

"What about the fortifications of Rinbao-Dar?"

The largest city on the eastern shore of the Bishak Gulf was by law the capital of an independent republic extending along the shore north to an area long in dispute with the Regality of Eneh. The republic's actual control over anything more than two commons' dreezanride from its massive walls was nominal, but even that modest territory produced wealth sufficient to make the city a notable stronghold.

"What about them?" the High Captain asked. I Hmilra would neither dislike nor distrust the old Farer himself, but he felt both sentiments about the bland tone of that question.

"I agree that they haven't been kept up after we suppressed the pirates in Luokka and the Empire drove them out of their enclaves on the western shore. But we've given them ample notice of our coming. They could have hired mercenaries, bought Imperial guns, used the labor levy to restore the walls."

"Assuming that all this is true—and we have no report of any of it happening—why should we fear their opposition?"

"Making friendly visits on training cruises is one thing. The waterfront folk get rich and we are soon gone. Asking for base rights even in their outer harbor is another matter. Particularly when we come to aid the Regality of Eneh, or has it been forgotten how long the Old Republic has had its quarrel with Eneh?"

"It has not," the High Captain said, in a tone that made it clear to I

Hmilra that he had stepped over a line which, if crossed in public, would require official action. I Hmilra mentally both praised and cursed this charity, kept his face blank, and replied in a neutral voice.

"We shall certainly make every effort to give no offense. Indeed, I have been looking at some of the Adinisi anchorages. Some of them are large enough, and a few are both large enough and close to Rinbao-Dar. I will pick one that can be fortified, so that we do not need to either fear the city's forts or trust to them for our own protection."

"You are being as long-headed as I expected, Farer Jossu."

The High Captain would not have said that if he'd known just how scanty had been the planning for bases in the Adinisi Archipelago, but matters would improve before he learned the truth. I Hmilra was beginning to agree with those who said that the Fleet needed a proper corps of commander-planners, as the groundfighters already had in spite of their lesser strength and duties.

"I could almost wish this expedition provokes the Empire to a fight," the High Captain said.

Now he seemed to be speaking to himself, the walls, his old commander, perhaps his ancestors—anybody except the living Jossu I Hmilra across the table from him.

"That fight must come," he went on. "I would not mind if it came while I can still take a ship out to sea. I fear that the battle will not come until it is your responsibility to face it."

The words might have been taken as a subtle criticism, but the tone said otherwise. I Hmilra smiled at the older Farer.

"If I command against the Empire, and you are still fit to come aboard, you will have a place in that war. Don't be too hasty to lose your sealegs and let your seaclothes molder!"

"I swear it," the other said, returning the smile.

From ahead came a hail, bringing Jossu I Hmilra's mind back to the present.

"Launch ahoy!"

The boat steerer replied.

"Expedition!" Meaning that the launch had the Expedition's commander aboard.

Above the smoke clouds, something small, silvery, and round now floated in the sky. I Hmilra had to look at it twice before he realized that it was not the Lesser Moon making an out-of-season appearance, but the balloon rising from inland.

Quick work by the detachment ashore. I Hmilra spared a moment's thought for the groundfighters, patroling the forest to keep possible enemies from slipping within rifle shot of the balloon base. One bullet into the gas generator could produce an explosion as violent, if not as deadly, as one aboard a powder hulk.

Then he stood up, unhooked his arm from the grab-rail, and began lacing up his waterproof. He'd need to be careful, going from launch to ship in this chop, if he wanted to arrive with either his dignity or his uniform intact!

DECK LOG OF KERTOVAN REPUBLIC SHIP *LINGVAAS*, SEVENTEENTH HARVEST:

> Six beats thirteen sunfade watch: Underway for Rinbao-Dar as part of Vanguard Squadron. Course 210, speed seven, moderate sea.

The "Vanguard Squadron" (a traditional name which gave nothing away to possible enemies) had sailed in three columns in no particular order. Establishing a neat formation with complicated maneuvering was something that could wait until they were clear of shoals, reefs, the rest of the Expeditionary Fleet, and the cable-layer *Minguuso*.

From Sean Borlund's post on the bridge, the converted coal-carrier was now falling astern to greenside. In the fading light the cable paying into the sea off her blunt stern, fed from the big tanks amidships, was almost invisible. Two torpedo-carriers steamed in slow circles around her, ready to catch or at least buoy broken cables and pick up Farers who fell overboard.

Minguuso had a technically demanding but short task: to link Skirmana Bay with the main submarine telegraph cable running south from Saadi to Cape Zibir and onward to Rinbao-Dar. Once her work was done, and the new length spliced into the old one, anything observed from the balloon at the bay *or* by the fleet off Rinbao-Dar could be known in Saadi in half a watch, in Kehua in less than twice as long.

All three of the major Kilmoyan nations seemed to have a knack for working with electricity. Borlund wondered how long it would be before someone invented radio (at least the old-fashioned code-using "wireless") and knew that would be a mixed blessing. Faster communications would help everyone—including those trying to penetrate the secret of the Drylanders.

Soon *Minguuso* had faded into the dusk astern, and Borlund turned his eyes forward. With less rigging blocking the view, not only gunners could clearly see what lay ahead. In this case, it was *Byubr*.

Byubr was going with the Vanguard to add some heavy gunpower and anti-torpedo protection. One or the other would almost certainly be needed before the rest of the Expedition came up. Another *Illik* steamed in the redside column, and both seemed to be having a fairly easy time butting into the chop. Their long rams still scooped green water over their foredecks at intervals, but the upperworks remained dry and the gunners could have cast loose their weapons without being drenched to the chin or flooding the magazines.

They'd done good work on the "floating turds." Borlund had heard how Farer gossip had turned from predicting doom for everyone aboard them to mild envy at the amount of armor between their crews and enemy guns. He could appreciate that, as his station in battle would be out on the deck with at most sandbags between him and the enemy.

The drum beat a familiar signal that Borlund recognized even before he heard the cry of "Captain on deck!" He stood with a deliberately stern expression by the binnacle, until he heard footsteps and sensed Barbara Weil's presence beside him.

"All well, Farer Borlund?"

"I think we really ought to sink this ship, let the ocean wash around in her for a few commons, then bring her up and rinse her out with fresh water. That *should* see off the last of the coal dust."

He heard laughter, then in a more sober tone:

"Anything else to report?"

Borlund swallowed and decided to gamble.

"Nothing except the sense that we are past the point of no return."

"Explain."

"Almost anything we do from here on is likely to do less damage than turning back."

"You seem to have more doubts than you've expressed in the past."

Borlund motioned to the bridge wing and led Weil toward it, until they were halfway between the Steerer Chief at the compass and the redside lookout, as well as out of hearing of either.

"I have," Borlund said. "I haven't said anything about them

because I know my duty. Naming no names, I would say that it's not only the Yoshinos who have doubts about this expedition. I didn't want to encourage them."

"Don't you trust me?"

"Personally, yes. Officially—Captain, I'm not sure you can *afford* to be trusted that way."

Weil said something pungent with a Germanic flavor. "Officially, I also have the duty to know the strengths and weaknesses of my command."

"Are doubts a weakness?"

In-drawn breath, followed by silence. "I could take that as an insult. Instead, I'll say that up to a point they're a strength. Naming no names, like you, I'd say that some of our people would cheerfully sack Rinbao-Dar to the bare walls if it would advance them or the Drylanders in the Kertovan service.

"I'm not one of them myself. So I can hardly complain about you not being one of them either."

Her voice sounded almost in Borlund's ear; she must be standing very close. "Duty is no excuse for bloodlust, and doesn't require mindless rigidity either. The more commanders we have who know that, the better."

Then she was gone, withdrawing so quickly that Borlund could imagine he felt the wind of her passage. He looked after the sturdy figure now briskly descending the ladder to the main deck. It gave him no clues about hidden meanings in those last words. At last he decided that there hadn't really been any, except in his imagination.

Which he did not need to have working overtime, as commander of the deck on a warship steaming toward battle.

chapter 17

"Flagship signaling," the signalman beside Sean Borlund said.

Borlund nodded wearily. This was the third time since she dropped anchor that *Valor* had broken out in a rash of flags and lamps. So far most of the signals had been general and the few particular ones to other ships than *Lingvaas*.

Trusting the signaler to at least recognize *Lingvaas*'s particular code, Borlund looked landward. Rinbao-Dar lay sweltering in the fiercer heat of this more southerly latitude, Rinbao on the north bank of the Fuinhazi and Dar on the south. The floating bridge that linked them was barely visible, around the famous last bend in the river.

The twin cities were a study in contrasts. Rinbao sprawled across an alluvial plain, its walls doubling as dikes when the Great Tides or the Fuinhazi's floods drowned the plain. A light railroad linked the city to its waterfront, and right now whole villages of tents sprouted to either side of the railroad, adding the smoke of cooking and ritual fires to the heat haze.

The south bank rose steeply, providing natural ramparts broken only by a few carefully carved and well-fortified routes, one of them a cog railway that through Borlund's glasses looked like Imperial work. Dar perched atop the cliffs, a mass of solid stone and timber houses with a few public buildings, the whole trailing off toward the north along another railroad that linked it to the docks above the bridge.

No fortifications; Dar had needed none even in the days when it had no weapons against ships in the river below except stones hurled over the cliff. Borlund thought he saw a few of the pre-dug gun emplacements, which could be equipped from the arsenal on half a common's notice. He couldn't make out any guns in them, which meant that either the city Matriarchs didn't think the Kertovans a threat, that they had the guns hidden too thoroughly for any casual observer to find, or that they had some other plan for dealing with any possible danger from the Expeditionary Fleet.

Borlund decided that half of a commander's job was listing what he didn't know and devising ways to fill in the gaps. Establishing the location of those guns—which could clearly sweep the whole Outer Harbor as far as Yatago Island, if they were eight-liners or bigger—was clearly a high priority.

Fortunately, it was also somebody else's responsibility.

"Flagship done signaling," the signaler said. "Nothing particular to us, but a general signal about preparing boats for the shore parties."

"That's particular enough for me," Borlund said. He turned, and cracked his elbow painfully on the breech of the foretop's crankgun. The signaler carefully looked elsewhere until Borlund had fought down the urge to curse.

Climbing down to the deck, Borlund once more had to fight mild vertigo. He still wasn't use to climbing down a naked mast surrounded by nothing but empty air, instead of by the vertical labyrinth of spars and rigging that the refit had removed.

By the time he reached the deck, Captain Weil was up from below. *Valor* had also finally sent *Lingvaas* a particular signal.

"We're to anchor inshore, off Yatago Island," she said. "How soon can you have your people in the boats, Farer Borlund?"

With *Lingvaas* and her crew on display among the whole Fleet, the formality of Captain to junior commander was now the rule between them. But they had a subtle private code of facial expressions and gestures to ease the stiffness of words mean for other ears.

Borlund pulled out his watch. "Half a beat, if nobody forgets anything and has to send back for it."

"If anybody leaves anything, you leave them and they can go ashore in the next wave," Weil said. "I want you on the way before we shift anchorage."

"We're rowing?" He was extrapolating from a subtle shift of tone.

Weil nodded. "I want the launch patroling tonight."

"The Kertovan mission didn't report any signs of trouble," Borlund said. For the sake of his boat crews, he had to at least formally protest against a long pull in the southern heat.

"The mission's staff is half local," Weil said, in a level tone. Borlund nodded, to show that he drew the right implications about possible spying or corruption. "Also, the fair has the Gurthagi in town, nearly the whole tribe, and some of their blood-kin from the Eggimai and Toroshi."

"No blood enemies, I hope."

"Not yet," Weil said. "Get the boats overside, Farer Borlund," she concluded briskly. "We haven't all day."

"Aye-aye, Captain."

EHOMA TUOMITTI CAST THE SKEPTICAL EYE OF THE SEASONED CHIEF ALONG the line of Farers from *Byubr*. In this heat and after coaling ship, she wasn't worrying about starched kilts or groomed fur. Unauthorized weapons or too much of the cheap local fruit-ales would be enough trouble.

She saw nothing—well, maybe one or two suspicious bulges, and definitely a couple of Farers who needed more help standing up than they should have. But the bulges could be snacks from the vendors who'd already rolled their carts up to the waiting Farers, and the heat could have even a sober Farer needing a helping hand.

She was about to commend everyone on their discipline, when the shriek of a railsteamer whistle made speech impossible. She closed her mouth, to preserve dignity and keep out the swarming insects, and watched the train up to Dar pull out. Commanders and Farers of the Purchasing Division of the shore party hung out of the windows of the rear coach. She recognized Sean Borlund from *Lingvaas*, and knew that Zhohorosh would be in there, too.

Sending only a small party into the city itself and leaving the rest of the shoregoers close to the water, ready to load the boats, had been a decision signaled from the flagship. Aboard *Valor*, they hadn't wanted too many from the Fleet in the city, with the tribesfolk between them and the water.

On shore, facing the tent-city of the tribes, Ehoma Tuomitti thought that old I Hmilra had the right idea.

"Heads up," she called. "We'll be one-third on duty and the rest off until the supplies come down. Duty Farers to be armed at all times. Off-duty can disarm inside our lines, but go armed if you leave them.

"Also go in parties of four at least, go easy on the fruit-ales, and watch your backs and purses. There's five thousand tribesfolk in town at least, selling hides, furs, pottery, silverwork—all their best goods.

They've also got enough rifles and ammunition to fight a small war, so don't make them think you're the enemy."

"What can they do with single-shot rifles?" someone asked, obviously trying not to laugh.

"One shot can kill you if it hits, and I've heard tales about tribal marksmanship," Tuomitti replied. No cause to take a name—this time. "Play games with your own life if you want, but if you get your mates killed, don't complain if they haunt you for the next ten Greats."

It took a beat fifteen after that to set the duty division at their posts. After that, Tuomitti wandered over toward the beach. The canteen boat had been unloading when she lined up her people; now its people had a fire burning in a pit and racks of hoeg and stew pots heating over it.

What she really wanted in this heat was iced fruit-ale, but she needed a clear head, and ice in this city gave you a flux more often than not even when you were as young as she'd been the first time she came to Rinbao-Dar. That was fifteen Greats ago, most of it spent living on shipboard or lodging-house fare, and she'd no inclination to spend the rest of the day squatting over a midden trench!

WITH ALL THE PORTS AND HATCHES OPEN AND A FAN TRYING DESPERATELY TO stir the air, Jossu I Hmilra's cabin still felt like a steam chamber. He wanted to snatch at the iced drinks on the silver tray his steward presented, but dignity prevented him from even moving until the steward had left.

I Hmilra's visitor was less inhibited. He had his cup empty and refilled before the door closed behind the steward, then let out a long gusty sigh of relief.

"Ah, blessings on your hospitality."

"Whose?"

"All those who can give blessings on a worthy host, and they are many."

That was the sort of answer I Hmilra might have expected from someone like this man. Vuikmar Drojin had a Kertovan name, spoke the Kertovan tongue without an accent, and clearly had more Kertovan blood than any other. But his dress was the short breeches and sleeveless tunic of the south, he had the shaven upper lip and nose ring of a high burgher of Rinbao, and on the back of his left hand he wore a tribal tattoo. Which tribe, I Hmilra couldn't remember—he hadn't studied the tribes of Rinbao-Dar, not expecting to have to deal with them.

So much for not studying the Rinbao-Dar calendar, I Hmilra thought.

He sipped from his own drink. "I rejoice that my hospitality pleases you. How do you propose to repay the debt I have thereby imposed on you?"

Drojin contemplated the overhead, as if he was trying to decipher obscure runes on the steel beam. Then he shrugged.

"I offer you a choice of many ways. But the best way, I think, is one that requires you to answer a further question of mine."

"You cannot require me to answer any question of yours, not without the orders of your superiors *and* mine," I Hmilra said, more politely than he felt. This was not the first time he had found Kertovans of the Rinbao-Dar mission believing they were outside the law, almost a sovereign republic of their own, bound as tightly to their hosts as to their native land.

It gave him more sympathy with the Drylanders of Yproga in their sometimes-strained relations with their Study Group in Saadi. It too seemed to feel that it knew best the interests of all Drylanders, even if they were barely one in fifty of their folk.

"That was perhaps a stronger word than circumstances justify," Drojin replied. "May I at least ask the question, without any obligation on your part to do more than listen?"

"An old Farer like me will listen to almost anything," I Hmilra said, with a smile. "But because of my Greats spent Faring, I doubt you will say anything that I have not heard before."

Drojin shrugged. "Perhaps. How well are the Drylanders, aboard their ship *Lingvaas*?"

I Hmilra chose to make a literal answer to that question his own opening move.

"They know civilized healing and self-care, have a newly refitted and cleaned ship, and have learned the special needs of Faring. I have heard of no disease and few accidents aboard *Lingvaas* since the Drylanders became her crew."

Disappointment was plain on Drojin's face. I Hmilra smiled in a way to expose as many teeth as possible. "Does my answer lack something to which you think you have a right?"

"Eh?"

"Highmale Drojin," I Hmilra said, using the Rinbao-Dar title, "may I see the message you bear, and your authority for bearing it? The alternatives are leaving my cabin, or remaining aboard in confinement. On second thought, the last is the only alternative."

Drojin's face now showed a vigorous contest between duty and some less agreeable emotion. He finally reached inside his tunic and handed over a sweat-stained leather flat-pouch. It bore the seal of the Fleet.

Inside was another flat-pouch, bulging with paper. Also a note, on the purple-hued scale-sheet used in the south for formal correspondence. The note was anything but formal.

> To Jossu I Hmilra,
> Vuikmar Drojin's manners are atrocious, but he's as honest as our purposes require. Answer his questions; they are reasonable. Also let him talk, if he wishes it, but don't leave him alone with your best table settings or any woman you care about.

The letter had no signature, only a red windflower.

For I Hmilra that was enough. He who had sent this was Captain-Born since nearly the time of the founding of the Republic. Ten Greats younger than I Hmilra, he had "gone south" sometime back, allegedly to escape a crushing burden of debt. Not everyone believed the story, but the matter was not one on which speculation was encouraged.

At least this saved I Hmilra the trouble of finding a school of fang-jaws into which he could throw Vuikmar Drojin. The Expedition commander thought he might still heave someone over the side, probably whoever had decided to make this a surprise, but would omit the fangjaws.

"There are no women aboard this ship with whom you could make free without their consent," I Hmilra said. "My valuables are locked up. So we do our work quickly, I trust."

"So it would seem." Drojin sighed and poured his cup full again. "I suggest that you open the inner pouch."

HOW THE RIOT STARTED WAS A MATTER ON WHICH THERE WAS NEVER REAL agreement. The best that anyone was able to do was annoy enough witnesses to piece together an account that satisfied them. Arguments over whether the riot was provoked or not went on until the last witness was dead, and afterward among historians of every folk and tribe involved.

Ehoma Tuomitti was a witness, and she remembered it this way.

"A Gurthagi rider on an ariyom—that's the southland riding beast, looks like a dreezan that's been starved for half a Great—he brushed against a walker.

"The walker fell over and hit a vendor's table. The vendor was selling fire-sticks of smoked fish and vegetables. His brazier went down with the table and landed on the next tent over.

"The people in the tent came out in a hurry. They didn't have anything on, and from the way they looked it was pretty plain what they'd been doing. The man hit out at the vendor. The vendor drew a knife, and the woman grabbed up a pistol and shot him.

"Then they noticed that the tent was on fire. They started to pull their things out, but I think the rider was a clansfellow of the vendor. He pulled out one of those arm-length throwing spears the Gurthagi use, and threw it at the man.

"It hit him, and he went down. Right into the burning tent, and he started screaming. Then somebody from *his* clan—I think—shot the rider out of his saddle.

"That was all I saw before I full-steamed it out of the tent city, me and the three with me. We drew our weapons, on the way back to our lines, but we didn't have to use them. We could hear shooting by the time we were as safe as we were going to be, but more shouting than shooting, if you take my meaning.

"I stopped being worried when the rest of our people turned out under arms. Or at least worried for myself. Some people I cared about were up to Rinbao, buying supplies. The riot was between them and the sea.

"Then we got orders to form in column of fours and march to the railroad bridge over the Ayot River, which was hardly more than a decent stream but still too big for trains to cross. That made sense, but what were the Matriarchy's groundfighters doing if they weren't guarding the bridge and the railroad?

"At least everybody got sixty rounds, a full canteen, and a biscuit pouch. Some of us were barefoot, but we were Farers, used to that, and the ground was soft underfoot anyway. Almost sickly soft, I thought.

"But we were also Kertovans. We weren't used to the heat, most of us, except the ones who'd spent a long while in Luokka. Even the march to the bridge seemed a bad one, and most of the canteens were empty when we got there.

"But we did make a—perimeter, the groundfighters call it—a guard-line, as we Farers say—around the bridge. We even put an outpost on top of the hill overlooking the bridge, which let us look all the way to the walls of Rinbao.

"We could also look offshore and see the ships signaling and getting up steam. So we knew they'd learned about what was going on, and maybe even knew more than we did. The whole tent city was dust and smoke, and it might have been in a fogbank for all we could make out.

"The Fleet might know what was happening and where we were. What I wondered was, what could they do to help us if we needed it?

"It felt a lot lonelier than I enjoyed, being out there by the bridge that day."

I HMILRA'S LUCK WAS IN. THE INNER POUCH HELD A MAP THAT HE COULD take in at a glance, and a stack of documents that would need several watches to read, let alone digest. He was able to finish the map before word of the tribal riot came from shore, and had his response firmly in mind already.

"Signal to the shore party: 'Take all measures for protecting Farer lives. Reinforcements will be sent as necessary for that purpose. Otherwise avoid taking sides.' "

When the messenger was off to the bridge again, I Hmilra could see that Drojin was less than happy. No doubt he had profitable business dealings with the tribes—the tattoo made that plain—and they were in danger. Or could his motives be more respectable?

Never mind Drojin's motives for now. "I see the map shows a fairly extensive network of Drylander sightings in the Bishak Gulf area. More on the west side, in Imperial territory, but some elsewhere. Is that what it was intended to tell me?"

Drojin nodded. "The—we can call him the Red Windflower, if you wish—"

"I do."

"The Red Windflower did not write this, but asked me to speak with his voice if you did not have time to weigh all the evidence. In the documents," Drojin added, then coughed at I Hmilra's glare. The commander expected him to reach for his cup again, but this time the visitor contained himself.

"Continue. It's become plain that we have little time."

"The Red Windflower asks that you consider assigning *Lingvaas* outside the Gulf."

I Hmilra did not need to look at the map again to understand the implications of that request. The Captain-Born turned chief of Kertovan spies in Rinbao-Dar had always been rather narrow of vision. He distrusted the Saadians, nearly joining the Ironbands faction at one time. Now it appeared that he'd slipped over into distrusting the Drylanders—or at least into making decisions that smelled of such distrust.

I Hmilra was not influenced by his old acquaintance's sending this request by a subordinate with dubious manners and a fierce thirst. (Drojin had emptied his cup again.) It was so outrageous that he would not have forgiven it if it had been borne on a golden platter by six Ladyspeakers. He would merely have refused more politely.

The air in the cabin grew a trifle warmer from I Hmilra's language. He was, to say the least, forceful in refusing to even contemplate any action that hinted of doubting the Drylanders' loyalty.

"At least the loyalty of the Drylanders aboard *Lingvaas*," he concluded. "Evidently some of those who did not place themselves under Kertovan protection when they were driven out of the Confederation serve other masters. This is neither new, secret, nor surprising.

"It is also hardly evidence that we need to worry about treachery from *Lingvaas*. Indeed, I forbid you to mention this to anyone except the Red Windflower."

Drojin frowned. "He will not be pleased."

"He does not have to be pleased, only obeyed. I trust that you have no doubts that I am his superior, and yours, and that I can give orders instead of merely making idiotic requests?"

"Eh—no."

"Good. Then I think I will ask you to remain aboard while I read through—"

I Hmilra had not finished the sentence when Drojin's hand darted inside his tunic. The commander acted with the instincts sharpened in the wrestling bouts of his youth and not quite blunted by the passing Greats.

He punched Drojin as hard as he could in the easiest part of his body to reach, which happened to be his chest. Then he hurled himself against the table.

It was light enough to topple from such an impact, and heavy enough to pin Drojin briefly. Long enough, anyway, for I Hmilra to snatch up the nearest heavy object, the empty jug.

He smashed it hard against Drojin's chest, hitting him there to keep him alive and maybe even conscious for a hasty interrogation. Unless Drojin turned out to have been simply suffering from a fever-induced fit, he would need that interrogation—plus several others, longer and as rigorous as necessary to learn what he knew.

Drojin screamed, and now his hand lunged inside his waistband. I Hmilra struck again as the hand emerged, and bone crunched. Fingers dangled limp, and a small two-shot pistol clattered to the deck. Then the door burst open, and for a moment I Hmilra was in more danger from being trampled to death by would-be rescuers than he'd been from Drojin.

It was then that I Hmilra realized that he'd never thought of calling for help. He hoped Alikili would never learn that—what she would say to his wrestling would-be murderers barehanded hardly bore thinking about.

Then he stood up, elbowed a clear space around him, and realized that he wasn't barehanded, either. He'd completely forgotten to draw his own pistol, a rather more potent weapon than Drojin's.

He pretended that the pistol needed examining, while the guards bound and gagged Drojin. By the he'd finished, his hands no longer threatened to betray him by shaking and the guards looked as if orders were long overdue.

I Hmilra took a deep breath.

"Confine him closely, and keep him alive at all costs. His name is Vuikmar Drojin, and he appears to be a traitor who fair-tongued his way into the service of our observers in Rinbao-Dar."

That was as much of the truth as anyone needed to know at the moment, and more than enough to keep wild rumors from spreading about the Fleet. Or at least to keep truth in hot pursuit.

The guards hustled Drojin out. Commanders and messengers remained behind,

I Hmilra reminded himself that being moderately clumsy in dealing with a murder attempt was no proof that his warrior's skills had wholly departed. Also, the shore party needed guidance, perhaps more help than he had expected.

"Have all ships beat to battle stations and make steam for getting underway. All boats not already ashore are to return immediately. Crews of those ashore are to join the shore party."

"Aye-aye, Captain," a commander said—I Hmilra now recognized the Weapons First. "*Lingvaas* has just got underway."

"Good. Send her in, no more than five hundred paces off our camp, steerageway, defend herself as required, otherwise wait for further orders."

These would come as soon as I Hmilra had changed his kilt and tunic, stained and rent beyond dignity, and had a few breaths to finish settling his jangled wits.

SEAN BORLUND CAREFULLY HID HIS RELIEF THAT RINBAO'S SPRAWLING market lay outside the city's walls. Those walls were ten meters high, thick enough nearly everywhere to mount light artillery, and surrounded by a flooded ditch as well.

The only way in or out of the city was through the five Great Gates, each equipped with a fixed bridge and a pair of massive gates. The gates themselves would be vulnerable to medium artillery, but every one of them was commanded by two or three well-armed bastions. As for knocking down the walls themselves, the only way to do that without a regular siege would be heavy naval gunfire from the river—and there was no deepwater anchorage in the river out of range of the batteries of Dar.

As long as the two cities were nominally under a single reasonably competent government and their people remained loyal, nobody but the Empire of Alobolir could seriously contemplate taking them. Even the Empire could not readily afford the price in lives, matériel, and time.

Borlund was surprised at how quickly he reached this conclusion. Two Greats ago, he would have called himself a total innocent on tactics, strategy, and weaponry. He might even have exhibited that ignorance with a trifle of self-righteousness, in front of the right audience.

No more. The last two Greats had administered a heroic dose of reality, curing him of a great many conditions from which he had not known that he was suffering. While he served with the Fleet, he would no more give up his warrior's eye than he would resume going clean-shaven.

Borlund stopped in front of a set of six stalls selling rawhide (very raw, from the smell) and scratched his chin. Then he corrected himself. He would shave off his beard if he was going to spend much time in tropical climes. The itching under it had gone from irritating to unpleasant and he could already foresee its going on to unhealthy.

Ahead were the factors' tents, almost a small town in themselves. Anything not on display in the market (and the tribes had a reputation for being light-fingered, so quite a lot wasn't) could be ordered in any quantity available from one of the factors—for a price.

Borlund was profoundly glad that he had nothing to do with negotiating most of the prices. The Fleet Treasurer would handle that; Borlund would only be bargaining for a dozen or so items on *Lingvaas*'s requisition list as provided by Captain Weil.

He still wondered if anyone else would rattle his ears with the Yoshino "anti-Imperialist" line. He also wondered what they would say if they learned that he was halfway inclined to their views.

Borlund knew this inclination might be more habit than reasoning, as for nearly three generations the Drylanders had been leaning over backward to avoid being empire-builders. (Not that you could seriously do much serious empire-building when you were outnumbered at least five thousand to one and had only a modest technological edge.)

But it also made sense. Piecing together what he knew of human and Kilmoyan history made him suspect that empires had a short period of being assets and a long period of being liabilities. Post-Skyfall Kilmoyn had restored a great deal of civilization on a rather limited resource base. They didn't need new and complicated ways of wasting what they had. Even the Aloboliri ruled much of their vast (and sparsely populated) lands with a light hand, and might have long since fragmented but for the work of the temple engineers, the Hands of God.

A breeze blew past Borlund. It wasn't strong enough to cool his skin, and it brought a whole stew of new smells, including the wall's ditch. Even in the dry season Rinbao-Dar had enough rain to keep the ditch from breeding plagues, but no one had ever bottled its odor to sell for perfume.

Borlund stopped, waited until his two guards were in position with a clear view around them, and pulled out his handbook on Rinbao-Dar. Long-distance tourism being practically unknown among the Kertovans, it was more of a businessman's guide than anything else, but it did include a general-arrangement map of the markets.

Right now he needed the tinkers' and brassworkers' area. The second item on his list was something as mundane as a dozen new chamberpots. *Lingvaas* had received a crate of necessary vessels either rejected by or retired from the Fleet. Most of them had not survived the voyage south, and the sick berths were using the survivors.

Borlund's next thought was that the tinkers had come to him. The clattering and clanging certainly sounded like metalworkers hard at it. Then he saw the four-dilgao team swing around the factors' tents and on to the main road south.

The quasi-bovine dilgao needed a high-sugar diet that could only be easily supplied in the south, so Kertovans only saw it in zoos. But properly fed and with a trained driver, a four-dilgao span was the most efficient draft animals on Kilmoyn.

What these were efficient hauling was a fieldgun, one of the old models without recoil cylinders, but a five-liner at least. Two more spans of dilgaos followed, one with a wagonload of gunners and tools, the other with what had to be an ammunition cart.

Two more three-span gun teams followed, a full battery from what Borlund remembered. As the last one passed, a mounted messenger with half a dozen escorts cantered past, raising a storm of dust. As the dust settled a column of groundfighters came trampling along in the wake of the guns, high-peaked helmets pulled low over dusty faces and plumes already sagging from the heat. But their equally dusty jackets also sagged with ammunition, and the bayonets on their single-shot breechloaders were fixed.

Somebody was about to shoot and somebody else was about to be shot at. Or at least the Matriarchy intended everyone who watched to think so. Borlund wondered whose minds were the Matriarchy's targets, if they were not planning to shoot at bodies.

He stopped wondering when he heard the crackle of small-arms fire, distant but unmistakable. It quickly blended into a steady roll, then lost its identity entirely in a din of voices, drums, trumpets, bellowing and screaming animals, and even the pop of signal rockets.

It didn't surprise Borlund to see smoke billowing up from the area of the tribal camp. It surprised him even less when the Fleet Treasurer emerged from the factors' area with more speed than dignity.

Spotting Borlund as the nearest commander, the treasurer rushed up to him.

"Gather your Farers and prepare to withdraw to the water."

Borlund decided that the phrase "your Farers" had to mean everyone, Drylander and Kertovan, in the market.

"At your orders, Honorable," he said, then added a salute to which the civilian treasurer wasn't strictly entitled.

The treasurer beamed. Borlund dispensed with further courtesies, but drew his pistol as he moved to guard the treasurer's back. A quick gesture sent one of his own guards off to round up *Lingvaas*'s shore party.

chapter 18

The Farers who had been ordered or at least thought they had been ordered to defend the railroad bridge had to run most of the way. This was no easy work under the southern sun and carrying their weapons ready for action instead of slung for convenient carrying.

Even Ehoma Tuomitti had her doubts before they were halfway to their destination. Whatever was boiling over in the tribal camp and fair, the tribesfolk seemed to have the sense not to let it scald Kertovans. Stray bullets kicked up dust within pistol shot of the marching Farers, and occasionally a blood-freezing scream would make some younger Farer shudder and claw at ear-tufts, but that was all at first.

By the time they reached the station, however, all thought the caution justified. A mass of tribesmen seemed agreed on one goal: marching on the station. A handful of Rinbao-Daran Patrol and second-line soldiers seemed agreed on another: defending the station.

"Stay here and help us!" someone shouted from the ranks of the Patrol.

A Kertovan commander (Tuomitti couldn't tell identity, let alone seniority, but hoped that the voice had the second) shouted an impatient reply:

"We have to move to the bridge. Our orders are not to take sides."

Tuomitti thought then and long afterward that the commander might have left out the last words. They drew a growl totally lacking in warmth or pleasure from the station garrison. Tuomitti forced herself not to aim her pistol, then had to raise it to knock down some young fool's lifted rifle.

No one opened fire, but wisdom outran folly by a bare neck's length. Tuomitti wasn't the only Kertovan slow to turn her back on the station. Even after the waiting train stood between them and the garrison, she felt a prickling between her shoulder blades, as if her flesh was recoiling in advance from a bullet.

By the time they were halfway from the train to the bridge, the tribal brawling had raised such a cloud of dust that no Kertovan eyes could make out what was going on under the cloud. As far as Tuomitti could tell, the tribefolk might have given over fighting in favor of mass copulation—*and if they plough themselves witless, so much the better for the rest of us*!

The railroad bridge itself was iron frames on stone supports, carrying two pairs of rails and a wagon road across a dry wash and the stream that ran down the middle of it. Except after a heavy rain, one could cross the wash dry-shod, but even when its water ran barely knee-deep the stream's banks were two men high and nearly vertical.

Another commander's voice ordered the Farers into position. Someone with wits between the ears, too—both ends of the bridge were covered, and riflemen sent down to watch the stream for anyone trying to slip up on the bridge along its bed. Half the Farers were sent down into the shade and told to catch their breath and drink; Tuomitti was among these.

Looking up at the dark iron lattice of the bridge against the blue sky, she wondered if defending the bridge had some purpose. Or was it just an order that some commander had given to hide the fact that he or she didn't know what ought to be done, so the Farers would be put to work doing *something* until wisdom came—or vanished entirely?

Tuomitti rather hoped this was not so. Dying to do something useful could hurt just as much as dying to no purpose, but afterward you felt less foolish when you faced Lord or Lady.

She was almost asleep when she heard, far off, whips cracking, drums beating, and even the bugling cries of dilgaos.

JOSSU I HMILRA HAD COME STRAIGHT FROM THE MEETING WITH *VALOR*'S senior commanders to *Lingvaas*. What he saw (or rather, could not see) from *Lingvaas*'s deck persuaded him to hurry straight from her deck to the foretop.

Now he braced himself with one hand on the crankgun mount and held his binoculars to his eyes with the other. He could look over the dust cloud now shrouding the tribal camp, and if someone had been signaling from the walls of Rinbao he could have read their message.

As it was, he could see enough to confirm the shore commander's wisdom. At first he'd wondered what defending the bridge could do except perhaps involve the defenders in a fight with the tribes. Now he could see that the tribes were nowhere near the bridge—weren't yet doing more than glower at the station—and trouble wasn't going to come from tribes fighting the Kertovan shore party.

Not unless those retreating from the city had to swing well to the east, between the city and the camp. They wouldn't need to do that if they could use the bridge.

But to the west of the rails, Rinbao-Dar's groundfighters were deploying. Guns—more than one battery—and infantry to defend them while they swept the camp with sprayshot and explosives, then follow up with a charge to close quarters.

Assuming somebody wanted a massacre of the tribes, for some purpose that I Hmilra at this point could no more guess than he could fly to the shore by flapping his arms. (Drojin was still drugged into a stupor; the story given out was that he had fallen sick with brain fever and needed sleep. Six people in the whole Fleet knew the truth, and I Hmilra intended that to be all until the meeting with his Captains tonight.)

I Hmilra thrust the tribes to the back of his mind and contemplated the best way of getting his Fleet's people back from the city.

Anybody attacking the shore party's waterfront camp would be declaring themselves an enemy and making themselves a target for ships' guns—those aboard *Lingvaas*, to begin with, and soon everyone that could be brought to bear. But "accidents" were another matter—if the shore party came down the rails just as the Rinbao-Daran artillery opened fire. . . .

I Hmilra scrambled down the ladder so fast that his guards were still halfway up the mast when he approached Captain Weil. Her relief at seeing him safely on deck (which, he supposed, was where she thought one of his age belonged) was unconcealed.

"Captain Weil. Will you be safe here even at low tide?"

"I'm keeping steam up. I'd rather weigh anchor if a north wind gets up. That could push the water out a trifle, and we've barely an arm's length under the keel as it is."

"Good. You won't be alone if you have to start shooting, at least not for long."

"Thank you. We've taken ranges on three or four points well clear of our people. We could start hitting them straight off."

"Even better."

I Hmilra made the old gesture of pressing the backs of his hands one against the other—the sign of a lord to a sworn follower that the latter deserved well of his chief. *Barely a third of the way down her life course, Weil is bearing the same burden of command as I did* and *a mighty weight of responsibility for the future of her folk.*

I Hmilra's guards came up just in time for him to send them to get steam up in the launch. Weil looked a question.

"I'm going ashore," he said. "That's why I was concerned about your gunnery."

"Oh," she said. He saw no flinching, but heard it in her voice.

SEAN BORLUND WAS THE FIRST COMMANDER TO DECIDE THAT THE RINBAO-Daran troop movements were cause for rallying the Kertovan shore party. The others, however, were only moments behind him.

In a great flurry of shouted orders, beaten drums, and people running as if they had neither plan nor purpose, the shore party drew itself together. By the time the last gun was out of sight, some four hundred Farers, a hundred pack animals, and fifty-odd loaded carts and wagons had assembled by a grove of trees just under a thousand paces from the walls.

Less pleasant for Borlund was the discovery that he was second in command of the whole motley flock. Three of the four commanders senior to him, along with some forty armed Farers, had gone into Rinbao a watch ago, to visit Trade House, the Matriarchy's Delegate, and a few other places required by protocol. They were also supposed to be arranging for a state visit by Jossu I Hmilra and shore-leave privileges for less exalted Farers.

Whatever they might be doing, they were not coming out of the city. Borlund learned this moments before some gunners on the walls further ruined what little appetite he had left by opening fire in the direction of the tribal camp.

A good many Farers yelled that they were under attack, others dove for cover in ditches (usually damp and filthy) or behind trees (most of which would not stop a stout club, let alone a shell). A good many of the hired teamsters leaped out of their seats, hit the ground running, and did not stop running before they were out of sight.

By the time Borlund had (mostly) succeeded in calming down everyone who needed it, the new senior commander wanted to talk to him. She was a hard-muscled woman named Fija Skorbeen, above average height for a Kertovan (which meant that Borlund didn't have to address the top of her head when he spoke to her). In general she reminded him of Ehoma Tuomitti, if she'd been a commander from her early Faring days, and he found her easy to talk to.

"We wait a bit, I think," she said. "Those shots weren't for us."

"Did you see where they went?"

"Over toward the tribes. Couldn't tell if they were crankguns or some of those little two-line swivels. Probably laying down a no-cross line for the brawlers."

The guns might also have been laying down a no-cross line for people coming from the city, but Borlund decided not to argue. "How long should we wait?" he asked.

Skorbeen pulled out her watch. "Half a beat, I propose. Then we'll send a message in. Nothing else. If the folk here want to let our people go, they'll be safe enough with their forty guards. If they're to be kept in, we can't get them out with only eight thousand groundfighters and the guns of the Fleet. Not without a war with the Matriarchy, anyway, and I doubt it's my job to start one on my watch."

Borlund nodded. It was agreeable to see eye-to-eye with Commander Skorbeen. It was almost more so, to hear her speak to him as one commander sharing a difficult problem with another. Kertovan or Drylander, both were Farers with a burden of responsibility that they could lift more easily if they shared it.

"Good. Now, one of us had better go and find if we have any teamsters among our Farers. All the locals seem to have run off, and I'd hate to abandon all the wagonloads."

What they really needed, Borlund thought, was a drenching rain, to dampen everyone's ardor for fighting, reduce visibility for the trigger-happy, and make everything except hard-surfaced roads impassable to cavalry and artillery. Looking up, he saw that the sky promised no such gift, saluted, and went off to round up wagon drivers.

THE SHOTS BROUGHT EHOMA TUOMITTI RUSHING UP FROM UNDER THE bridge, pistol in hand. She measured the distance of burst with a practiced eye, then decided that nobody but the tribal brawlers and maybe not even they were the targets.

She was less sure about the guns to the west of the road. From where they were going into position, they could strike anywhere from the city walls to the shore, although not too accurately in the second direction. Even if they were aimed at the tribes, they were going to be firing over the road and the bridge, with Kertovans already where the shots would land, and more to come if the people who'd gone to market came out, as Tuomitti sincerely hoped they would—and soon.

Tuomitti also hoped that the tribes would know who was shooting at them if it came to that, and attack their real enemies. She suspected that was a vain hope, because the tribes would come boiling out of their camp in no mood to spare anyone in their path.

Against a mob of enraged tribesmen, Tuomitti had a pistol and twenty rounds, a boarding sword and clasp knife, a sun helmet, canteen, and bread pouch, and two whole field-dressings already impregnated with wound-cleaner. Also her hopes, and whatever favor her prayers and offerings at godhouses had given her.

Enough for a valiant last stand, of the sort thrilling to read about but not to be part of. She spat into the dust and her lips twisted in a wry parody of a smile. She remembered a time when someone of thirty-eight seemed so old that she'd thought being dead was better. Now she'd seen thirty-nine Greats flow by, and she desperately wanted to see many more.

JOSSU I HMILRA RAN BACK TO THE GANGWAY AND SCRAMBLED DOWN INTO his launch fast enough to leave Captain Weil tight-faced and pale. Then the launch cast off, smoke already pouring from its funnel, and thrashed toward the shore.

Once ashore, I Hmilra had to slow his pace. He could not leap into the saddle of the nearest ariyom and ride off to save the rest of the shore party for two reasons. He had to observe the camp's situation, listen to its commander, and read any messages received from farther inland.

Also, it was fifty commons since he'd last ridden. A dramatic leap onto any riding beast's back would likely end in an ignominious tumble off the other side, injuring dignity or more.

The camp commander approached and saluted.

"We're in a state of defense, Lord. All posts manned, ammunition either issued or secured, and double lookouts for sun-mirror signals."

Someone behind the camp commander coughed, spat out dust, then looked at I Hmilra. The Farer's eyes had a quality of desperation in them, such as what I Hmilra remembered seeing in the eyes of the last few stokers out of a flooding engine room.

"Yes, Farer?"

"Ah—the city party—the ones who went all the way—don't have a sun-mirror."

I Hmilra counted to eighteen before his fury could find words. The commander flinched. So did the messenger. I Hmilra was obscurely glad of that. It made it less likely the second Farer had spoken up to advance a feud.

I Hmilra ran out of colorful phrases about the commander's ancestors and took a deep breath. "Where is the farthest sun-mirror, and do you have another mobile one?"

"At the bridge, and no."

The commander's stern face made it plain that he would not accept blame for the missing sun-mirror. Perhaps he didn't even deserve it; that could, in any case, be settled later.

The heavy thump of a naval gun forestalled a further explosive reply from I Hmilra. A moment later the tearing-canvas cry of the flying projectile clawed a path across the sky, ending in another, more subdued thump.

I Hmilra started for the watchtower, but the lookouts were as alert as their duty required. One shouted down to the commanders:

"Some of the tribals were pushing over toward the railroad station. *Lingvaas* fired a shell, but it didn't explode."

That was probably just the way Captain Weil had planned it. Pulling the fuse from a shell before firing it made for a good, harmless warning shot, since the conical shells would dig in instead of rolling like the round solid shot.

"*Lingvaas*?" the commander asked. His eyebrows rose and his crest seemed to be twitching.

I Hmilra wanted to reach out and smooth the twitching crest, as he had with his children when they were no taller than his waist. The commander seemed as far beyond his limits as a child alone in the dark.

"Does that make you uneasy?" I Hmilra asked, softly. He himself was uneasy over the commander's not noticing what ship was assigned to direct support of the camp, but that was yet another matter for later discussion.

"It is hard to feel otherwise, with the rumors—"

I Hmilra cut the other off with a raised hand, opened his own mouth to speak, then chose silence.

If he cursed the commander again the man would have no authority left. The commander's friends would also question I Hmilra's reasons, wondering aloud if he had done this out of fondness for his pet Drylanders.

Within the Fleet at least, everyone had carefully steered around the minefield of the loyalty of the Drylanders. Making more of this matter would be setting a course straight into it, while expecting the Lord of the Waves to watch out for fools.

Neither I Hmilra's parents nor his teachers had raised him to behave that way. He took refuge in a manner so rigidly formal it might have been cast in steel.

"I wish enough mounts for myself, my four guards, and a guide. I wish to go forward as far toward the city as safety permits. Please have messengers ready to ride if you receive any signals from the Matriarchy or from our people within Rinbao."

It had not been necessary to ask if the delegation had safely left the city; the silence and the strained looks spoke clearly enough. The closer to the city, the more likely it was that someone would know at least where the delegation was.

I Hmilra spent the rest of the time before the ariyoms arrived doing mental calming exercises. These worked well enough so that he found the stirrups on his first try, and a firm seat in the lightweight saddle on the second.

That was a much better effort than usual, for his first time back in the saddle after a long break from riding.

BY THE TIME THE COMMANDERS DECIDED IT WAS TIME TO MARCH, THE KERtovan market party had risen above chaos without reaching the level of order.

They had most of their essential purchases, thanks to several-score Farers who *said* they could drive wagons, lead pack animals, or carry critical items in improvised backpacks or on shoulder poles. Some of the bearers were too heavily loaded to handle weapons, so they left these in the carts and distributed the ammunition among the guards on the flanks.

This left forty or fifty people nearly helpless if somebody *did* get inside the column with as much as a Gurtagi skinning knife, but Borlund had long since given up hope of guarding against every danger. He was only trying to pick the most critical ones, instead of leaving matters to chance.

There'd been no rain, and the day seemed to have grown hotter as it dragged on toward evening. Certainly the last trace of breeze from the water had died, and every step by Farer or beast raised dust that seemed to hang in the stifling air until someone came along to breathe it in and add another layer to the hair of nose, mouth, lungs, and eyes.

Borlund used the last of his water to moisten his kerchief and wipe the dust out of his eyes, then looked south toward the cliff-crowning fortresses of Dar. Was it just his imagination, or were figures moving on housetops and—much more disquieting—around the gun pits?

Another moment's standing and staring into what in a decent land would already be twilight told Borlund nothing. He shrugged and quickened his pace, relentlessly putting one foot in front of another, passing sagging bearers and pack animals with their dust-yellowed tongues hanging out and saliva dripping onto the road, until he was back at the head of the column.

The bridge was in sight now, barely a kilometer away, and the road to it was clear. Not clean—discarded clothing, the odd glinting cartridge, and even a body showed where the tribal fighting had briefly spread onto the road. But no obstacles, and figures in Kertovan garb standing on the bridge already waving—

A Rinbao-Daran trumpet let out its high-pitched cry and found echoes. Borlund jerked his head right and saw some of the troops he'd seen earlier coming out of the city. Many more seemed to have joined them on every patch of high ground that offered a good field of fire. Below and between the clumps of groundfighters were crewed guns. A few of them were much larger than anything Borlund had seen earlier.

When the Rinbao-Daran troops opened fire, they would sweep the whole stretch of road between the bridge and the head of the column.

They could sweep anything on the road at that moment into oblivion.

Why the troops had been ordered into this position didn't matter, nor did what other orders they might have received.

Behind his back, Borlund made a Saadian good-luck gesture, left thumb between the first two fingers. Then he pointed at two of his Farers.

"You! Run back to the First Gun and ask him to halt the column. You can describe the situation; bring back any orders."

Another finger stabbed at a second Farer. "Run and unload one of the pack animals, or unharness a wagon team. Somebody's going to have to ride up to those people and ask what's going on."

Both Farers and several others followed Borlund's gesture with their eyes.

"What about somebody riding to the Fleet and telling them to blast those sons of stingfish if they sneeze?" a Farer called.

Borlund pretended to laugh. "In this dust, anybody could sneeze. Better wait until they start shooting."

But how long would that be?

Not long at all, he judged, as three more guns rolled up, unlimbered, and went into position. A detail of groundfighters surrounded a wagon, formed a living chain, and began passing ammunition to the newly arrived battery and two others.

The second Farer returned, with the sorriest-looking ariyom that Borlund had ever contemplated riding. It was docile enough to need no saddle, but so swaybacked that Borlund's boots nearly reached the ground.

He'd just persuaded the beast that lying down and rolling to crush him would accomplish nothing when the first Farer returned.

"Commander's orders—we are to proceed as before. Halting would make it look like we were cooperating with the local grounders against the tribes."

Borlund looked and saw that where it was the column gave the Rinbao-Daran artillery a clear field of fire against the tribes. He realized that he must have spoken aloud when the Farer replied.

"Don't know, commander. But Old Lady Skobeen was really stiff about it."

Walking onto ground beaten by that much firepower might make a lot of other people of both races even stiffer, as they lay dead, mingling their blood in the dust. Borlund agreed with the commander in principle, as he'd grown even more suspicious of what might lie behind this oddly timed tribal riot or whatever you wanted to call it.

He did not agree that a wholesale slaughter of his people was a necessary mark of neutrality and good faith. If somebody was going to be slaughtered, it ought to be a single person, far enough ahead of the rest so that his or her death would be a timely warning.

Borlund realized that he'd been thinking of this move ever since he ordered up a mount. He'd even decided on the single person. It had to be a commander, and that meant him or Skobeen. Being a Drylander would earn him more attention, apart from his being able to reach the spot more quickly.

If the Rinbao-Darans did kill him it would prove the Drylanders' good faith and loyalty to the Fleet. If they didn't, he stood a better chance of learning about human activities in the south—not that he knew the local language, but he could always keep his ears open, listening for Kertovan speakers or reliable translators.

Now it was time to move, before too much analysis of the course of action he'd already chosen made him regret his choice and hesitate to act.

Borlund wheeled his sorry mount to the right with the pressure of his knees, then unstrapped his knife from his belt, sheathe and all, and prodded the beast with the end of the leather. It said something probably unprintable in its own speech, and lurched into a trot toward the bristling heights to the north.

EHOMA TUOMITTI DIDN'T KNOW IF SHE WAS THE FIRST TO SEE THE APPROACHING riders, but thought she was the first to draw a weapon. Her reasoning for that gesture was simple: no sun-mirror signals meant no proof they were friends.

She was ready to go one step farther and fire a warning shot, when the riders slowed and she recognized the most awkward of them. The Fleet Commander had come out to inspect the outposts. She thanked Lord and Lady that she hadn't fired that warning shot, which could have spilled the commander in the dust.

Tuomitti decided that while she was on duty (as was everyone, since the shot from *Lingvaas*), her position as a watch chief required her to know immediately what was going on. So she slipped toward the end of the bridge, where the riders dismounted and the commanders of the bridge garrison came up to meet them. She ended up close enough to hear, but not so far from her position that she couldn't watch her own people.

"All seems well," I Hmilra began. "I commend your sense of duty. Have you received any messages that you did not choose to send?"

This drew blank looks. I Hmilra seemed to sigh. Then he continued.

"Who saw most clearly the fall of the shot from *Lingvaas*? They intended it to be a false-fire by way of a warning, in case you've doubts."

Tuomitti hadn't doubted that *Lingvaas*'s gunners knew when to slaughter and when to scare, and hoped that the commander's words put no doubts in minds where there'd been none before. Sometimes, though not often, the best way to deal with a mystery was to treat it as a simple, common matter until people grew bored with trying to find something complicated or unusual in it.

A watch chief Tuomitti didn't know spoke up.

"The tribesfolk did seem to be getting on their bold shirts," he said, "but the shot changed that right off. Some of them didn't run right away and we thought they might have taken rocks or dust where it hurt. But they all got up in time and ran back to their friends."

"We owe *Lingvaas*'s gun crew a few gifts for that," I Hmilra said. "My orders are for you to hold the bridge until our people from the markets join you. We will then be out of the way of the local groundfighters and too strong for the tribes to attack, and can return safely to the camp."

"What about our people in the—?" a commander began. He broke off as I Hmilra stiffened in his saddle, nearly sliding out of it. The commander raised his binoculars, and Tuomitti would have given a foot for a half-height's better vantage to let her see it as well.

I Hmilra dropped his binoculars, drew his pistol with one hand, and gripped the reins of his mount with the other. Tuomitti supposed he didn't ride much worse with one hand than with two, and perhaps some of those tribal bodies weren't as dead as they looked.

"Our people from the market are coming on, the local forces look ready to fire on the tribes over or through our ranks, and someone is riding out from the column." He dropped the reins and raised his binoculars again.

"The one riding out is a Drylander."

"Damned fool," came from several throats, but not loudly, and even straining her ears Tuomitti didn't hear anyone doubting the Drylander's loyalty. She wondered if it was Sean Borlund—the Lord of the Waves seemed to have made him so that he was given to that sort of gesture.

Then nobody could hear anything for a moment, as I Hmilra and his guards heel-spiked their mounts and rode from the bridge in a cloud of dust.

SEAN BORLUND WAS A THIRD OF THE WAY TO THE RINBAO-DARAN POSITION before he'd decided what to say to them.

In the simplest terms, it was that the market shore party wanted to pass in peace, without taking sides in the confrontation. The faster they were allowed to march clear, the less they would be interfering with either side. He himself would be prepared to remain as a hostage for his people's quick passage and neutral conduct.

Another third of the way, he spent weighing his chances of carrying out this plan. He decided that he wasn't likely to be killed outright; shooting either parley parties or Drylanders could be a chancy business. As for finding someone who spoke Kertovan, that was the second language of virtually every educated Rinbao-Daran who had not learned the southern dialect of Alobsi, the common tongue of the Empire.

How educated were the people responsible for this situation, Borlund didn't know. But he had long since learned that a high level of formal education was compatible with a low level of common sense. If the world proceeded in any other way, his own problems with the Study Group and its Directorate would never have arisen.

The last third of the way, Borlund concentrated on keeping his saddle and dignity, and making sure that everyone saw his empty hands.

He succeeded well enough that when he rode into the infantry positions, groundfighters swarmed out of firing pits and from behind boulders and bushes to crowd around him. They mostly had new if dirty Imperial-made single-shot breechloaders and new and filthy boots, but their uniforms were as ragged as their discipline.

Their commanders called them to order quickly, with explosions of oaths that would have made Ehoma Tuomitti envious, and blows with fist and stick that would have appalled her. Borlund was making such copious mental notes of the state of the local army that it was some time before he realized that one of the commanders was standing beside his mount, trying to get Borlund's attention.

"Who in the name of the River Spirits sent you?" the commander asked, in heavily accented Kertovan. The commander appeared to be male, and he wore a modern uniform tunic over more traditional southern-style short, baggy trousers. He also wore boots and a belt with not only a sword but two pistols.

Borlund saluted. "Honored commander, I come on an affair of peace."

He spoke as formally as he could, slowly enough to be understood but (he hoped) not so slowly that he would seem to be condescending to the uncouth southerner. The Kertovans had bad habits in that direction, one reason why Imperial sympathies had been gaining ground in the south during the last generation—or so rumors ran.

Two things seem to run in war, Borlund decided. *Bowels and rumors.*

He explained the desire of his people to leave the area without harm to either side, as they had no quarrel with either. Also, they did not wish to endanger the negotiations now in progress within the city between the commanders of the Fleet and the representatives of the Matriarchy. (Borlund puffed up the phrasing of that last point like an observation balloon, until a listener might have thought half the Matriarchs and half the Republic's Senate were meeting in the holiest of the Mother's temples to devise a way to universal peace for the next ten generations.)

He himself would be quite happy with peace between the locals and the Fleet in and around Rinbao-Dar, for a watch or so, or as much longer as needed to get the commanders and guards to safety.

At least he kept his audience's attention, from commanders on down to music-boys (most of them looked male, anyway). When Borlund had finished, his throat was dry, the breeze seemed to have revived a trifle, and the column was still moving down the road. If the Rinbao-Darans opened fire now, at least the head of the column would be massacred.

Of course, the only reason that was not true for the tribes as well was that they had no artillery. (Or at least they had shown none. Borlund remembered an adage from *The Book of the Soldier*: "Invisibility is not the same as nonexistence.")

"Is this all?" the commander asked.

"All that is within reason," Borlund replied. "We ask you to face no dangers—"

"What if it is the tribes who shoot first?" the commander asked. His fingers (with tinted but field-short nails) tapped a monotonous rhythm on the polished butts of his pistols.

"We are under orders to defend ourselves," Borlund said. "We would have that right and duty even without orders. The tribes or anyone else will pay for any harm they do us."

The commander looked—"dubious" seemed a polite way of putting it. Borlund couldn't help sympathizing. In the same position, he would probably look worse, particularly if he had (as he suspected the commander had) no clear orders about what to do to anybody except the tribes with the imposing forces under his command.

Borlund decided to make a gesture of trust by dismounting. He bent forward—and, as he did, something went *wheeeet* past his head.

A bullet.

Borlund turned his forward bend into a tumble that brought him down on top of the commander. The man gave a half-stifled yell of protest mixed with pain, then quieted as another bullet whipped overhead. The third time, Borlund listened for the shot, heard it, and heard instead the solid *chunk* of the bullet sinking into flesh.

Ariyom blood sprayed over him, as his mount reared with a bubbling scream. It reared again, spraying more blood from its gaping throat, then collapsed on its side and very nearly on Borlund. He rolled clear, then roughly pulled the commander after him.

By now enough city groundfighters had realized, however dimly, that somebody was shooting at them. Fortunately, the artillerymen (who seemed a good deal better trained) kept their eyes and their muzzles pointed front. But from every infantry unit, bullets began to fly.

Borlund raised his head, tried to peer over the fallen animal and the half-panicked groundfighters to see if any of the bullets were hitting his comrades, but couldn't make out any details. At least the column was still marching, although he thought some of the guards on the near flank had unslung their rifles.

A long burst of firing, a score of rifles shooting so close together that they sounded like a crankgun in action, made Borlund flatten himself again. If he could have dug a firing pit with his nose, he would have done so. He was frightened, frustrated at the apparent failure of his mission, embarrassed at the thought of dying while looking like a fool, and eager to get his hands around the throat of that unseen rifleman.

Not to kill him outright, of course—he had secrets to reveal first. Just to remind him not to make a fool of peacemakers.

It was then that shouts joined the shooting and made Borlund raise his head again. It was a moment before he believed that what he saw was real, and decided that five mounted Fleet Kertovans really were riding toward the column.

One of them even had a sword in his hand.

JOSSU I HMILRA RODE THE LAST FEW HUNDRED PACES WITH HIS SWORD rather than his pistol in his free hand. It was more traditional for grand gestures, and tradition aside, it also looked less threatening. A pistol could kill from a distance, a sword less easily.

He even contrived to holster pistol and draw sword without dropping either one, falling off his mount, or even losing control of it. This was more good fortune than good riding as the shooting began only just before he finished the exchange of weapons. Moments earlier, it would have made him a most undignified and dusty figure.

As it was, he flicked his sword over his head, in signal to his guards. All five ariyoms hastened from a slow walk to their faster, sidling trot, hard on the teeth and buttocks but covering ground a good deal faster.

It was when smoke puffs told of the infantry opening fire and faint *wheets* told of bullets coming I Hmilra's way that he wished that some of the dreezans had been unloaded. But, then, after the voyage south they were hardly more likely to be in shape to gallop than these dubious mounts.

He kept his heels still and his head erect, as he and his guards closed the distance to the Rinbao-Darans. Mostly Rinbao infantry, he saw, with batteries of the Matriarchy's gunners (drawn from the best of both cities) interspersed among them; everything needed to slaughter anything within their field of fire, either the Fleet column or the tribes.

The Fleet column was coming on with admirable discpline. Whoever had ridden into the local ranks had not ridden out, but a flurry of action in the front line might tell of his present position—pray to all Powers, not his death.

The tribes had drawn back, leaving a space some five cables wide littered with much more debris but few bodies, and most of those were still moving. It was hard to tell if the chiefs had taken the feudists and brawlers in hand yet, but it was easy to see that placed where they were, the tribes had only three choices.

One was a parley with the Matriarchy. Some among the tribes would rather die—enough to bring on a fight. A second was a death-or-freedom charge, certain to bring death rather than freedom even if it didn't involve the Fleet column and force it to fight on the side of the Matriarchy in self-defense.

The third was for the tribes to swiftly and thoroughly learn the art of swimming.

I Hmilra flicked his sword again. One of the guards raised the truce flag, a golden harp on a black field, and began waving it. The sacred truce flag implied conceding superiority to the people one was approaching, but it also imposed on them a rigorous obligation to stop shooting at those under the truce flag.

The first response to the flag was further scattered shots in all directions. One of them plucked a guard out of his saddle like a small child snatching a cake. He landed on his back, rose with one arm dangling bloody and useless, but cursed too fluently to be mortally hurt.

The truce violation was enough to send the Matriarchy's commanders running about among their people, urgently trying to restore discipline. They knocked up rifle barrels with swords and halberds, snatched weapons from stubborn hands, and generally threw their own ranks into such confusion that if I Hmilra had been leading five hundred mounted fighters instead of five he could have broken the Matriarchy's infantry in moments.

He would also have died soon afterward as the guns swung about and opened fire. On the walls or in the field, the Matriarchy's gunners had stood between their cities and disaster at least seven times that I Hmilra had read of. They took pride in their craft, and knocked that pride into any laggard who remained in their ranks more than a single Great.

To diminish both the confusion and the target he presented, I Hmilra slid out of the saddle and completed his approach to the lines on foot. Two of the guards went with him, leaving a third to act as mount-holder and take care of his wounded comrade.

The Fleet Commander's eyes had not deceived him. The rider from the column was a Drylander—Borlund of *Lingvaas*, to be precise. He was an appalling sight, covered with so much blood that I Hmilra was astonished to see him alive and standing.

Borlund shook his head. "Not mine, Lord. If you wouldn't take it amiss, I'd like to see you in a firing pit before I say more. We've taken long-range shots from the rear, which is what started the firing."

From the look on their faces, the three Matriarchal commanders in earshot both understood Kertovan and agreed with Borlund's sentiments. I Hmilra allowed himself to be led to a gulley, which turned out to be proof against rifle fire from nearly all directions but also filled with crates of rifle cartridges and artillery shells.

I Hmilra felt an obscure sense of grievance at this choice of location. He badly wanted to light up his pipe, if only to give his hands something to do while his mind weighed and rejected various approaches to the situation.

As it was, Borlund spun out his account of recent events until I Hmilra had his thoughts in order and the Matriarchy's commanders had begun to fidget. When the Drylander was done, I Hmilra stood up.

"Have you done anything to capture the snipers?"

The city commanders looked insulted, and the first one to start talking had the least command of Kertovan. Fortunately his comrades helped, as did I Hmilra's modest knowledge of the local language. (Time to search out other speakers of Southern Alobsi in the Fleet; at this rate they were going to be needed in swarms.)

Apparently the shots had come from so far back in the scrub growth on the low hills to the north that a thousand could comb the ground for a whole common without much chance of finding even a trace of the snipers. Or so the commander said, and from the maps and I Hmilra's memories, they probably told the truth.

"Very well," I Hmilra said. "As Fleet Commander, I declare that we have no serious grievance with the Matriarchy over these shots. We will accept blood-money for the Farer wounded by the wild firing."

The commanders had just time to look relieved before I Hmilra continued.

"This is, however, on condition that we receive unmolested passage for the column to our camp on the shore. Also, that the Matriarchy guarantees the safety of our folk within the city of Rinbao, which they entered lawfully, with full diplomatic rights, and by written agreement sworn and signed in the sight of all gods and holy ones by those having the right to swear and sign for both sides."

I Hmilra contrived not to yield to a coughing fit after uttering the entire last sentence without taking a breath. Borlund and the guards looked as if they wished to applaud.

The Matriarchy's commanders looked less pleased.

"We can hardly halt everything else we have in hand to bring your people out of the city!" the commander who appeared senior growled. He (or maybe she, inside a shapeless tunic but with elaborate earrings and a fertility tattoo on one cheek). "Could you promise the same, in our situation?"

I Hmilra made an emphatically negative gesture. "No, nor are we asking it. We only ask that none of our people be put in danger by the crisis in the Matriarchy's relations with the tribes."

"Are you breaking off negotiations, then?" a younger commander snarled, drawing glares from his (definitely his) associates.

"What are we negotiating, besides the amount of time spent on ceremonial?" I Hmilra asked. "If you wish our people to continue these discussions in a city about to be surrounded by a battlefield, and think this is useful, please say so. But I assure you in the strongest terms that we disagree with any such—conclusion."

He wanted to say "folly," as he had wanted to use "massacre" about the Matriarchy's plans for the tribes. He had avoided both. He might be able to go on containing his impatience with the Matriarchy for all of another beat, if he was lucky.

"I suggest that I order our Farers in Rinbao to proceed to the Water Gate, and at the same time order a vessel of ours upriver to the gate. It will proceed under a truce flag, load our Farers, and return at once to the bay."

I Hmilra caught looks passing among the commanders and raised his voice. "I realize this will interfere with the guns of Dar, which are being placed as we speak, from firing on the tribes. However, I am sure there will be no danger to anyone from that necessity.

"There will be more danger than any of us cares to face, if we begin shooting at each other through either malice or mischance."

The commander looked as if he had no quarrel with that proposition. Before he could voice his agreement, half a dozen groundfighters ran up, half-carrying, half-dragging one of their comrades. A score of people all around promptly raised weapons, and were just as promptly cursed into silence by the senior.

I Hmilra could not follow all the cursing, but had the feeling that the senior was relieving a good deal of frustration on the hotheads.

Finally silence returned, and the groundfighter (with a blood-soaked bandage on his thigh and another across his belly) was allowed to speak. He was half-dead from loss of blood and half-mad with pain, but with a courage that I Hmilra had to respect, he forced himself to tell the story of getting a clear view of one of the snipers.

It had been well to the rear, deep in the bushes, and indeed beyond what the fighter had thought was rifle shot. Unless it was one of those big telescope guns, but the weapon the sniper (if it had been the sniper) was carrying hadn't been more than half the right size.

"Looked like a toy, the fellow was that tall," the fighter said, in a burst of clear speech. "I think—ahhhh—think—it—he could have been—one of his folk."

The fighter jerked a thumb at Sean Borlund, and lost consciousness. I Hmilra was too busy ordering his churning thoughts to notice when life followed consciousness.

A Drylander, with a rifle shooting farther than any comparable weapon known to any of the three northern nations? Either one created interesting possibilities. Together they created real danger—possibly great danger, if added to intrigues among the Kertovan community in Rinbao-Dar and Imperial plots. None of which could be averted by anything done or said here today.

The primary task, the safety of his people, remained firmly before I Hmilra's eyes.

"I suggest that this makes it even more important for our Farers to leave the battle area," I Hmilra said, addressing the commander. "I would wish upon no one, not even a declared enemy, the burden of fighting with foes to the front and treachery to the rear."

"What will you do if we don't give safe passage?" the loud-mouthed commander said.

The senior (definitely female, I Hmilra decided) shot him a look which said that *he* might get safe passage to a prison cell if he opened his mouth again without orders. I Hmilra thought, however, that the question gave him an opportunity.

"We will leave the area regardless. Our Farers in the city will find a defensible house and remain within it until peace returns or they are overcome by sheer weight of numbers. Neither body will yield without resistance.

"If you open fire while we pass before you, then we may decide you are attacking us. Then we will have the right to extract our people from Rinbao by force.

"If the tribes open fire, we shall of course defend ourselves—and if we fight your enemies, how can you justify harm to our people in the city?"

"And if neither of you attacks, but our people in the city do not go free, we shall take appropriate action short of force, to secure their safety."

The commander looked at the sky, which had darkened with more than the passing of the daylight. Failing to find the answers she sought written on the gathering clouds, she appeared next to wish to extract them from the ground at his feet. Finally she stared at I Hmilra, then slapped the hilt of her sword.

Orders snapped out too fast and in too many different dialects for I

Hmilra to follow. But he understood that messengers and riding animals were to go up to Rinbao and bring out the northern folk, and that crankguns were to move out to the flanks of the present position, ready to fire both forward and back.

That made sense. A well-handled crankgun could equal the range of even some exotic rifle in the hands of a Drylander marksman, and keep his head down if not kill him. From the flanks, it could also hammer any tribal attack without hitting the Kertovans.

Now all they needed was luck or heavy rain—which would in itself be a form of good luck, at least for the Farers of the Fleet of the Island Republic. I Hmilra would wish good luck to others when his own people had all they needed.

EHOMA TUOMITTI KNEW SHE MUST HAVE BREATHED FROM TIME TO TIME while the column from the city marched to the bridge. She could not remember doing so, but the proof was there: she was alive.

She didn't breathe easily until the sun-mirror signal came that the launches picking up the Farers from inside Rinbao were safely downriver. By then it was nearly dark, any part of the sky not gloomy with night was gloomy with clouds, and the air smelled of rain.

All during the fading daylight, Farers had been leading pack animals up to the bridge and unloading heavy sacks, which they placed in pits dug under its supports. Then they filled in the pits—and all the while, anybody who wandered too close was sent scurrying away, and anybody who asked questions met tight-lipped silence.

Even an old friend and bedmate, a gunner watch chief from *Valor*, refused to answer Tuomitti. She then thought briefly of asking Sean Borlund, who had remained with a handful of Drylanders on watch over the bridge.

If his look was that of a hero, Tuomitti hoped she would be forever spared that splendid ordeal. Borlund had the look of someone who could barely answer to his own name, let alone any more complex question.

At last light and the work below the bridge were both done. Urgent signals, passed along silently with hands and shielded lanterns, pulled the last defenders from the bridge.

The nearest was three hundred paces from the bridge when firing broke out inland all along the tribal front and all along the Matriarchy's position as well. Tuomitti saw a commander she didn't recognize watching the darkness, binoculars raised and head cocked to one side as if listening.

Then Tuomitti heard it as well. Firing well out to the Matriarchal flank. Tribes, the horde of Drylanders rumor had placed in the scrub and hills, the lost Marines of Captain Tuusivi? A problem for both Matriarchy and Fleet, if the fighting spilled over toward the shore.

A problem, however, for which there was already a solution. Tuomitti saw the commander nod—then saw nothing for quite a while, as blazing white-orange light snatched away her night vision like a gale shredding a topsail.

The bridge heaved and the roadway bowed upward, twisting itself apart as it rose. Fragments of iron mingled with fragments of stone, both black against the eye-searing flame of the blast.

Then darkness returned, more complete than before, and after a while so did silence that was not from temporary deafness. The bridge lay in ruins, and no one could bring heavy equipment across the stream against the Fleet camp.

Tuomitti turned, and without waiting for orders, began to retrace her steps toward the camp and friends.

chapter 19

The commanders' hall aboard *Valor* was below decks and behind armor. The rain and the whine of the ventilating fans (about all that kept the cabin habitable, on this close hot night) fought off most other outside sounds. The speakers finished the work of making it impossible to tell how the battle ashore was going.

Not that the battle ashore was Barbara Weil's greatest concern. All of her people were safe, and Sean Borlund was even rumored to be due for a commendation—which she thought he richly deserved. The camp would hold, and the only shooting its garrison might have to do would be in self-defense—a right that reasonable folk on all sides would certainly concede them.

But not all folk were reasonable, and there was also the matter of what to do with the Fleet and the groundfighters whom the Island Republic had sent so far, to what seemed at the moment little purpose. It might be a sign of doubt in Jossu I Hmilra that the Fleet Commander had called this Council of Captains, but if so, he was not the only doubter afloat or ashore.

In such a Council, it was required that the Fleet Commander hear the voice of every Captain or the Captain's authorized representative. It was further required that each Captain or representative speak. Finally, it was required that after all Captains had spoken, they obey without further question any orders given by the commander. Anything else was mutiny.

One could not run a ship or fleet by committee, still less by democracy, but in the old days the Island Republic's fleet commanders had been only first among equals. The Council had grown up as a way of reconciling old custom with new technology.

The Captains spoke in order of seniority, which put Weil a long ways down the list of twenty-nine speakers. She was twenty-fourth, ahead of only two transport captains and two of the torpedo-carrier squadron leaders. However, most of the senior Captains had spoken briefly, in favor of intervening on one side or the other. Now Rytko Muisk was speaking at greater length in favor of abandoning the whole voyage to Eneh and returning home, to sail south at a better time. Weil would be the next speaker.

She realized that Muisk's proposal would never be accepted, but that she could do herself and *Lingvaas* a kind of favor by supporting it. This would prove her opposition to Kertovan Imperial expansion, a concept which seemed to have more than a few supporters—as well as more human opponents than the Yoshinos.

The Kertovans' apparent lack of Imperial ambitions had heavily influenced the decision sixty Greats ago, to link the fate of the human exiles to the future of the Island Republic. Not only would the humans not become Gods from the Sky, they would not become the tools of ambitious local potentates.

And now—well, it seemed that the folk of Kilmoyn would change on their own, however self-restrained the "Drylanders" chose to be.

"—the bloody feud between the Matriarchy and the tribes. However much blood may flow before it is resolved, none of it will be ours, and the total may well be less than it would be otherwise. Then both sides will be stronger, and neither will be our foe."

Weil realized that she should have been listening more closely, even while she was trying to come up with a sensible suggestion. Muisk was not much of a speaker, and that was a soggy peroration, but it was one nonetheless.

My turn now.

Fortunately I Hmilra chose to call a halt in the speaking, to allow the stewards to refill the water jugs and clear away the plates. Most of the biscuits and cakes departed uneaten; between heat and tension few had much appetite. Weil was one of the few who turned in an empty plate.

As she did, she realized that she hadn't worked so hard and sailed so far just to tamely turn and go home. She also hadn't done worked and sailed to become involved in a local war—for all practical purposes, a civil war.

Either would raise a good many questions among the Drylanders, and perhaps ignite that long-stifled brawl between the Study Group Directorate and its supporters and the rest of the Drylanders. That brawl would answer no questions and do little else, but it would surely leak many secrets—too many, with someone like I Hmilra watching. Not to mention other humans, with fewer resources but more knowledge of what to look for.

Those humans would also, most probably, have fewer scruples about playing Gods from the Sky. Or, situated as many of them were, aiding the Island Republic's enemies.

So what offered a middle course?

The Expeditionary Fleet itself was not of much consequence. This war would be settled on land. But the eight thousand Eneh-bound groundfighters the Fleet escorted could play a potent role in that land settlement.

Suppose the groundfighters were somewhere else? Back home would be much too far. If they were thoroughly occupied, somewhere else closer—as indeed they would have been, if they'd been landed *before* the tribes and the Matriarchy went to war. . . .

A tinny-sounding gong signaled the end of the break. Weil felt eyes on her even before I Hmilra rose and pushed the speaker's staff down the table. Eager hands carried it the rest of the way—too cursed eager, or so it seemed to Weil.

She swallowed, gripped the staff, and spoke.

"It seems to me that both sides ashore expect much of our groundfighters. But these good people have another mission, the one we brought them here to carry out.

"Our voyage to Eneh will not be complete, until they are ashore where we intended them. . . ."

RAIN AND THUNDER NO LONGER DROWNED OUT THE BATTLE SOUNDS, AT least at Ehoma Tuomitti's post at one corner of the camp. There were also fewer battle sounds to drown out.

The artillery was silent, except for an occasional flat thump as something—probably less than five lines, possibly a signal gun—went off. She heard plenty of small-arms fire, and from every direction—which suggested that either the two sides had become thoroughly mixed together, or that the tribes had more modern weapons than previously thought. Metallic-cartridge weapons could fire in wet weather; spark-ignition open-pan ones could be drowned out by a heavy dew.

Not that the Matriarchy's dubiously disciplined troops would be all that better off for their better weapons, in a sprawling, brawling night battle at close quarters. The tribes also had knives, swords, and curious long-handled, light-headed axes that they could use either mounted or on foot. At close quarters in the dark, against unseasoned troops soaked to the skin and muddy to the waist, Tuomitti herself wouldn't have minded using steel.

Time to go round the sentries. The corner post was a series of half-flooded trenches built around the last crumbling building of an old villa. On the soundest portion of the roof, a crankgun squatted behind sandbags. More sandbags hid riflemen, a mixture of Farers and groundfighters from the Seventh Bohoians.

In spite of her Farer's conviction that groundfighters were drawn from the weak-stomached and the palsy-fingered, she was glad to have at her side people who'd spent more time than the average Farer with a rifle in their hands.

By the time Tuomitti was half around the trenches (and from alternately wading and falling, wholly covered with mud), the rain had stopped completely. It was only a few breaths after this that she heard a voice calling from the darkness beyond.

At first it sounded like the dying bleat of a gyurok, sound without sense, and no telling what folk it might be. Then she heard what sounded like a Kertovan cry for mother, and a moment later an unmistakably Kertovan:

"Wounded—help. Hellllp—"

—mixed with gasps and moans.

Trap? Not necessarily. Half a score of Farers were still unaccounted for. Everyone hoped they would lie low until the fighting was done, then come in. Here, however, might be someone who had rushed matters.

No reason for her to do the same, however. Tuomitti made her way to the two sentries at the next bend of the trench.

"There's someone coming in—one of our missing, sounds wounded. I'm going out. One of you go and alert the crankgun crew. The other stay here, and be ready to cover me. Do you have a flare?"

The two sentries were groundfighters but not reluctant to obey a Farer who knew her business, which was more than could be said for some. One of them held up a hand-thrown stick-flare, with the igniter cord already hanging free, ready to pull.

"Good."

Tuomitti undid her boots and dropped her raincloak on top of them. This rescue would not take long if it succeeded at all, and she would need swiftness more than anything else.

The groundfighters slapped her on the shoulder as she put her hands on the rim of the trench, then vaulted and rolled into the open.

BARBARA WEIL WAS TRYING TO READ THE ATMOSPHERE IN THE COMMANDERS' hall as she finished her presentation. Splitting her attention between that and a fine flourishing conclusion, she ended up accomplishing neither. By comparison, Rytko Muisk had been an orator of historic prowess.

She poured herself a glass of water and made a great business of drinking it, to keep from having to raise her eyes and face the others around the red-covered table. A peremptory throat-clearing from another Captain finally forced her to move. That throat-clearing had the sound of an order, if ever one did.

To her suprise, she saw more than one slowly nodding head, and more than a few looks of deep concentration. That was as much approval as she had expected, and more serious consideration.

She also saw one or two looks that could be easily translated: "To the backrooms with Drylanders who dare dispute seasoned Farers." She was afraid to look at Jossu I Hmilra for fear of what she might find on his face.

Then Muisk spoke again, and she recognized his as the cleared throat.

"With permission, Farers?"

I Hmilra nodded, Muisk looked and saw no one disputing, and spoke.

He spoke at excessive length for a comparatively junior commander (in rank, if not age) taking the privilege of a second turn. Weil could not even remember afterward most of what he said, other than its being in her favor. This pleased her, but not to the point where she took much attention away from organizing her thoughts to deal with the inevitable questions.

She had spoken more or less off the top of her head. Many details remained to be filled in. If God (or some other source of power) was not in the details, her chance of carrying the debate certainly was.

Muisk finally sat down, as I Hmilra seemed to approach the moment of ordering him to do so. The last four Captains spoke, only one openly in favor of Weil's suggestion, but none of the others openly against it.

By then everyone else had their questions ready—and Weil was equally prepared with her answers.

Would the troops be safe, on the eastern bank of the Bhir River?

Unless the Empire wished a war, yes. The territory was claimed if not settled or held by Eneh. The Empire had never made any claim on it. Their marching into it in force would be a simple invasion.

Would Eneh consider the troops so far south a real means of support?

Probably. Certainly they would understand that the landing force could not sail up the Bhir, past the rapids and all the other obstacles, with the situation in the Gulf so unsettled. The groundfighters and the Fleet would have to be much more careful about locking shields and guarding each other's backs than the original plan had intended.

This might well be true. But what if the Empire had, as some said, shipping and men to seize the islands off the coast of the Matriarchy?

A force of groundfighters could stay behind to build and guard a base for a squadron of shallow-draft ships. From that base, launches, torpedo-carriers, and chartered local steamers could patrol the islands and warn of any hostile moves in time to bring the Fleet south again.

Why shallow-draft ships?

Because she thought (hoping that she remembered the charts accurately) that there were few deep-water anchorages and fewer still deep channels in the islands.

The next question about shallow-draft ships did not come in words. It came as a look of blatant hostility. Weil decided that she had no choice but a bold counterstroke.

"As to my reasons for wishing for *Lingvaas* to be one of the ships remaining here—yes, it has something to do with what my compatriots may be doing here.

"But in that, I am only obeying ancient customs of both Kertovan and Drylander, to say nothing of other civilized folk. If one's brother steals the dreezan of a friend, one helps the friend track down and punish the brother, replaces the dreezan as necessary, and helps clean up the stable.

"Also, I think my crew alone knows more about the likely habits and methods of our compatriots than the rest of the Expeditionary Fleet combined. I would prefer not to see that knowledge wasted.

"If anyone thinks it better than our knowledge be wasted than our loyalty be tested, let him say it to my face in plain speech. But do not be surprised if I ask satisfaction."

The challenge, technically illegal as it might have been, drew no reproof. Several Captains, including the original offender, sat bronze-faced. Others nodded, still others actually grinned.

Weil counted noses and sighed openly in relief. The skeptics were badly outnumbered, and no duel they forced with her would gain them much sympathy.

Of course, that merely presented them with a motive for treachery in the dark. But they were not fools; they knew that such treachery was treated as a capital offense in time of war.

She realized that she was becoming a trifle casual about deaths that were not hers or her friends'. Did this make her a warrior, as some would have it, or a monster, as the Study Group Directors and their allies might put it?

That question could wait until later. In the corner, a small printing press was already clacking, producing copies of the proposal for a formal vote. Weil hoped I Hmilra hadn't ordered the printing so fast that essential details would be left out and room for debate or even disobedience remain.

He had not. The ink was still wet on the paper, but everything was there. Seven thousand groundfighters north, to hold an enclave on the Bhir. A thousand with naval support to remain behind in the island off the coast of the Matriarchy, to observe and if necessary offer relief to the homeless and the hungry. The bulk of the Fleet to remain wherever it seemed most likely to forward its mission, the interests and neutrality of the Island Republic, and the revelation of plots against it by any and all persons of any or all lands.

Most of the Captains waited just long enough for the ink to dry a trifle more before signing. The junior captain collected the papers (with a wink to Weil as he passed by; he'd been the open supporter among the last four, no doubt because of the lively work it promised his hot-for-combat torpedo-carrier crews) and handed them to I Hmilra. He shuffled, counted, coughed, and rose.

"Nineteen to seven for Captain Weil's proposal. Do all consent to be recorded as having spoken?"

"Ayes" rose in order from around the table, some clearly reluctant, all audible.

"Then I declare this ordering of the Expeditionary Fleet to be lawful and binding. Let us commence the development of it."

"Development" meant filling in all the details, as Weil had

expected. She had not expected, until she came back from the head to find everyone waiting for her, that she would now lead the discussion.

Law and custom both made sensible this Kertovan version of the old saying "You kill it, you eat it," sensible. It also promised Barbara Weil a very long night.

THE EXPEDITIONARY FLEET HAD SAILED WITH AN ABUNDANCE OF SPIKEWIRE but unloaded none of it. Coils upon coils sat in the holds of the transports, rusting as the bilgewater trickled over them and doing the camp absolutely no good tonight.

Not to mention that there were too few trees to allow raising the older kind of barrier, of trees stripped of all but sharpened stubs of branches and piled every which way so that an attacker could not climb over or under them without making himself an easy target even for a boy with a slingshot, let alone riflemen and crankguns.

Ehoma Tuomitti had felt a trifle naked even in the trenches and now felt as if she'd left her skin behind and was crawling about the battlefield in her bones. At least the lack of barriers had one virtue: it was as easy to get out unpunctured as it was to get in. She could move a good deal faster with nothing to snag or stab her, only mud and bodies to impede her progress.

The wounded fugitive kept moaning intermittently all the while. Twice he was silent so long that Tuomitti lost her bearings, but she had the sense to lie flat and wait for the moans to begin again. The third time, she'd judged where he was, kept on crawling, and reached him just as he started moaning again.

It was indeed a male Kertovan, in Farer's garb (much muddied and shredded), and covered with so much blood that Tuomitti marveled he was still conscious. But consciousness did not mean in one's right senses, and the eyes that stared up at her seemed lacking all intelligence.

Tuomitti knelt beside the Farer, thanked Lord and Lady that he was not too big for her to carry for a short distance, and began looking for the best way to grip him that would not hurt him worse. She kept watch on his eyes while she did this, and it was those eyes that gave her the lifesaving warning.

They widened suddenly, the mouth followed, in what should have been a scream but came out a gargle and a hiss, and Tuomitti heard over that pathetic sound stealthy footsteps behind and to her right.

She half-vaulted, half-rolled over the wounded Farer and came up with her knife in hand.

"Owerigo!"

The single shrill tribal battle cry set off an eruption of sound. Someone shouted a curse, in Alobsi, Tuomitti thought, but in what seemed a Drylander voice. Someone else let out a wordless shriek and leaped forward with a spear held ready to thrust down into the fallen Farer. Tuomitti got inside the spearman's guard with her knife, sank it between his ribs, jerked it free, and thrust again to cut his throat almost to his spinal cord.

The night was heavy with blood-reek—then night faded before the light of hand flares, as the people in the trenches started igniting them. In the next moment a mortar coughed, and a more powerful bomb-flare burst high overhead. Then the crankgun in the bastion opened fire.

The bullet stream whipped just over Tuomitti's head, close enough to singe her fur. She wished she could make herself as thin as a sheet of paper—but then, she'd probably dissolve in the mud—

The crankgun chopped air again, and this time something more solid. A death-scream died away in a gurgle, somewhere beyond the edge of the light, a death-scream that could come from no Drylander. Tuomitti slid under the wounded Farer and began half-carrying, half-dragging him toward the left, out of the crankgun's line of fire.

That put her squarely in the path of a groundfighter squad lumbering out of the trenches, making more noise than mating dreezans and carrying their rifles so that if anyone tripped he was likely to shoot a comrade. Tuomitti could still have kissed the lot of them. Even when one of them stepped on her foot, he had at least the grace to apologize.

"I've our friend here," she said. "I think he was bait for a prisoner snatch." The groundfighters snapped into a circle, with her outside of it and rifles pointing in all directions, including back toward the trenches. Tuomitti cursed softly, and by judicious use of elbows and knees cleared the way to pull the wounded Farer inside the circle.

The dead spearman lay where he'd fallen, too close to the groundfighters for his friends to reach him. But more sounds came from the darkness, including once more a voice that might have been Drylander. That drew a blast of rifle fire, quickly drowned out by the crankgun, sweeping a wide arc all across its front and narrowly missing one groundfighter who stood up to get a better view.

Tuomitti and her squad chief both dragged him down, the crank-gun rattled again, the last flare faded, and silence returned to the camp perimeter. When it had lasted as long as a drinkshop might take to prepare a snack, the squad leader tapped his people on the shoulder, the two-tap signal that meant "Return to previous position."

Tuomitti had to hold one of the groundfighters back to help with the fallen Farer, but two others picked up the dead spearman on their own initiative, so Tuomitti was reasonably content with her work when she slid back into the trench, for all that she felt as if she'd been swimming in mud and smelled as if she'd been bathing in ordure.

The lot of the groundfighter, she decided, was not one she would willingly accept, even if she might know the work better than those paid to do it!

THE FIRING ASHORE BROKE OUT JUST AS BARBARA WEIL REACHED *VALOR'S* stern, to join the other Captains waiting for their boats to come around to the gangway and return them to their ships.

In dress uniform she couldn't carry her binoculars, and they wouldn't have been much use anyway. The mortar flares were lighting up the ground battle quite nicely for the camp, but *Valor* lay too far out to let the unaided eye make out much by flarelight.

One or two Captains suggested that they form their launches into a patrol force, sweeping the anchorage for hostile boats. More prudent voices spoke in favor of not giving enemies easy prey and friends problems with identifying targets. Weil sweated in silence, knowing that *Lingvaas* was likely to be the first target for any such enemies, lying as she did close inshore, immobile, and crucial to the defense of the camp.

The firing died, followed by the flares, and Weil discovered that the whole battle hadn't lasted as much as a single beat. The mixture of relief and alertness kept her silent until the launch carried her back to *Lingvaas*—where the relief vanished the moment she mounted the gangway.

Crouched in the shadows of the railings and the fore and aft gangway were nearly a hundred of the Matriarchy's people, mostly women and children, and with a look that would have told Weil they were refugees even without that. Fortunately Second Captain Sharil Kund was on hand before she could ask rude questions of those without answers.

In spite of Weil's impatience, Kund began his story at the beginning and only came to the refugees near the end. The fight on shore had been too short for *Lingvaas* to take any action, but he'd called all hands to battle quarters. All guns were loaded and the searchlights were fully crewed but not turned on, and two more boilers were coming on line so that the ship was at half a beat for getting underway.

"I also had Mr. Borlund turn out the landing party and get up steam in the launch. When no call for assistance came from shore, I put him to cruising around the ship to keep watch for torpedo attacks or swimmers with towed mines."

"Is that where the refugees came from?" Weil asked.

Kund nodded. The fighting ashore had moved inland but had not ended. Many tribal warriors had broken through the Matriarchy's lines on the left, and some had stolen boats and slipped upriver beyond Rinbao, undetected by the defenders of either city. Now they were rampaging among the villas, small farms, and factories outside the old walls of Rinbao. The paddle-steamer that Borlund found adrift was only one of several boatloads of refugees that had already set out, fleeing what seemed demon fiends let loose upon the peaceful of the world.

"We agreed to let them go if they left their ship for the night while we searched it for weapons. She's out there off the red quarter, and we have the sternchaser trained on her in case there's any funny business."

"Borlund and his people are aboard?"

"Yes, but they've got the launch with them."

That might help if the ferry began to sink suddenly, but if the search parties detonated a booby trap—

Weil shook from her mind a thought that seemed to make the still, hot night almost wintry. To finish the process, she gave Kund an edited version of the Captain's Council and its decision.

The Second Captain surprised her with a grin. "Good for you, ma'am, and even better for the rest of us. Empire-building's dirty work, and the less we have to do with it, the better."

Weil's tongue ran ahead of her brain. "You've been converted by Farer Yoshino?"

Kund took a pose of injured dignity. "Not in the least. Justice and morality are fine, but I'm practical. The Kertovans don't have the experience to build empires, and there aren't enough of us Drylanders to compensate for that. Better to let the Empire and the Confederation make enemies, then exploit that mistake."

Weil would not normally have let such cynicism pass without comment, but she was too tired. All she said was, "We'll want a commander's conference in my quarters as soon as everybody's awake. Meanwhile, feed the refugees, don't let them wander around the ship, and wake me up if Mr. Borlund reports anything unusual aboard the ferry."

"Aye-aye, ma'am."

SUNBRIGHTEN WAS ONE OF THOSE SULLEN, COLORLESS AFFAIRS THAT FRIGHTened the Farers new to southern seas. Sky, sea, and land all seemed to flow into one another.

Even Ehoma Tuomitti might have found it hard to tell up from down without the help of the smoke columns to the north. The fires set in the night's fighting were mostly still burning, and every so often a new dark plume would scar the horizon.

At least there was no smoke from Rinbao, save the usual grayness of wood-fueled forges at work, and an occasional white puff as someone fired a signal gun or let loose at some phantom of their imagination. Dar stood pristine on its bluffs, although the river was still dotted with boats, carrying fugitives one way and soldiers the other. (Tuomitti had even heard tales of working parties on barges, laying a boom loaded with mines across the river to keep out *everybody's* Fleet.)

She wrinkled her nose as a puff of breeze surrounded her with the reek of bodies left unburied in the heat for the best part of a day. She'd thought the caked mud from last night made her the foulest-smelling thing around; now she knew better.

Arms went around her from behind, even as she heard the footsteps there.

"Greetings and good health, hero."

She turned and thrust the palms of both hands against Zhohorosh's ribs.

"How so?"

"Did you or did you not go beyond the trenches to bring in one of our people? And in doing that, did you or did you not break up a night attack on our fort?"

"I hadn't heard the last part. Is this another of your jokes?"

"May my vital forces fail—"

"Swear by something that doesn't concern me so nearly, dear friend."

"May I be hairless if I lie."

"The last nakedness wouldn't improve you, but your mother must have loved you as a babe and I'd try to turn a blind eye as she did."

"I cannot express my gratitude."

"Express what brings you here, and you'll have mine."

It didn't take Zhohorosh long to explain, although Tuomitti knew he had to be leaving out a good deal of what he knew, let alone what the higher commanders knew and were keeping to themselves. *Lingvaas* staying here, with the rumors of Drylanders at work among the tribes (or the Matriarchy's troops, or the Seakin, or among little green folk left behind by a second, secret Skyfall) had to be part of *somebody's* deep scheme for learning the real nature of the Drylanders. She'd wager on it's being I Hmilra's notion, but not anything she couldn't afford to lose.

"What's to feed the groundfighters who go north?" she asked, at the end. "They'll be farther from the borders of Eneh than we'd expected?"

"They've a half-Great's rations to be unloaded with them," Zhohorosh said. "Or at least that's what's being put about. Might even be true, if this filthy heat hasn't rotted it.

"Even if it has, there's fish aplenty, fruit, game, and not many folk about to argue who eats what. Just as well, too. Brawling with the folk here or up north when we've still the Saadian problem at our back—"

Tuomitti raised a cautioning finger and strangled laughter at the same time. Zhohorosh might be no school-taught commander, but he had the wits not to pick more fights than he could handle.

He continued. "*Byubr*'s one of the stay-behinds, so. . . ." This had quite a list of consequences, including Zhohorosh's being chief over a new shore party to relieve all Farers whose ships were sailing north.

"We'll probably blow up the camp fortifications tonight and leave the mainland to the people with a taste for that sort of fighting," he concluded.

"Here I was hoping that my people would be on their way back to the ship, thanks to you."

"There'll be time," he said, grinning, then picking a clot of mud out of her crest. "After a bath, though."

She punched him in the ribs. "Don't worry about that, I'll just swim out to the ship."

From seaward a whistle sounded. She looked, and even without straining her eyes, she could see a string of flags soaring up to *Valor*'s masthead.

SOMEONE STINGY WITH EXPLOSIVES (BORLUND SUSPECTED I HMILRA) CHOSE instead to strip the camp of everything movable, then burn everything burnable, with a few drums of stove oil to hasten the fire. The foul smoke drifted offshore in the breeze and reached *Lingvaas* even at her new anchorage, to trickle below.

Borlund was trying to finish a sponge bath between fits of coughing when Barbara Weil walked into the bath chamber wearing a robe and a bath bag slung over one shoulder.

"My bath drain's blocked," she said. "An artificer's trying to work it clear with a worm-pusher."

"What about steam or air?"

"The engineers don't trust some of the piping," Weil said. She unslung the bag, took off her robe, and hung them both on hooks.

She wore nothing under the robe, and the sight of her nude was hardly a novelty to Borlund. However, he did not fight back a thought that had come to him a few times before—that Barbara—Captain Weil—looked better nude than clothed. Her solid-boned, well-fleshed build became bulky, almost squat, when fully clothed. With the clothing gone, a man could see the muscle tone, the firm *and* shapely breasts—

A cough interrupted Borlund's mental cataloging of Barbara Weil's anatomy. At first he thought the smoke was also getting to her, then he went hot all over at the knowledge of part of his own anatomy misbehaving, no doubt brought on by that anatomical catalog.

Not, to be sure, misbehavior under any and all circumstances, but certainly under any and all he could foresee with Barbara Weil. His bearer-partners might raise no more than eyebrows. Others would raise more, in the Study Group, among human conservatives in general, and worst of all, aboard *Lingvaas*.

Then Barbara Weil reached up, pulled Sean Borlund's mouth down to hers and kissed him. It was not a sister's kiss, either, and she followed it by running her free hand over his ribs and belly, almost down to the level of the offending anatomy.

Confusion replaced embarrassment. He would not allow it to become delight or anticipation, because nothing was going to happen now and the sooner all of his body got back to business and out of here, the better. But Barbara knew sexual etiquette as well as anybody he'd ever met, and her gesture under these circumstances had only one ultimate meaning according to that etiquette.

Borlund also had only one acceptable response (actually two, but the one that meant an unequivocal "never at all to the last days of the Universe" was the farthest thing from his mind). He returned the kiss thoroughly, then rested *his* free hand on her shoulder and let it drift lightly down over one of those suddenly no longer untouchable breasts.

He was grateful that she did not continue the kiss beyond that, or stand closer against him. Instead they drew apart, and Borlund was quite sure that it wasn't only his anatomy that showed signs of arousal or his breathing that was a little irregular.

"Actually, I wanted a bath and to talk to you about something else," Barbara said finally. She turned on the faucet and filled her own bucket, then tossed her sponge in the water. "I wanted to ask you to be *Lingvaas*'s shore-party commander."

"That's turning into my speciality, it seems."

"Do you have a problem with that?"

"Well, the younger Fleet commanders I listen to say it's not a common road to higher postings."

"They're assuming we'll run our Fleet the way they run theirs."

"What Fleet?" Borlund asked.

"Given time—" she began, then shrugged. "I suppose there are arguments on both sides. At least they're letting you listen, which can't be a bad sign."

She'd wetted her skin, which made it gleam subtly—and now desirably. She soaped herself, and as she did, she went on.

"The stay-behinds would have to garrison one island, preferably one with a high peak for an observation post. The assigned groundfighters would provide most of the garrison, although each ship would also be represented.

"The ships would also have to assign smaller parties, to embark in the shallow-draft vessels of the squadron—not just the torpedo-carriers; they burned too much coal and their engines were delicate—and patrol the rest of the archipelago."

"Looking for what?"

"Anything that might affect the Republic's safety or neutrality."

The whole Fleet of Kertova would be too small to make that thorough a search, Borlund pointed out, and Weil didn't contradict him. She did add that she'd picked him because he was experienced, popular, and unorthodox.

"Unorthodox?"

"Enough to match wits with whatever our—fellows—are up to."

Borlund was quite sure that he did not deserve that high praise, likewise that he couldn't get out of the job, and furthermore that if he'd asked to go where history was going to be made he couldn't have been given a better spot. Not that he had any desire to be part of history-making events, to be sure. But like the rest of the human population of Kilmoyn, he knew his people were too few and too close to the edge of survival to afford the luxury of always being somewhere else when events took an unexpected turn.

Which, when you think about it, makes two unexpected turns in one day. At this thought his eyes lingered on Barbara Weil and he fleetingly wished his hands could do the same.

Aloud, he only said, "I volunteer. I've always wanted to ride a torpedo-carrier."

"Good," Weil said, and began rinsing herself off with a clean sponge.

THE BURNED FLEET CAMP AND THE FIRES AROUND RINBAO NO LONGER smudged the sky. The Fleet was doing that, as funnels belched black and one ship after another reached the channel buoy and headed out to sea.

It was a scene out of one of those books of sea adventure written to make young ones wish to join the Fleet. With a southerly wind, some ships had even set sails, slack now but soon to be full-bellied. The battle flags and signal flags were already stiff in the breeze, and curls of foam grew even where no prow cut the water.

Jossu I Hmilra rested a hand on the railing of the flag bridge as *Valor* reached the point of her turn. It was a relief to be outward bound again, even for a voyage of three or four Tides at most. It was even more of a relief to be bound for the completion of the Expeditionary Fleet's original mission—if that was still possible—without running aground on the Matriarchy's brawls and intrigues.

If Alikili's last letter was true, he would receive some honor even if nothing came of completing the voyage to Eneh. He had no difficulty conjuring up words that he'd read a dozen times.

> The ones who call themselves "the best sort" seldom call on me. But our servants and their servants are busy folk indeed, and much passes between them.
>
> By what I am told, these people have more confidence in you than they would in most other Fleet Commanders. They believe you love action at sea so greatly that you will steer past anything which might draw you into shore fighting.
>
> Of course, this overlooks the fact that we have no declared enemies in the south and none of them have any seapower worth the name. Also, that when the day comes for the Fleet to uphold the Republic against the Empire or the Saadians (whom these folk sometimes speak of in one breath), it will hardly do so by great battles on the open oceans.
>
> However, folly in some has often left an opening for the wisdom of others. May it be so in these circumstances, is my most earnest wish, next to your swift, safe, and honorable return. . . .

I Hmilra laughed too softly to be heard above the churning bow wave and the rumble of the engines. "The power behind the throne" was a name sometimes given in the chronicles to rulers' lovers. So far no one had been so minded to apply it to Alikili.

He would not be surprised if the day was not far off, however. Nor, in truth, could he deny that she had power—only that he had a throne, or that she was behind it.

It began to seem that making her an independent fortune, to keep peace in his family, was no longer necessary. A change in his opinion, which might well be assuming virtue to disguise failure, because the chances of bringing home much of a commander's prize-share out of this expedition had shrunk until one needed a powerful telescope to see them at all.

He also wanted to learn a good deal more about the servants' underground than Alikili could have dared to put in the letter. She had hinted in some past letters that a certain lady once rescued from Saadi Bay by Sean Borlund was still communicating with her; how to discreetly ask for more than a hint?

Time for that later. *Valor* was turning, the deck was heeling, and ahead one of the transports had spread sail at exactly the wrong moment, so that she'd been taken flat aback and wind and steam were fighting to command her. Somebody was likely to collide with her before that fight was finished.

I Hmilra's gesture brought a signal messenger to him. "Signal to *Sguizaan*: 'Take in sail until clear of channel.' "

interlude

The Bhir Delta, Second Fullripe:

Whips cracked, team drivers shouted, and every sort of hauling creature except slaves gave tongue in their own fashion. Ungreased wheels and overburdened metal and wood added their notes to the concert.

Given a choice, Jossu I Hmilra would rather have listened to the apprentice musicians of Fort Huomikki practicing. However, the choice was not his. The fort and all the rest of Saadi were half a midtide away.

Also, the din now assaulting his ears meant that the landing of the expeditionary force in the Bhir Delta territory was almost complete. Drawn by ten-pair teams, the heavy guns were going ashore. By tomorrow's sunbrighten most of them would be emplaced, in locations the gunners were keeping so secret that they did not even show on Jossu I Hmilra's maps.

When that was done, the Fleet would be free to deal with any Imperial efforts to cut it off from home, whether by intrigues in Rinbao-Dar or by open force. The groundfighters would be able to block any Imperial advance by land around the northern edge of the gulf, while extending a hand (actually, patrols) north up the Bhir to the southernmost outposts of the Regality of Eneh.

It all looked very fine on maps, but Jossu I Hmilra had been been Captain over his own ship before Barbara Weil was born. She could hardly know as well as he how the final proof of the wisdom of any strategy was found not on maps, but when the enemy came at you armed and ready to kill.

With that said, Weil's strategy was mostly admirable and sound. Short of the kind of disaster which he himself was unlikely to survive, I Hmilra would see that she had her reward. There was already talk of the Drylanders having enough Farers to provide crews for two ships, one of which ought to be a proper war vessel. If Barbara Weil continued to prove herself, it was I Hmilra's intention, if it lay in his power, that she should command that new ship.

The last heavy gun rumbled and squealed off the barge. The whistle of the tug at the barge's stern shrilled, spewing white steam into the already sodden air as tow lines went taut. The nearly empty barge came free with a rasp and a rumble, so suddenly that it nearly collided with the next gun barge, inbound with a smaller tug lashed to one side and a steam launch on the other.

I Hmilra wondered if with the time and tools available, it would be possible to strengthen one or two of the barges to stand the recoil of heavy guns, then arm them and hide them in the winding channels of the Delta. Aimed by observers perched well forward, in the tops of rathome trees if necessary, they would be a first-order headache for any Imperial commander approaching from the sea.

An improvisation, probably not even practical in the time available, and one that should not have been necessary at all. A pity that they had been able to win so few of the heavy gunboats from the dedicated watchers of the Hask. Perhaps the Rinbao-Darans could be persuaded to sell one or two of their rivercraft, through intermediaries, of course. It would need to be a devious route they took, before they ended up under the Republic's flag, or all the short tempers and long memories in Rinbao-Dar would again be inflamed.

The breeze shifted direction while the shore parties wrestled with barges. It had been blowing mostly from the land; now it blew along the foreshore, from the open water to the east. The water was as hot as the land, so the breeze was no cooler, but it now carried fewer ripe smells. Seven thousand groundfighters and a thousand hauling beasts had done their best to add to the rich odors of a tropical foreshore; I Hmilra drew in a deep breath from sheer relief.

"Permission to come on the bridge?" he heard from behind. Turning, he saw the bridge guard looking dubiously at Leader of Scouts Juinjijarsa, who was standing at the head of the port ladder.

"Be welcome, Scout," I Hmilra said.

"I am grateful," the commander said. She was about equally of Enehan, Rinbao-Daran, and tribal blood, and the mixture had given her longer legs than most folk. Indeed, at sunfade, from a distance, she might have almost been mistaken for a Drylander.

That mixed blood would have kept Juinjijarsa from even being considered a lawful resident of Rinbao-Dar, except that one of her grandmothers had been the First Matriarch. Fewer questions were asked about one of such blood; fewer still when she proved to have a natural genius for the demanding work of the mounted scouts.

She had volunteered to accompany the Fleet north, saying that her kin would rather have her aiding the northerners than be a standing target in the cities. That this was not the whole story, Jossu I Hmilra had known, when some twenty more Scouts ("kin-bound or oath-sworn," she said) and their blooded ariyoms came north with her.

"Reporting that our mounts and gear are ashore, and asking permission to join the scouting line," Juinjijarsa said, bending at the knees in the formal greeting of a Matriarch-kin to an outlander of superior rank. Then she put both hands over her heart, a rare gesture from Matriarch-kin to any outlander. It meant that she would shed her heart's blood before she would betray the Island Republic.

Jossu I Hmilra was certain she would not be foresworn. He and others among the Captains were equally certain that the Scouts included spies for every faction in Rinbao-Dar that the fleet knew of, as well as all the others it would only learn of too late.

The spied weren't likely to learn anything about the expedition that was not known already. Their work among the Scouts pushing north would doubtless be aimed at Eneh—and did the Island Republic know so much about its would-be ally that it could not find that help useful?

Another delicate problem of ethics, and one that could not be rendered less delicate even by plain speaking. I Hmilra fought a brief delaying action by sending for a cold pitcher of fruit-water (*Valor*'s icemaker had come to life again, after two commons' desertion of its post in spite of the engineers' best efforts).

"I cannot bind the groundfighters as I could Captains in the Fleet," I Hmilra said. "Not concerning the work on land. But I can commend you to all their commanders, especially those of the Scouts."

The woman raised her drink in a toast, so that the sunlight passing through it turned ruddy. "You give only what you can promise in good faith," she said. "No one can ask more."

I Hmilra asked for pen and paper, and would have asked for the Lord of the Waves to inspire his wits. What could he say, beyond extolling the Scouts' reputation (which he knew was high) and Juinjijarsa's skill and honor (about which he knew much less)? He wanted to suggest that it was worth some danger to avoid insulting

Matriarch-kin but could think of no words that would make that plain without usurping the authority of the groundfighters' Captains.

Juinjijarsa seemed content with the letter when she read it, however. She even repeated the oath of heart's blood before she climbed down the ladder to the launch ready to take her ashore. I Hmilra watched her go, then watched the last gun barge sliding off the beach. Meanwhile, a double hauling team and fifty groundfighters heaved on the ropes of the barge's load, a fifteen-line bomb-thrower, to get it across the sodden ground of the foreshore to where a steam tractor could take it in tow.

I Hmilra wondered. Could there be a way of building a steam tractor inside a boat's hull, with the wheels acting as paddles in the water? Such a machine could move from water to land without stopping, even if it might not be able to carry the heaviest loads.

And suppose one also built shallow-draft ships, with their engines in the rear and most of their hull one long hold? Perhaps even a hatch in the bow, or, better yet, doors, so that they could run up on sloping shores, open their bows, and let beasts and men, guns and tractors, run straight on to dry land?

Such a vessel might be too expensive to build strictly for war—but would it not have other uses? River ports were often shallow and ill-equipped. Also, those who wished to have rock-oil more widely available had been wrestling for ten Greats with the problem of keeping the flames of a boiler's firebox apart from the cargo of inflammable oil. Would not putting the engines aft serve the purpose?

I Hmilra could not leave *Valor*'s bridge at once, not while the unloading continued. By the time it was done, he had mentally registered a half-score new designs and devices, and made his kin so rich from these registrations that he could leave everything else he owned to Alikili without their uttering a word of protest!

Even if only a part of this dream came true, it remained certain that the more wealth there was to divide, the less folk quarreled over dividing it.

SAADI, SECOND FULLRIPE:

The offices and training camp for the Women's Squadron was too far from the dockyard to let the women use the dockyard's godhouse. So they used a smaller one near the Street of the Forsaken, named for a sickhouse for victims of joint-rot that had stood there in the days of the Saadian princes.

The name was still appropriate, Alikili thought, as she led her company in step around a cobblestoned bend. They passed five orphanages on the way from camp, three of them in the Street of the Forsaken. Four more lay west of the godhouse.

None of them, to everyone's sorrow (except perhaps that of employers who wished to procure both cheap labor and favor in the sight of Lord and Lady), seemed to have fallen on hard times lately. Indeed, three of them sent their children to prayer at the same godhouse as the Women's Squadron.

The marching Squadron rounded the bend, half a cast short of the godhouse. As always, the bend gave an excellent view uphill, to the Drylander Study Group's home in the old princely citadel. This morning it rose against a sky gray more with cloud than smoke. It was so little past high clearsky that few needed to keep fireplaces alight, save the old and sick.

It occurred to Alikili that the godhouse where she would do Reverence this morning was also the closest one to the Study Group's citadel. Yet she had never seen a Drylander there, at least to recognize.

What or whom the Drylanders worshipped was a mystery that might have troubled folk giving more importance to faith than the Kertovans. Alikili granted some truth to the most common opinion: they could not worship the Lord of the Waves at all and worshipped the Lady of the Rocks under other names.

But not complete truth. She had heard Jossu talk in unguarded moments; she had even studied some of his confidential correspondence. Some Drylanders clearly worshipped the male principle, which they called Jeshu, Ullah, Bowda, or Lurd (which last might be a title rather than a name). Others worshipped a Lady Muri. Most did not worship at all, or at least pretended not to.

Why anyone should pretend to have no faith at all (as opposed to merely pretending one and believing another, as was sometimes necessary in the City-States) was a mystery Alikili could not solve. But then, no doubt the best minds of every folk who had met Drylanders these past fifty-odd Greats had struggled with that mystery with equally little success. She would not solve it in the short time before they reached the godhouse.

The godspeaker for the Lady was in good voice this morning. The godspeaker for the Lord barely had a voice; he croaked, wheezed, and coughed as if lung-rot would take him off in the next moment. Alikili hoped not, for the orphans' sake as well as his own. They lived cold and hard in the winter, and it was no secret that too many of them died young from wasting diseases.

The godspeaker coughed again.

"Bless most particularly those commonly in the care of your kinswoman, who are among us today. For they have stepped forth from the Rock to serve among those who ride the Wave. They do not ride your creation themselves, but honor them for all that they have done and bless them that they may do more."

Alikili did not dare twitch an eyebrow, let alone turn her head. But she felt glances boring into her like crankgun rounds, and not only from the Women's Squadron. She suspected that if she had looked around her, she would have seen the same question on a score of faces.

Is someone at work, to allow the Women's Squadron to serve at sea, even the fertile? And has Jossu I Hmilra told you about it, even if it is not his idea?

She would have had to say "I do not know" to the first question, and "No" to the second, for all that she would have been called "liar" both times. Jossu I Hmilra had responsibilities to more than the jouti of the Squadron, and would hardly have time to agitate on this matter, even if he were not far off in the south.

But everyone who heard of the godspeaker's words today would be chattering about them tomorrow, from the leaf-scrap posters up to the Chamber of Delegates. Alikili was prepared to hear any amount of such chattering around her, as long as she heard none of it *at* her.

The long-drum rolled, the speaking-sticks rattled, the pipes gave their soft, distant moan. Five hundred voices rose in the chant, "Give Us Now Your Blessing, Lord and Lady Fair," voices ranging from children barely able to pronounce the words to the splendid soprano of the godspeaker for the Lady, loud enough to make those standing close to her wince for all its beauty.

Keeping the five hundred in harmony on the chant was a game compared to getting them out of the godhouse in some sort of order afterward. The Women's Squadron Captain ordered her charges to halt and let the children go. Only then did she let the Squadron piper sound "Withdraw."

As Alikili's company reached the door, she heard hooves clattering outside, and prayed that no early-morning recklessness would stretch a child lifeless on the stones. Once outside, she saw a two-wheeled single-pole in Fleet colors draw up, and a young woman in Squadron uniform spring lightly from it.

That light, quick movement identified the woman even before she approached Alikili. Quiusa I Shtuur came from a family that had been Captain-Born as long as the rank had existed. They owned half an armorclad, three torpedo-carriers, and twenty merchanters, besides considerable land and financial interests in half a score of different enterprises.

To complete confusion, Quiusa I Shtuur was as proven fertile as a woman could be without actually having borne a child. Her family had threatened to disinherit her if she joined the Women's Squadron, but her reply had routed them with enviable speed.

"If I have no inheritance from my blood-kin, then I will have my inheritance from the honor of the Fleet in which we serve," she had replied. That had given her a case for serving that few dared dispute. As she had also quickly won promotion to Farer First Class on sheer ability, she now had more than a nimble tongue fighting for her.

I Shtuur looked no better than anyone else who had been on duty since sunbrighten was a distant gray spot on the horizon. She blinked as she held out a message pouch to Alikili.

"Thank you, Farer I Shtuur."

"It is from your—from the I Hmilra estate. The duty commander said that she would authorize emergency leave if necessary."

That was hardly tactful, in hearing of the Squadron's Captain herself, but it was not maliciously meant either. I Shtuur had merely spent her whole life in circles where no one dared take offense at anything said by someone of her name. It was a miracle that she had more wits and courtesy than the average.

"I agree," the Squadron Captain said. "If you care to read it now, I can arrange for you to return with the driver, or even go directly to the station and find an earlier train."

Alikili would rather have taken off her clothes than read the letter with so many eyes on her, but the Captain's suggestion had the weight of an order. She unsealed the pouch, opened the letter inside, and read.

Her face must have said what her lips held back. The Captain and I Shtuur both stepped close. "Bad news?" they said, almost together.

"Not the worst. He is alive and well. So is everyone at the estate. But we are having some trouble with robbers. I have more authority with the rural Watch than anyone there now. So I suppose I had best go upcountry for a few days, until the panic is over."

That was not just to even the estate servants, and ten times over unjust to Moi Kekaspa, who would not panic if facing death by torture. But the situation must be nearly dire, so, if she would write so openly to Alikili.

"Very well," the commander said. "The driver can take you straight to the Northbound Station. There's a train north at sunglow ten. I'll have Farer I Shtuur pack whatever you think you'll need at home and bring it out—"

Alikili was about to say that she would lack for nothing at home, then saw I Shtuur's face. It seemed more than likely that her family had warned her to have nothing to do with Jossu I Hmilra's irregular companion. Now she was being ordered to spit in her family's eye.

Alikili could not find it in her heart to turn I Shtuur's barely suppressed grin into a frown. She nodded. "Very well, Farer I Shtuur. But if they make a pack-dreezan out of you, they will hear from me."

I Shtuur saluted. "Service to the Fleet."

"Service to the Fleet," Alikili replied, and darted for the two-wheeler.

Puyasa Island in the Adinisi Archipelago, Second Fullripe:

Sean Borlund wore long, baggy trousers and low groundfighter boots, a sleeveless Farer's tunic, and a groundfighter's light marching order, without either a commander's sword or a fighter's rifle. Instead, he carried a second pistol, an extra box of cartridges for both his weapons, a heavy bush knife with a saw-toothed edge, and an extra canteen.

He would gladly have carried little and worn nothing, like the mythical Father-god avatar Adam—or the first human, depending on one followed the Rationalist or Observant orthodoxies. The Adinisis seemed to form a barrier to the slightest breeze, as well as a ripe collection of tropical stenches that the nonexistent breezes let accumulate over them like flies over a dunghill.

There were some of those, too, near the refugee camp whose care and maintenance had quickly become the largest single work for the observation force. A thousand groundfighters and the crews of *Ling-*

vaas, Bybur, nine torpedo-carriers, and several transports had been expected to be more than ample for the work to be done.

But the refugees who clambered aboard *Lingvaas* the night of the riots were only the vanguard of an endless (or at least not yet ended, even if diminishing) flow. Not all of them remained on the islands under Fleet care, of course. Some had money or were sent it by their kin in Rinbao-Dar to buy them safe passage until the Matriarchy was quiet again.

Even those needed at the very least food, water, and transportation to their destinations. One of the torpedo-carriers was serving practically full-time, running up and down the coast with refugees clinging to practically everything above-decks except the funnels and the torpedo warheads. Two other torpedo-carriers had escorted the light-transport *Juumsan* down the coast to the town of Dlee, on a voyage that began with five hundred and six refugees aboard and ended with five hundred and ten (one dead and buried at sea, five babies born).

This left a mere two thousand or so camped in improvised shelters (less improvised each day, thanks to both the Kertovans' efforts and those of the refugees), fearing or believing that they had no place to go. A few Kertovans and even some humans muttered that the refugees were simply trying to use the Fleet's generosity for a few midtides of easy living, but Sean doubted that.

"It's been a while since they had a pitched battle close to either city, I'll admit that," Barbara Weil had told him after a commanders' meeting two nights ago. "But they've had a dozen factional or feud killings every night for the last five commons. About as many more bodies turn up every sunbrighten because somebody wanted to settle a personal score and thought one more corpse wouldn't be noticed under a whole pile of them.

"So anybody who says the refugees are lazy or parasites, I am personally going to throw overboard." She'd said that in voice that carried from one end of *Lingvaas*'s main deck to the other, and made heads turn.

It made Borlund try not to wince. Captain Weil's temper was growing shorter with each passing day. It had begun to seem that the observation force ought to be spelled "farce," at least as long as it couldn't do anything about the simmering civil brawls in Rinbao-Dar.

If it was a farce, what would this do to the status of the Drylanders in the eyes of the Fleet? Could even Jossu I Hmilra be trusted to reward a Drylander, if her best advice did little to get the Fleet out of a strategic and political dilemma?

Borlund wanted to be there for Weil, to share as much of the burden as any junior could take from a Captain. He would even let her cry on his shoulder, and half-anticipated, half-feared the consequences of holding her that closely. Everyone was losing weight in the heat, and Barbara Weil was one of those improved by doing so.

Sean Borlund had been properly socialized, was considerate by nature, and in this kind of heat had very little desire for anything except cold baths. He still trusted himself less than he once had to hide ill-mannered and worse-timed desire.

It was a relief when Weil told him to lead a heavily armed shore party to the patrol line west of the refugee camp and stay there for two nights. *Lingvaas* had been contributing her quota of guards to both camp security and the distant patrol ever since the camp went up, but this was a different matter.

"I want to see how fast we can get thirty people ashore with a crankgun on wheels, supplies in pack saddles, and everything else for a serious fight," she said. "I want to see how many of those thirty know their arses from their elbows about groundfighter work, and make sure the ones who don't stay ashore.

"And I want to find out just exactly *what* our Kertovan friends may really be doing in the camp."

Borlund had nodded, there being nothing to say. He and Barbara still had few secrets from each other, as short-tempered as they had both grown. They both knew that more than a few troublemakers in the Matriarchy accused the Fleet of keeping the refugees in camp against their will, of using them for forced labor or worse, and of trying to make them serve Kertovan interests in the cities.

Borlund and Weil thought this was nonsense. But other humans, not just in the Study Group, might do so. Then all the suspicions of the motives of those humans who had accepted the Fleet's invitation to honorable service might erupt like a geyser, scalding the reputations of everyone serving aboard *Lingvaas* or training for Fleet service.

Losing so much to the gaping mouths and empty heads of Rinbao-Daran demagogues was unbearable.

So as the quick sunfade of southern lands swallowed the shore, Sean Borlund strode up the beach toward the road to the camp. It had begun as a forest trail, been widened to a path by trampling feet, and then widened and smoothed further into a proper road by work parties from both camp and Fleet. Ahead of him marched four Farers with their rifles held at the ready, as if they were moving in hostile territory. (Weil had picked those four herself; none were too quick to shoot but all could hit with the first round when they did.)

Then came Borlund, then came four pack dreezans with bulging saddlebags. A fifth towed a small still for brewing up fresh water; a sixth towed one of *Lingvaas's* crankguns on a field carriage. It was supposed to be a light carriage, but if this was the chief metalsmith's idea of a light carriage, Borlund hoped he'd never be asked to make a heavy one. Even on level, hard-packed ground, the gun's dreezan was panting.

Borlund dropped back for a while, to help the gun team. As he returned to his original position, brush cracked on a side trail and four rifles and several pistols swung toward the noise. More cracks and clanks from cocked hammers and thrown bolts—then Ehoma Tuomitti and Zhohorosh led a dozen of *Byubr's* Farers out onto the road.

"Good Faring," Borlund said. "Do you come to ask help or give it?"

Zhohorosh laughed out loud, which drew a poisonous look from Tuomitti. "Our Captain wondered how fast we could move to help the camp if they needed us. So tonight we learn."

Borlund would have laughed, except that he suspected more than coincidence. A useless suspicion, when he could not discuss the matter here or be sure of a straight answer when he could.

"I trust the groundfighters for what they know how to do," Tuomitti went on, "but cursed few of them have served in this kind of jungle. If they were closer to the camp, that might not matter, but where they are. . . ."

Borlund had to agree. To avoid the appearance of keeping the refugees prisoner, and to take in several good observation points and springs of fresh water, the groundfighters' perimeter was well beyond the camp. In tropical forests where visibility might not reach pistol range, that left gaps wide enough for a whole army with evil intent and silent feet to slip through.

"Very well," he said. "Fall in behind us. The road's not wide enough for us to march abreast, more's the pity. And I command, if anybody needs to."

That shouldn't be necessary, as the patrol commander was always someone senior to both Borlund and Tuomitti. That seniority might even help twist an answer out of Tuomitti or Zhohorosh, about why *Byubr* and *Lingvaas* were carrying out the same training exercise on the same evening.

The single combined column had covered about two-thirds of the distance to the patrol line, with the lights of the camp's fires fading into the forest behind them, when Borlund heard a single flat crack from ahead. It was too loud to be a twig snapping, but didn't sound like a shot.

Had some of the camp children found another box of old fuses and decided to throw them into a campfire? That had already happened once, a few nights ago, although mercifully with no damage except to adults' nerves and children's bottoms.

The crack came again, loud enough to raise echoes. As the echoes died, Borlund heard a peculiar metallic *clang* that sounded like a spring-loaded metal door slamming.

That could hardly be a children's prank.

The next sound ended all doubt. It was an explosion—a shell burst, Borlund thought, maybe a dud but at least a six-liner.

No children, and nothing on the patrol line or even friendly. The nearest Kertovan artillery was on Outpost Flanker, four-liner pack guns. They'd hardly be firing into the patrol line.

Somewhere up ahead, those folk with evil intent and silent feet were coming.

chapter 20

None of the feet behind Sean Borlund were silent. It seemed that everybody in both parties tried to break into a run at the same moment. Also, some of both races started shouting. If they had no evil intent, they had a good chance of telling both friend and enemy exactly where they were.

Borlund halted the forward rush by shouting louder than anybody else, and also spreading out his arms. On the narrow path, that pose made him a good roadblock.

Meanwhile, farther back in the column, Ehoma Tuomitti was also trying to restore order if not quiet.

"You want to run into an ambush or have friends mistake you for enemies?" she snarled. "Or run off the path one way into the spikewire or the other into the swamp?"

Borlund doubted that any spikewire had been strung out here, but the thought of the swamp made even him shudder. The swamp that protected the right flank of the Fleet position ran all the way from the base of Outpost Hill to the shore and swarmed with minumbiklis.

On minumbikli could be ignored, but you hardly ever found just one. The swarm seemed to be their basic social unit, even if they reminded Borlund more of reptiles than of insects, and hunger seemed to be their normal condition. Even a swarm would not attack a live and healthy human or Kilmoyan, but a helpless one was doomed and a dead one skeletal unless rescue came quickly.

The column had just started off again when two of the Scouts hurried back, carrying a wounded Kertovan groundfighter between them. A healing-trained Farer stepped forward from the *Byubr* party, although even dim lantern light showed too much bleeding for there to be much hope.

Tuomitti and Zhohorosh deployed the two parties so that they wouldn't be an irresistibly large and vulnerable target for whoever was slinging shells out of the darkness, or even for prowling snipers. Borlund interrogated the Scouts.

"We came up to where the telegraph line to the artillery crossed the trail," one said. "We saw a dead gunner lying on the ground. We started to spread out, but somebody shot Stark. Sniper, I think."

"Local weapon or—?" Borlund asked. This might be violating security, but rumors of Drylander snipers were all over the Fleet. Ignoring them was bad leadership and plain stupidity.

"Local," the other Scout—Klimova, from the name on her shirt—said. "It had that heavy black-powder boom to it. Big slug, though. Stark's head just came apart. Then somebody else started lobbing shells—too big for grenades—and one hit close enough for the fragments to hit Ruag. Pedersen and I were already on the ground, but Ruag was trying to spot the sniper."

Another distant *clank*, but this time a dull *thud* followed, along with cracking branches, instead of an explosion. Pedersen bit his lip and stared wildly about him, but said nothing. Klimova was clearly doing the better job of keeping her nerve. Borlund remembered that aboard *Lingvaas* she was an oiler who worked every day with hot, fast-moving machinery.

"Nice to know that they sometimes have duds, too," Borlund said, pitching his voice to be heard by everyone under his command. He signaled for the watch chiefs to gather around him.

"All right. We can't stay here, I won't retreat and leave our dead, and going up the path into the sights of a sniper is stupid. We're going to strike off to redward of the path, and try to find our patrols or at least the wire-post between them and the camp. We may even be lucky and get around the sniper's flank. We'll unharness the crank-gun and hand-haul it as far as we can, so that if we find the sniper—"

"Or snipers," Tuomitti put in.

Sometimes Borlund wished that Ehoma Tuomitti couldn't see more clearly with one eye than most people could with two. As usual, she also made sense. Listening to her would hardly weaken his authority, certainly not with Zhohorosh.

"Of course. I don't like the idea of even one sniper this far inside the perimeter, but if I were attacking, I'd send in several. Just in case that fancy mortar or whatever it is didn't work."

To prove that the enemy hadn't been *that* optimistic, another explosion echoed through the trees, this time from almost directly ahead. It seemed to Borlund that the enemy was firing into the perimeter almost at random, without having observation on the most profitable targets. That might reduce the damage, unless the enemy was simply trying to harass or divert, wanting to draw attention whether they hurt anyone or not.

Another shell exploded before the echoes of the first died. This time Borlund heard falling branches, the crack of a toppling tree, and screams.

Borlund, Zhohorosh, and Tuomitti exchanged looks. *Two of those guns?* Borlund asked the chiefs.

Then it's a serious attack came the reply.

Unless those guns, mortars, whatever are as cheap as clay pots was Borlund's thought. He fell in behind Klimova, who seemed ready to take the lead.

Pedersen, now calmer, moved to Borlund's flank. As he stepped off the trail after Klimova, Borlund's final thought was *If something that potent is that cheap, whoever has it is a serious menace. Whoever they are, and* wherever *they learned how to make them.*

THE WIRE-SPEAKER NOW DIRECTLY LINKED THE WAN'WA CROSSING STATION and the I Hmilra estate. It had done so, in fact, since before the last snow melted. But along several passages through forest and along one stretch of road where no forest provided windbreaks, falling branches and snapping poles could break the wire as easily as a string asked to moor an armorclad.

So Alikili had no way of telling the house when she reached the station, near the end of sunfade. The first train she could have caught from Saadi was a local that actually arrived later than the next one, an express; she decided to wait for the express.

However, its railsteamer broke down halfway between Gaanaus and Wan'wa Crossing. Since the line was single-tracked, the fastest way out for the passengers was in carts hauled by steam tractors hastily gathered from the nearest builders' camps and road gangs. Alikili was glad she carried no baggage, but hoped that they would clear the line in time for what I Shtuur was sending after her to reach the house tonight.

Not all of it was material she cared to leave at the mercy of fate and strangers. Still less did she want it exposed to strange or hostile eyes as well, for a whole common.

Her uniform seemed to speed matters, and certainly helped one of the tractor drivers recognize her as Jossu I Hmilra's tuunda companion. Ignoring indignant protests, he allowed her to ride in the cab, but himself protested when she wanted to relieve the stoker—who seemed hardly more than a boy—at his work.

"A lady shouldn't have to do that work," he muttered.

It would have been quickest for Alikili to reply that she was no lady but a garcik, and if he doubted her word perhaps he would take Jossu I Hmilra's? Instead, she shrugged.

"But she has the right and duty, if it needs doing and there's no one else? True?"

"Suppose so," the driver muttered, barely audible over the hissing of the steam and the clank of the wheels. He spent the rest of the journey with his eyes fixed firmly on the gauges, or on the stoker, as if daring him to become too comfortable.

When Alikili and twenty other passengers dismounted in the station square, it was darker than it might have been otherwise, with the lowering gray clouds of an oncoming storm. The wire-speaker had already died, as if in anticipation, and Alikili was reluctant to send a messenger out to the house in a storm while she remained warm and dry waiting for the carriage.

At last she compromised by visiting the hire-stables. The owner's son was outspokenly disapproving of her and her connection with Jossu I Hmilra, so much so that she thought it a tribute to her companion's honor that he had not had the young man exiled from the town. But (perhaps out of an old-fashioned fear of the lord's displeasure), the man did not go beyond rude words and making her pay the dreezan-hire in advance.

As Alikili rode out of town, head bowed to keep the wind and flying debris out of her face, she heard the first roll of thunder.

IT TOOK SEAN BORLUND HARDLY MORE THAN A SINGLE BEAT TO BEGIN WONdering about the wisdom of taking the crankgun cross-country. It took less than a second beat before he knew that they should have left it on the trail. Disabled, of course, so it could not be carried off or turned against them, but somewhere it did not make them sweat every moment and every pace!

The manual for the crankgun did say that one needed extra animals or Farers to haul it cross-country. Borlund thought it could have added that the Farers needed the wings of gray stoopers or the strength of the legendary giant Sovmraaki. He felt a grievance at this lack of accurate information.

He also felt sweat pouring off him, and half a dozen muscles strained or torn. Being not only the commander but one of the largest and strongest Drylanders in the party, meant doing his share of the brute-force lifting and hauling or maybe a little more.

All the force of all the brutes in the party, however, managed to move the crankgun no more than three hundred paces before Borlund had to call for a halt. Along that trail of sweat and straining, they had made so much noise that he was sure only the continued mortar bursts had kept the enemy from marking every step of the crankgun's progress.

If an enemy attack did burst out of the forest now, he suspected that nothing would save *Lingvaas*'s landing party except the enemy's laughing themselves into a fit at the sight.

Borlund wasn't too short of breath to give a few orders, however. The Farers of both races weren't too weary (or perhaps were too afraid of the chiefs) to obey them. They heaved the crankgun around until it was aimed across the largest stretch of open ground in sight, perhaps two pistol shots wide and half that long. They loaded a drum of the thumb-sized brass-jacketed slugs, then locked the hammer back while they cranked one into the firing chamber.

After that, it would take only the flick of a thumb and a hand on the crank before the gun started spewing death. Of course, it would help if there was somebody to spew it *at*, and Borlund had begun to wonder if anyone would be willing to provide the legitimate target.

The mortar barrage seemed to have ceased. He heard the random round-popping of sniping and skirmishing, but hardly any explosions. Even those were the flatter, milder *craaak*! of hand grenades or homemade throwing-charges.

There had to be an enemy out there, making that murderous din with those two curiously silent and alarmingly inexhaustible mortars. The idea of having rushed his people cross-country on a fool's errand was too embarrassing for Borlund to contemplate.

At least he had more orders to give, by way of distraction. The crankgun wasn't the only weapon that needed to be ready. He and the chiefs collected volunteers for an outpost line under Zhohorosh, set up exchanges of ammunition, assigned a watering party to fill canteens at a small spring thirty paces to the right rear, and in time kept everybody including himself too busy to worry.

It helped that Pedersen and Klimova both volunteered for the outposts. He had regained his nerve; she had never lost hers; Borlund hoped that everyone would follow the example of those who'd been closest to the enemy so far tonight.

He still sent Pedersen off as escort to the watering party, letting Klimova join the outposts under Zhohorosh. The watering party was returning with dripping canteens slung all over them like puffpods, and the outposters' messenger had just returned when Borlund heard a familiar *clank* in the forest ahead.

It was not only familiar. It was much closer than he had heard it before.

ALIKILI'S MOUNT STARTED AT THE FIRST ROLL OF THUNDER. WHEN A CRASH like a salvo from an armorclad's turret guns followed, the beast reared.

Alikili was trying to stay in the saddle without doing anything that would make the dreezan harder to control when she caught sight of riders on the road behind her. Four of them, coming on briskly.

She now added drawing her pistol to everything else she was trying to do. Bandits hadn't prowled these roads for twenty Greats or more, but the times had already spawned worse than bandits, seeking more than money. Why shouldn't they take to the roads in search of prey?

Before Alikili could even finishing drawing her pistol, let alone aim it, the four riders were up with her. Without slowing, they trotted on past. She would have sworn that one of them was a woman, and that they had a fifth dreezan, a pack animal humped with a heavy load, clattering along behind them on a lead rein.

But she couldn't be sure of any of this, before the loudest thunderclap yet burst over the landscape. Then landscape, riders, and everything else more than ten paces away vanished.

It seemed like the Skyfall Rains had come again. Alikili abandoned compassion and thrust in her spurs. The dreezan quivered, took one step that an infant might have equaled, then halted again. It raised its head and began a plaintive grunt, instantly lost in more thunder.

Alikili did not try to outcurse the thunder. But in her mind she cursed the whole race of dreezans, the hire-stable owner's son and all his line to the last generation of the world, all powers commanding weather, and the whole household staff who couldn't find their hindparts without her drawing them a map!

After that, she felt sufficiently eased to dismount. She would lead the dreezan until the rain or at least the thunder ended and its nerve returned. The satisfaction of doing something lasted three or four breaths, until the water lying across the road spilled over the tops of her shoes, so that she squished as well as splashed at each step.

Sadly, she realized that she had exhausted her stock of curses.

WITH CLANGS AND CRASHES, THE CRACKLE OF SMALL BRANCHES BREAKING and the thud of something heavy bouncing off larger ones, the mortar's projectile plummeted down onto Borlund's party.

Borlund had a moment to glimpse it—a shape like a large food can, with a stubby tail ending in a ring—before Pedersen dashed forward. He left a trail of canteens behind him as he ran, bursting the last two as he flung himself on the projectile.

A silence that seemed to last longer than the time since the coming of humans to Kilmoyn followed. When it did not end in an explosion that shredded Pedersen into bloody rags, Borlund breathed again.

Once he'd caught his breath, he started whispering orders.

He knew that he should whisper, to avoid giving the enemy Scouts dangerous knowledge. He could not have said how he knew it, but he knew it as surely as his own name or the desirability of Barbara Weil.

Somewhere in the eternity of Pedersen's intended self-sacrifice, Borlund's mind scanned all it held about groundfighter tactics. It discovered how much it had retained, sorted it out, developed a plan, broke the plan down into orders, and told Borlund what orders to whisper.

Somewhere about the fifth order, Borlund wondered if this was a good plan.

It took him only two more orders and the breath between them to realize that almost any plan was better than no plan at all. That would leave him standing in sight of both friend and enemy with his mouth so wide open that everyone could look into it and see how vacant his skull was.

Orders put eight human Farers—muscle was everything, now—bodily lifting the crankgun and carrying it off to the left. It still had a clear field of fire but bushes half-hid it.

More orders held the rest of the watering party where it was, to guard the left flank. Pedersen rejoined them, now coolheaded enough to pick up the canteens he'd dropped and check each one for leaks.

Still more orders sent a few Farers assigned to the outpost off to the right, to watch the way they'd come, back toward the trail. The guards he'd posted on the trail had either fallen silently or met no enemy, but four Farers couldn't watch much besides the trail. More flank protection—even if in the end, Borlund suspected he would have more flanks to protect than Farers to protect them.

The messenger from the outposts volunteered to return, to warn them of the crankgun's shift of position. Borlund realized that the outposters needed to know this, but didn't want anyone wandering around alone. He asked the messenger to pick a companion and go quietly, then turned his attention to the mortar projectile.

It did look like a large tin can, the kind used aboard ship or in eating houses for cooking oil or vegetables. From one end sprouted a long metal rod, strengthened with three flanges set equally around it. At the end of the rod was a circular plate, lightened by several cut-out sections.

The thing did not look particularly strong, and from the fact that it had dug only a shallow hole in the ground it could not be very heavy, either. The can was probably light cast iron or, more probably, rust-barriered sheet steel, filled with explosives. Borlund had no idea where the fuse was, why it hadn't gone off, or what it would take to set it off now.

He very much wished that one of the *Lingvaas* landing party was a gunnery expert. Even a senior gunnery chief would know more than Borlund did about things that flew through the air and were expected to go *bang* when they landed.

Zhohorosh was the closest thing to a gunnery expert with Borlund's party. However, he was also the farthest leader from Borlund himself. Calling him back from the outposts now was hardly practical.

A hope and a necessity remained. The hope was that someone among the Drylanders had acquired contaminating knowledge of weaponry, and would be willing to reveal it. (Borlund performed three Kertovan and one Saadian rite of aversion with his hands behind his back, to keep away spies for the Study Group Directorate.)

The necessity was to get the projectile out of the middle of the party's position. Then they could examine it at leisure, if they had any, or at least be safer if it went off. A light projectile loaded with explosives was most likely intended to damage by blast rather than by fragments—Borlund remembered that much weaponry. But "light" was a relative term. That much sheet metal reduced to hurtling fragments could clear most of the position.

Borlund stood up. "I want a volunteer to help me take this—thing—out of the line of fire. Right now, before the enemy attacks and somebody puts a stray bullet into it."

Nobody rushed forward. Several did stand and look at the projectile, then at Borlund. "Just one," he added. "It doesn't look heavy, but we can't risk dropping it."

In fact, Borlund could have tucked the projectile under one arm and walked into the bushes with it. The help of Senior Farer Boxxen let him move faster while avoiding bumps, then set it down gently inside a hollow tree that, rotten as it was, ought to be at least bulletproof.

Borlund was sweating all over again when he turned his back on the projectile. Wasn't there some old Terran nation-state, the Kinai or some such, who had a traditional curse, "May you live in interesting times?"

They would have thought human life in exile on Kilmoyn a very potent curse indeed. Life had often been short for Drylanders but seldom dull, in spite of the Study Group's apparent intentions. Borlund suspected the next sixty Greats would be even less dull than the preceding sixty.

As if to confirm that prophecy, the whole outpost line suddenly burst into small-arms fire. Borlund heard the heavy boom of black-power weapons, the flatter crack of friendly smokeless ones, once the sharper crack of a grenade, but no *clanks*, no crankguns, and no war cries. The screams of the wounded and dying, yes, but nothing to give away anybody's position or identity.

Borlund liked that even less than he liked the attack itself. That kind of discipline smelled of trained Imperial groundfighters or the best of the Rinbao-Darans. He hoped Zhohorosh could do as well with his outposters and confuse the enemy as badly.

Then one scream found an echo—several echoes. What seemed half a hundred throats were all tearing themselves to pieces with screams that might have been war cries or might have been the plaints of damned souls in Hell as Bridget described it. (Borlund was briefly glad that he did not have to believe in Hell, if it made people scream like that.)

The screaming went on, and now thudding feet and cracking branches swelled the din. Borlund drew a pistol and wished he had a rifle; the ranges would be short but the more accurate rifle would reduce the danger of hitting friends.

Then as if a theater curtain had risen, the far side of the clearing suddenly boiled over with hurrying, armed groundfighters. Half a dozen paces behind them, conspicuously taller than the rest, came an unmistakable human.

THE RAIN DID NOT BEAT ON ALIKILI'S SKULL HARD ENOUGH TO STOP HER thoughts. She could spare a few, from the work of leading the dreezan "not into error and vice," as the Reverence gave it, and not herself stepping off the road into the ditch or even into the larger potholes on the road.

There was no law that said a woman could not be riding abroad tonight, with three companions and a pack-beast. To say otherwise was to think like the hire-stable owner's son, which was hardly thinking at all.

But it had to be some unusual business bringing the woman out, or perhaps an unusual woman about something usual for her. The name Moi Kekaspa did not come unbidden into Alikili's mind; she not only called up the woman's name but imagined her face and put a question to it.

The answer to that question was the *screeep* of a high-velocity bullet passing Alikili's ear. The dreezan was suddenly more lively than it had been for several beats, rearing until Alikili feared that either the reins or her wrist were going to snap.

A second shot ended the dreezan's liveliness by hitting it in the head. The shot also ended Alikili's contemplation of the mystery woman. She remembered Jossu's advice—"When there's shooting and you can't join in, *get down*, even if it's friends doing the shooting."

Alikili seriously doubted that the unknown rifleman ahead in the gloom had killed her dreezan as a gesture of friendship. Also, even if the rifleman had shot at the wrong target, he had a rifle and she only a pistol. She could do nothing with the pistol except reveal her position without being able to hurt her enemies.

She now had time to look through the rain at her dreezan. It must have been dead before it hit the ground, with a small hole in one side of its skull and a larger hole on the other. Alikili carefully did not look too closely at either hole; she would be not just an easy but a helpless target if she had to spend the next five beats heaving her stomach empty.

It occurred to her that a good deal of effort had been devoted to ensuring that the Women's Squadron would not touch serious combat. It had not occurred to anyone (her included), or if it had, these wise heads had been silent, that combat might reach out to the women.

She would have something to say on that when she returned to Saadi, if she did—and she pushed that dark thought vigorously aside. It *was* different, facing someone with a weapon and intent to use it to end your life, instead of an impersonal force like the pull of the ground threatening your handhold on a cliff or fire and smoke ready to end your life with no more malice than they would show toward a mite.

Alikili promised thank-offerings to all concerned with giving her a modern cartridge pistol that could be trusted in wet weather. She rummaged in her cloak pocket, for the ten spare cartridges, which gave her a total of fifteen.

Then she crawled behind the dead dreezan, conscious that her back was still exposed as well as sodden. It still felt better to be crouching with a weapon in hand rather than lying wondering what hit her, and that her movement hadn't drawn a third shot was encouraging. Random shooting in this murk needed luck to do damage, and luck played no favorites.

chapter 21

Borlund couldn't tell from the human's face and stance whether he was leading the Kilmoyans' wild charge or trying to keep them from being easy targets. The human was surely a legitimate target: he was armed with a sword and pistol, among at least a dozen Kilmoyans equally well armed and wearing Imperial uniforms or at least badges.

In another moment Borlund counted twice as many Kilmoyans, mostly wearing the sashes and caps of militia, but all armed and some of them shooting—not very accurately, but they sent bullets close enough to Borlund to let him give with a clear conscience the Kertovan Drylanders' first order to fire on another human in many years.

"Hit them!" he shouted—or rather, screeched. Even to his own ears, half-numb from explosions and excitement, his order sounded like a bird's mating call.

No one laughed. A few didn't obey, more of them human than Kertovan. Enough obeyed to hurl a squall of rifle bullets into the advancing ranks.

Suddenly those ranks were thinner and even more disorderly. Borlund saw the human go down. His feet took him forward of their own will, before his mind could give any reason.

Haul that idiot out of the line of fire and interrogate him. His being here has to be a misunderstanding.

Borlund managed about three steps before the enemy reinforced their attack. Crushed bushes crackled as nearly a hundred Kilmoyans shouldered their way forward, trampling fallen comrades as they came. Few of them wore any insignia, many of them wore hardly any clothing, and more than a few of them had no firearms at all, only spears or long two-handed swords. Most of them also had empty sacks slung over their shoulders.

Borlund recognized locally recruited tribal levies when he saw them. He knew that they might have been carried away by misplaced enthusiasm for battle, rushing forward against orders. He also knew that if their enthusiasm carried them to close quarters, those blades and spears could do appalling damage.

The crankgun roared.

Its crew had reached the same conclusion as Borlund, moments earlier. An entire drum of rounds staggered the enemy line, soldiers, militia, and levies alike dropping from crippling wounds or knocked off their feet. So many went down that the second drum found fewer targets.

The third drum spewed as a few hardy souls tried to arm and throw hand grenades. One grenade bounced off a tree, slicing the air and several living bodies with fragments. Three others fell back into the enemy ranks and exploded there, maiming more of the throwers' comrades than the throwers' enemies.

The combination of three drumloads from the crankgun and the self-inflicted grenade damage ruined enemy marksmanship. Even those who survived to use their rifles and pistols mostly had black-powder single-shot weapons. Quite a few bullets flew toward the defenders; few hit. Borlund had only moments to be aware that the enemy seemed to be able to miss even a target his size. Then suddenly the battle turned hand-to-hand, and Borlund was glad of his size. Previously, towering over the average Kilmoyan had made him self-conscious. Now it gave him a survival edge.

He emptied his pistol without knowing what the bullets did, except that he had fewer enemies in front of him after he stopped shooting than before he started. But some of them might be on his flanks, so he backed away, punched one attacker with his free hand, abandoned the idea of reloading the pistol in the other, and was about to reverse the weapon and use the butt when Ehoma Tuomitti used the butt of her rifle on the same enemy.

Then bullets flew in several directions at once. Tuomitti swept Borlund's feet out from under him and rolled on top of him as he crashed to the ground.

"Cursed fools—!" she snarled, then laughed. "This would be indecent, if we lose our clothes."

"If somebody drops another grenade, we might," Borlund said. He rolled over, to see the ragged levies and a few militia streaming toward him, some of them falling as they ran, a very few turning back to shoot.

Then the tree line spewed still more armed groundfighters, the crankgun let fly with another drum, and Borlund recognized Zhohorosh running with the newcomers.

He rolled out from under Tuomitti and leaped to his feet. "Cease fire!" he shouted, then less formally, "Stop shooting, you idiots! You're hitting friends!"

All this did was make the crankgun fire swing toward him. This drew it away from the oncoming reinforcements, but Borlund had to dive for the ground again. This time Tuomitti guarded what was left of his dignity by not trying to be a living shield.

The crankgun ceased fire, but not before the last burst chewed up trees and ground all around friendly positions. It inflicted no friendly casualties and few hostile ones, and Borlund was about to organize a pursuit of the fugitives when Zhohorosh bent over him.

"Commander, there's something you ought to see, back in the trees." He pointed in the direction from which the attack had come. "It looks like a Drylander matter."

"Another Drylander in Imperial colors?" was all Borlund could say.

It was hard to tell when a Kilmoyan's eyebrows were rising, particularly when they had as much facial hair as Zhohorosh. The watch chief still radiated surprise, and Borlund realized that he might have given away too much.

"Was there one up here?" Zhohorosh asked.

"Yes, and I think we killed him. Have a search made for the body, and when you find it, guard him."

The two chiefs saluted, and Borlund remembered just in time to respect the chain of command by repeating the orders to the human chiefs. Then he lurched to his feet.

"What is back in the trees, if it's not a Drylander, alive or dead?" he asked.

"Nothing I've ever seen," Zhohorosh said, "nor any of the groundfighters either. We think there was a second, but the people with it got clean away."

"A second what? Zhohorosh, are we talking about their portable mortar, or something else?"

"You can call it a mortar if you want," the chief said. "But it's like no mortar I've ever seen. It looks as if it tosses bombs with a spring."

"A *spring*," Borlund repeated, glad that this time surprise didn't turn him into a soprano. "I have to see this."

"Then follow me," Zhohorosh said.

* * *

ALIKILI WAS CERTAIN BY NOW THAT SHE HAD CROUCHED BEHIND THE DEAD dreezan through the whole night, and that sunbrighten must be close. She also suspected that the first storm had blown out, and that its third or fourth successor must be blowing now. Or had there been another Skyfall, which was the only thing that could have produced so long a storm . . . ?

She shook her head, half expecting water to spurt from her ears. The rain had been coming and going, and at its height the road had been a finger's length deep in water. Alikili had been less wet bathing.

The wind, rain, and thunder had also made so much noise that listening for enemies in her rear had been futile. Someone could have driven up a steam tractor towing a twelve-line gun, most probably, then unlimbered and loaded before Alikili noticed.

More practically, she was concerned about water getting down the barrel of her pistol. It was well-oiled, but this kind of storm could still leave damage that it would be hard to explain without explaining why she had been out in the storm in the first place.

One set of instincts told Alikili to hold her tongue and take any punishment for neglecting her weapons. She had been happy to see that the Women's Squadron was expected to observe Farer customs in that respect, even if they were not expected to use the weapons; the punishment would be almost a badge of honor.

Also, silence would reduce the number of people who knew about this incident—and she thought that number should be as small as possible.

The other set of instincts told her that she, the house, and perhaps the Women's Squadron were all in danger from the same set of enemies. They should put their knowledge together when deciding how to fight back; if a few secrets trickled out onto the street, better embarrassed than dead. Nor would everyone at the house be sufficiently alert if she held her tongue.

Alikili did not doubt her own good sense when it came to deciding between the two calls of instinct. She spent a wistful moment wishing that Jossu would be here when she had to decide, and not only because she valued his advice—yes, and cherished his approval, when she received it—she also missed his embrace, which was a warming thing to feel or even think about when one was cold and wet.

Jossu I Hmilra had the fire of youth and the steadiness of age. She hoped that the enemies of the Republic would continue to find him impossible to kill, and that he would die in his own bed from the sheer weight of the Greats pressing him down into the Lord's realm—

The first shot aimed at her in some while made a *wheet* as it flashed overhead and a *chunk* as it tore into a tree. Then the sodden darkness ahead was darker still, with solid shapes. No, not solid, but wavering—which Alikili realized came from their moving fast.

She was ready to empty the pistol into them when she remembered Jossu's tales of disastrously mistaken identities. There had also been some training—one common of lectures, another common of exercises—in Watch duties. The Women's Squadron was not expected to see combat, but neither were they expected always to be able to call on male Farers to guard their quarters or their offices, and had not been issued pistols and quick-healing kits for their personal adornment.

Alikili tried to make herself invisible, inaudible, and invulnerable all at once, which would have let her rank with the great magic-workers of legend if she had succeeded. Before she could so much as draw breath to laugh at the conceit, the running figures stormed past, making as much noise as a galloping herd of unbroken dreezans.

Then lightning blazed, showing Alikili the receding backs of several hooded heads. Darkness returned quickly, and as her night vision did the same, the sky's thunder again crashed across the land.

Not sure if she was safe or if she could hope to *be* safe tonight, Alikili didn't move until she became aware of someone standing over her. Even then it was only to draw in a deeper breath, so her mind would be clear and her hand steady when she aimed her pistol at one who probably would shoot first and at this range could not miss—

"Greetings, Farer Alikili."

It was unmistakably a woman's voice. Alikili looked up, and saw eyes staring at her from above a scarf and inside a rainhood. The rest of the clothing was just as distinctly male, although the holster and pistol lurking half under the new arrival's cloak was the twin to Alikili's own.

Alikili braced her hands on the dead dreezan, refusing to think about what she might be touching. If she *did* soil herself, after so much wallowing in mud, nobody would be able to tell!

"Are you by any chance—one—who serves Jossu I Hmilra against—enemies he and the Republic share?"

The laughter was harsh but genuine. "You do very well at trying to be polite, accurate, and discreet all at once. I am grateful."

Alikili stood up. "I was also thinking of your husband and babe—who was your own true-born, wasn't he?"

"Oh, yes," and Alikili heard yearning in the woman's voice. "But my sister gives him the care of one of her own, though that was not my first plan. Those shared enemies, as you call them, had other plans.

"They sought your life, the ones we drove off," the woman concluded. "I doubt if they will fail to strike at the house if they have an opportunity. You are there, not to mention more than a few secrets."

"I—what do you intend?"

"After taking you home? What you do not know, you cannot tell."

"What I do not know, I cannot use to defend the house," Alikili said, in a bared-teeth voice. She doubted that her ear-fur could bristle, as sodden as it was. "And if I or anyone from the house were to be captured and tortured, then you would already have failed. Why not try to succeed from the beginning?"

The woman rocked slightly on her feet, then started a laugh that vanished in another thunderclap. It was lighter and they saw no lightning; perhaps the storm was dying.

Alikili thought that she might do the same if she had to stand here arguing much longer. "If I have to walk the rest of the way home, I will. I will not trust myself to anyone who will not tell me what I need to know." She held up a hand. "And do not think to take me by force. That would prove you a poor friend to the Captain-Born."

"I was not thinking of any such gross stupidity. My oath to both Lady and Lord upon this," the woman said. "Are you fit to ride?"

"I think I have doubled my weight with mud and water, but if you have a stout dreezan—"

"We captured several."

"Good. Then mount me on one, and perhaps you can tell me what I need to know as we ride home."

SEAN BORLUND HAD BATHED, EATEN, AND CHANGED CLOTHES SINCE COMING back aboard *Lingvaas*. He had not slept, and did not dare even rest his chin in his hands, for fear of dozing off.

He had to be awake and even coherent right to the end of the commanders' meeting. He didn't know if he had led the bloodiest ground action since the Drylanders came to the Island Republic. He hadn't even read all the public histories, and the secret ones might hold almost anything.

He definitely held the ground-combat record aboard *Lingvaas*, the first and so far only Drylander-crewed ship of the Fleet. This made him the center of attention for now, even if the future might reduce him to footnotes.

The bath had helped, although he still thought he smelled of the battlefield—leaf mold, human bodily wastes, gunpowder, and other undefined odors. So had the meal, although he hadn't been able to eat much. The queasy stomach he'd dreaded during the shooting came afterward.

He'd therefore been able to look everyone in the eye while giving his report. Sometimes he saw underneath the sweaty, weatherbeaten faces the ruin a bullet or grenade fragment could make of flesh and bone, or even the bare skulls that alone would remain after half a Great of weather and insects. Then he wanted to look away, but he'd seen the real thing; he did not starting at fancies.

Once he'd finished, he drank lukewarm water until his throat was no longer dry, and listened to the arguments flying back and forth like crankgun bursts. It quickly became obvious that *Lingvaas*'s commanders were divided over what risks they should run in dealing with this undeniable appearance of humans working with the Empire.

The Kertovans had at least one photographer and one sketch artist with their garrison. But would the two dead humans be recognizable from the Kertovan work? If not, did anybody (the Study Group being carefully not mentioned) have a secret-technology camera that would take more useful pictures—which could then be treated so that the copies turned over to the Fleet would not look suspicious?

Another point: did the secret-technology files have anything definite on the portable spring-activated bomb-thrower? It would clearly be a formidable weapon in far too many situations, against trenches, crankgun positions, or exposed Farers in close-range sea actions. How could it be discreetly learned whether Drylander stay-behinds had started played "Gods from Space" with gifts of advanced weapons designs, or whether the Empire's cult of the craftsman/engineer had started bearing military fruit at a particularly bad time?

"It might not matter, after all," Second Captain Kund said. "The—Imperials—seem to have a bit to learn about using the thing, even if they can make it. They sacrificed surprise, by putting it into the hands of half-trained people in an outpost action."

Borlund shook his head. "We don't know how many more they have. Perhaps they have enough so that the loss of surprise won't make much difference, in the next fight. And the actual crews may have been perfectly well trained, just not knowing where we were and trying to—what's the term—scout by shooting?"

Nobody was groundfighter enough to correct Borlund, but he detected some sideways glances. Knowing too much about war had been at least a social offense on Esperanza since before the first subassembly for *Ramparts* reached orbit. Maintaining that standard on Kilmoyn had been a rearguard action since within days of the landing. It was now about to become an exercise in complete futility—but some of those glances were from people too senior to Borlund for him to tell them that, to their faces, in public.

"That's a point," Kund said. "But even then, the Imperials seem to have had problems with discipline among their levies. What if they depend on the levies for ammunition bearers?"

"The levies could be replaced with militia or even Imperial regulars," Borlund said. "As you said, this was an outpost action. Perhaps the local Imperial commander didn't have the regulars to spare.

"Also, the levies did their duty until they ran into the crankgun. By then, they'd kept their oath to bring back their weapons bloodied or die trying?"

Kund's face hardened with frightening speed. "How did you learn that?"

From the faces around him, Borlund knew his stomach wasn't the only one twisting. He wished he could interpret those faces. Were the other commanders just surprised, or ready to take sides, and, if so, which?

It would not help if they wound up taking sides, even if some of them took Borlund's. Every commander aboard *Lingvaas* was here. Weil had made it clear that missing this meeting now or being indiscreet about it afterward would be a beaching offense.

"The people from *Byubr* had interrogated some of the prisoners and weren't trying to keep it a secret," Borlund said. "All I had to do was listen, and ask a leading question every so often."

Kund had opened his mouth again, when Captain Weil spoke, in knife-edged tones. "I'm glad to see that someone realizes we aren't alone here in the Gulf. Not counting the refugees, I would say we're outnumbered five to one by friendly Kilmoyans, and by who knows how many enemies.

"So let's not waste time discussing any plan that involves trying to keep a human presence secret."

"I was not suggesting anything of the kind," Kund asserted. Borlund recognize's Weil's facial twitches as an effort not to laugh.

"I do ask if we should investigate Commander Borlund's communication with the *Byubr* Farers. Protecting the secret of our identity demands no less."

Borlund wanted to suggest where the identity secret should go, and how. An even sharper look from the Captain reinforced discretion in silencing him.

"Commander Kund," Weil said formally. "I do not have to authorize any such investigation, by you or by anyone else who cannot establish their right to conduct it."

"I—I know those who can," Kundelin said.

"Good. I also hope you know that *Lingvaas*'s joining the Fleet was authorized jointly by several bodies within the Drylander community. It would not be in anyone's interests for such an investigation to proceed without either my consent or that of the other authorizing parties."

Borlund hoped that he was hearing a confirmation of rumors, not a pure bluff. Kund might not be equal to calling a bluff; the Study Group Directorate certainly would be.

"I will authorize that investigation under one condition," Weil said. "Apart from you and your—staff—being extremely discreet, so that the Fleet does not suspect we are trying to hide anything from them."

That drew nods from all around the table. Borlund was relieved to see everyone apparently united against stupidity, even if they might not agree on what would be good sense.

"Yes?" Kund looked as if he would agree to dance on the table if it ended this embarrassing situation any faster.

"Help us in the matter of identifying the Imperial humans and their weapon," Weil said. "With your own resources, those of your friends, and those of anybody you report to. I will even let you use Fleet facilities for messages using—ah, private codes—if it will bring us more intelligence faster.

"As you yourself said, anytime the identity secret is in danger, we all have to bend the rules a trifle to defend it."

Borlund felt a perverse combination of a stomach twisting again at the thought of the investigation, and a head so light it threatened to float off his shoulders at being able to do serious work on tonight's mysteries. Possibly the identity secret wasn't directly in danger, but cooperation between Fleet and Drylander easily could be. Then the Fleet would have more reason than ever to be curious about matters they had let lie for two generations.

More reason—and more resources, if Jossu I Hmilra had anything to say about the priorities. Borlund hoped his face would not crack from the effort as he tried to smile.

"As the central exhibit in the investigation, I'd like to vote in favor of the bargain. The only thing I ask is to advise the investigators on how to question the *Byubr* Farers without giving up secrets. There's probably not much that Tuomitti and Zhohorosh don't know about Drylanders, and that's not counting anything their commanders or fellow chiefs might have learned."

He wished that everyone around the table, Weil included, didn't look so relieved to see him consenting to be thrown into the killpit. But then, according to what he'd heard of Saadian sacrificial customs, it was always a bad omen if the sacrifice did not go consenting through the gate!

ALIKILI WAS WEARING DRY CLOTHES WARMED OVER A FIRE AND HAD DRUNK A cup of sgai heated over the same campfire, when they mounted for the last stage of the ride home. Moi Kekaspa had even had one of her people dry and oil Alikili's pistol, so that it would show no signs of mistreatment.

"It's more important that it shoot when I need it," Alikili pointed out.

"I'm glad to hear that wisdom," Kekaspa said. "But it will help if no one in the Squadron has to ask questions about the pistol."

"What about the house?" Alikili asked.

"What about it?" Kekaspa said.

"It just came to me. Some of the servants are old Farers. They will wonder about the pistol looking so fine. And about my dry clothes, too."

"Just say that you visited the house of Young Dorpaad," Kekaspa said, with a dismissive wave of her hand.

"I suppose that Dorpaad is one of yours, and will uphold this story?"

"Ask me no questions and you'll learn nothing that can be taken out of you," Kekaspa said.

"Do you tell everyone that, including your mate and mine?"

Kekaspa actually looked bemused for a moment; the sunbrighten grayness let Alikili read her face clearly. Alikili felt briefly ashamed. The spy did not really deserve that kind of question, not after saving Alikili from grave danger if not death, and facing the prospect of some commons' riding the country roads, until Jossu I Hmilra's enemies either abandoned their plans to attack the house or tried to carry them out and were defeated.

Or broke through Kekaspa's guard and took the house, Alikili reminded herself. She remained aware of that possibility, for all the other woman's reassurances that the house was hardly more than bait in a trap that could be expected to do all the necessary work.

She was not sure how strongly Kekaspa felt about having the household left ignorant, lest some of them talk where hostile ears could hear. Therefore, Alikili had resolved to tell her people as little as allowed them to remain safe—but to tell Kekaspa nothing at all about speaking to the people.

That would only ignite an argument. Such an argument would go nowhere and yield nothing—except perhaps a loosening of Kekaspa's authority over her companions. Alikili doubted that even the most remarkable of men could be wholly free of doubts about obeying even the most remarkable of women, particularly in Saadi.

When Kekaspa replied, it was in a somewhat remote voice.

"My mate is kin to a family that once gave Saadi five princes. He holds to the old notion that both sire and bearer must breed courage into the babes. So I tell him much about dangers but little about where they come from, and he thinks I am braver than I am.

"But at least the old tales seem to have it right. Our babe healed swiftly after his little swim, and thrives now in my sister's care. I know he misses me, and I hope he knows that I miss him, but where he is, it will be hard to make a hostage of him."

Alikili almost softened to the point of abandoning her resolve of silence. Moi Kekaspa might end leaving her mate and babe alone, if she did not know everything the house would have ready for its enemies.

"He also thinks it is better I serve where I do," Kekaspa added, with a twisted grin that bared exceptionally white teeth. "Otherwise, he fears that I would serve those who believe that justice for Saadi can never come from the Republic."

"Would you?" Alikili said.

Kekaspa started to glare. A cough twisted her face.

"Perhaps we should find some dry clothes and hot sgai for you," Alikili said mildly.

Another glare began, then turned into soft laughter. "Perhaps we will. And perhaps I will turn my kilt—I and many others of the blood of this land—if those folk prove right.

"But so far, we have found justice among Kertovans, Drilions, even Drylanders from beyond the known Seas of Kilmoyn. Not always, but often enough that we can fairly be asked to seek more, and not turn Saadi into the City-States for no certain gain."

That burst of eloquence brought on another coughing fit. Alikili was tempted to invite Kekaspa to the house, but knew that the other doubtless had a refuge close by. Besides, an invitation to abandon secrecy would be a waste of breath.

They spoke little more, except for Kekaspa's pointing out a few places along the road that Alikili and her people should avoid during the next few commons. After a while it was full light, and Kekaspa reined in near a grove of gnarled and fungus-splotched mellownut too old to give either nuts or timber.

They pressed hands to hearts in farewell, and Alikili did not look back until she was a hundred paces down the road. But by then, Moi Kekaspa and her companions had vanished so thoroughly that they might never have been there in the first place.

SEAN BORLUND DID NOT SLEEP LONG, BUT HE SLEPT SO SOUNDLY THAT EVEN his cabin mate's snores didn't wake him. His own sweat woke him before sunbrighten, and he lay in the sodden bedding for a while contemplating whether it would be safe to "discover" the electric fan.

Probably not now, he decided. The Kertovan knack for compact, high-powered steam engines had reduced the market for expanded uses of electric power. On the other hand, those handy little engines would make wonderful generators, particularly if they could be adjusted to burn "rock oil"—and the technical journals had mentioned that this was being worked on.

It shouldn't be long before electricity was in sufficiently widespread use for various "inventions" to be made without contaminating Kilmoyan culture—assuming, that is, that the stay-behinds had not sold themselves to the Empire (with or without the aid of the Confederation) and embarked on a systematic program of inventions. After two generations in exile, the ragged handful of stay-behinds must be ready to contaminate anything and everything, if it could give them leadership among the humans of Kilmoyn.

Unless their ancestors had stayed behind not out of a desire to play Gods from Space, but out of a genuine disagreement with some of the principles of the *Ramparts* group? That had not occurred so clearly to Borlund before.

The more he thought about it, the clearer the possibility became. Also the greater. If systematically lying to your hosts to protect them from your imagined power to harm them had begun to look like a cure worse than the disease to someone like Sean Borlund—who was definitely no scholar. . . .

To puzzle that one out, Borlund decided he needed fresh air. He shaved quickly and went on deck.

It would have been an exaggeration to call the air "fresh," but an occasional puff of morning breeze blew away some of the sweat and stench. It also brought the smell of wood smoke from shore, where the watchfires were dying down and the cookfires were starting up.

They had the cooking for the refugees well organized by now, Borlund recalled. But sooner or later the area around the camp would be stripped of firewood. Then the wooding parties would have to go farther afield—closer to where enemy ambushes might find them.

A tug steamed past just offshore, towing a bargeload of logs. They looked too big for firewood, and Borlund wondered where they were going. He also noticed that the tug now mounted a crankgun on the cabin just aft of the funnel, and that a torpedo-carrier followed the barge. All the torpedo-carrier's crew except for the engineers and stokers seemed to be on deck, and with a crew at the crankgun forward.

Not wanting to interfere with the watch commanders, Borlund walked aft. A work party was already doing something mysterious to the training gear of the redside quarter gun, and gears, oil cans, and rags littered the deck. Borlund knew that Gunnery work parties liked commander-level spectators even less than the deck Farers, and was turning to go forward again when he saw Barbara Weil coming toward him.

She put a hand on his arm and without a word or much effort steered him to a secluded area amidships, under the flying-deck just forward of the funnel.

"We're going to have a problem with reaching the Study Group," she said. "The telegraph link now runs through Rinbao-Dar, which makes it too insecure even for coded messages. At least that's the Fleet decision."

"So we have to solve the puzzle of the bomb-thrower ourselves?"

"That, and a few others. But the bomb-thrower will be a good start. If we at least make a good try at solving that, the Kertovans shouldn't suspect that we already know the answer."

"That assumes we do," Borlund pointed out.

Weil smiled. "You have little faith in our leaders."

"If I thought they were leading us anywhere it was worthwhile to go, I would have more faith in them," Borlund said.

Weil's smile faded. "Didn't I warn you about preaching your conversion in the streets where the Study Group can hear you?"

"A long time ago. Or it seems that way, at least. Besides, a lot has happened now that hadn't happened then."

A whistle blew off to greenward. Another torpedo-carrier steamed past, towing a smaller barge also piled high with logs.

"What are they doing?" Borlund asked.

"Getting out a boom across the mouth of the anchorage," Weil said. "We don't know what the Empire has on or around the island. But *Byubr* and *Lingvaas* are all the heavy guns we have now if the camp is attacked."

"Do we have enough chain to make something that will hold in a storm?" Borlund asked.

Weil nodded, acknowledging his prudence, then shrugged. "We only have to keep torpedo-carriers out of the anchorage for a few days," Weil said. "And the weather seldom gives worse than rain at this time of year. Once Jossu I Hmilra returns, we'll have plenty of searchlights and guns for a more active defense.

"But it wasn't big guns I was thinking about when I carried you off. It was the bomb-throwers. You mentioned that Chief Zhohorosh is a gunnery expert. Can you and he work together on the local investigation of what the—the Empire has come up with?"

Borlund thought that they ought to send one of *Lingvaas*'s gunners and said so. Weil shook her head.

"It's not expert knowledge we need to send, it's someone our friends trust."

"If I go with that label pinned to me, the Study Group people will be watching me every step of the way."

"Afraid of the Study Group suddenly? Sorry, that was not well said. But I have to meet with Captain Impanskaa of *Byubr* and Commander Shvotz of the groundfighters this morning. I'd like to be able to report as much progress as possible."

Borlund could see Weil's point. He also could see no real argument against taking the assignment.

Except for the danger of being overworked. No, make that a certainty. But what's new about that?

"Aye-aye, ma'am," Borlund said.

Weil didn't quite hug him, but she gripped him by both shoulders, very tightly.

chapter 22

Ehoma Tuomitti usually slept unclothed when she did not sleep alone or when it was almost too hot for a sane Farer to contemplate sleep. Tonight was the second sort of night.

She shared a cabin with three other watch chiefs, but two were women and Huusen the devoutly faithful sire of eight children. She did not fear temptation, only drowning in their own sweat.

The *Illik*-class vessels had never been designed for warm waters and hot winds, when there was a wind, which there usually was not (as tonight, for example). What could be done with clockwork-driven fans, windsails, and sleeping on deck had been done, but the first two were falling apart and the third was no longer safe. Since the Imperial attack, the only Farers allowed on deck were those clothed, armed, and on duty.

Tuomitti rolled over, with the care needed not to jostle the Engineer Chief in the bunk above. The woman was a light sleeper and ill-tempered when awakened.

Spending half the day in the boats and the other half with a work party in the chain locker had taken its toll. Tuomitti found herself yawning, then felt vision grow dim and muscles slacken. Then she was floating along on a current of luminous purple water that seemed to form a border between waking and sleeping.

She thought she saw her father floating not far from her, with the sober look he had always seemed to wear. Had he worn it from foreknowledge of his fate, torn to pieces in a gun accident?

Her father's features gave way to Zhohorosh's. He was smiling, and she wanted to ask him if he and Borlund had penetrated the mystery of the Drylander bomb-thrower. Mysteries, rather. How it worked, how it was made, how it had come to be in Imperial hands, why it had been used for the first time in no more than an attack on the Kertovan patrols on Puyasa. . . .

With the clarity of a waking mind and the fantasies of a dreaming one, Tuomitti wished Zhohorosh good luck and careful hands in seeking the enemy's secrets. And if he won those, then something more, the luck to teach Sean Borlund what Zhohorosh knew of gunnery, for by learning guns Borlund would be a very complete Farer indeed, for a Drylander—

A tight grip on her shoulder. Voices—whispering, but angry, excited, or both. She'd slipped back into the waking world.

"Unh?" was her first reply.

"Stations, everyone," came the voice of the Senior Watch Chief, "but quietly."

"Who's broken into the medical herbs now?" floated querulously from above.

"Swimmers on the boom," the Senior said. "Not ours. We think."

"Who says they're thinking?" came from the top bunk.

"Ask, *after* you're at your posts," the Senior snapped. "We want to be battle-ready before we open fire. Otherwise we might give away our position to folk ready to take advantage of it."

That was an explanation for Farers with two Greats at sea, not watch chiefs. But the Senior was likely enough as hot, weary, and impatient as the rest of them.

Action could cure at least impatience, and Tuomitti would have wagered on action. The Imperial battle-swimmers were half-legend, half-rumor, but there'd been suspicious incidents that could hardly be explained otherwise.

They were one reason the Island Republic's ships did not anchor too far up the Hask, even in City-State waters. They were also one of several good reasons for the three days of backbreaking labor to lay the boom across the mouth of the anchorage.

Tuomitti slid out of her bunk, landing with her heel on a rivet in the deck. Pain burned the oath out of her mouth; she groped blindly and felt Huusen holding her up.

"Easy, there, girl," he said.

"Girl?" she snapped, then remembered that his eldest daughter was only a few Greats younger than she. Except for wanting to be part of this last great voyage to Eneh, he would doubtless be home with them, and *their* children.

She'd do her best, Lord and Lady helping, to see that he went home afterward.

* * *

ALIKILI COULD NOT SLEEP AND WONDERED WHY.

It could not be that she was alone in the bed she had so often shared with Jossu. She always slept poorly for a few nights after he went to sea, but he had been in southern waters much longer than that.

Nor was it injury or illness; she had not so much as a dripping nose or earache from her battle on the storm-swept road. Perhaps it was just that she had slept so long the first night at home that now her body needed less rest than usual.

Certainly she had little enough to do. Coming home, she had found that the house was as ready for defense as could be contrived, short of spikewire in the hedges or crankguns on the roof.

Either Moi Kekaspa had been lying about keeping the situation secret from the house, the house had drawn their own conclusions and taken their own measures, or Kekaspa's people in the house had talked freely whether she wished it or not. It would be both interesting and important to find out which, after their common enemies had been routed.

Meanwhile, Alikili knew of at least three of Kekaspa's people in place, and trusted otherwise to the natural loyalty and good sense of her household. Some might not approve of the southern campaign; she doubted that any would let their disapproval make them play traitor or even give ear to criminals.

Now it was the evening of the third common since her homecoming. She had not done work decent for a Farer since then, and she had begun to wonder if she had protected her home or deserted her post.

Perhaps what now left her sleepless was the thought of not doing her duty with the Women's Squadron? She not only missed the long commons of handling the thousand and one aspects of administering the Fleet, she missed the comradeship that came with sunfade and the end of duty. She suspected that some of those comrades missed her too, and not only because her age, experience, and position gave her advice what could pass for wisdom among the younger women.

She had not been *needed* by anyone save Jossu I Hmilra and her kin for more Greats than she could count on her fingers. She doubted that this discovery would warp her life, draw the wrath of any god, or even much unsettle Jossu.

She did not, however, wish to put it in the letter that lay on the nightboard beside the bed, half-written (or perhaps less than that, seeing how much had been crossed out).

She could perhaps give herself the sense of doing something useful by making a fair copy of the mangled opening of the letter, and thereby find inspiration for finishing it as it and Jossu deserved. A cup of something hot, however, would speed the search for inspiration.

She rang.

"Hot hoeg," she told the servant who appeared. He looked like one of the old Farers in the house, who spent more time laying fires and shifting crates and barrels than he did bringing refreshments to the lady. He was immaculately clean, though, and both his muscles and his garments bulged reassuringly.

"Aught else?" he asked, with a pronounced Saadian accent.

"Plenty of greenmist in the hoeg, say half," she added.

"You'll not sleep, after that," the man said.

Alikili grunted in frustration. She hadn't had this many nursemaids when she was a newborn babe!

"I should think there's enough to keep anyone awake," she replied.

"Mayhap," the Farer said. "But if they come, it won't be tonight. Quiet, clear, and those of us who need to be awake will stay that way."

Alikili muttered a Drilion oath that made the man's ears twitch. He would not meet her eye as he backed out, but his shoulders shook.

It was only after the door closed that Alikili discovered that the inkpot was dry. She lay back on the pillows, setting herself to compose the rest of the letter in her mind. When the hoeg came, it would be soon enough to ask for fresh ink.

UNDER OTHER CIRCUMSTANCES, SEAN BORLUND WOULD HAVE SAID THAT HE was wandering. On a larger ship with a broader deck or even aboard *Lingvaas* on a night when he had fewer duties, he might actually have done so.

But tonight each change in the direction of his steps, from redside to green and back again, was deliberate. He wanted to keep an eye on the lookouts, who probably didn't need a commander or even a chief looking over their shoulder to make sure they were intently watching the sea. He also wanted to look out into the darkness himself, if only to reassure himself that nothing was out there that hadn't been visible the last time he looked.

This time he stopped at the railing and rested one hand on the slick metal of the forward greenside davit. It was slick with condensation from the damp air, not spray from a sea that looked like an oily pond. Smelled like one, too—the land smells of vegetation, both living and decaying, mingled with water smells. Water that held life, but lay motionless so that the life might be in suspended animation.

Lingvaas was steering a random course up and down the west side of Puyasa, just outside the shoals and with the best leadsman in the chains to make sure she stayed outside. An outpost with one torpedo-carrier picketed the mouth of the Lhub River; it was there they had found the most signs of Imperial landings.

Not that the next wave of Imperials was certain to come there. But certainly it was the best-hidden place with water deep enough for anything more than a canoe, so both tactical sense and the known Imperial habit of falling into a routine made it worth guarding.

To seaward of *Lingvaas,* three other torpedo-carriers roamed in the darkness. They were as thoroughly blacked-out as she was, but had extra lookouts chosen for their night vision. One had also landed her torpedoes and shipped an extra crankgun and a double allowance of ammunition. Light craft or troop barges were bad targets for torpedoes, but horribly vulnerable to crankguns for explosive shells.

Also, on a quiet night like this, the uproar of a crankgun opening fire would be all the warning *Lingvaas* needed—and she had extra signalers posted, to flash warning to the outpost that was connected by the field wire-post to the camp. If survivors of the first Imperial landing force hadn't found the wires and cut it again. If the Imperials didn't risk a ship bristling with crankguns or fast enough to ram the torpedo-carriers—

Borlund ended the mental parade of "ifs," looked into the darkness, and then at the launch on the davits. The canvas cover was snugged down tight, to keep rain out.

Find out when the cover was last undone, to give the launch an airing. Tropical molds and fungi had a voracious appetite for damp, closed spaces, like the bilges of a launch too long sealed.

That kind of detail was really the chiefs' duty, but it never hurt for a commander to remind them that he knew about the details. Borlund thought he'd finally learned to walk the fine line between standing back so far the chiefs thought he was careless and standing so close that they thought he was doing their job for them out of mistrust.

At least Zhohorosh said so. Borlund sometimes wondered if Zhohorosh's praise of him these past few commons was sincere. The Kertovans certainly seemed to be engaged in the next thing to a conspiracy of tact, to assure the humans that finding Drylanders among Imperial troops didn't make them distrust the Farers of *Lingvaas*.

Borlund now walked aft, studying the lashings of the launch's cover. All snug, none showing any signs of being undone to let a pair (or more) of lovers crawl into the launch for a quick meeting.

Zhohorosh said that was a problem, in tropical waters after a midtide or so. "Something in the air," was how he'd put it.

Human sexual codes should make that less of a problem aboard *Lingvaas*—but "should" was as important a word here as "less." Borlund had noticed a few exchanges of the same kind of looks he exchanged with Barbara Weil, when they were absolutely sure nobody could see them.

For a few commons he had found himself aroused at the thought of what might happen if nobody could see him and the Captain for a really long time—even half a watch. But that was letting himself grow frustrated over the absence of a miracle—he found himself using that Observant term for gross anomalies, more and more often.

He came out from behind the launch and looked out to sea again. The leadsman called out:

"Sixteen and a half, muddy bottom."

Plenty of water, and if there was any kind of bottom around here except mud—

Out to sea, a lamp flickered.

Borlund watched it long enough to know that it wasn't a trick of his vision or sweat running into his eyes. So he missed the reply, from the shadowed bulk of the land to redward.

He did not miss the yellow spark of a crankgun firing, or the orange flare from the muzzles of heavier guns replying. He did not hear the shout to the signalers and the clacking of the lamp-shutters as they flashed "Enemy in sight" to the outpost, because for a moment the long boom and longer rumble of the seaward guns drowned out every sound aboard *Lingvaas*.

On deck, Borlund was already at his post. But in the interval between the second enemy salvo and the arrival of its sound, he heard the thud of feet on wood and their clang on ladders, as *Lingvaas* went to battle stations.

VALOR'S BOW WAVE HISSED AND SPLASHED IN A FAINTLY SHIMMERING ARC TO either side of the ram. Jossu I Hmilra looked at the traces of seaglow with what would have been a sour expression, if Captains Over Captains were allowed that.

The southbound Fleet was running without lights, and he had taken great trouble (as well as greatly annoying certain Captains) to choose a formation that would make this safe. Safe, from both the hazards of the sea and the fury of the enemy, from both collision caused by unexpected course changes and enemy torpedo-carriers slipping between the columns and firing from barely outside the arming range.

Now seaglow threatened to make the Island Republic's ships visible from several-score casts farther than they would have been otherwise. Only slowing still further could douse the seaglow now, and some of the ships could not maintain steerageway at any lower speed. The half-empty coal-carriers and at least two of the transports were among these.

Then it seemed for a moment that the sea off the redside bow caught fire. Seven parallel lines of green fire seared across the dark water, as if a seven-fingered hand had clawed at the sea. I Hmilra gripped the railing so tightly that his knuckles ached by the time the first of the Seakin blew.

Seakin. *Not* Imperial torpedoes or some mystery out of Farer legend. I Hmilra knew quick relief, unclamped his hands—then heard the other six Seakin blow also at precise intervals. Too precise, to have any meaning except one.

This was a message party.

"Send for the Speaker to Seakin," I Hmilra said.

The watch commander saluted with great discipline and grinned with equal triumph. "Already done, Lord. Do you want her up here or down on the bow?"

"Down on the bow, with relay talkers to a Farer on the whistle."

"That could warn the Imperials as well as tell the rest of the clan."

"Not being able to warn the rest of the Seakin risks offending every last one of them in the Gulf, at least," I Hmilra said.

"At least?" the commander asked, plainly controlling irritation at being ignorant in front of both seniors and juniors.

"The message we received before the Fleet sailed south was said to be from the entire race of Seakin. *If* they communicate that well, and if the Speakers know their—"

"I assure you that the Seakin do communicate that well," came a level voice apparently from around I Hmilra's knee. He looked down, to see the Speaker to Seakin on the ladder to the bridge. She climbed the last few rungs briskly for one old enough to have lost most of her ruff, nodded by way of greeting, then looked forward.

"I can handle the whistle myself, Captain," she said. "It will save time, and they seem to think that important."

The Seakin sense of time was still a complete mystery to even seasoned Farers, and largely one to the Speakers. I Hmilra let the bold statement pass, however, not wishing to insult the Speaker a second time.

This was only the fifth time he had been present at a conversation between Speakers and Seakin, which was about four more times than many Farers. It was only the second at which the Speaker had used a ship's whistle to reply to the water-dwellers' blowholes. The first time, the Speaker had made a hideous din that gave I Hmilra a crashing headache and the Seakin reply was nothing that the Speaker would swear to being even approximately the truth.

This time he was luckier, or the Speaker was more sure of herself, or the Seakin were more eloquent in the Twin Tongue, or *something* was on the side of communication. Certainly the Speaker's prowess on the whistle was; she had to have been a Farer, to be able to play *Valor*'s massive steam whistle like a Saadian songpiper in a park concert.

The last howl of steam was fading away, and the Seakin were circling *Valor* in pairs, before I Hmilra's patience finally overcame his self-command.

"Well?"

"What they said, Captain?"

"No, whether the sky is green or pink!"

"Temper, Captain."

"The correct address is—" the watch commander began.

The Speaker looked not so much at the young commander as through him, to the Seakin beyond. Then she jerked the whistle cord again. Anything the commander might have been about to say was lost in a triple blast. The Seakin replied, each with a single blowing, and sounded.

"As I was saying, Captain Over Captains," the Speaker resumed, "they did come to warn us. They said that those not Landkin—I do not like that translation, but—"

"Does that poor word affect the truth of what they told you?" I Hmilra said. "I too delight in a fine choice of words, but not when time presses, as you seem to be saying it does."

The Speaker looked annoyed. I Hmilra swore to himself that if she was angry enough to sulk until he had counted to ten, she would never sail with the Fleet again. (The Speakers had a powerful guild, so that was the most he could do; throwing her overboard would be only briefly satisfying and doubtless end his career nearly as quickly hers.)

At the count of seven, the Speaker was continuing.

"Those who are not Landkin have come against the rest of our tribe in—it translates as the south. Not Luokka, the people off Rinbao-Dar, on that island I never could remember and the Seakin have no name for—"

"Puyasa," the watch commander put in,

"Thank you," the Speaker said, more graciously than before. "On Puyasa there is—or will be, I can't be sure—fighting. The unfriends have come by sea but will fight both on land and on the sea. The water is too shallow for the Seakin to help, if their—we call it *law* but it's really not translatable—"

This time I Hmilra held his tongue as the Speaker went off into a long display of her erudition. She might be telling him nothing that he needed to listen to, but she was giving him time to organize his thoughts.

"I thank you," I Hmilra said at last. "Signalers!"

The Speaker understood the dismissal and looked as if she wished to protest. Then she met I Hmilra's eyes and this time thought the better of it.

"Signal to the Fleet," I Hmilra began. "All ships burn running lights and crew searchlights. Torpedo-carriers cast off and take station by threes, ahead of each column, distance twenty casts.

"On flagship's signal, all ships change course to greenside five, maintaining column and individual intervals and speed."

The first signal was going out with the clacking of the lamps before I Hmilra had finished speaking. Once the Fleet was on its new course and properly lit, he would increase speed.

He was making an unsubtle response, a mating dreezan's charge of a response, bringing the whole Fleet south in a solid wall of ships. But he was bringing them in on a course that would take them well out to sea, in deep water where even *Valor* and the still-loaded coal-carriers would have maneuvering room.

Also, where the Imperials might with luck be trapped between the Puyasa garrison and the guns of the Fleet, and cut off from any Confederate or other naval help.

Now, all they needed was for those tales of someone tinkering up a wire-post that needed no wires and could send coded signals through the air at the speed of thought. . . .

Dreams, for now. Reality was the solid deck of *Valor* under his feet and the solid railing under his hand.

chapter 23

Everyone on *Byubr*'s deck was still on duty. Not all were clothed, because they had scrambled on deck hastily. Nor were all armed, because not all had duties that allowed them to carry personal weapons.

Ehoma Tuomitti wore enough for street decency and more than enough for battle modesty; she also carried her pistol. It was on her belt now because she needed both hands free to signal or push her anchor section into position.

Whistles, shouts, anything that made noise—Captain Impanskaa had forbidden them. His plain intent was to have *Byubr* fully alert and ready to open fire without giving any sign of this to the enemy.

If there was an enemy.

On the prow, forward of the capstan and just above the tarnished scrollwork on the stem, Tuomitti had as good a view as anyone on the main deck and better than most. For all she could see, the Imperial combat swimmers might have vanished back into legend or at least into the dark sea.

They might also have left gifts behind them—waterproof explosive charges tied to the boom, or mines set adrift in the anchorage. Or they might even now be swimming for shore, to slit the throats of sentries at the refugee camp, or for *Byubr*, to board and grapple, shielding themselves among Farers too afraid of hurting a friend to defend themselves against a stalking enemy—

Tuomitti slammed the hatches in her mind on such fancies. She wished she could slam real ones on the prying fingers of Imperial visitors. Then she felt a subtle vibration in the slick deck planks under her feet.

The stokers had been keeping a low fire in two of the ship's four boilers. The two would give enough steam for getting underway. Hot coals from the first two boilers, spread across the grates of the others, would bring them to steaming pressure much faster than stoking from cold iron.

Tuomitti looked up at the tall, stout funnel, now serving as part of the support for two searchlight platforms. She trusted that the last funnel-cleaning had left no pockets of soot in the uptakes to flare brightly and warn everyone of *Byubr*'s presence.

The vibration underfoot turned into a faint but audible rumble. The hiss of steam into the capstan and, farther aft, into the training gear of the twelve-line gun joined the padding of bare feet and the occasional clink as someone brushed metal against metal.

Tuomitti raised both hands over her head, then dropped them palms down. Five Farers of the anchor section took their positions. The other three raised weapons, two rifles and a sword—although what good the sword would do unless the Imperials really *did* board—

The darkness to seaward shattered in a thundering explosion and a towering column of water, lit from within as if by spirit-fire. The shattered darkness rained down in unidentifiable fragments of every shape and size, raising splashes halfway to *Byubr*.

Spirit-fire and column vanished, but before they did Tuomitti saw three black-painted shapes on the water just outside the boom, and two larger ones barely visible farther out to sea. It was too brief a glimpse to more than hint, but the hint was of Imperial torpedo-carriers.

On *Byubr*'s decks, discipline strained but did not part its moorings. The one anchor Farer who raised her voice above a whisper stared briefly down the muzzle of Tuomitti's pistol, then nodded and turned back to her work. Around the main gun, the crankguns, the searchlights, everyone gripped ammunition, tools, or handles, posed with them for a moment like a troupe of hill dancers, then eased their stances.

They had just done this when a second explosion sprayed water and flame across the beach in front of the camp. The roar echoed around the anchorage, joined by screams from the camp.

From pain or fear? Tuomitti wondered.

Byubr's seaward searchlight snapped on. From beyond the boom, the spitting yellow flame of a crankgun replied—or, rather, from beyond where the boom had been. Searchlight and gunflash together showed a gap wide enough to pass three ships the size of *Byubr* steaming abreast.

Fire sparked in the darkness of the forest-covered point to the north of the anchorage. An enemy landing party trying to clear the way for their comrades, or Kertovans moved so secretly that *Byubr* hadn't been told, trying to defend the anchorage?

No bullets touched *Byubr* or her Farers from land or sea. That left Tuomitti and everyone else still ignorant of who was shooting at whom, but usefully informed the crankgun crews that they did not have an identified target. The four crankguns with clear bearings remained silent.

The searchlight's beam lifted now, briefly gilding the funnels of two unmistakable Imperial torpedo-carriers, both of them now using their crankguns. Tuomitti shouted to her people to be ready to lie down. The enemy could find the range at any moment, and sweeping an enemy's decks with crankgun fire was listed in most books on tactics as a preparation for boarding.

If the crankguns lacked range or targets, the same could not be said of the main gun. Tuomitti heard metal squeal, as the gun turned; clangs as the breech opened to receive a shell, then shut behind it; more squealing.

"Down!" she called.

She barely had time to obey her own order and clap her hands over her ears when the main gun fired. The yellow-orange flare from the muzzle not only shattered darkness but drove it back to the remote corners of the world. The muzzle blast swept over the anchor section like a stormblast, and would have knocked Tuomitti up against the railing if she hadn't taken a two-handed grip on a bollard.

She lurched to her feet, ears ringing but eyes not too dazzled to see the first shell hit. It had gone high, but the funnel of a torpedo-carrier was almost solid enough for the fuse of a common shell. It was a flat, almost subdued explosion, but it must have sent one fragment into a boiler and others into one of the torpedoes.

Steam wreathed the little vessel, but not so much that Tuomitti didn't see the stump of the funnel topple overboard and the dark shapes of the crew leaping after it. The carrier slewed around, without a hand on the wheel, nearly collided with its mate, then lost way. It was almost dead in the water when *Byubr*'s main gun fired again.

This time Tuomitti took the shot standing up. Her head might have flown off her shoulders or the rest of her overboard, but she couldn't take her eyes off the squat shape revealed by the torpedo-carrier's death and plainly the target of the second shell.

Target, but not victim. The second shell struck the water and burst, showing more clearly still a broad-beamed, shallow-draft river-steamer, of the kind the Imperials built by the score. She was throwing up a bow wave such as she could never have done in ordinary service, as she swept toward the gap in the boom. On her deck the fire-sparks of groundfighter weapons began to dance.

This time Tuomitti heard the *wheett* of bullets passing, and the *spanngg* of them hitting metal close by. She did not hear any cries of wounded Farers, because *Byubr*'s crankguns opened fire, now sure of their range. Their bang and clatter made a din fit to kill the living as readily as to wake the dead, and drove silence back to the same remote corner of the world as darkness.

Tuomitti had to ask the messenger tugging at her arm to repeat himself three times before she understood that *Byubr* was going to weigh anchor and get underway. The main gun fired a third time as the anchor section took their posts, knocking them down again without the shell's hitting anything. The fourth shot drowned out the clanking of the capstan, and this time a Farer went down so that he would have been caught in or maybe under the chain if two others hadn't snatched him clear—

Tuomitti saw a fifth shot going into the main gun, and this time remembered to open her mouth as well as clap her hands over her ears. Without the orders she'd forgotten to give, two of her section pried the hatch off the chain-locker and scrambled down, to be sure that the chain was coming in properly.

Then the main gun fired its fifth round.

BY THE TIME ALIKILI FINISHED COMPOSING THE LETTER, SHE HOPED THE HOEG was scalding hot and loaded with greenmist. Otherwise she might not be awake long enough for the servant to bring the fresh ink, let alone finish the letter.

She also wanted to be particularly delicate in her choice of words. Jossu would not object to her new sense of duty to the Women's Squadron, unless he thought that meant diminished regard for him. He concealed his pride under the Captain-Born's customary armor, but it was there and capable of being wounded. Nor could he wholly ignore the gap of so many Greats in their ages, not when he was alone with his conscience.

She could be sure of one thing. Jossu I Hmilra would never dismiss his conscience or even give it a leave of absence, as many men (and to be truthful, women) had done under such circumstances.

Alikili was running her description of the number of jouti in the Squadron who wished to go to sea, when she heard a knock.

"Enter."

The door opened. As it did, Alikili thought she saw two figures silhouetted against the light in the hall when she had only expected one. But the man in the lead was the old Farer with a tray held gracefully aloft in one hand and a basket covered with a napkin in the other.

"The cook had just finished baking—" he began.

Then the light in the hall went out. Not before Alikili saw the second figure take a long step, not before her mind and nerves together screamed:

"Treachery!"

She screamed aloud what she hoped would be taken as a warning and flung herself out of bed on the side away from the door. Either scream or movement warned the Farer; he spun around, dropping the basket to free at least one hand.

One bare hand and a tray were still no match for any weapon. It was Alikili's good fortune that the intruder did not realize this. His long knife first drove between the servant's ribs, piercing so many organs that the Farer must have been dead before he struck the floor. He did not fall, however, before his last gasp sprayed blood all over his killer.

Wiping his face and retrieving his knife delayed the killer just enough for Alikili to slip a hand under her pillow and withdraw her pistol. It did not fail her.

What failed her was her battle judgment—not wholly surprising in only her second battle. She concentrated so completely on putting three shots into the knifeman, that she failed to see the second figure in the doorway. When she did, she saw nothing about him that said "enemy"—until he threw a lantern at her.

She ducked and shot, so that the lantern missed her and she missed the new attacker. Then the lantern crashed to the floor, shattering as it did, spewing flames and the stench of rock oil.

Alikili felt the scorching at her back as well as the stench pricking at her nostrils. If she stood to escape the flames, she would be silhouetted against them. If she crawled around the end of the bed, she would be a slow-moving target. If she crawled under the bed, she would die a coward.

So she slipped the pistol down the front of her nightrobe, then lay flat, feigning being stunned or frightened into helplessness, watching with half an eye as the second attacker stood by the bed.

Would he draw another knife, use his comrade's, or risk the noise of a pistol? Three shots must have waked the whole house by now, and every loyal soul in it must be rallying. He was big, though. If it came to a grapple, Alikili doubted she had much chance. Pistols evened that kind of odds, but only if you could hit with them—

The man climbed onto the bed and stood, looking down at Alikili. Rage at muddy boots ruining her bedding nearly drove her prematurely into action. But she waited, until he flexed at the knees, ready to jump down and subject her "corpse" to a close examination.

In the moment that he was off-balance, she rolled over, drew her pistol, and fired at the largest target, the man's belly. The heavy bullet knocked him back and down into a sitting position, which for a moment was all that told Alikili she might have hit him.

Then the man started screaming.

In a part of her mind, Alikili both marveled and stared in horror at her own self-command, rising to examine the knifeman and find him dead, then realizing that if she wanted a live prisoner the second attacker had to be kept alive.

But not screaming like that. Not anywhere under the rule of Lord and Lady, screaming like that.

She did not want to take her hand off the butt of the pistol, so she knocked the man senseless with the barrel. Another fragment of her mind now commanded her ears, so that by the time the man fell back, bleeding now from scalp as well as belly, Alikili knew that she had heard other shots and other screams.

She was fumbling more cartridges out of the drawer of the bedside table and into the pistol, when Moi Kekaspa strode in like the Lady of Cleansing.

"I thought you were riding the—out there," Alikili said.

"I was. But there were more than we thought out there, and traitors in here. I thought we'd best fall back around you." Her tone was of one taking command as a natural right, even if it was in someone else's house. Alikili would have resented this, if she had been able to think clearly.

Then Kekaspa seemed to take in the carnage in the bedroom for the first time.

"Both yours?"

"My what?"

"Kills?"

"Kuh—keh—?" Alikili's stomach churned and her mouth filled.

Fortunately, the chamber pot was empty, so she managed to preserve the rug if not her dignity. It was only after her stomach was empty that she realized what kind of a mess turning a bedroom into a battlefield really made.

Her second battlefield. But the first one, where she had not only been an intended target but had to *kill* to keep herself alive. A first as important, no doubt, as realizing her sense of duty to the Women's Squadron. Unlike that other first, one that she would rather forget.

She pulled herself to her feet, and Kekaspa chased everyone out into the hall to give Alikili some privacy. She needed clean clothes, to be sure, but what she really wanted was a hot bath and some hotter hoeg.

But there was no time for the bath, if she was besieged in her own home. As for the hoeg, she took one look at the Farer who'd been bringing it, face-down in a puddle that mixed his blood with the spilled hoeg. She would have heaved again if her stomach hadn't been too dry and empty.

It would be whole Greats before she could order hoeg again.

IT TOOK LONG ENOUGH FOR EVERYONE ABOARD *LINGVAAS* TO BECOME THOROUGHLY uneasy, before they learned the strength of the attack from the sea.

Lingvaas's Farers would have been worse than uneasy if they hadn't been busy preparing their ship for action. At least that occupied their hands; but to Sean Borlund they seemed so well trained that they could run out and load the guns, stock the dressing stations with bandages and splints from the sick quarters, and so on, without thinking.

Borlund was able to keep both hands and mind busy. Battle Stations was an all-hands job; good commanders were expected to work up a sweat if necessary. With his size and strength, Borlund was able to find it "necessary" quite a few times.

At last the ship was ready for action, and his good luck did not desert him even then. Signals swarmed in from the scouting line. Some were broken, some fragmentary, and many hard to tell from the gunflashes.

Barbara Weil had a notebook full of signals within a few beats, and summarized them for every commander within hearing.

"Eight-plus large merchant vessels, one with heavy guns on deck. Several torpedo-carriers and unidentified light vessels, some towing barges. Looks like a major reinforcement for the island, obviously."

"What kind of troops?" Borlund asked. "Imperial Regulars or more tribal—"

He wanted to say "scrapings," but that would dishonor at least the courage of the people he'd fought—what seemed like four Greats instead of four commons ago.

"Don't know," Weil replied. "Tribal warriors come cheap around here. Regulars have to be brought in. Also, if they're after the refugees, to prove that we can't protect them and so turn Rinbao-Dar toward the Empire, they might not feel they need their best fighters. Just their fiercest."

Not everyone here was allowed knowledge of the bomb-thrower and all that it implied about human assistance to the Empire. The time was coming when curing poisonous rumors would be more important than guarding the Directorate's pet secrets. Meanwhile, Borlund had drawn his own conclusions.

It was simply that there were as many misguided, stupid, or plain dishonest people of both races on the other side as there were fighting for the Republic. The enemy was never a supernatural being.

However, a whole convoy of any sort of groundfighters could mean more *natural* beings than the defenders of Peyasa could handle. At least more than they could meet and still protect the refugees, which meant that *Lingvaas* was about to go down fighting on her side of the island and *Byubr* on hers, because neither race would care to live on knowing they'd deserted the refugees.

Not to mention handing Rinbao-Dar to the Empire—or at least putting the Matriarchy where the Empire could make trouble in the cities any day it chose.

Diplomacy and decency asked the same sacrifice.

Borlund realized that he'd been drawing conclusions while Weil had gone on saying things he should have heard. He thought it was only his not having heard the first part of her plan that made him start when she said:

"—get out to sea, then close in as fast as we can and try for that armed transport. She means command of the sea around Peyasa. If we're close enough, and she can't use her broadside without hitting the other transports. Unless they scatter.

"If they scatter, that will delay them. Delay them, and our groundfighters can post sentries on every beach with access to a trail. The Imperials will have to fight their way off the beaches.

"I'll wager half of them will still be on the beaches when *Valor* and the rest of the Fleet come back. Then we won't have anything more to worry about."

Borlund was inclined to agree, if only because *Lingvaas* might not be afloat or her Farers alive by then. But they had a fighting chance, against even a heavily armed vessel with no more armor than they had and almost certainly inferior gunnery.

That was not underestimating the enemy. That was a realistic assessment of risks, unless the Empire had bought not only ships but entire crews of trained gunners from the Confederation. Borlund decided to keep *that* possibility to himself.

Weil had finished while Borlund was assessing risks. He had decided that he was dismissed along with the rest—*Lingvaas* was already heading out to sea—when Captain Weil signaled with one hand.

In the shadow of one corner of the bridge, she gripped his hands and looked down at his feet. "I hope this comes off. I hope the Kertovans will stop worrying about Drylanders not making good Farers. And I hope we come through it, so we can keep our promises."

She did not kiss him, because a messenger scrambled up the ladder just as she swayed forward to do so. The messenger was Roald Chaykin-Schmidt, with a look on his face that said he had heard everything and was disappointed not to see more. Borlund's glare sobered him quickly.

The boy was hardworking and a promising Farer, but his "uncle" was still Directorate Security.

IT NOT ONLY SEEMED ONLY A BEAT OR TWO SINCE JOSSU I HMILRA HAD LAIN down on his bunk to try sleeping. It actually had been.

He set his feet on the deck and glowered at the messenger. His orders about being called in any kind of Fleet emergency were strict; they had been obeyed; he could not honorably or wisely abuse anyone. The same rules bound the commander of a Fleet as bound the Captain of a single ship.

He would still have offered a Great's celibacy for another watch of sleep. (On second thought, he would not. Alikili would flay him alive.)

"Yes?"

"Captain's respects, lord, and we hear gunfire to the south. Heavy guns."

"Our position?"

The position report took away Jossu I Hmilra's last hope. From here, southward meant Puyasa, and heavy guns in action there probably did not mean *Byubr* going out for night firing practice.

"My compliments to the Captain, and have him order steam for the maximum sustainable Fleet speed."

"Ah—"

"Well? If the Captain doesn't know it, we'll just have to find out what it is when ships begin to break down."

The messenger fled with great haste and no dignity whatever.

chapter 24

Thoma Tuomitti had too much else to do to follow the path of the fifth round. As the gun blazed, the anchor started moving, the vibrations in the deck told her that the propeller was turning, and every drum, trumpet, and whistle aboard *Byubr* signaled "Getting underway."

Being half-blinded by the muzzle flash and more than half-deafened by the discharge didn't help either.

She crouched by the capstan, closer than she would have allowed most Farers, alternately watching the chain come in and shouting reports on the ship's position to the Farers below. Two more of the section wielded a hose hooked to the foredeck pump, washing the mud and filth of the bottom off the chain as it came in. *Byubr* generated enough reeks and smells of her own without help from the southern seas.

The last of the section was mounting guard but had no other work until after the seventh round. By then *Byubr* was backing down slowly, and the anchor chain was so taut that Tuomitti heard the winch groaning and squealing under the strain. She supposed that the Captain knew what he was doing; backing down would put the ship in water too shallow for torpedo attacks and open arcs of training for more crankguns and searchlights.

She still fought the urge to order the Farers in the chain locker back on deck. If the chain snapped under the strain, they'd have no hope of dropping flat or leaping overboard. The flailing chain and flying links would slice them apart before they could say "Take my spirit—"

The seventh shell round flew, Tuomitti started to look out to sea again, and a dark shape burst over the railing.

It was on her blind side and she could barely recognize it as a Farer, let alone what kind or which side. The sentry had a better view and fewer problems. She fired from the hip at the same time as the newcomer swept a long knife upward into her belly. She screamed, the newcomer flew backward several paces, the sentry fired again, and the newcomer's head disintegrated.

Then the sentry dropped to her knees, no longer screaming. She whimpered softly as she bit her lip and tried to keep her guts from slipping out on to the deck.

Tuomitti hated to leave anyone to die alone, especially like that, but where there was one war swimmer there might be more. She picked up the rifle and handed it to one of the hose crew. Then she strode aft, looking over the side as she went, hoping that as *Byubr* picked up speed the wash alongside would keep any more war swimmers from finding a handhold.

She did not let herself think about what a beautiful target she made, head silhouetted against the sky. Or at least when she did, she reminded herself that a shot to the head would be a clean, painless death, compared to what a Farer of her section faced tonight.

By the time the anchor broke water and clanged onto its seat, *Byubr* had fired three more rounds from her main gun. The crankguns were now firing intermittent bursts, which Tuomitti hoped meant they were short of targets rather than short of ammunition.

Most of all, somebody aft must have seen the war swimmer's attack and spread the warning. Lanterns and lamps hung all along the railings, with rifle-armed Farers on the deckhouse peering into the water alongside. A large insect would have been sighted trying to board now.

Then *Byubr*'s engines shifted from slow back to slow ahead, and from that swiftly to one-third, two-thirds, and at last full speed. The main gun fired three more times before Tuomitti saw a decent bow wave, but after that the stokers must have shoveled like fire-sprites. *Byubr* was throwing spray higher than her anchor when she passed through the gap in the boom.

Tuomitti stared around her, wishing that some of the spray would splash high enough to wash her face. She felt ready to shave her hide bare, if nothing else would get it clean.

Crankguns raved again, from out to sea, from the north point, from *Byubr*, and from alongside. Tuomitti watched spray rise from the shallows, sand and gravel from the beach. Running figures also rose from the shallows and ran toward the camp. But groundfighter rifles on land and crankguns aboard *Byubr* and a Kertovan torpedo-carrier chopped them down like mad cane cutters.

It was not a good night for the war swimmers.

The main gun ceased firing, and a stretcher party came forward to pick up the gut-slit Farer. She was mercifully senseless now, from the blood lost before one of her comrades packed the wound with an emergency dressing. Tuomitti hoped the woman would never awaken—then started and nearly slipped in the pooled blood.

The beach on the north point now swarmed with dark figures running with as little apparent purpose as fingernippers in a panic. Fires in the trees and flares overhead showed up the runners as Imperials. The Kertovan defenders seemed to have fallen back on the camp, with only a few fire-sparks in the trees to show where the rearguard stood.

The river-steamer lay broadside to the beach, hard aground. Bodies littered her decks, blood streaked her sides, and her deckhouse and funnels had been ripped off by shells where they hadn't been hammered flat. A fire blazed amidships, adding light and what Tuomitti would swear was the reek of burning flesh to the battle scene.

The little ship had done her duty. She had landed her groundfighters where the survivors could advance on the camp, using the trees for cover from both the camp's defenders and the ships in the anchorage.

Tuomitti wondered why *Byubr* was heading out to sea, instead of remaining in the anchorage. From there her guns could sweep the open ground between the trees and the camp, and even punch through the trees to smash any bomb-throwers or crankguns the Imperials brought up.

But in the anchorage *Byubr* would also be a sitting target for torpedoes, now that the boom was gone, or even another wave of war swimmers. And if the Imperials ashore couldn't take the camp, they could still hold the point for the landing of reinforcements. At sea, *Byubr* could intercept those reinforcements.

That made sense to Ehoma Tuomitti. It also made sense that she was a watch chief, not a commander. She could play with this sort of decision. She didn't have to make it, then see Farers die if it was wrong.

Engine thumping, *Byubr* headed north. A torpedo-carrier fell in behind her, then moved up to her greenside. Any waterborne attack would come from there, at least for the next tenth-watch.

To landward, the searchlights swept the trees, making the grease-vines shimmer eerily. At least one Imperial crankgun was ashore; it fired a single burst and *Byubr*'s crew replied with four crankguns and a round from the main gun. Destroyed or merely discreet, the enemy crankgun fell silent.

Tuomitti remembered that with the anchor raised, her next duty was to lead a repair party. Or inspect it, anyway, since *Byubr* seemed to have no damage to repair.

She walked aft, past the main gun with its bent stanchions, scorched paint, and gunners black as if they'd been rolling in the coal bunkers. She waved; they'd done well enough that she could forgive them the ringing in her ears and the bruises where they'd knocked her down.

In fact, she'd have been almost content, if Zhohorosh had been aboard to share the coming sea fight.

WITH HER BACK SAFE FOR THE MOMENT, ALIKILI TURNED TO THE WORK OF keeping the bedchamber from going up in flames. Fortunately the lantern's rock oil had not fallen on anything that would burn like dry tinder such as the bed hangings.

In the bath, Alikili soaked a blanket until it was dripping, then flung it over the heart of the fire. A servant with an equally sodden pillow attacked the rest. Then more of the household appeared, sooty and grimy, holding mostly empty buckets, which they promptly ran to fill.

They were even sootier and grimier by the time the fire was at last out, as well as coughing from the smoke. Alikili thought of opening a window, then realized that with the room lit from within, this would tell anyone lurking outside exactly where to strike, with gun or bomb.

She would have given much to be able to chop a hole in the floor. The firefighting water lay toe-deep even where the rug had soaked up some.

More water that hadn't drenched the floor had ended in Alikli's wardrobe chests. She had a long search for clothes that would preserve decency, keep her warm, allow her to move quickly, and not make her as plain a target as if she wore a Lady's headdress set with candles!

By the time Alikili was dressed, so many people had come into the bedchamber that Kekaspa had to chase some of them out again. Leaving too much of the house unguarded or gathering too many people into a single unmissable target seemed less than wise, although Alikili was glad that the more experienced fighter was the one to give the order.

Six remained—Alikili, Kekaspa, and four men, three from the house and one of Kekaspa's. Alikili hoped this didn't mean heavy losses among Kekaspa's people.

The woman shook her head. "Now that the enemy is in, we need to take you *out,* so I have most of my people surrounding the house. We can think about taking it back when we don't have to protect you and the others who can't fight—"

"*Those* who cannot fight, please."

Kekaspa looked at Alikili, then managed the first laugh Alikili had heard all night. It was only a small-laugh, but then it had been only a small joke.

"Very well. We need to have everyone who might be a hostage either safe or dead. If we're lucky, we can do that before the enemy calls for help. I've already sent off a well-escorted messenger to bring help to us, and the Watch, groundfighters, and local citizens can move faster and more freely than the people attacking."

Which meant odds turning in favor of her side, and soon enough that she might see another sunbrighten. It diluted Alikili's brief joy that this new hope meant leaving the house at the mercy of those who had already shown themselves willing to leave it rubble and ashes. Ashes that already included toys from her childhood, the first night shift that Jossu I Hmilra had ever given her, and much else she would be sorry to see spaded into the garden.

But she would be sorrier still to see others die for the house when she could save them by leaving it. The books on tactics she had read made much of choosing when to retreat and what to abandon when you did.

"What is the weather like?" she asked.

One of the household shrugged. "No rain, but the wind's up enough to hide a good bit of noise. A deal of mud, from three nights ago."

She would get no drier or warmer tonight, then.

"Let me get a heavier pair of boots."

Aliliki was sitting on the ruined bed, pulling the boots on, when Kekaspa knelt beside her and handed her a slim envelope.

"Guard this carefully. It's what I had time to write down about tonight's enemies that is not in the files that Jossu knows."

"If you fall, I will be the next place they think to look for it." Alikili realized that might sound like fear, so shrugged. "So let's agree to live out the night."

"And many nights beyond this one," the other woman said. "Oh, and you almost forget these." The bag she handed Alikili *clinked* faintly, and Alikili realized that it was all the spare cartridges from her nightstand drawer, for the pistol that she had only begun to reload when everyone suddenly claimed her attention!

SEAN BORLUND COULD NOT CONSOLE HIMSELF THAT HE WAS NOT A COMmander, as *Lingvaas* headed seaward. But at least he was fifth (or was it sixth?) in the line of command. *Lingvaas* was likely to be sinking or sunk before he had to take command of her survivors.

Not to mention that at his battle station amidships he was standing on one of the most likely targets. Some of his seniors were far more likely than he to survive tonight if it came to heavy action.

Borlund knew that it would, unless by sheer ill-luck they could not *find* the enemy. Then solemn curses on Drylanders in the name of the Lord and Lady and more ancient powers would be the most charitable response from the Kertovans. To say nothing of the kin of the Rinbao-Dar refugees, or the refugees' own spirits.

Spirits. Something he was not supposed to believe in. But on this night, on these waters, he found it easier than ever to wonder if those who spoke of gods, spirits, and other supernatural entities might not have grasped another part of the same truth that the Rationalists thought they knew entirely?

He peered out into the darkness, hoping that his imagination would not conjure anything out of it. A piece of wreckage floating by less than pistol-shot off? Yes, but too old and too far inshore to be from the torpedo-carriers' battle. The seas of Kilmoyn ate a hundred ships a year, and wreckage from the lost could wash ashore ten Greats later and a thousand leagues away.

A clinking almost in his face. Borlund turned, to see Corinne Yoshino standing with a covered tray.

"Something to eat, Commander?"

It was bowls of fish stew, with so many kinds of fish and all of them so salted that Borlund couldn't tell which ones. But it was hot, filling, and not too hard on the taster. He had emptied his bowl and was scraping the bottom with the wooden spoon when Yoshino returned.

Her tray was empty and he thought he wasn't imagining a smile on her face.

"Nervous, Commander?" she asked.

That was technically insubordination. It would take more than technicalities to make Borlund willing to lie. A clean conscience never hurt in this world, whether or not you feared traveling into some other one.

"Yes. It takes more than being shot at two or three times to make people—well, to make me, anyway—used to it."

"I thought I'd be nervous, too, and I am. But I don't feel guilty."

Borlund wondered who Yoshino might have been bedding, then remembered her politics.

"It doesn't look as if the Kertovans want Rinbao-Dar in an empire of their own, does it?"

"No. I think they would bar the door against the Matriarchy if it asked to join. The Island Republic has enough plots and counterplots of its own without buying a cargo of somebody else's. Eneh may turn out to be a different matter, but we're not there yet."

"Also, they've been independent too long to be more than allies, even if the Kertovans wanted more. And I couldn't ask the Kertovans to abandon the refugees, even if they were helping them for the wrong reasons."

Another new believer in the complexity of the Universe—or at least of Kilmoyn, Borlund decided. Saying that out loud would sound condescending, so he smiled and nodded.

To seaward, complete darkness had now returned, along with silence. Double and even triple lookouts kept every wave and patch of sky watched every moment, and listened for any sound lounder than fissioning jellyfloats.

Borlund turned Barbara Weil's decision to go for the armed transport over and over in his mind, as if it were a problem set in a tactics class. Except that he had much less than half a watch before the answer had to be in, and every prospect that a wrong one could kill a great many Farers.

No, not quite. *The Captain* faced those limits. Fortunately, so did the Captains on the other side, and it could be they who came up with the wrong answers.

Barbara Weil was making sense, Borlund decided. Without their escort, the other troop-carriers might not be able to fight off *Lingvaas* or *Byubr*. They would probably be unable to bombard the camp or Kertovan groundfighter defenses. They would be more vulnerable to torpedo attack, even if *Lingvaas* herself did not survive the battle.

Borlund wondered how many others aboard realized that Weil's plan called for treating *Lingvaas* and every Farer aboard her as expendable. That kind of thinking was clearly labeled "militaristic" everywhere Borlund had seen it—at least in Drylander writings.

But if the plan brought a victory, the Kertovans would raise strenuous objections to punishing anyone for winning it in the wrong way. If the plan failed, there would be very few from *Lingvaas* left for the Directorate to punish.

The Study Group would hardly follow dead Farers into a next world in whose existence its members were not allowed to believe!

Borlund would still have given much to make a single change aboard *Lingvaas*: torpedoes. If she was going to be facing larger opponents or multiple targets, a pair of torpedo-launchers on either side (with maybe a spare torpedo for each launcher) would give her a bigger punch.

The Kertovans had plenty of torpedo-launchers on their river flotilla, that guarded the mouth of the Hask. But those launchers were behind armor that *Lingvaas* didn't have, and unprotected torpedoes were vulnerable even to crankgun bullets that could wreck the flywheels, burst the air tanks, or even explode the warheads.

Put the torpedo launchers underwater? That would help, if you could solve the problem of expelling the torpedo against the water pressure and keeping it from striking its own ship. Borlund had read hints in even some of the permitted Terran histories that the problem had once been solved by putting the whole ship underwater. There should be simpler ways, too.

Time to think on that later. They were coming up on where the scouting line had been.

A lookout's hail floated down from the aftertop, reporting two friendly torpedo-carriers in sight, one under steam, the other sinking.

Borlund was still trying to see the second vessel when he heard Weil on the bridge order a turn to redward. The helm went over so sharply that *Lingvaas* heeled and Borlund braced himself against a stanchion.

Now he saw them, one Kertovan torpedo-carrier standing by another, half on her beam ends. Swimmers were climbing aboard the first one, while others were trying to work a torpedo out of the after-launcher. Salvage it, Borlund guessed.

Abruptly the deck quivered, as if *Lingvaas* had scraped a rock. The beat of the engines changed—unmistakably into reverse.

Borlund tried not to stare wildly around him, searching for what made this engine-wracking command wise or at least safe. Quickly, he saw and understood.

Dead ahead, a high-sided dark shape was sliding past, a silver curl of water at her bow. Almost as dead astern, a column of smaller shapes slid past on the same inshore course. Borlund thought he saw something even smaller, about the size of a torpedo-carrier, trailing the column.

Lingvaas was exactly between the two columns of the—

The enemy?

The passing ships were no hallucinations, but their shapes were too vague to identify. Had I Hmilra sent transports on ahead, while he turned toward the Imperial shore of the Gulf to patrol against seaborne intruders?

All Borlund's sweat was suddenly as cold as the ice water only dreamed of for much too long.

Then a reminder came that the enemy always has the same problems you do. A searchlight blazed from the column astern. Its beam painted a glowing line across the sea all the way to the other ship, then began groping about, seeking what some lookout must have vaguely glimpsed.

Before the beam touched *Lingvaas*'s mast, it had settled the question of the strangers' identity. In the yellow glow, the brown and red sword-and-sceptre flag of the Empire showed up plainly, at bow, stern, and after-masthead.

Before the beam swept lower on *Lingvaas*, Borlund heard three separate voices shout a single order.

"Commence firing, all guns bearing!"

A MESSENGER BROUGHT JOSSU I HMILRA WORD FROM THE LOOKOUT, THAT gun*flashes* as well as gun*fire* could now be made out. Definitely to the southward, on about the bearing of Puyasa. No Seakin in sight.

I Hmilra swore to promote the lookout. No Seakin meant no need to wake the Speaker again, and then slow down while she and the whistle talked to them, sending a warning down the wind and making the Fleet an easier target for enemy torpedo-carriers that might have been sent this far north to chance their luck and provide warning.

One problem off the board. How many left? I Hmilra mentally unrolled a chart of the local waters. But his memory and therefore the mind-map lacked some of the soundings he needed before he could plan.

A visit to the chartroom settled matters before the next report from the lookout. I Hmilra printed with exquisite care on a message pad, then read off aloud to the Flag Captain.

"Signal to *Shuumiba, Relentless,* and Torpedo Squadron Two. Follow me, course red six-zero. Remainder of Fleet, take course green one seventy, half speed, until abreast of Guari Point. Then form line abreast and sweep toward Puyasa at one-third speed, with scouting line both ahead and astern."

The Flag Captain looked from the message to the chart, then at I Hmilra.

"I see. We're leading a fast squadron to—or through—the North Channel, to guard the landward side of Puyasa. The main Fleet moves straight down to guard the seaward side."

The Captain ran a finger through his scanty ruff and contemplated the hairs that came loose. "What if the main attack is to landward?"

"Then we'll have plenty of targets, and the main body can come around Cape Joibor and join us."

"Or if they have the North Channel mined and picketed with torpedo-carriers?"

"The faster we get there, the less likely they are to have time for that. Or do you expect the Drylanders of *Lingvaas* and our people aboard *Byubr* to lie down and die?"

"I expect nothing of the kind, Lord. But I did not expect the Empire to show itself so arrogant on the high seas either."

"This is hardly beyond coastal waters yet, Captain. As for arrogance, I think our Fleet has a few proven cures for that."

chapter 25

Under the thump of *Byubr*'s engines and more and more distant sputter of groundfighter weapons, Ehoma Tuomitti kept hearing a faint rumble. She hoped it was not the ship scraping the bottom. Probably not, since *Byubr* did not turn or slow at the rumbles.

This left a great many things it could be, up to and including some new Imperial weapon invented with the help of the Drylander traitors and now turned loose against the Island Republic for the first time, with *Byubr* the experimental target!

For the tenth time she wished Zhohorosh had rejoined the ship before tonight's fighting broke out. Not only because she could talk more freely with him than with anyone else and draw on his greater knowledge either. She would miss him horribly if he died, but less so if he died a Farer's death at sea and not at all if they went together.

It would be more painful than she wanted to think about—his dying because his sense of duty had taken him ashore into the path of some ragged-arse Imperial tribal levies, equipped only with breech-guards, long knives, numbers, and bad tempers.

Tuomitti told herself that she needed no calming rituals. She had given over those when she first put on the badges of a watch chief, to set a good example to unsalted Farers. But she found that she was going over the equipment of her repair party with uncommon care. From time to time she also walked forward to see how they were coming along with swabbing the blood from the deck by the capstan.

Each time she walked forward or aft, she passed the main gun. The gunners were now hard at work oiling and greasing the breech mechanism, training gear, and hoists, adjusting the sights (with judicious taps of a small hammer), and making sure that the ready ammunition locker was watertight, flash-tight, and full.

Then it was always back to her repair party and its supplies. She could count woven-fiber mats, compressed-fiber and wooden plugs, patches, props, and shoring for weakened bulkheads and pierced plates (in all, enough wood to build a small house), entire baskets of hammers, saws, axes, and smaller tools, and a metal can of fastenings varied enough to make the landbound builder claw her hair. Not to mention two hoses, six buckets, a breathing helmet for entering flood or smoke-filled compartments, and a hand-cranked air pump to make sure the helmet lived up to its name and the wearer lived to breathe the Lord's and Lady's air again.

She could also count eight seasoned Farers, two from the anchor section and six others whose battle station was repair from beginning to end. The pile of repair stores was in good hands able to put it to proper use, save it from fire or flooding, at the last resort throw the lumber and fiber overboard to help swimmers keep afloat, and at no time to steal so much of it that she or the repair chiefs would have to notice what was missing.

Tuomitti wished she could be sure that this lull in the battle meant the situation was also in good hands. It wasn't out of doubting her Captain that she doubted this. It was also not as consoling as it had been, that the enemy was probably as confused from stumbling ashore as the island's defenders were from being attacked. Ashore the enemy had the edge in numbers; afloat the odds were still anybody's guess.

At least the shoal water meant that any torpedo not running so shallow it could easily be seen was likely to hit the bottom and explode. Tuomitti was fairly sure that the first two explosions had been two torpedoes intended to sink *Byubr* at her moorings, but one had blown away the boom and the other run up on the shore to explode there.

Of course, the shoal water also kept *Byubr* on a straight course, good for her gunnery, good also for making her an easy target for anything able to fight from the shallows where she could not go. Shallow-draught vessels here tonight should include any friendly torpedo-carriers that had survived to get to sea. But they hadn't signaled once since *Byubr* reached open water, and when even spar-torpedo craft had accidentally attacked friends, those who could launch free-swimming torpedoes from beyond crankgun range might have trouble telling friend from foe—

And what was that alongside?

It wasn't quite alongside, as Tuomitti saw in the next moment as searchlights tore the darkness. It was a cast or more away.

Now it was also easily recognizable—one of those Imperial gunboats that looked like a gigantic pressing iron. On a low flat hull sat a deckhouse that looked like nothing so much as a handle for a dressmaker fifty spans tall!

Pressing irons didn't carry heavy guns forward. Tuomitti saw a movement aboard the enemy, heard the same aboard *Byubr,* then heard nothing but the snarl of crankguns opening on both sides before the roar of two heavy weapons drowned out the smaller ones.

Her repair party had already dropped flat. So neither the muzzle blast of *Byubr*'s gun nor the crankgun fire from the enemy hurt them. They clung to any handhold as the blast swept over them, and were still clinging when the enemy's shell arrived.

Byubr's new bulges had decreased her speed, maneuverability, and draught. They were also intended to keep torpedo explosions a safe distance from her vitals. Now they proved they would do the same for shells.

The enemy shell burst against the redside bulge well aft of Tuomitti's position. Fragments of shell and hull plating whistled in all directions, including harmlessly upward and outboard, as well as less harmlessly inboard. Tuomitti heard screams from Farers as if they had their mouths against her ear.

She heard more distant screams from the enemy. Looking through a new gap in the railing, she saw the Imperial gunboat slewing bow-first toward *Byubr.* She was either out of control or trying to ram, with steam pouring from her deckhouse and driving overboard Farers who had survived the shell's explosions and the spraying with crankguns.

The enemy's main gun—ten lines at least, Tuomitti thought—was still crewed, though. It fired again, before *Byubr*'s second shot. The aim was high, but the shell punched a hole in *Byubr*'s deckhouse and passed almost all the way through before exploding. Most of the blast and fragments wrecked empty cabins or flew out to sea.

Some of both flailed the crew of *Byubr*'s main gun from greenward. Tuomitti heard more screams, also the sound of a butcher's cutter as one fragment bounced three times and ended in the skull of a repair Farer.

Then *Byubr*'s main gun fired again.

Shot or shell, it was impossible to tell which. It struck the gunboat's main weapon squarely on the muzzle. One or two explosions—again, no way of telling—flung bodies and fragments masthead-high but also poured out smoke that hid the worst of the shambles.

Flame spewed from the heart of the smoke cloud. This time the whole gun rose higher than the gunboat's bridge, hung in the air long enough for Tuomitti to see the peeled-back muzzle, then plunged into the water. Smoke hid the whole enemy vessel for a moment, but even Tuomitti's ringing ears heard a frenzied hissing as water poured into the flaming hull.

She lurched to her feet, reaching for a handhold and scorching her fingers on the hot lip of the second shell hole. Her ears still rang, but she heard moans from inside the superstructure, above on the boat deck and forward from the gun.

She also saw water lapping over the edge of the first shell hole. The Farer hit in the head was barely twitching and probably doomed, but the rest of the repair party seemed fit.

"All on deck, there!" she called, taking one end of a rolled-up fiber patch. "Somebody ask the Captain to slow down so the bulge doesn't flood through the hole before we can patch it. Healer, wait here for orders, unless we take casualties."

A moment later Tuomitti was certain that there would be casualties among the repair party, probably including both herself and the healer. A torpedo-carrier shot between *Byubr* and the sinking gunboat. She turned sharply, opening her broadside, which including two launchers and a crankgun.

Then Tuomitti recognized the two funnels, and the Republican flag spread between them, a bit tattered and smoke-darkened but unmistakable. She was not the only one worried tonight about shooting at friends.

The torpedo-carrier was slowing to pick up Imperial survivors. Tuomitti hooked her safety line on to a stanchion and climbed down onto the top of the bulge.

ALIKILI HAD EXPECTED TO BE MORE AWARE THAN BEFORE OF THE WEIGHT OF her pistol as she and the others crept toward the door. Keeping silent focused her mind elsewhere, as did the need for silence and passing one place where clearly attackers and defenders had fought to mutual extermination. (She counted five bodies there, two of them from the household and three strangers.)

But until tonight the pistol had been mostly a mark of rank. Now she had killed with it. Shouldn't this make a difference?

Apparently not. She wondered if this was good or bad. Turning into a warrior was a fate to which she was now resigned. But there were good warriors and bad warriors—most especially, warriors who could tell friend from foe and those who could not.

Jossu had made this entirely clear. What he had left darker than the hall before her was how to tell the two kinds apart. He had not even hinted at how to keep from becoming the bad kind oneself. Alikili felt a moment's grievance against Jossu, even as she felt it knowing that it was unjust. He had not anticipated the fighting coming this close to her. Neither had she. The fault, if any, was shared.

Also, Moi Kekaspa might be able to give a better answer. She must have made her first kill many Greats more recently than Jossu. And she was jouti, walking out alone into a land from which her kind was usually supposed to be barred.

They were a good deal closer to the entrance hall when a muffled shot sounded from somewhere above. A second followed quickly. Then a scream and five lighter shots replied from outside.

Everyone stopped. Most stared at Kekaspa. Some looked as if they would have liked to flatten themselves into the carpet, like roof-worms. Some of those staring seemed to want Kekaspa to turn into a magical war engine out of the old tales that came from before Skyfall.

Alikili tried not to stare but would have rejoiced at seeing the woman so transformed. She wondered idly if the Drylanders had such tales. She had never learned enough of their history to know how much of it they lost at the time of Skyfall.

Jossu was more likely to know that than to know how she could train herself as a warrior. She hoped his knowledge of the Drylanders was a secret he was willing to reveal. It had begun to seem knowledge needed for carrying on his work, as she would have to be ready to do, being in the course of nature likely to outlive him. Except for unanticipated circumstances like tonight, of course.

Kekaspa was tugging at her shoulder and nodding toward a corner.

"I don't know if the sniper's an enemy and the people outside friends, or the other way around," the Saadian woman whispered as soon as they'd crawled out of the other's hearing. "We need to divide. One party to go out, the other to climb up and take the sniper in the rear. Even if it's an enemy, we can distract him long enough for the ground party to reach cover."

"What if it's a friend here and enemies out there?"

"Then we help the friend keep the heads outside down, while the ground party goes for more help."

"I thought as much. You make sense. Young Fuomin—the one with the yellow half-gloves—knows the grounds better than anyone else with us. He can guide the ground party.

"I know the house better than you do. So I can guide you upstairs."

That line did not have the effect Alikili had feared. Kekaspa merely looked at her.

"You share bed and spirit with the best man of our time," she said. "Don't throw that away."

"I throw nothing away," Alikili said. "I merely help defend something else that he and I share."

Briefly, she wondered if Kekaspa and Jossu had ever been lovers. That was strictly forbidden among jouti of fertile years, even when they were not married, even more strictly among the Saadians than among the citizens of the Island Republic. But the *knowledge* in that woman's eyes. . . .

Still more briefly, Alikili fought to stifle laughter. Knowledge could be of many kinds and from many sources, even among men and women. Also, she would *not* sound like a woman ready to throw a jealous fit.

If anything could ensure her being sent out into the darkness, denied the right to defend her home, it would be making Kekaspa worry about her back as she crept up on the sniper!

"ALL GUNS BEARING" INCLUDED ALL THREE HEAVY GUNS, FORWARD AND AFT, and the crankguns bearing forward. The midships five-liners and Borlund's crankguns couldn't bear on any target within range.

The din was still ear-battering. Borlund hoped all the noise led to some results. Forward, he was pretty sure it would. The big armed transport was within rifle shot, let alone heavy-gun range.

The transports aft were a different matter. They were a third of a league off at least. Borlund only hoped the guns there would hit something even if it wasn't what they were aiming at.

Gunners, Zhohorosh had once said, came in three kinds. One could hit only with modern sights and calculation arcs, one could hit only by Farer's eye, and one couldn't hit anything at all.

It would appeal to Zhohorosh if *Lingvaas*'s gunners could hit the old-fashioned way; he was of that school himself. But with the latest sights on all of her guns, if her gunners couldn't use them, *Lingvaas* faced the unappealing prospect of hitting nothing and probably being sunk in the next few beats.

The opening salvo destroyed what was left of Borlund's night vision and left a whine in his ears. He could still see the torpedo-carrier close alongside, and someone leaning from the wing of *Lingvaas*'s bridge and shouting to it. As his hearing returned, he recognized Barbara Weil's voice but not her words.

She was shouting in pure Saadian, and as the next salvo drowned out her words he understood why. There were almost certainly Kertovan speakers aboard the transport, which might be close enough for them to hear Weil's orders. It was long odds against anyone speaking Saadian.

Weil had finished her orders when the transport returned fire. Four guns, as big as *Lingvaas*'s heavies, bellowed with one ragged voice. All four rounds flew high, clipping wire-stays and yardarms and spraying fast-moving bits of metal onto *Lingvaas*'s deck and the sea around her.

Borlund shut his ears in anticipation of screams or even the piercing of his own flesh, and concentrated on getting his redside guns into action. The torpedo-carrier was getting up steam, and turning as she did. The redside guns fired, Borlund saw the flash of at least one hit aboard the transport, and now *Lingvaas* herself was turning hard to redside and the greenside battery was the one with the target so big and so close that the gunners there fired without waiting for Borlund's orders—

Eyes dimmed by the flashes, Borlund could still make out the torpedo-carrier swinging around *Lingvaas*'s stern. Two flashes on deck told of the powder-impulse pistons flinging the torpedoes out of their launchers. Borlund wanted to hold his breath but didn't dare; that was dangerous to the ears when heavy guns were going off all around you, and by now every gun aboard *Lingvaas* was in action.

One torpedo vanished into the night. A shock that made *Lingvaas* herself tremble, a column of water climbing the side of the transport, and a ragged third salvo told Borlund that the other torpedo had struck home.

But it could not have hit anywhere immediately fatal. The transport did not spew smoke and flame, only trailed silvery steam. She also did not slow. Instead she heeled over as she turned sharply toward *Lingvaas*.

As the glare of the next exchange of salvos faded, Borlund had a remarkably good view of the transport's high curving bow, growing larger with each moment. She was coming down fast, to ram *Lingvaas* and put this pesky opponent forever on the bottom of the Bishak Gulf, or at least out of the fight.

The lookouts and steerers aboard *Lingvaas* were working together too well for that. The two ships passed broadside to broadside, with *Lingvaas* able to hurl everything that two heavy guns, two light, and four crankguns could produce into the transport. In the lulls Borlund heard riflemen shooting in both directions; if he'd been nearer the railing he could have probably hit the transport with his pistol.

If *Lingvaas* had carried torpedoes, they could not have missed. They also might not have had time to arm themselves.

The transport's crew was still working their guns, but *Lingvaas* was so close alongside that everything was flying even higher overhead than before. It was a long burst from a crankgun, more easily depressed to reach a low-flying close target, that first drew blood from *Lingvaas*.

A series of sharp explosions tore at Borlund's ears. Screams followed. So did the *whup* and *wheet* of more flying fragments passing him on all sides, and not passing some of the people around him. More screams shrilled, practically in his ears; he saw Farers reeling, bleeding, falling.

He also saw a gaping hole in the transport's redside quarter, with torn and split plates all around it and steam trickling out. He didn't know if he had a voice or anyone around still had ears to hear him, so he waved as well as shouted.

Both of the midships guns still had crews; they did not fire together, but both shells tore into the transport close to the torpedo hole. The steam turned from a trickle to a cloud. The transport began to lose way, as the crankguns that would bear raised their muzzles and sprayed the transport's decks.

Then the two ships had passed each other, *Lingvaas* after guns both had a target, and they let go together. It was a narrow target but they punched nine-line shells into the transport's stern, one into the rudder post and the other into the hull right on the waterline.

With two big holes to flood her aft and her steering lost, the transport was not going to be an effective warship for the rest of tonight's battle.

She did have one well-crewed gun aft, however. Even with the stern flooding under them, they knew their business. *Lingvaas* was an even narrower target for them than they for her, but she was also a long one. A shell that would have flown clean over *Lingvaas* if she had been abeam to the gun struck her at the base of her foremast.

It was either a dud shell or a solid; Borlund heard only the clang and screech of sundered metal, not an explosion. But the mast tottered, then swung aft and toppled. Stays, shrouds, and everything else attached to it parted like thread. Arm-thick fiber ropes and thumb-thick wire ones lashed about like demented serpents.

Borlund stood and let them flail about him, not to show his courage but because he was too frightened to move. Somehow he was still on his feet, unharmed, when the mast crashed down on the bridge, knocking him into the hot breech of a crankgun.

He recoiled from the scorching hot metal and this time he did stumble and fall, onto something soft that said a much ruder word than "Ouch!" He ignored it for a moment as he watched the bridge collapse on to the main deck. Dark figures tumbled from it, some on to the deck to rise, some to lie still, some right overboard.

On hands and knees, Borlund found himself staring into the face of Corinne Yoshino. Rising, he saw that her mouth was set into a rigid line, her eyes wide, and her left leg missing just below the knee.

Borlund was fumbling for his own dressings when Roald Chaykin-Schmidt scrambled up the ladder. He unslung a drum of crankgun ammunition from his back into the hands of the gunners, then knelt beside Yoshino. He no longer wore much of a shirt, but he stripped off the powder-blackened rags that were left and twisted them as a tourniquet around the bloody stump. Then he unpacked his own dressing and started tying it over the wound.

An explosion that came from no gun rolled across the water. Borlund looked up from his healer's effort to see the enemy transport brightly lit by several fires, most on deck but one gushing flames from ports below and aft. She was also nearly dead in the water and noticeably down by the stern.

It would take longer than a night for the transport to become a fighting ship again. If sunbrighten found her afloat at all, it would be good work from her crew. The thought of how many Farers and groundfighters might be struggling amid the bits of wreckage made his stomach twitch for the first time since the battle opened.

He calmed it, rather to his own surprise, by calling for a muster of his own division. Yoshino and some others answered from the deck, and some did not answer at all. Borlund could put not only a name but a history and a personality to all the still, blank-eyed faces. When he knew all the names, he felt a little better about the coming fate of the Imperials aboard the transport.

He even felt a trifle better about his own people, once he started preparing a list of the dead and wounded. The doctor would need it, and so would Captain Weil—or her successor (a thought which nearly destroyed the barely regained calm).

Then he heard Weil's voice from near the ruins of the bridge, calling to the torpedo-carrier.

"Fine shooting. We're going after the other transports. Can you keep up?"

"We need a couple of fresh stokers. Two of ours are down and the survivors of *Number 67* aren't fit yet."

"I'll call for volunteers."

What she should have said was, "I'll keep you from being swamped by volunteers." There was no time for the torpedo-carrier to lay alongside *Lingvaas* before a general rush to the railing aboard the larger ship. Borlund saw two survivors of the bow gun's crew be the first overboard, and saw Chaykin-Schmidt starting for the ladder.

Corinne Yoshino promptly grabbed the boy by the ankle. He lost his balance and would have fallen if Borlund hadn't gripped him by the shoulder.

"They need men over there," the boy protested. "Are you saying I'm not a man?"

"We need them here, too," Borlund snapped. "Can you load a crankgun as well as carry the cans to it?"

"Yes."

"Then you're the new second loader on Gun Four. As soon as you've helped get the wounded down to the sick berth, anyway."

Lingvaas's deck was trembling from the thrust of her engines rather than the firing of her guns when Borlund followed the stretcher party down onto the main deck. They went aft to sick quarters, he went forward to report to Barbara Weil.

She was standing with her back to a ventilator, so close against it that he wondered if she was hurt too badly to stand without help. Reporting his division's casualties helped calm that fear and control the impulse to kiss his Captain on her own deck.

"Well done, Commander Borlund. When we develop a gunnery

speciality, I'll endorse your application. Any casualties you didn't report?"

"Only to my pants, Captain."

Weil chuckled. "I won't be able to say that I had all my wounds in front tonight."

She turned, showing a bloody flap of trousers and underwear hanging like a broad tail halfway to her knees. Above it was a slightly less bloody dressing over a wound that must have cut across both cheeks of her buttocks.

"One of the few times I've really regretted not being thinner," she said with a forced smile. "Two fingers less of me astern, and nothing would have happened. Now I can't even say I have an honorable scar. Or at least one that I can show."

"Those of us who were here tonight won't insist on proof, and it's nobody else's business."

"Thanks, Sean."

Weil laid one hand against his cheek briefly, and he felt the sweat on it mingling with hers. He also felt the tautness in her muscles, and remembered that buttock wounds were more than embarassing. There was a lot of flesh and nerves down there, the pain would be serious and long, and meanwhile *Lingvaas* would have a Captain who could lie down or stand up but not sit!

"Now, let's see about getting a repair party on the bow gun," Weil said. "A captain shot in the stern is one thing. A stern chase with no bow gun is another."

"Aye-aye, ma'am," Borlund said. He turned another impulse to kiss Weil into a regulation salute, then headed back toward his post.

IT DID NOT TAKE JOSSU I HMILRA LONG TO MAKE A SUM OF THE LOOKOUTS' reports, from *Valor's* tops, both cruisers, and the torpedo-carriers on either flank.

Somebody was in action to both the southeast and the southwest, off Puyasa and also well out to sea.

Further calculations suggested that the fighting out to sea was not the rest of the Fleet encountering an enemy. It seemed to be closer than the westward squadron could have been, unless they had sighted an enemy invisible from *Valor*, closed, and engaged.

If so, no harm done. The westward squadron had less than half the torpedo-carriers but considerably more than half the armorclads and heavy guns. Nothing that the Empire and the Confederation put together could send into these seas would stand against them.

I Hmilra leaned back in his chair on the wing of *Valor*'s bridge (time to get behind armor in the stifling-hot command tower later). With paper and a pencil he reduced his plans to brief orders.

The westward squadron would not be recalled nor would he change course to rejoin it. *Valor*'s squadron would continue toward Puyasa. The defenders there did had no armorclads except *Byubr* and no more than four armor-piercing guns afloat, apart from lucky shots.

Valor's squadron would, however, change its formation. Three torpedo-carriers would lead, with *Valor* behind, then *Relentless* flanked by two more torpedo-carriers. The rear would be *Shuumiba*, with two more torpedo-carriers.

Relentless had heavier guns that *Shuumiba* but lighter armor and less speed. *Shuumiba* could more easily survive any surprise attack, then outrun the attackers and rejoin her consorts. Any enemy off Puyasa who ignored the torpedo-carriers would find themselves confronting *Valor* and a cruiser that outgunned any class of armorclads except *Valor* and her sisters.

Any ship identifying an enemy should immediately signal the flagship *and* engage, without waiting for orders. Neither Imperial nor Confederation Fleets were quite as battlewise on the open sea as the Island Republic's. They would be easier to surprise and to demoralize by engaging promptly after that surprise.

Which did not mean that if the Imperials had a Captain Over Captains here tonight, he would not be thinking just as hard how to surprise the Kertovans. A good commander of anything from a stoker watch to a Fleet needed luck, and that fell where Lord and Lady would have it in spite of all the well-drafted orders than mortals could issue.

chapter 26

Ehoma Tuomitti was too busy with her repair work on the bulge to pay much attention to her ship's maneuvers. But she had the vague notion that *Byubr* was wandering up the North Channel toward the open sea. She was certain that the main gun was firing toward the island every dozen beats or so.

She hoped they were not going to waste too much ammunition on what could be hardly more than a gesture as far as she could see. The shore was a mass of trees with not even a patch of glow-moss showing, let alone fires or anything that might have been a battle.

That dense a forest would soak up the fragments of a shell before they'd gone twenty paces. A solid shot would do nothing except to the tree it hit, and if the tree was big enough, not much even to that.

Keeping up the hearts of the groundfighter ashore was hardly worth even a single round for which they would surely find better targets soon enough. Unless the groundfighters had been driven back out of the forest to open ground, where weight of numbers and tribal fierceness might count?

Tuomitti jerked her mind away from that thought and swung her sledge with extra force as if to crush it thoroughly. That kind of a retreat almost certainly meant Zhohorosh's death. Otherwise he would have stood behind the cowards with pistol or even sword, threatening to have their thumbs hanging from his belt if they moved back another pace.

Maybe he had. And maybe Imperial tribal levies had frightened the groundfighters more than Zhohorosh.

By the time the patch on the bulge was as finished as it was going to be, *Byubr* was well up toward the mouth of the channel. The land to either side was only dim, blurred shapes. Tuomitti had seen more clearly defined fogbanks.

She looked forward and aft. At a quick glance, *Byubr* looked ready for action, even if some of the crankgun crews included Farers with dressed wounds and there were holes and bloodstains in many places that had been intact and clean last sunfade.

From where she lay, *Byubr's* main gun could reach all the way to the land on either side, even if the range to the north would be long shooting against anything smaller than a large town. She herself was at last in deep water where she could maneuver freely—and where torpedoes could swim freely.

It was not her imagination, either, that *Byubr* was lower in the water than before. The patch kept water from pouring openly into the shell hole, but the bulge could have sprung seams elsewhere. Sprung seams could let in enough water to sink a ship—or at least make her list enough to ruin her gunnery.

With hands out of sight behind her, Tuomitti made selected gestures of aversion. She had just finished the third, when two lookouts shouted, one screamed, and out to sea everyone saw the flash of a gun.

It looked like a light gun, firing to seaward, which said little about who might be coming in from the sea. *Lingvaas* was the most pleasant possibility—unless she was being chased by a superior force. After that the possibilities quickly grew worse, up to the superior force having sunk *Lingvaas* and now coming to finish off *Byubr* before helping the landing party overrun the camp and slaughter the refugees.

Tuomitti reminded herself that the night could bring far worse than Zhohorosh's death.

The torpedo came out of the darkness with only a single wordless cry that held both fear and warning. Any further cries were lost in the explosion of the torpedo against the greenside bulge.

No glare dazzled Tuomitti's eyes this time, but a waterfall poured down all over *Byubr's* decks. The shock of the explosion made even her fat hull flex and twist, and Tuomitti went sprawling.

The explosion faded into echoes rumbling back and forth between the two shores. Tuomitti gripped a stanchion, slashed her palm on a jagged end where it had spilt, then lurched to her feet.

Beside her one of the repair party lay moaning, one foot at an implausible angle to his leg. Explosion shocks could sprain or even snap ankles. Tuomitti was relieved to discover that both of hers could support her weight. They ached, and those weren't the only aches, but apart from her hand she was fit.

One-handed, she fumbled a dressing out of its wrapper. By the time she'd done that the Farer with the broken ankle had recovered enough to help her dress the wounded hand. By the time they were done, Tuomitti could see that *Byubr* was still lower in the water, and listing to greenside.

Steam roared up from the funnel, as the engine room vented a boiler. That meant likely enough a cracked boiler shell or a cracked steam line. Tuomitti hoped that they could keep enough boilers on line to steam *Byubr* into water shallow enough to beach her.

The Captain's voice cut across the roar of steam. "Main gun, stand ready. Do not fire without my orders. Repair parties, lay below to the greenside boiler room."

Tuomitti winced. Even one-handed, she could still climb down the ladders if her Farers needed her, which they probably would. Nobody enjoyed being in the engine spaces of a torpedoed ship, with steam already loose and flooding water ready to swallow Farers in moments. Not even the engineers, still less those sent down from the open deck to the inner darkness.

ALIKILI KNEW ENOUGH ABOUT COMBAT NOW TO BE READY TO DROP TO THE floor or flatten against the wall at Moi Kekaspa's signal. In turn, Kekaspa let her pick the safest route to the sniper's position, and pass warning of any dangerous places.

Now, if they could only have done it by speaking mind to mind, as in old legends, so that the snipers could not be warned by their ears. . . .

But in those same tales, the enemy always had an evil wizard who could read minds, and some hero always had to die first to bring victory.

Alikili reminded herself firmly that she believed in neither old tales nor omens.

A rifle blasted echoes past them, and they heard plaster *skritch*. Then, without hearing a bolt work, they heard another shot.

The two women looked at each other.

Two snipers.

Alikili drew her pistol. It *was* loaded; she'd had plenty of time for that. She'd even had enough light in one hallway to handpick the rounds. Nothing dented or tarnished was in the cylinder.

Kekaspa signaled with one hand for those behind her to pull back. Everyone started to obey until they saw that Alikili was hesitating.

Again she prodded her memory. Spread out, the attackers were a harder target. Gathered up close, they could follow Kekaspa in faster.

They didn't all have to be up front and close, of course. But Alikili wouldn't send others where she wasn't going. She'd had enough of that for tonight.

And the others wouldn't move to the rear if she didn't.

She rolled over and signaled those behind to move to either side, against the walls. That seemed a compromise that everyone could live with, except the snipers—and their opinions didn't matter.

Another *skritch* of plaster, and the muffled sounds of shots from outside. Alikili could now tell that that the outside now had rifles, pistols, and shotguns in actions. To her, that suggested friends—the game guards would certainly have turned out with their game pieces.

Kekaspa had been lying with her head to one side, listening as intently as a healer to a sick child's breathing. Then she turned and gave Alikili the signal.

First finger curled into the base of the thumb—enemy.

The next moment, Kekaspa leaped up and plunged forward. Alikili felt herself lifted as if by invisible wires, and jerked forward in the other woman's wake.

She did not know or care who followed her. She slapped her free hand down on the wardrobe chest laid across the doorway and vaulted into the room a breath after Kekaspa. Bullets raved through the air toward her, then gouged dust and splinters from the walls and kept on going.

Something seared across the back of Alikili's left leg. She rolled, coming up with the pistol aimed at a shape half-hidden in the faded and ragged curtains over the window. The half she saw let her recognize an enemy, and gave her a target.

She'd fired three times before the enemy started to fall out of the curtains. Then screams and curses jerked her around, to see Kekaspa grappling with two opponents. One of them was holding his rifle by the barrel, to swing it and smash Kekaspa's skull with the butt.

Instead, Kekaspa wrestled her pistol free and shot the rifleman at such close range that Alikili saw the bullet rip out of his back. The other man now broke away and fired his pistol into Kekaspa's back.

He had time for only two shots before Alikili shot him through the head. She would have tried for the larger target of his body if Kekaspa hadn't still been too close.

Kekaspa swayed, and blood trickled from her mouth. She went down on hands and knees, then onto her side. She rolled over, and Alikili could have sworn she was smiling.

"Might be more—" she said. Then she coughed, the coughing brought up more blood, and she curled up into a ball. Alikili knelt to find a pulse, and was surprised to find one.

She also knew she had to identify herself to the people in front, if they were friends. Kekaspa might have been warning her against more enemies, but the wounded needed help.

"Guard the hall and stairs, all of you," she called to the rest of the party. "One up on the roof, and take the rifle with you. Don't expose yourself until we know who's out there."

Her tongue seemed to have an authority that her mind could never have given her. That, and the blood on her, and the fact that they'd just seen her kill two enemies in not much more than five breaths.

"Oh, and somebody dress Moi's wounds," Alikili concluded, as she strode to the window.

Standing to one side, she drew the curtain back and held out the palest piece of cloth she could find. Shouts greeted it. She thought she heard bewilderment, but at least nobody shot at it.

The dead enemy who'd fallen out of the curtain had a small lantern—City-States work—on his belt. It had gone out, but his belt pouch held unruined matches. Alikili crouched low, relit the lantern, then without rising set it on the window ledge.

Nobody fired, and the next time she held out the rag, someone hailed her.

"Hallooo, the house! Who stands?"

"Alikili, companion to Jossu I Hmilra. We hold the house. Let our friends out the front door, and bring up healing for our wounded."

A farmyard din of voices ended with a sharp, wordless command.

Then:

"Stand in the window, Alikili."

Before anyone could protest, she obeyed, throwing back the curtains and holding up the lantern to light her face.

No bullets tore into her. Instead, she heard, even with battle-stunned ears, sighs of relief. Then someone cheered, and a second, a third. In another moment everyone seemed to be cheering.

Alikili stood motionless, glad that everyone was too far off in the night to see the tears trickling down her cheeks. All she could think of was that this cheering wasted time that might bring healing to Moi Kekaspa. But her voice had left her.

It was finally one of the household who stepped forward, broke through and beat down the cheering with Farer's oaths, and brought a healer forward to the main door.

LINGVAAS WOULD NOT HAVE HAD MUCH OF AN EDGE IN SPEED OVER THE transports unless she had been able to hit one or two of them. With them undamaged and her own engineers treating her engines delicately, she closed so slowly that it was hard to see that she was closing at all.

Furthermore, she was chasing at all in order to keep the transports nervous and try overtaking them when they slowed for the mouth of the North Channel. With no bow gun, she could not even chance an occasional harassing shot without yawing to open an arc for one of the undamaged after-guns. That would cost too much distance, and also turn her broadside to an enemy not so nervous they couldn't strike back.

One of the transports at least had a long-range light gun, probably one of the river-fortress antiboat guns on a shipboard carriage. The shot it fired left a hole hardly larger than a fist when it punched through metal, but if it hit someone they had to be picked up with a broom and a bucket.

Borlund did his best to ignore the enemy's persistent sternchaser and not get in the way of the party trying to put the bow gun back into action. It was easy to assume that it had lost only its crew and taken no damage from the spray of crankgun rounds, but too many Farers had died from that kind of assumption.

Borlund was about ready to go forward and help at least with the heavy lifting when Chaykin-Schmidt stepped up beside him.

"Captain Weil's compliments, and would you report to her aft?"

"On the way. Oh, that was good work, with Yoshino. How is she?"

The boy shrugged. "They're not letting anyone below who doesn't have business, and sick quarters are a madhouse. I haven't seen her body laid out, leastways."

Negative evidence was always frustrating, but right now it seemed about all he would get. Borlund hoped that someone would think to get a message to Adrianna Yoshino in the engine room about her twin's wound. Then he thanked the boy and walked aft.

Barbara Weil's face was tight and sweating from the pain of her wound when Borlund saluted. "Shouldn't you have something for that wound?"

"You're not the surgeon and I've already talked with him. Anything that would kill that much pain would keep me off my feet. I can't command lying on my stomach."

She obviously would not be receptive to the suggestion that she turn over command to Second Captain Kund or whoever else was the senior surviving officer, not when her wound was not dangerous and there might be no surviving officer senior to Borlund.

He wondered briefly if that was why he'd been called aft, to take command of *Lingvaas*. That would definitely be getting dragged into the pages of the history books, feet first and protesting. It would also be his duty, which somewhat reconciled him to having another complicated situation to untangle.

Weil looked over the side to where the torpedo-carrier was keeping station with no apparent effort. Her crankgun was crewed, and rifle-armed Farers perched on the empty torpedo-launchers.

"They picked up a prisoner from one of the transports up ahead," Weil said. "He confirmed what we suspected—a landing to take the Puyasa and kill the refugees, or use them as hostages. Either way, the Empire would have the high hand in Rinbao-Dar, which would cut us off from Eneh."

"The Directorate might not like that highly intimate pronoun 'us,'" Borlund said.

"Oh, flush the bilges with the Directorate," Weil said, in a voice that shook with pain and fatigue. "The secret of our stay-behinds helping the Empire will be all over the Republic by the time we drop anchor back in Saadi. The only way we can keep it from blowing us up too is to make sure everyone knows we're too valuable to be destroyed or exiled."

"Tonight's battle won't hurt."

"No, and neither has everything you've done before you joined *Lingvaas*. The Directorate may never admit it, but you've done more good work for them than you could have in ten years on that damned rock."

Weil shifted a foot and winced. Then she started. Borlund did not, because his ears hadn't quite recovered from standing so close to the guns.

But he did see the flashes. He combined memory with a look at the compass and realized that one set of flashes was off the mouth of the channel. Another was well to the north. Neither seemed to be the enemy transports, unless they'd altered course or increased speed—which was perfectly possible, of course.

Planning for the enemy's capabilities instead of estimating their intentions was a sound concept. It also led straight to paranoia when you didn't know who was the friend and who was the enemy.

Weil gripped Borlund's arm. "We'll keep on the tail of the transports. If it's more Imperials, they'll be coming to help the transports. If it's our friends, they'll be coming to sink them. We'll be in the fight on the right side either way.

"Now go back to work. I want that bow gun ready for action before the transports pick up any friends."

Borlund walked forward, passing a working party scrubbing the decks. What they were cleaning up, he didn't want to look at too closely.

He also hurried past the ventilator leading to sick quarters. They had plenty of anesthetics for surgery, but not much to use on those wounded who were only moaning, not screaming.

FLAME STREAMED FROM *VALOR*'S STACK AS SHE READ TOWARD THE CHANNEL mouth. Probably she needed a boiler-cleaning; that was more flame than one could get from soot in the stack.

But for now boilers and engines were both giving their best. *Valor* had not churned through the water at this speed for this long since her endurance trials, and I Hmilra had not been aboard for those. His Fleet shares had been in *Fearsome* and *Kuipaso*.

The Captain had wondered about the flames from the stack. I Hmilra had taken time to reassure him, even keeping the edge out of his voice as he did.

"If they don't see us, no matter. If they do see us, they'll likely aim at the stack and fire high. We absolutely *cannot* slow down enough to douse that flame without risking everybody on Puyasa."

The Captain did not need telling that this was unacceptable. This was fortunate for him. His ears might not have survived I Hmilra's language. Nor would his career have survived being relieved of command, which I Hmilra was prepared to do.

Again, lookouts aloft aboard both *Valor* and *Relentless* saw the gunfire before the torpedo-carriers did, and the torpedo-carriers both ahead and astern saw it before I Hmilra did. He ordered no course changes, because the squadron was already headed where it had to go and in formation to fight in any direction from which an enemy might appear.

It was only when the trailing torpedo-carrier and *Shuumiba* both reported transports overtaking from astern that I Hmilra ordered the helm put over.

Valor heeled as she turned hard to greenward, *Relentless* following in her wake, torpedo-carriers maneuvering to cover both the seaward flank of the heavy ships and the mouth of the channel.

"What about the command tower . . . ?" The Captain sounded as if he was embarrassed to remind I Hmilra that there was such a place.

"Wait until we know who they are," I Hmilra said. He moved to the wing of the bridge and braced himself so that he could use both hands on his binoculars. He willed the darkness to lift as he peered into it, even for the moment that would let him tell friend from enemy.

Then a searchlight thrust out from *Relentless*. It lit up a high, rusty gray hull hung with netting and topped with boats swung out ready for lowering. A gilded broadwing topped a straight bow, and the railings were crowded with brown-capped figures.

Imperials.

I Hmilra thought it, the Captain and others shouted it, and those with hands on lanyards or cranks acted without thinking or speaking. Suddenly the searchlight was only one light among many, and not even the brightest one.

chapter 27

By now, *Byubr* could hardly be said to be on course toward anything. Even finding water shoal enough to beach her before she sank would be more chance than steering. She had enough water below that she wallowed even in the flat calm.

It amazed Ehoma Tuomitti that the engineers hadn't drawn the fires and ordered the strokers and her repair party out of the boiler rooms. It also infuriated her, because if her people were down below she ought to be there with them.

The Second Gunnery Commander had other ideas. He told her that her people below had other chiefs, but the ammunition party for the crankguns did not. With enemy torpedo-carriers probably still lurking in the darkness, he needed her help to keep the guns firing.

Tuomitti thought of simple insubordination. She thought of appealing to the Gunnery Commander, who turned out to be dead. She even briefly considered appealing to Captain Inpanskaa, who undoubtedly had more on his mind than petty squabbles over the best place for a watch chief who wasn't entirely fighting-fit anyway. (Tuomitti had a nosebleed now, and her hand was plainly going to need salving if it wasn't to fester.)

It took her two breaths to consider all these choices, then only another one to nod (she refused to salute such a painful order) and say:

"Aye-aye."

ALIKILI BROUGHT ALL THE RESCUERS INTO THE HOUSE, IN HER MIND PERFORMING rites of aversion that there should be no more traitors or enemies among the new arrivals. However, they could do harm as easily outside as inside, and any stray gun-toters or knife-wielders from the first attack could strike much more easily if she kept everyone milling about outside. There were too many stone walls and bushes in the garden that would allow slipping up to shooting or even stabbing range.

This did not make her think the house's stone walls a solution to all her problems. She posted armed sentries on stairs and in halls to block any attack from the rear. She posted the two best rifle shots on the roof, and had torches set out on the lawn to reveal anyone trying to attack from the front. She used her own and the household's knowledge of the ground to take several other precautions that she hoped she would remember well enough to describe in detail to Jossu.

By the time she was done, the only ways to attack would be light artillery, or else a bomb in the rear of the house powerful enough to knock the front down as well or set everything on fire. If the enemy commanded such weapons, then Lord and Lady had forsaken her and her people. She would just have to make the best fight she could when she had lost even much hope of its becoming a tale told to those in Greats to come.

When she had done all this, and thought she could command her voice, she went to see Moi Kekaspa.

They had laid the wounded and the dead in two of the guest bedchambers. The master chamber was unfit for anything except laying out the enemy's dead. Two healers attended the wounded, and a gardener and a cook's helper who had learned some quick-healing helped them.

Alikili nearly lost her self-command when she found Kekaspa not only alive but conscious. From the pain in the woman's voice, she would have been far better off senseless. Or so Alikili thought, but Kekaspa took her hand and squeezed it so hard the other was sure she felt bones creaking.

"Not much—to ask," Kekaspa whispered. Her wounds were dressed, front and back, but she sounded as if she was speaking with half of one lung and just enough blood to keep her heart beating.

"Ask anything you wish," Alikili said.

"Ah, but—what can you do?"

"What I can't do, Jossu surely will. Between us—"

"What I hoped. But—he might—take care—the baby—"

"We'll take care of your babe," Alikili said. *If I have to stand over him with a pistol every night for ten Greats, I will see him safe.*

"Don't—understand. Be careful—he stays—with sister and—father's sister."

"Your sister and your husband's sister should keep him?"

"Yes. Murku's kin—will help—if Saadians raise him. If Kertovans take him in. . . ." Her voice trailed off, leaving Alikili torn between maddening frustration at hearing no more and chilling fear that there would be no more to hear.

Presently, Kekaspa's breathing stopped. Alikili went on holding the dead hand, but closed the staring eyes with the thumb and forefinger of her free hand. She only stood up when the hand she held began to stiffen.

By then, her own legs were nearly as stiff as Kekaspa's hand, and outside a new voice was calling her name in a tone more usually found among herders driving stock to pasture.

BORLUND ENDED BY DOING ENOUGH HEAVY LIFTING TO STRAIN EVEN HIS MUScles. He also felt twinges of pain that came from no strains, and discovered that his left hip and calf were peppered with tiny fragments and splinters. Some hadn't even penetrated clothing, let alone skin. Others had gone in far enough that he could anticipate a little while in sick berth with his trousers down and the attendants yanking at him with tweezers and smearing him with salve.

Meanwhile, he hadn't lost a dangerous amount of blood and he wasn't going to before the next round of shooting began. He intended for the bow gun to be pulling its weight by then, even if he had to lift its entire five tons himself.

By the time the gun was back in action, he felt as if he had very nearly done so. He was stripped to the waist to keep from ruining his uniform even more thoroughly than it was already, and the clothes he still had on were clinging with sweat. He kept his boots on, however; they helped support a half-sprained ankle and keep loose bits of metal and wood out of his feet. The deck crew had swept down fore and aft, but working in darkness they couldn't possibly have found everything.

He put his hat back on so that he could salute properly when he reported to Captain Weil that the bow gun was ready for action.

"Well done," she said. "Somebody's engaging the transports already, in case you hadn't noticed. It's time for us to join the party.

"Gunnery Chief Gann is back on duty—it was just a scalp cut. Let him take over the bow gun, and you get back to your own battery. Don't worry, I plan to take us in to biscuit-tossing range. Those crankguns will have all the targets they can use."

"Aye-aye."

Borlund had barely pulled on his shirt when the bow gun fired. The blast snatched his coat out of his hand and set it whirling overboard, and made the ladder he was climbing sway like a mast in the wind. He could hold onto something like that now with one hand, though. A Great ago he'd needed both hands and both feet and wouldn't have minded being able to grip with his teeth as well.

He was a Farer now. He was also a Farer with shipmates and battle-comrades to avenge, and if the notion of vengeance made milk-suckers on the Directorate cringe, let them change places with him for the rest of the night and see what they said then!

Lingvaas was turning to redward, heading out to sea again, when he reached the flying deck. Looking off to greenside, he saw the bulky silhouettes of at least two transports, lit up by their own gunfire as well as that of someone firing into them from inshore.

A flash that had to be either an explosion or a heavy gun lit up a third transport. Borlund thought he glimpsed another large ship beyond the transports. He hoped his eyes told the truth. I Hmilra might have returned; if he had, even with only a handful of ships, there could be more than *Byubr* on the other side.

Borlund hoped so. He liked the idea of catching the enemy between two fires. Fires straight out of Hell—which he now definitely hoped existed, even if that meant he could no longer call himself a Rationalist but not yet be Observant!

"Ah, sir, we're in range, I think," came a chief's voice. It had the tone of a chief who sees a commander with his mind elsewhere and isn't sure how to bring it back to the work at hand.

"Loaded?"

"Since before you came back, sir."

"Captain, fire as our guns bear?"

Weil's reply was lost in the second round from the bow gun. Her second effort blew away on the blast of the after-guns firing together, although at different targets.

After that Borlund decided that since he'd received no orders *not* to open fire, he would assume that he could do as he pleased. He cupped both hands and shouted, to the three crewed midships guns and the three working crankguns:

"Open fire as your guns bear!"

IF THE ENEMY HAD AN ARMORCLAD OR EVEN ANY HEAVY GUNS AMONG THE transports, Jossu I Hmilra hadn't seen it. He feared, however, that

Valor had done herself as much damage as a serious opponent might have done.

The steam line to the training engine for the after turret had carried away on the third broadside. No enemy metal had come within a cable of it; the concussion of Valor's own guns had done the work. Fortunately the loading gear was hydraulic and pressure in it kept up by a second engine, so the turret could still fire, but it could not turn to follow a target, and the transports seemed to be scattering like a flock of sea fliers.

"Signal to *Relentless,*" I Hmilra shouted. He was shouting as a matter of course now, because even when the guns weren't firing everybody on the bridge was half-deaf. Being inside the command tower might have shielded ears, but it would also have blinded eyes. When the enemy had nothing that could hit *Valor* at this range I Hmilra preferred a good view.

"Signal to *Relentless?*" someone asked. Without looking to see who had replied, I Hmilra ordered the cruiser to steam out to sea, steering a course to pass to greenward of the transports and hitting them at close range as she did.

That would reduce the transports' chances if they turned and fled back the way they had come. Meanwhile, *Valor* could maneuver off the mouth of the channel if the enemy tried to press on through. With her five-gun broadside reduced to three, it made more sense for the enemy to come to her than for her to chase them.

Besides, any more high-speed steaming and she might cripple more than a training engine.

The signal lamp flashed. I Hmilra hoped it could be picked out amid the gunfire. That was always a problem in a night action, except when you were the only friendly ship about and could shoot in all directions with a clear conscience and a full magazine.

"Ship to redside, two-five-zero!" a lookout shouted. He must have felt the news was urgent; he yelled loud enough to be heard over one of the citadel guns letting go. He shouted again as I Hmilra watched the shell go home with flaring orange flame and a torrent of sparks. He was shouting a third time as I Hmilra turned to look to redward.

The newcomer seemed to be low in the water—indeed, dead in the water. Sinking? Hard to recognize that, or whether she was friend or enemy. Then I Hmilra saw movement alongside the other ship—on both sides, indeed—and raised his binoculars.

The ship was *Byubr*, so low in the water that if she wasn't already resting on the bottom she would sink before long. The moving shapes to either side were torpedo-carriers.

Searchlights were on them before I Hmilra could even think of the order. He thanked variously Lord, Lady, Fleet training, and the other seventeen Captains sharing in *Valor*. Then the greenside tower gun, which had been silent thus far, spewed flame.

I Hmilra hoped that it also spewed a well-aimed shot, because those two torpedo-carriers looked Imperial and might have a clear shot at *Valor* with as many as four torpedoes.

EHOMA TUOMITTI RECOGNIZED THE ENEMY TORPEDO-CARRIERS IN THE SAME moment as the lookouts did, also the gunners on the crankguns, who let go with everything they had in both directions. She felt as if she'd walked into a door, and held both hands over her ears. At least her bandaged left hand was good for something.

The Imperial torpedo-carrier to greenside was sliding past just outside crankgun range, however. Tuomitti could see the splashes in the water. The enemy wasn't returning fire either. All hands seemed to be amidships, around the torpedo launchers. Tuomitti hoped that meant they had a faulty torpedo or launcher, preferably both.

Then it seemed as if the door opened in her face, flinging her outward against the railing. The gouged and nicked railing gave under the impact and she felt herself in midair. She had time to thank the Lord that the bulge was now nearly submerged and she would not break too many bones by falling on it. Then she plunged into the water.

When she broke the surface, she saw what had hit her. Firing abeam, with its muzzle thirty paces from her, the main gun had hit the torpedo-carrier squarely amidships. It was a solid shot, two Farers' weight of chilled steel, aimed high.

Not too high to do its job, though. It had cleaned one torpedo launcher off the carrier's deck like a knife trimming the stem of a squan-fruit. Air blast and fragments had swept the crew off the decks. More fragments had certainly pierced the funnel, possibly riddled the bridge, and perhaps even reached the engine room.

Certainly the torpedo-carrier was steering like the last and drunkest Farer back from leave as she vanished into the darkness.

Tuomitti swam only a few strokes before her left hand struck something solid. The pain sharpened her senses; she realized she had swum onto *Byubr*'s bulge. She used her right hand and both legs to push herself onto the rounded iron, scraping one knee on a rivet.

Then she stood up—and as she did, she saw a silhouette hard to mistake, well out to sea but lit clearly by her own gunflashes—and then suddenly, by two searchlights as well.

Valor was out there, in among the transports.

Crankguns snarled, aimed to redward. The main gun fired again. The next sound to pummel Tuomitti's ears was an explosion from well clear of *Byubr*. She tried to make out if it was anywhere near *Valor*, could no longer see the flagship, recognized *Relentless* even farther out to sea on the flank of the transports, and only hoped that the explosion was a torpedo-carrier blowing up, not a torpedo hitting *Valor*.

Then she crouched with only head and shoulders above the water, looking about her to see if anybody else had fallen overboard and needed a helping hand. She did have one, if somebody else needed it worse than she did.

THE HERDER-VOICE BELONGED TO THE YOUNG DRILION COMMANDER WHO had accompanied Jossu on his race to Fort Huomikki on the day of *Aygsionan*'s accident. He had not come alone either; half his company was with him, ready to fight anyone without artillery and hold anyone who had it until friendly guns came up.

Doubtless someone had ordered him up because Jossu had mentioned him as an example of honor, discretion, and skill. Alikili hoped that the judgment was correct; also, that his groundfighters followed his example.

Alikili walked out to greet her new defenders, at the head of a solemn procession carrying the dead. The company also had a surgeon, who took one look at the procession and sprinted for the house, followed by a dozen groundfighters with their rifles slung and their sleeves rolled up.

The commander looked down at the blanketed form on the litter.

"Is that—?"

"Yes."

"One heard—tales. I am sorry we were not in time to save her."

"A full surgical chamber might not have done it, nor could she have been taken to one without dying on the way. You have nothing to be ashamed of. And do not be so Drilion as to go looking for things to be ashamed of either."

"Do not you be so Kertovan that you see everything as inevitable, like the rise and fall of the tides," the commander said.

He turned away and shouted some orders whose words Alikili understood but not the sense.

"We have the other half of the company coming up on a sun-brighten train," he said, answering her look. "A messenger is returning to the station to tell the guards we left there that we have matters here in hand—"

"That you *found* matters here in hand," Alikili said. Had her voice been steel, the commander would have been clutching a bleeding throat.

"That we found them in hand at the house, and are now scouting the country for any fugitives or folk too stupid to know defeat?"

Alikili could not help smiling. "I can accept that. But do not pull ruffs in every village and farmstead within a day's march. Jossu enjoys peace with his neighbors."

"We will let him enjoy it when they are at peace with him," the other said. "When they are not—both of you are too precious to the Republic to put foolishly in danger."

Alikili had no reply to those words, and after a moment decided that this was no great loss.

SEAN BORLUND HAD ONLY TWO MIDSHIPS GUNS LEFT NOW; ONE HAD A round go off from the heat in the open breach. Only one Farer was surely dead, but some of those sprawled dark shapes below looked as if they would be a long time moving.

However, healer-attendants were working on them. That was oddly encouraging; it meant that everyone below was either dead or at least fit to be left alone briefly.

The greenside gun was ready to fire again when Borlund recognized something in its target.

"Hold your fire! That's *Shuumiba*!"

Somebody sounded ready to argue, but the redside gun also had a target and let fly, drowning out the arguer. Then a searchlight lit up *Lingvaas*, and five gun flashes lit up the ship carrying the searchlight.

She was indeed the armored cruiser *Shuumiba*, with blistered patches all over her elegant green topsides and holes in her yellow-brown funnel but otherwise looking ready for a Fleet review.

Signal lamps winked. "Follow me. Watch out for Imperial torpedoes. Do not fire on transports except at my signal."

Borlund's curses weren't the only ones. A chorus of them swelled, loud enough to war with the guns forward and aft. That was an order Weil would have to obey; *Shuumiba*'s Captain was substantially her senior even if they had both been of the same race.

He was also openly skeptical about sharing the seas of Kilmoyn, let alone the honors of the Fleet, with Drylanders. Not enough to disobey I Hmilra's orders, but if I Hmilra had gone where he would give no more orders, and Acht Fobeen now commanded—?

"Hold your jabber or they'll hear us!" Borlund shouted. "*Valor*'s got to be in there mixed up with the transports, and maybe other friends, too. The Axe knows more of who's where than we do!"

One searchlight swung away from *Lingvaas*, probing into the tangle of transports—and lighter craft, Borlund saw—where there was already so much light from burning ships that you could have read a leaf-scrap poster at least. The other searchlight swung until its beam was aimed upward and aft, as a beacon for *Lingvaas* to follow.

"Think we're blind, do they?" someone muttered.

That hadn't been said loud enough to be worth noticing, Borlund decided. Besides, the searchlight aimed upward could also be swung to either beam, to illuminate targets for both Kertovan ships.

He still doubted that the battle at sea was over. And he *knew* that the battle for honor hadn't even begun, might take longer, and probably had to be fought with just as much determination.

Otherwise the Directorate's opponents of humans going to war and the Republic's opponents of Drylanders going to sea would have time to form an obscene alliance to deny *Lingvaas*'s Farers any reward for what they had done this past Great *or* tonight.

EHOMA TUOMITTI DISCOVERED THAT SHE HAD NO LIVE COMPANY IN THE water. But the top half of a body floated close enough for her to recognize the Imperial cut of the ruff and the tattoos above either ear where the scalp had been shaved bare.

It was supposed to honor dead foes, to think about those who would mourn them as your kin would mourn you. It was pleasing to the Lord, and those who obeyed the Lady more than most Farers thought it was nearly a duty.

But Tuomitti decided that such thoughts now would more likely addle her wits. Tonight had been the longest fight of her life, and the bloodiest. She tried to climb back aboard *Byubr*.

Unfortunately, one hand wasn't quite enough for climbing. The roar of the guns out to sea kept everyone's eyes turned that way and deafened everyone's ears to her croaking calls.

So she squatted on the bulge and looked at the body, and decided that she might as well honor him as not. She might be keeping company with him for much of the night.

Be well, Farer who fought us. Be well, you whose kin will mourn. Be well, kin who mourn.

Those ritual words were over too quickly. Tuomitti thought of questions she would have liked to ask the living Farer, if they had met at some drinkshop.

I never served aboard a torpedo-carrier. Ours have a reputation for cramped quarters. But yours was bigger than any I have seen in our Fleet. Tell me about her—oh, that's right, you call ships him.

It kept her from fretting over the outcome of the battle out to sea, even if the dead Farer didn't reply.

VALOR WAS NOW DOWN TO BARELY HALF HER GUNS, AS THE GREENSIDE citadel tower gun had sheared bolts in the recoil mechanism. The gunners didn't want to fire it unless it was life or death, because they could repair it after the fight unless it jumped its mounting, which it might do if fired again, and then it would be a dockyard job.

This left the forward turret and the redside citadel gun, plus the after turret when it would bear. The repair parties were still working on the steam line to the training engine. It had taken them until just a few beats ago to make sure hot steam would not scald several compartments' worth of Farers or leak into the magazine and ruin the powder.

I Hmilra was glad that he'd favored the study of electric motors for shipboard tasks, such as turret-training and anchor-weighing. Electric cables could be made harder to break than steam lines by armoring them or keeping them below the waterline for most of their length. Hydraulic systems might also have their uses.

He was also glad that he'd favored keeping rams on the bows of armorclads and the larger cruisers and gunboats. A wise Farer always had a final weapon tucked into his sleeve.

Also, the ram was a weapon that could, with luck, kill ships without killing Farers. On his orders, I Hmilra's squadron had been using solid shot instead of shell and no torpedoes since the battle joined. He wanted to keep the transports from landing their groundfighters, not massacre the groundfighters in numbers that the Empire would not be allowed to forget, if only by the kin of the dead.

But ramming meant coming in close, to crankgun or even rifle range. Best do it from inside the command tower—where you could not see well enough for the fine maneuvering ramming needed!

"Everyone off the bridge, except the lookouts. Command tower party, to your stations. Maneuver on my orders!"

For a moment he thought the battle roar had cost them their wits as well as their hearing. For another moment, he feared, if not mutiny, at least rude remarks.

Discipline held, though. They went in silence.

Now, if my voice and the speaking tubes hold so that I don't have to ask for messengers. . . .

Valor heeled in another sharp turn, letting the after-turret fire—encouragingly, with both guns. I Hmilra gripped the railing, wished that it was possible to keep one's night vision in a night action, and started picking his first ramming target.

SHUUMBIA'S SEARCHLIGHT PICKED OUT A BATTERED TRANSPORT NEARLY dead ahead. The enemy was brightly lit, by three fires and a searchlight of her own.

Her decks were also crowded with brown-uniformed Imperial groundfighters, and her railings seemed pierced for too many guns. Crankguns or light artillery at most, but solid splashes to either side of *Lingvaas* said that the artillery at least had the range.

The cruiser was turning now, hard to greenward, to pass the transport astern and rake her deck. The signal winking to *Lingvaas* told her to pass ahead of the enemy, meanwhile engaging her on the broadside.

Once more Borlund would have given ten Greats of life to have torpedoes aboard *Lingvaas*. That wasn't the only discontent, either. He heard muttering from below.

"Hope they don't rake when we're in the line of fire."

"Awful careful about us not hitting friends. Maybe they'll take their own advice."

Something about Captain Fobeen that would, not too many Greats ago in Kertovan history, have demanded a blood-duel.

Weil was swinging *Lingvaas* hard to redward now, so that two heavy guns and the last midships weapon would bear. Borlund hoped the heavy guns still had ammunition left. His own midships weapons would have been run out a tenth-watch ago if two of them hadn't been silenced in the fighting.

As for crankguns, Weil was clearly going to stay out of range of the enemy's. *Lingvaas*'s were now under orders to fire only if the enemy attempted to board. Borlund fingered his pistol. He really hoped the fighting would not come down to that.

Lingvaas could not be steaming fast enough for her engines to be roaring. But in the intervals between her own guns and the enemy's shells whistling harmlessly by, Borlund could swear he heard a wild-animal noise from deep within the ship. A large, hungry, predatory wild animal.

The two guns bearing to greenside fired. The redside stern gun also let fly, at what Borlund did not see. He turned to look—and a blaze of light poured over him, blinding him so that the idea of looking at anything was absurd.

He held on as *Lingvaas* heeled, continuing her turn to redward even more sharply. He held on as a roar like mountains colliding swept over him, along with air at the speed of a winter storm on the fringes of the Ice Sea. It was anything but cold, however. It held pure heat as well as a dozen stenches, burned flesh among them.

"Down!" Borlund yelled.

He knew what had to have happened. The last salvo from *Lingvaas* had reached the artillery ammunition in the transport's hold. Or maybe it had touched off a chain of explosions among the ammunition carriers feeding the guns, that had reached the magazine.

Borlund obeyed his own order and briefly thanked Barbara Weil for risking the contempt of Captain Fobeen, by staying out of crank-gun range. He heard more wires parting, metal clanging, and at least one scream. But he didn't hear the sounds of wholesale slaughter, as if *Lingvaas*'s decks were being scoured clean of live Farers by the debris from the explosion.

He gripped what was left of the railing and pulled himself to his feet. The transport was still afloat, but with her bow half blown away and fires burning all over the rest of her. Astern, *Shuumiba* was vanishing, beyond the transport was another Imperial ship, even bigger, and something loomed even farther away, with a mast like a warship's.

"Cease-fire, all midships guns!" Borlund yelled. "All" was only one, for now, but that was too many to have firing into a tangle of ships that certainly weren't all enemy.

VALOR WENT ON WREAKING DESTRUCTION WITH HER REDUCED BATTERY EVEN as she maneuvered to ram. Her gyrations kept opening the arcs of fire for the immobilized after turret. It kept firing. I Hmilra even authorized them to use shells if they ran out of solid shot. He dreaded the Imperial casualty list after too much of that, but they weren't surrendering and his ship was now in crankgun range.

Fortunately both sides had crankguns. What bothered I Hmilra was the times when he was within rifle range of troop-crowded decks. It was just as well that there were only three people exposed on the bridge at any moment, although the lookouts had been changed twice. He knew that he'd felt bullets clip his clothing, and he knew he'd gone far beyond what Alikili would allow to pass without a few sharp words. As for what his tailor would say—

Well, the little dear will have her profit either way. Either a complete outfit of new uniforms for further service, or a chance to create a masterwork for my burial.

The searchlights were dying on both sides now. Shattered by crankgun rounds or shell fragments? Abandoned by crews too weakened to crank them? Without power? Or simply turned off because so many ships were on fire in such a small area that everybody could see clearly?

Even me, I could do without seeing that transport ahead, that is going to pull clear of any thrust we could make with the ram unless she had to slow—

Darkness vanished. Where it had been was a transport, lying squarely across the bows of I Hmilra's intended target. She was also doing a good imitation of an erupting fire-mountain. Old nightmares, handed down to every Farer from Skyfall, made I Hmilra grip the railing.

It did not choke his voice. "Redward ten and full speed. All hands, stand by to ram."

The transport he aimed at was already slowing. She might turn toward *Valor* or away, but she could not steer around her sinking consort in time to avoid the armorclad's ram.

The forward turret belched. A shell tore the transport amidships. One funnel went down. The tower gun fired. A mast vanished.

Crankguns on the flying deck aft now had the range. They raved, and I Hmilra saw bodies flying or jumping overboard.

A ship swept out from behind the target. Another ship swept across *Valor*'s stern. The first ship was a perfect target for the jammed after-turret. The second was in a perfect position to rake *Valor*.

I Hmilra hoped the after-turret would fire without orders.

Then he was screaming into the voice tube. "Cease-fire, cease-fire! Full astern, full redward helm!"

He had recognized *Lingvaas* ahead and *Shuumiba* behind. He had also recognized the dozens of yellow flags suddenly waving from the transport's deck. Some of them looked like uniform waistcoats or parts of a nobleman's wardrobe, but they were all the ritual color of surrender.

It was still a near thing, as *Valor* careened across *Lingvaas*'s bow at pistol-shot range. But Weil had lost none of her shiphandling skill. *Lingvaas* was turning hard away from the collision point. It would have been a glancing blow at best, although not well done, in the moment of victory, with damaged ships far from a friendly dockyard.

We have to do something about that, if we are going to keep the sea route to Eneh open year-round, I Hmilra decided.

The bridge suddenly seemed to grow people. He decided that he could forgive their coming out with no orders. Victory ought to be celebrated in the open air.

Not fresh. Death-stink all around, every kind of smoke. Lord of the Waves, forgive what we've done to your air.

The last intact signal lamp was flashing, and *Shuumiba*'s reply came back quickly.

BYUBR GROUNDED TO PREVENT SINKING. SERIOUS DAMAGE AND CASUALTIES. THREE TORPEDO-CARRIERS MISSING. ONE ENEMY TRANSPORT KNOWN SUNK, ONE ASTERN DEAD IN WATER, NOT SURRENDERED.

I Hmilra replied:

REQUEST TRANSPORT ASTERN TO SURRENDER IMMEDIATELY ON PAIN OF BEING SUNK. IF OBLIGED TO SINK, PREPARE TO CARRY OUT RESCUE OPERATIONS. GOOD SHOOTING ON OUR FRIEND WITH THE MAGAZINE EXPLOSION.

It seemed a long time before the cruiser replied:

TRANSPORT ASTERN HAD SURRENDERED. MOST LIKELY CAUSE OF MAGAZINE EXPLOSION GOOD SHOOTING BY *LINGVAAS*. WILL CLAIM ASSIST, HOWEVER.

I Hmilra stared from *Shuumiba* to *Lingvaas*, and then to the transport they'd been arguing about, which looked as if she would need a rescue operation before long. Her ruined bow was already nearly level with the water.

So Captain Fobeen had enough honor to overcome his dislike of Drylanders and praise them for what they did. They indeed assisted, and with something more important than a single battle.

The Drylanders might be many things, but some of them were certainly no friends to the Island Republic. It would be well if those who were continued to be so, on land or at sea, whether they rose to Captain Over Captains or merely tended their dreezans better than most.

I Hmilra did not tumble to the deck because someone pushed a stool under him before he sat down on the empty air. He looked thanks in all directions, not knowing who was responsible. He signaled for water.

Then, when they brought the water quickly, and soon afterwards a signal from *Relentless,* relayed through a torpedo-carrier. She had cleared the North Channel, left boats and repair parties to help *Byubr,* and was proceeding unless ordered otherwise to bombard the enemy groundfighters on Puyasa Island.

Thanks to the water, I Hmilra was able to acknowledge the signal and send a reply. All he needed for that was his voice. The water could never have helped his legs, working down the list of orders for cleaning up this battlefield. He was glad his legs did not have to work for him to give those orders, or he would have been mute.

epilogue

Puyasa's anchorage was no longer as crowded as it had been a half-midtide ago when several hundred refugees were returning to Rinbao-Dar every common. A single paddle-wheel-steamer lay off the beach, with a steam launch towing a barge carrying more lumber than people heading toward it.

Few signs of the battle remained. The hulk of the river-steamer lay rusting where she had grounded that night. A gallant effort, Jossu I Hmilra realized, but without a victory at sea a futile one.

The groundfighters had been too scattered in landing to attack the camp before the Kertovan defenders rallied. Their thin line held until sunbrighten, when word came (or was sent) of the disaster at sea.

Even then, a few Imperial commanders whose heads held so much honor there was no room for brains wanted to continue the fight. Most of these fools had their wish of death before surrender, even if some of them died at the hands of their own fighters.

The rest of the battle marks were trees shortened or trimmed by shells or burned by the fires of unnatural lightning. The refugee camp was not being abandoned; the Kertovan garrison on Puyasa would use it. But the quick-growing vegetation of this warm land was already blending its outline into the landscape.

The next set of answers to the querulous wire-posts would not wait much longer, I Hmilra realized. But he could answer them better if he organized his thoughts. Since he owed Alikili a letter, why not accomplish two things at once?

The last convoy from home had brought spare parts for all of *Valor*'s ventilators; his sea cabin had as much air as possible on a still, hot afternoon like this. He tried not to sweat on the paper as he wrote.

—treaty ratified in the full forms of both our laws and those of Rinbao-Dar. However, our making our base on Puyasa continues our policy of taking no sides in the cities' disputes, but providing help whenever those disputes force people into flight.

It is therefore likely to be acceptable to both our leaders and the cities'. Nor do I forget the Drylanders, who clearly have among them some who would not like to see their gifts and their blood used to build our Republic into Empire.

They need not fear. Even without the aid of renegade Drylanders, the Aloboliri and the Dhandarans are much too formidable for us to think beyond our own survival for many Greats to come.

Captain Weil has been admirably frank about the renegade Drylanders. I shall do my best to protect her from any revenge the Study Group or others among her people may wish to take for her giving me this knowledge.

I would not care even in a letter to you to write all she has said. But she is sure that the renegades will not be as great a gift to their allies as either side thinks. Nor does she believe they and their devices will always be used as foolishly and carelessly as they were in the fighting on Puyasa.

So the future is only a trifle less cloudy than before—which is not saying a great deal, it having always been cloudier than the sky in a thunder squall. Nonetheless, the future holds you—and so may I, before much longer.

Not being a poet, I cannot find words to say how much I have missed that. Nor can I say how frightened I was at the thought of losing you, without seeming more of a coward than I wish to sound even to you.

All blessings to you, and my hopes that *Valor* will outspeed this letter homeward.

I Hmilra read over the letter, realized that the weight of what he could say on paper had made him sound awkward, and blotted the letter nonetheless. Alikili could read well enough what he did not say, even though she might feel like boxing his ears for not having said it.

A whistle blew, to seaward—one I Hmilra did not recognize. He peered out the port.

The high red hull and the green banner floating from the third of the four stubby masts were unmistakable. The new Enehan ship (in fact, the only seagoing steamship under the Enehan flag) had arrived.

Even though this was not her first visit to Puyasa, her coming called for I Hmilra's presence aboard her sometime before sunfade. He called for his steward and pulled the water jug toward him.

ABOARD *BYUBR*, EHOMA TUOMITTI, ZHOHOROSH, AND TWENTY OTHER chiefs and senior Farers stood at attention, while a trumpeter and a drummer rendered honors to the Enehan ship.

They remained that way until Tuomitti was certain that her good eye was going to melt and her saluting hand become as weak as the wounded left one. They remained that way, for what she knew was half a common longer.

Then at last the Enehan ship blew her whistle five times, acknowledging the honors. The Enehan choice of signals was still a mystery to Kertovan Farers, but since the Regality was rather new at sea, perhaps that explained much.

It did not excuse it, but one did not say that where any senior, let alone any Enehan, could say it. Fortunately, few of them spoke any tongue but their own or Alobsi. After the blood price of the voyage to Eneh, Kertovan Farers were still being cautious.

With the ceremonies over, the two chiefs walked forward. Their eyes cleared the odd Farer from the capstan, which they used as their seat.

Tuomitti looked up. The canopy overhead and Zhohorosh beside her weren't the only changes on the ship's foredeck since the night of Imperial war swimmers and dead Farers. *Byubr* no longer felt like a living ship, even though she was afloat again.

She was now a "station ship," like the old hulks in anchorages along the Luokkan coast. *Her* ship, reduced to one of those, after helping to win the biggest sea battle ever fought against the Empire. The battle of Puyasa probably wouldn't hold that title for long, although the Aloboliri had publicly denounced two provincial viceroys for "adventurism and banditry."

But it had been the biggest sea battle Tuomitti was likely to see. She resented seeing *Byubr* turned out to pasture like a dreezan too old for breeding but too young to slaughter. She said so.

Zhohorosh shrugged. "It's another part of the same road as the bargain over the Enehan ship. She was legally the property of a

Matriarchy company, so the Fleet bought her from them at a huge price. Then we sold her to the Enehans to become their flagship, for about ten slyn."

"I can remember how much we're spending to bribe those people," Tuomitti said. "I don't have to like it."

"Nobody's asking what you or I like," Zhohorosh replied. "But I can tell you straight about this old lady. "We bought Puyasa to have an offshore base on the way to Eneh. It needs a station ship. Either we bring one all the way down from the north, or we use one that's already here.

"*Byubr*'s here, and she's not going to fight again. Not without a pot of gold sent on repairs. So the pot of gold is going to the cities, to pay the 'maintenance fees' for keeping her afloat."

"Another bribe," Tuomitti said. "Has Fleet worked out a bribe for us, to make us stay?"

"The tales run that everyone aboard has their choice of taking their pension and staying, or going home to a post of their choice." he hesitated. "I will go where you go, my friend. Or stay where you stay."

She looked at him. He shrugged again. "I am too old to put love into stronger words. My heart might not stand it. You might even tell me to go. That one eye sees pretty clearly."

She tucked his arm through hers. "I see a good man. That isn't the most common sight. Maybe I can do something with him."

"I won't fight it if you try."

LINGVAAS STEAMED IN THE REAR OF THE FIRST CONVOY BOUND NORTH FROM Puyasa to Eneh. The convoy carried a good part of what would be needed to build the fort, repair the canals and railroads, and establish permanent harbor facilities on the north shore of the Bishak Gulf.

Or at least as permanent as the Empire allowed. The Aloboliri still had more than enough groundfighters that they could in a purely military sense write off their losses in the Battle of Puyasa. Their pride might make scrap of purely military calculations.

Hence the convoy, with *Relentless*, four gunboats towing torpedo-carriers, and *Lingvaas*, for ten merchant vessels, two of them smaller than *Lingvaas*. Provincial viceroys could be replaced with remarkable speed when the Empire's ministers wished it, and a purely land route for attacking Eneh's seaward connection remained open to them.

So enough matériel was going north, to make a tempting target if it traveled unescorted, which it would not. The escort duties would also keep *Lingvaas* in the south for much longer than Sean Borlund had expected *Lingvaas* to be allowed to remain in these waters.

"But we're a Fleet unit, which means Fleet orders are the only *legally* valid ones," Barbara Weil reminded him. Neither of them was on watch, the convoy was in the open Gulf, and with everyone else looking forward, they had the extreme stern to themselves. With only a little more privacy, they could have sunbathed.

"The Directorate could put that to a test."

"Not unless they're bigger fools than even I think," Weil said. She leaned against the railing and finger-combed her hair. It was shorter than it had been when Borlund met her, almost shorter than he would have found attractive before then.

Of course, where Barbara was concerned, he would admit that he was not particularly objective.

"I don't think they will," she added. "Having Corinne Yoshino come home a wounded hero and a convert to the Kertovan viewpoint will be something all by itself. Add all her sibs, kin, and friends, and she'll be talking to a good fraction of the anti-Empire fanatics.

"What you did won't hurt either," Borlund said. It was against military etiquette to compliment one's commander. However, he'd learned a few delicate phrases to outflank that rule.

"What *we* did," she said. She did not quite touch him, but the air between them seemed to sparkle for a moment.

"My one question is whether I Hmilra is keeping us down here because he wants to know what I didn't tell him, about the 'renegade Drylanders.' He may think that if we're down here long enough, we'll be indiscreet, he can read our mail, or we'll tell just to get home."

"What didn't you tell him?" Having helped compose the report, Borlund wondered that there was anything she'd left out. Certainly it couldn't be enough to save her from the Directorate, if they caught her outside Fleet jurisdiction for long enough.

"Remember why *Lingvaas* can't become an independent Drylander community, even if the Fleet asked us?"

"No headroom," Borlund said. Service aboard any ship designed for Kilmoyans was a sore point with him. (Also, quite often, sore head from bumping or sore neck from ducking.)

"The real reason."

"Too small a genetic base."

"Exactly. Now, I've probably seen more secret material than you have. But even what I've seen doesn't give the stay-behinds more than two hundred people. That's sixty years ago, so all but the handful of children will be going or gone. Two-thirds of them were men."

Borlund needed only a moment's mental arithmetic. "A small population. Village-sized, if that. Much more inbred than we are, no matter how hard they try. Getting more so with each generation, too."

"Precisely. So small that even if each one was an Einstein or a Feisal, they'll know that time is running out for them.

"They've never had numbers on their side. Now they don't have time. They may be desperate. What happens if desperate stay-behinds find an Imperial ally smarter than those Emperor's bad bargains we just fought?"

Borlund decided not to suggest making a free gift of this knowledge to Jossu I Hmilra. It might not be knowledge, anyway—just a guess, not even a probability.

He liked it no better for that.

"Speaking of gene pools," Weil said, "ah—how to put this? I'm old-fashioned in some ways. I want your bearer-partners' permission to—court you."

"Court" was a ludicrously delicate way of describing what Barbara Weil wanted to do with him and he with her. But she was describing the custom accurately, and in the traditional language.

"I've sired one offspring by each of the ladies," Borlund said, using a proscribed term. "They may make a condition that I sire the other one they're allowed by a single partner before they'll let me go."

"Hmmm," Weil said. "A good man is hard to find?"

"Well. . . ." There was enough sea breeze that Borlund could feel himself flushing. He covered it with a coughing fit from a pretended lungful of funnel smoke.

"Sorry," Weil said, resting a hand lightly on his forearm. "But you are a good man. I have found you. I don't want to lose you, to custom, the Directorate, your bearer-partners, or an Imperial shell."

How little what either of them wanted might influence the future was too obvious to require comment. Borlund merely covered Weil's hand with his for a moment.

"Another reason for finding our way north soon," he said.

"As long as we take *Lingvaas,*" Weil added. "The old term for taking command of a ship has the same root as the old term for marriage. I used to wonder why."

They stood watching the wake, without any more touches, but not needing any.

IT WAS STILL TOO EARLY FOR THIS KIND OF CHILL RAIN, ALIKILI DECIDED. Nonetheless, those who heard oaths would be as present or absent as on any fine day. She doubted they would give her any special honor for getting wet, but they would also not shame her for soothing herself in a hot bath afterward.

She walked with the brisk stride that now came easily in her uniform kilt, out into the garden. The memorial stone was at the far end, between two dwarfed silvernuts. There would never have been room for Moi Kekaspa's grave there, not without undermining the wall, but her kin and her husband's had taken it, as they had taken her child. Good people all of them, and not ones Alikili would have cared to have as enemies.

The grass was too sodden for the ritual prostration. Instead she knelt, head bowed but eyes raised so that her spirit touched both the memorial here and the earth fifty leagues away that actually held the woman's body.

"Shimosh Kekaspa shall be raised by his kin, on both sides. This is right and proper, for they know the ways of Saadi and I do not.

"Yet I swear this, by all who listen, who uphold oaths and punish oathbreakers.

"What the child may need to become all that he may wish to be, and his kin cannot give, I promise to give it."

That was the easy part. Now came the part that had cost her sleep, although she knew that the oath would not be complete without it.

"If Jossu I Hmilra, by word or deed, does what might cause me to break this oath, then I will consider his oaths to me and mine to him likewise broken. This too I swear by all who listen and who uphold oaths or punish oathbreakers."

She rose, and felt the wind on her face. She also felt a wind blowing inside her, from nowhere to nowhere, a wind that seemed to chill and warm her at the same time.

For a moment she felt as if she held within herself a space as vast as all the seas of Kilmoyn.

selected glossary

ALOBSI
Lingua Franca of the Empire of Alobolir.

ARIYOM
Southern relative of the dreezan; longer-legged.

ARMS WATCHER
Chief in charge of security (also the small-arms locker) aboard a ship.

BEARER-PARTNER
In human society, equivalent to "mother."

BEAT
Kertovan unit of time; one-hundredth of a watch.

BREATH
Kertovan unit of time; one-hundredth of a beat.

CAPTAIN-BORN
A family that has produced Captains in four successive generations; hereditary nobility in Kertova.

CAST
Kertovan unit of measurement; approximately three hundred meters.

CITY-STATES
Loose federation of petty states between the mouth of the Hask and the border of the Empire.

CLEARSKY
The sunniest and warmest season in Kertova; roughly equivalent to summer.

COMMON (TIDE)
Day; 28.62 hours.

CONFEDERATION OF DHANDARA
Dominant political unit on the eastern continent of northern Kilmoyn; a militaristic oligarchy more friendly to the Empire of Alobolir than to the Island Republic.

DAUGHTER OF THE ROCK
Sworn servant of the Lady of the Rock; allowed to preside over Reverences in her honor.

DILGAO
Quasi-bovine southern draft animal; enormous strength when fed a high-sugar diet.

DISSTUL OIL
Inflammable extract of the sap of a Luokkan tree.

DREEZAN
Most common riding and draft animal; resembles a long-legged rhinoceros, about 1.8 meters at the shoulder.

DRILION
Minority in Saadi; descended from an extinct City-State and consider themselves oppressed by Saadians.

DRYLANDER
Common name for humans, based on their cover story of being from a distant southern land that remained dry during Skyfall.

DZRIK
Highly edible shellfish common in northern waters.

EINSEIN
Kertovan household spirit.

EMPIRE OF ALOBOLIR
Largest political unit on western continent; main rival of the Island Republic.

ENEH (OR THE REGALITY)
Moutainous kingdom stretching from the southern border of the Empire to the Bishak Gulf.

ERSKIN
Large deep-water fish; staple of the Kertovan diet.

ESPERANZA
Utopian colony; home planet of the *Ramparts* expedition.

FALSE FIRE
In Fleet gunnery, a blank or dud round.

FARER
One who goes to sea. In Kertova, has become a generic term for any adult citizen.

FINGERNIPPERS
Small carnivorous fish found in ponds in Kertova.

FLEET
In Kertova, all vessels legally registered as available in time of war, whether built for the purpose or not.

FLOWER FOWL
A Luokkan bird known for its spectacular plumage and evil-smelling droppings.

FUGITIVE *OR* STAY-BEHIND
Negative human term for those who did not sail to Kertova. Also called "tribalists."

FULLDARK
True night.

GAISOL
Synthetic fireproofing compound; one of the first products of the rock-oil industry.

GARCIK
Obscene term for a sterile female; implies that her sterility was the result of vice or neglecting her health.

GHATYS
Luokkan pirate knife with a heavy curved blade and a single razor-sharp cutting edge.

GIGNEL
Edible root, usually served either pickled or baked into a pie.

GREAT (TIDE)
Year; the Kilmoyan year is 355 Standard days.

GUIT
The Saadian male nature spirit.

GRAVELTOES
Rude but not quite obscene term for one who does not go to sea.

GREEN-GULLET
Predatory ocean fish; about 1.5 meters long and hunting in schools.

GREENSIDE/REDSIDE (OR GREENWARD/REDWARD)
Starboard (right) and port (left).

GROUNDFIGHTER
Replacing "landfighter" as a term for one who fights on land.

GRUUYAN
Popular fermented Kertovan beverage; available in varying degrees of potency.

GYUROK
Common domestic animal most closely resembling a small llama; raised for both meat and hair.

HASK
Principal river of the Empire of Alobolir.

HEIGHT
Kertovan unit of measurement, roughly 1.5 meters.

HIGH FARER
The chief judge of Kertovan Farers, presiding over their governing body, the Council of Delegates.

HIGHSHIP
Semi-archaic term for "flagship."

HOEG
Most common Kertovan herbal beverage; can be served hot or cold, in any strength, and with many combinations of additives.

HOST
Army or other large aggregation of groundfighters.

JOUTI
Kertovan term for a fertile female.

KANIK
Kertovan obscenity; implies incest.

KERTOVA
Republic ("the Island Republic") occupying most of the islands between the Imperial coast and the Greater Sea. The principal seafaring power on Kilmoyn.

KILMOYN
Best possible transliteration of the Kertovan name for their homeworld.

KRIMO
A common seaweed with a mild nicotine content; harvested with the help of Seakin and cured for smoking in pipes.

LINE
Kertovan unit of measurement for the bore of a gun; roughly two centimeters.

LORD OF THE WAVES *AND* LADY OF THE ROCKS
The principal Kertovan deities, also known as the Gray Lord and the Green Lady.

LADYSOUL
For the Kertovan believers in reincarnation, a honorific term for someone whose soul has been in existence since the original creation of the world by the Lord and Lady. Usually applied to a female.

LUOKKA
Kertovan colony on the equatorial continent; formerly infested with pirates.

MARITIME COMPENDIUM
The standard Kertovan reference on seamanship; *The Practical Farer and Commander* is its equivalent for commanders and senior chiefs.

MATRIARCHY
Popular name for Rinbao-Dar (q.v.), derived from the fact that its highest governmental body is a council of fifteen fertile women.

OBERVANT
Perjorative term for a human who practices one of the (officially) proscribed traditional religions.

MIDTIDE
Month; the Kertovans divide a Great into thirteen midtides.

MINUMBILIKI
Carnivorous insectoid found in warm climates.

MKLK
Juice of a pearlike fruit; a favorite Kertovan children's drink.

MUIKKEN
Omnivore, the size of a large dog, often trained for guard duty.

MUSTEKKA
Mule-sized, largely herbivorous quadruped; when well trained has great drawing power because of its sureness of foot.

RAMPARTS
Starship whose drive failure marooned the Esperanzan colonists on Kilmoyn; in a cometary orbit around Kilmoyn's primary.

RATIONALIST
One who rejects any of the traditional human religions.

RECUIN OIL
An edible nut oil.

RIISVAL TEST
The basic Kertovan test of female fertility.

RINBAO-DAR
A pair of cities on the Bishak Gulf loosely controlling territory north to the border of Eneh. Also see "Matriarchy."

SAADI
Formerly a theocracy opposite the mouth of the Hask, constantly at war with the City-States. Now a protectorate of Kertova. The name can refer to either the city or the whole territory.

SEAKIN
Omnivorous mammalian pelagic species resembling small orcas; highly social and recognized as sapient by the Kertovans.

SHTRUG
Epithet; feeble-minded.

SKYFALL
An asteroid strike on Kilmoyn c. 1000 years before the opening of *Eneh*; massively destructive to civilization and life in general.

SLYN
Basic unit of Kertovan currency; forty slyn is one day's wages for a skilled worker.

SOLVARSEN THEATER
Largest and newest entertainment establishment in Saadi (city).

SONG-STORY
Dramatic presentation combining both singing and narrative or dialogue, usually in verse.

SPAN
Kertovan unit of measurement; approximately twenty-seven centimeters.

STINKWORM
Waterborne parasite; exudes a foul-smelling, irritating slime through its skin.

STUDY GROUP
The de facto government of the humans on Kilmoyn, so called because its cover story is "studying" the Kertovans in Saadi. The *Directorate* of the Study Group has become something of an oligarchy.

SUNBRIGHTEN
Sunrise.

SUNFADE
Evening or twilight.

SUNGLOW
Noon.

SUN-MIRROR
Heliograph.

TUUNDA
Kertovan term for a sterile female (non-perjorative).

UKKIO
Kertovan demigod; the discoverer of navigation.

WATCH
Kertovan unit of time; approximately 4.77 hours.

WIRE-POST/WIRE-SPEAKER
Telegraph/telephone.

WATCH CHIEF
Petty officer.

WATCH COMMANDER
Junior officer (equivalent to lieutenant).

YERIS
Domestic animal resembling a small, long-legged pig.

YPROGA
Island holding principal human settlement in Kertova.